A HOME FOR THE
HOT-SHOT DOC

BY
DIANNE DRAKE

KU-765-723

MILLS
BOON

Published in Great Britain 2014
by Mills & Boon, an imprint of Harlequin (UK) Limited,
Eton House, 18-24 Paradise Road, Richmond, Surrey, TW9 1SR

© 2014 Dianne Despain

ISBN: 978 0 263 90776 6

Harlequin (UK) Limited's policy is to use papers that are natural, renewable and recyclable products and made from wood grown in sustainable forests. The logging and manufacturing processes conform to the legal environmental regulations of the country of origin.

Printed and bound in Spain
by Blackprint CPI, Barcelona

Dear Reader

When I went to Louisiana for the first time a few years ago—specifically New Orleans, and all the deep, dark backwoods of the bayou surrounding it—I knew I wanted to set a book there. It's a beautiful place, and there's nothing else quite like it in the United States. In fact, descriptions don't do it justice...but I've tried in this duet titled *Deep South Docs*.

Both stories, A HOME FOR THE HOT-SHOT DOC and THE DOCTOR'S CONFESSION, centre around the Doucet family and their daughters, all of whom work in the medical field in some capacity. In this duet you'll meet Mellette, who has to overcome one of life's greatest tragedies in order to find true love again. And you'll also meet Magnolia, who just can't seem to find time for love in her life.

Both meet men who try to capture their hearts, but it's not an easy thing to do as the Doucet family is filled with eight mighty strong women and one man who sits at the head of it and who's the biggest softie in the world. But, as both Justin Bergeron and Alain Lalonde discover, the fight is worth the effort...most of the time. At other times Mellette and Maggie are almost too much to handle.

When I was taking a boat ride through the swamps in the Louisiana bayou, perhaps the thing that fascinated me most were these little communities of people who live out there in the swamp, almost totally cut off from society. I could see the shacks almost everywhere. In fact we even took a detour by our tour guide's shack and saw a whole lot of alligators lounging in his front yard. He said that as long as he didn't bother them, they didn't bother him. Well, I don't know about that, but it certainly made for an interesting trip. So did the alligators that would swim right up to the boat.

I hope you enjoy your trip to the Louisiana bayous. It's fascinating. And after *this* trip to the bayous I'm going to hang around to write a few more books based in that part of the world, so look for Sabine and Delphine's stories coming next.

I like to hear form my readers, so please feel free to contact me at diannedrake@earthlink.net, or visit my website at www.dianne-drake.com, from which you can link to either my Facebook page or my Twitter page.

As always, wishing you health & happiness

DD

Now that her children have left home, **Dianne Drake** is finally finding the time to do some of the things she adores—gardening, cooking, reading, shopping for antiques. Her absolute passion in life, however, is adopting abandoned and abused animals. Right now Dianne and her husband Joel have a little menagerie of three dogs and two cats, but that's always subject to change. A former symphony orchestra member, Dianne now attends the symphony as a spectator several times a month and, when time permits, takes in an occasional football, basketball or hockey game.

CHAPTER ONE

NIGHTS LIKE THIS made him glad he was home again, if only for a little while. The far-off sound of bullfrogs bloating up and erupting with a courtly call to a lady love; the peculiar rhythm of the barred owl, who called to his own love from high atop the cypress trees; the warm breeze blowing in over the water and carrying with it the unique, earthy scent of the swamp... This all meant home to Dr. Justin Aloysius Bergeron. Home, but with that came so many mixed, even conflicting feelings.

With a mug full of sassafras tea and its bitter, soothing flavor, and a plate of his own homemade beignets made from his grandmother's recipe, Justin was ready to settle in on the porch swing for the evening and simply relax after a long day of doing nothing. Absolutely nothing. Nothing took a lot of effort for someone who was used to being active, all that sitting around and thinking. Down here, where life was slower, it wore him out more than a day on his feet in the O.R. did. Those were physically exhausting days, but here his exhaustion was emotional and far heavier. It dragged him down to a place where a good night's sleep didn't bring about any kind of recovery.

At a month shy of thirty-six, Justin was at the top of his game back in Chicago. He was well respected as a general surgeon with a career pointed in the direction of chief of services, or so he hoped. Equally well respected as a medical mystery writer with a couple of prestigious awards under his belt and talk of a movie in the works. It took a lot of effort, cranking out all that career, which was why all this nothingness seemed so strange to him.

He wasn't used to it, wasn't used to being lazy. But lazy was exactly what he was being, and it was turning him dull and lethargic, which, for the moment, suited him just fine. Because until he figured out his next move, nothing was truly all he wanted to concentrate on. He wrote in the early, early morning, as was his habit, but then there was nothing to occupy his time or to occupy his mind for the rest of the day. He was trying not to think outside the pages he'd managed to bang out. He was succeeding, intermittently.

For sure, life was simpler here in the Louisiana bayou than it was back in Chicago, his home for the past decade. He hadn't appreciated that singular simple fact when he'd lived here before. In fact, from the time he had been a teenager, all he'd ever wanted had been to get away from the simplicity. Go to the city. Any city. Seek out excitement and anything else that didn't resemble the upbringing he was accustomed to—an upbringing with a down-home flavor that could only be found in the bayou. Or the backcountry. Or godforsaken nowhere. Or, as this area had been named by its early settlers, Big Swamp.

And he'd done all that. Molded himself into what he'd wanted to be, and set off to become it. Self-made man, he'd called himself in the early days, even though now he knew better. Nobody with the kind of love and support he'd had was self-made, and just thinking about how he used to brag about his self-sufficiency caused him to cringe now. Even so, he was successful. Wealthy. Some considered him a player, although he wasn't sure he liked that description since he really didn't have time to play. But it bolstered the image. Playboy. Sports car. Condo on the lakeshore. Medical practice in the high-end Magnificent Mile. Everything about him shooting to the top.

But Justin was also part of Big Swamp—something he was just now beginning to admit. Big Swamp, where his grandmother had done her level best to raise a way-ward young boy who hadn't wanted to be raised, hadn't wanted to follow the rules, hadn't wanted anything to do with an old-fashioned set of values that had done his grandmother well for her eighty-nine years on earth. Yes, that was all him, too. The part of him he didn't talk about, or admit to. The part of him he wouldn't deny but certainly wouldn't confirm, either. It had been part of his embarrassment back then, part of his pride now.

No, none of this had been good enough for the young Justin. In a way it wasn't even enough for the Justin who existed now; he certainly hadn't made himself right with it. Hence the emotional exhaustion. But at least Justin felt more remorse for his attitude than he'd expected he ever would. And now that Grandma Eula was gone, his regrets weighed him down. Especially on an unsullied night like this, the kind of night she would have loved, where Big Swamp was at peace with itself. And yet Justin was not.

He missed Bonne-Maman Eula, as she'd been called by the people who loved her. More than that, he lamented…so much. And his grief felt so heavy against his heart, at times almost stopping it from beating. He'd owed her better, had always thought there was more time to do better for her. He'd always intended to.

"Now it's too late," he said to Napoleon, his grandmother's big, lazy, orange-striped tomcat. A fourth-, maybe fifth-generation Napoleon, actually. There'd always been a big, orange-striped tomcat living here for as long as Justin could remember, and his name had always been Napoleon. This Napoleon seemed especially mellow, he thought. More mellow than the earlier ones, and it made Justin wonder what the cat knew that he did not.

"I've been thinking lately that she'd want you to stay on here," Amos Picou said as he stepped up onto the wooden porch and took his customary seat on the well-worn wicker chair next to Justin's porch swing. The same chair he'd been sitting in for every one of the twenty-five years he'd come visiting.

It had been Eula's favorite chair—her chair of honor, she'd called it, because of its high, fan-shaped back. She'd loved that chair as it had reminded her of a throne, and she had spent many of her evenings sitting in it. Said it made her feel like royalty because she sat so high and mighty, which was why she'd always offered to let her guests sit in it, because in her house guests had always been treated like royalty.

In a way, Eula Bergeron had been royalty in that part of Big Swamp. There'd been no one more trusted or respected. With the way she'd been held in such high esteem in her community, there was no other way to describe it. Justin's grandmother had been treasured, and that was something he hadn't seen so much back in his childhood as he'd been too busy seeing other things—dreams, or delusions, of a better life mostly. Life away from here, somewhere, anywhere other than Big Swamp. Something other than what his grandmother had given him.

He hadn't appreciated her enough, and that had played on his mind more than he probably even recognized. Those sleepless nights, guilt trips, wanting to make it up to her when he could, feeling like hell after it was too late.

Now that he was back for a little while to tie up loose ends, he was reminded of all the respect for his grandmother everywhere he looked. "Not sure what I'm going to do, Amos," Justin said, his voice betraying his lackluster mood. "Can't stay here, but I don't want to walk away from the people who depended on my grandmother and leave them with nothing."

"Folks in these parts need them a good doctor now that your Bonne-Maman Eula has left us. They'd be mighty grateful if you stayed on to look after them. I think Eula would have approved of that, getting you back home where you belong."

"Except I don't belong here now." Justin exhaled an exasperated breath. "Too many years, too much separation… Besides, she knew how I felt about coming home for good. Knew I didn't want any part of it, that short visits to see her were the best I could do."

"She knew that, boy. Knew you loved what you were doing, where you were doing it. All she wanted was for you to be happy."

"And I was…am. But…" He shrugged his shoulders. "I don't know how to explain it.

"Torn between your worlds."

"Did she ever tell you I asked her to come live with me in Chicago?"

"She had a good laugh over that. Appreciated the gesture, laughed at the idea of living in such a city. I lived there for a while once upon a time. Can't say that I hated it, but it sure didn't fit me. And it sure wouldn't have fit Eula, either."

"I wanted to buy her a condo in New Orleans."

"Which kept her closer to home, which would have probably been even worse for her, so close and yet so far away from it." He shook his head. "Eula was a single-minded woman and it was a mind you weren't going to change. Not for any reason outside of you needing someone to take care of you."

"Maybe I should have lied."

"Or left it the way she wanted."

"The way she wanted it…" He pulled a crumpled letter from his pocket. "'You'd be a good doctor here, Justin. Promise me you'll think about it.' Well, I've been thinking. That's all I've been doing and I don't understand how she could have asked that of me. She knew better."

"I supposed she did, but do you?"

"I can't stay here and dispense herbs. That's all there is to it."

"Dispense herbs, get the folks in the area used to traditional medicine. Sounds to me that's exactly what she wanted from you."

"But I can't do it! She'd asked me before, I'd told her no. Then she'd told me I'd know when it was time to come home. But I can't just come home. Home is Chicago now. In a penthouse overlooking the lakeshore, senior member of a general surgery practice. That's home."

"You're sounding awfully defensive about it, boy."

"Because I am defensive about it. I've worked hard at setting up the life I want, and I'm not about to change that to come back here."

"Ah, but you could compromise, couldn't you? You, know…practice what you want most of the time, slip in a little bit of what they want every now and again? Make everybody happy."

Yes, right. Make everybody happy but him. "You are persistent, old man. Gotta give you credit for that." In spite of the man's almost daily nagging, Justin liked him. Always had. Amos Picou was ageless, with his unflawed black skin that showed no wrinkles, no age. Like Napoleon, Amos had come around for as long as Justin could remember, bringing his grandmother gator steaks, crawfish and whatever other food he managed to scrounge in Big Swamp. He'd always gone herb hunting with Eula, too, claiming Big Swamp was no place for a woman alone. Unrequited love, Justin suspected. Although he'd never asked and Amos had never told.

Rumor had it, though, that Amos had a little herb patch of his own, something he grew, cured and smoked. Perhaps that was the secret to his longevity and youth.

"That's the only way you get what you want, son. If you want it bad enough, you go after it and don't give up till it's dead, or till you're dead. That's what my grand-daddy always taught me." He grinned. "Compromise is good for the soul, too. It'll make you feel like you're in a giving spirit, yet you have the good feeling that comes along with a victory of getting what you want. Best of both worlds, I always say."

"But when you say you want me to compromise, you mean give up everything I've worked hard to get, just so I can come here and dispense swamp morning glory to cure centipede bites to a bunch of people who hate me? Because that's not me, Amos." He shook his head vigorously. "I have a great respect for my grand-mother's herbal cures, but for me life here is tough. Too tough. I don't fit in and I never have. That's what I ran away from when I was a kid, and I'm sure as hell not planning on coming back to it. That's why I hired that nurse to come in and help my grandmother—to keep me away from the medicine here. So maybe she's the one you should be trying to convince to take over, since all I've heard for the past year is glowing reports."

His grandmother had called Mellette Chaisson a god-send. He'd called her the compromise he'd needed to assuage his guilty feeling at not being the one to help his grandmother. The worst of it was, a traveling nurse who spent two days a week here assuaged a lot of his guilt. Just not all of it.

"That nurse was a real blessing for your grandmother, especially getting on toward the end. But she's not the solution here now, and you know that."

Yes, he did know that, which was why he was passing his days and nights only writing. Writing was where he could escape, a different world. A place with no guilt. "What I know is that I'm doing the best I can for the people here. I support that nurse coming in, and I'll continue to do that. Even up her presence here if that's what needs to happen."

"But what about the other days of the week, Justin? If we get sick, if somebody gets hurt, do we just wait until she comes back? Put our aches and pains on hold until her next day on duty?"

"You take a twenty-five-mile trip to the nearest hospital. This area of the bayou may be remote, but it's not entirely cut off from civilization."

Amos laughed out loud over that. "Whose universe are you living in, boy? Because you know the people here aren't makin' that trip. They keep to themselves, don't step foot in the big city unless it's absolutely necessary, go over to Grandmaison only when it's necessary, and they never, ever, look for medical help outside Big Swamp. That's just the way things are around here."

"Then that's their problem, because help's available."

"And it was your grandmother's problem, because she doctored these people every day of her life."

"She gave them herbs, Amos. The rest of it was…"

He wanted to say hysteria, or emotional dependence, but that would be downplaying what his grandmother had done for the isolated people in Big Swamp, and he sure didn't want to do that. "I'm not my grandmother. I don't have her knowledge of herbs. Can't be what anybody here wants."

"Can't, or won't?"

"Same difference. Anyway…" He shrugged. "Let me think on it some more, try to figure out what's best."

"You know what's best, boy. Seems to me you're spending all your time trying to figure your way around it. And it's not like we expect you to be here all the time. Keep that nurse coming in two days, then use some of that city money you make and fly down here for two days yourself. Or maybe transfer your fine medical skills to one of the hospital establishments in New Orleans to make it easier on you. That would work. Would suit us just fine, too."

Amos pulled out one of his homemade cigarettes, tamped down the end of it, then stuck it in his mouth and lit it up. "But here you sit, all bound up with some heavy confusion," he said, letting the first long draw settle into his lungs.

"Here I sit because I'm tying up my grandmother's affairs," Justin said defensively.

A deep, rumbling laugh started from what seemed like the pit of Amos's belly and burbled its way out. "Tying up her affairs, my ass," he said, offering Justin a hit of his cigarette.

Justin refused.

"You're here because you got yourself caught someplace between heaven and hell, and you don't know which way to turn. Part of you is pulling to go one way but part of you is holding back for some reason you probably don't even understand yet." Amos took another draw of his cigarette, and chuckled. "You're confused, boy. Just plain confused."

"Not denying it," Justin said, taking another sip of tea. "I'm confused, and I feel guilty as hell that I didn't know she was sick. Guilty that I didn't come back to see her as much as I would have if I'd known. I mean, I loved my grandmother, but..."

"But you didn't make her life easy."

"Not when I was a boy." He'd tried harder when he was a man, though.

"And now that you're a man you're paying for something she'd long ago forgot. She didn't hold it against you, boy. In fact, she was proud of what you made of yourself. Bragged on it all the time."

"And didn't tell me she was sick."

"Because you would have stuck her in some fancy hospital where she didn't want to go."

"If she'd gone she might not have..." He bit his tongue to hold back the bitterness. It didn't matter. Choices had been made; he hadn't been included. "Anyway, I'm trying to figure it out. I'll be talking to the nurse, and I'll see if she can give you another day. But that's the best I can do."

"The best you can do is admit you're still one of us, and give us that day yourself. Would have been Eula's wish."

"Damn it, Amos! I can't just commute from Chicago one day a week, and I'm not going to transfer to a New Orleans hospital to be closer. Also, I'm not one of you, which is the biggest problem. I never was. Not even when I was a kid, and you know that."

"That's right, city boy. You come from spoiled uppity folks who never would step foot in Big Swamp for fear something might bite them, or dirty their pretty little leather shoes." He kicked his foot up, showing up a well-worn, holey sneaker that had seen better days a decade ago. "I do have me a fine pair of alligator boots I save for special occasions, but that's not good enough for the Bergerons who left these parts."

"Would that be me?" Justin asked, knowing in some ways it was. He'd been from the city, raised there until he was five, then dumped on a grandmother he'd never met when his parents had died in a plane crash.

"If you want it to be, boy. Only if you want it to be."

The problem was, while his formative years had been spent in Big Swamp, he'd turned uppity, as it was called in these parts. But only after walking a long, hard road to get there. "Never mine, *mon cher,*" his grandmother had said to him on many occasions. "You've still got the good in you." *The good.* Whatever that was.

After the way he'd behaved he wasn't sure the good she'd seen was still there. If it ever had been.

His grandmother had loved him dearly, though. Taken him in without question when asked, raised him the best way she'd known how. And loved him. Dear God, that woman had possessed such a capacity for love. Along with the same generous capacity for forgiveness and understanding. "What I want…" Justin paused. Listened to the same barred owl he'd been listening to earlier, then sighed. "Don't have a clue." Not a clue, except that he couldn't stay here.

"Sure you do, boy. It's just going to take some strong medicine to cure you—something that's stronger than anything you can prescribe." Amos took another draw on his cigarette, then stood up. "Got me a couple dozen fresh eggs and a loaf of Miss Minnie's bread, made fresh this afternoon. Caught me a whole mess of crawfish today, too. So I'm fixing up a fine scramble for breakfast in the morning. Bring some peppers and onions and I'll see you around six."

"Nine," Justin countered. "And no chicory in the coffee."

"Seven-thirty, city boy. And it's not coffee if it doesn't have chicory. So don't be late, or I'll be startin' without you." He smacked his lips. "Havin' those crawfish all for myself."

Okay, so part of Big Swamp was in his blood. He loved crawfish and wasn't ashamed to admit it. He missed the way his grandmother had fixed them. "Fine, seven-thirty. But not a minute earlier. And go easy on the hot sauce, old man," Justin said as Amos ambled off the porch. "Don't want to burn my tongue off."

Amos's only reply was another one of his belly laughs.

Rather than dragging a reluctant child up the sidewalk, Mellette gave in and picked up the protesting three-year-old Leonie and carried her the length of the pavement. Passing by the red azaleas and pink bougainvillea, walking under a drape of lavender wisteria, which she'd dearly loved since she was a child, she struggled the squiggling bundle up the steps of the white plantation mansion, on past the massive columns supporting the front porch overhang, and straight to the mahogany doors. "I'll be home before you're in bed," she said as she fought to grab hold of the doorknob.

"Why can't I come with you?" Leonie whined.

"Because I don't have time to watch you." And there were alligators, and the swamp, and all manner of other outdoor things that weren't safe for a three-year-old who lived to escape her mother's watchful eye. "Mommy has patients to see all day." And Mommy was beginning to wear down from the daily grind of her work, which meant she wasn't as alert as she needed to be. Not alert enough, anyway, to take care of a day's worth of patients as well as look after a rambunctious toddler who, every day, in every way, was growing to be more and more like her daddy. Something that warmed Mellette's heart, and broke it at the same time.

"I told you we'd take care of those bills," Zenobia Doucet said sharply as she took Leonie from Mellette. "You're killing yourself, working so hard. And your daughter needs you. Just look at her—she's wild. And you… You're a mess. Doucet women should look better, Mellette. And if you weren't working out there in the bayou…"

Instinctively, she pushed her short hair back from her face. "But I am working in the bayou. And I'm hoping that job is still there for me now that Eula's gone." She worked there to help pay off medical bills left over from

Landry's illness. They were her responsibility, and she took her responsibilities seriously. "One more year, and I'll be free and clear. Then I won't have to moonlight." One more year and she'd be so ready to move on.

"Darling, you lost your house, they took away your car...you and my granddaughter live in a one-room apartment. You need better than that, and your father and I—"

"And we're making it work, Mother," she interrupted, brushing a kiss on her mother's cheek.

"But you don't have to be so proud about it. We're family, and family's supposed to help."

Sometimes it was still hard to believe that Landry was gone, because everything in her life revolved around him. But he was, had been for over two years now. A short bout with a devastating cancer, and she'd been widowed with a baby. Left with insurmountable debt she wouldn't let her family take over for her. Landry had been a proud man and she'd loved that about him. She had her own pride, too. And sure, a bailout from her family would have been easy. Move in, take money. But it wasn't right. She and Landry had agreed on that before his death. Although now Mellette was sure Landry hadn't known the extent of debt left to her. But that was okay. It was their agreement, something she had to do to honor his memory. And, yes, she was prideful, because she wanted to be an example for her daughter. Wanted not only to teach her strength but show her strength.

So she worked two jobs, raised a daughter and made one concession on child care, not just because her family doing it for free was helpful—which it was. But if she couldn't spend much time with her daughter these days, she at least wanted her daughter in the arms of people who loved and cherished her. Mellette's father, a retired anesthesiologist, spent his days with Leonie. Her mother, an active physician and chief of staff at New Hope Medical Center, spent evenings with Leonie when that was necessary. Her six sisters—all medical in one capacity or another—took turns when they could. And it worked beautifully.

They were an eminently qualified family to care for one little girl. And a family who loved Leonie with a passion. So Mellette had no qualms about leaving her daughter with them, except that she was missing out, and that hurt. Because her mother was correct. Leonie needed more of her. "I love you and Daddy for wanting to help me but, like I've told you, it's working out."

"But it breaks my heart, seeing how hard you're working. Seeing how it's dragging you down like it is."

"What I need most is to know that Leonie's in good hands. She's my biggest concern, and it makes me feel a lot better knowing you all have her when I can't."

"Your father and I would never refuse her, and you know that. And if you ever change your mind..."

"I know," Mellette said, glancing at her watch. One hour until her first patient arrived, and she still had to take that hellish boat ride in. Sure, she could drive in, but it took twice as long and that extra time the boat afforded her was time she spent with Leonie. "Look, I'm running behind. Got patients to see, and I'm barely going to beat them to the door. I'll be back tonight, but it's going to be a late day because I need to get some things straight with Justin. So go ahead and keep Leonie for the night, and I promised her I'd be back to tuck her in. Although I'm not sure she'll be awake when I get here. And if you don't mind, I'll probably crash here tonight, as well."

"Or you could just move home," Zenobia said again. "Lord knows, we have plenty of room."

Yes, they did have the room. But Mellette needed her private time with Leonie, and their tiny apartment suited them for now.

Mellette gave her mother another kiss on the cheek. "Tell Daddy I love him, and that maybe I'll see him later tonight." She gave her daughter a kiss. "And you, young lady, need to be good for your grandmother. Promise?"

Leonie gave her mother a sullen look and didn't answer. Which made Mellette's load even heavier to bear. But there was nothing she could do right now. One more year, though, and things would be different. Just one more year...

Mellette Chaisson. Justin really didn't know much about her. He'd hired her from the registry, had liked her credentials. Had liked her voice over the phone during the interviews. Liked what he'd seen of her bedside manner, as well. But when she was here he pretty much stayed away because the people trusted her with their problems. Whereas they were wary around him. So he didn't want to shake up that dynamic, which meant that the days she was here, he wasn't. From what he'd seen in passing, though, he did like her. Especially the way she threw herself into her work.

Except she always looked tired. "They're lining up today," he told her, as she rushed through the kitchen and quickly stowed a couple of bottles of water and a sandwich in the fridge.

"There's a flu virus going around. Ever since we had that malaria come though, people get nervous with the least little sniffle."

"People overreact."

She arched her back, bared her claws at that insensitive remark. "Four people in the community died of malaria, Doctor. If that causes the rest of them to overreact, then I suppose they have a right to. And you know what? While you may pay my salary, you're really not entitled to an opinion since you don't get involved in anything other than putting a signature on a check."

Okay, so maybe liking her was too strong. He admired her dedication to her work. Didn't know a thing about her, though. Not a single thing. Except she wore a wedding ring. Had a fiery temper. And she was a good nurse. Of course, his grandmother had liked her, too, and that said a lot. "So what you're telling me is that your employer isn't allowed to express an opinion about his employee's work."

"Yes," she said, quite sternly. "And, technically, I was not your employee. I worked for your grandmother, who worked for the community."

He couldn't help but smile. "Then that makes me... what?"

"Right now, a nuisance. Go to work, see a few of

those couple dozen people out there who want to be seen, and I could be persuaded to change my mind about that. Otherwise get out of my way."

Mellette slammed through the kitchen door, hurried down the hall and into the area Eula had set aside for her clinic. The people waiting there were orderly and polite, no one pushing and shoving to be seen first. But there were so many of them, she was beginning to wonder if she'd be able to make good on that promise to tuck her daughter in tonight, because if she wasn't out of here by dusk, she wasn't going.

Travelling during the daylight was one thing, and she'd gotten used to that. But Big Swamp at night was a whole different story, and not one she particularly wanted to face. Call her a coward, call her a chicken... she'd answer to it all because she was a city girl. Hadn't even known these isolated pocket communities existed in Big Swamp until a year ago when she'd seen the ad for a part-time nurse. And she'd spent her entire life living so close to here.

Talk about an isolated existence! Raised with all the advantages, she was almost embarrassed to admit where she'd lacked. Landry had made up for that in a lot of ways, not being from that proverbial silver-spoon family, like she was. But all this... Areas where an entire community of people existed, totally out of step with society, living a good life independently. Nothing was taken for granted here. And every kind gesture was appreciated.

"I don't work here," Justin said, following her into the clinic, which had actually been his grandmother's parlor. Now it was a plain room with several wooden chairs and a curtain to separate the waiting area from the person being seen. There was nothing medicinal here. No equipment, no real medicines. Of course, Eula Bergeron hadn't practiced medicine. She'd been a self-taught herbalist. Someone who'd known which swamp herbs cured what.

"But you could, since you're not doing anything else."

"The people don't trust me."

"Probably because you've given them good reason not to."

"You're actually right about that. So what's the point of wasting my time?"

"What's the point of even being here if you're not going to make yourself useful?" she snapped. "Look, we need to talk. Today. Later."

"You're right. I was thinking about asking you to put in another day every week."

"Another day?" Mellette sputtered. "And just where would I get that?"

Justin shrugged. "I assumed…"

She stepped around him, and gestured her first patient to the area behind the cabinet. "Don't assume anything about me, Doctor. And while you're at it, don't presume, either. Now, if you'll excuse me, I have patients who need medical care. If you're not willing to provide it, get out!"

She pointed to the front door without another word. But what was there to say? Justin Bergeron was an annoyance. If she hadn't heard Eula mention him so much this past year, she would have never guessed this man and the veritable *saint* Eula had talked about so lovingly were one and the same. But they were, and she wondered about the discrepancy. Wondered a whole lot.

CHAPTER TWO

It was hard watching her work, and doing nothing himself. She had such a look of determination, though. Brown eyes narrowed to her task. Biting down in concentration on her lower lip. He did have to admit Mellette was a looker. Tall, with legs that went on forever. Nice athletic form with well-defined feminine muscles. Smooth, dark skin, boyish-cut black hair with just a hint of natural curl, and all of it thrown into her work while he stood on the sidelines, casually observing.

But that was the way his days went since people around here would hardly even speak to him outside a stiff hello or an unfriendly nod accompanied by a muffled grunt. So what the hell made him think they'd accept him as a doctor? Someone to trust, someone to confide in. Someone to take care of them the way his grandmother had.

Clovis Fonseca, for example. He was waiting in line to have Mellette see him—Justin wasn't sure why—and if it weren't for the fact that Justin had stolen his canoe some twenty-five years ago, then gone and torn a hole in the bottom of it by racking it up on a cypress stump, Clovis might have been inclined to let Justin take a look at him. But Clovis held a grudge, and Justin had seen it every time he'd looked in the man's eyes since he'd come home. There was no way Clovis would ever consent to a physical exam from Justin, probably just as Clovis would probably never even greet him with anything other than a snarly sort of a snort.

And Ambrosine Trahan. He felt really bad about her because she'd loved him when they'd been kids, but he'd blatantly asked out her younger sister, Emmy Lou, the prettier of the two girls. It hadn't been so much that he'd wanted to go out with Emmy Lou, because he hadn't. She hadn't been his type, either. But he'd simply been trying to rebuff Ambrosine because back in the day he hadn't gone out with girls who hadn't been pretty. In fact, he'd been known to be intentionally cruel to them. So she was waiting in line today, a beautiful woman now, by all estimations, probably hanging on to horrible memories of the way he'd treated her, and he seriously doubted she'd want to claim him as her doctor. And rightfully so. He was so embarrassed just remembering the way he'd treated her.

The problem was, the line of waiting patients was full of bad experiences left over from his ill-mannered youth, and he didn't trust any of them to trust him. And who could blame them? He'd been a repeat offender on all fronts. After he'd taken Clovis's boat, he'd had pretty much the same experience with Rex Rimbaut's pickup truck. Taken it, banged it up. Then there had been that time he'd flaunted a date with Ambrosine's cousin, Ida, in front of both Ambrosine and Emmy Lou. Ida had been pretty. He'd done the same with their other cousin, Marie Rosella, as well, who had been even prettier.

So nothing gave Justin reason to believe that any one of those people waiting to be seen by Mellette would believe that he'd turned over that new leaf. Especially when each and every one of them assumed he'd neglected his grandmother at the end of her life. It was something that overshadowed everything else. And no one knew the real story, that she'd purposely not told him she was failing for fear that he'd want to do something drastic, like move her to the big city, rather than let her die where she wanted to.

No, history wouldn't repeat itself on his account. But as far as the people here were concerned, twenty-five years ago was the same as yesterday, and time wasn't healing the bad thoughts they had of him. He was Justin Bergeron, bad boy. Poor Eula's pitiful excuse for a grandson.

And poor Eula's pitiful grandson wasn't welcome to touch them, not for any reason. They'd just as soon go without medical help as accept his.

Which made Justin feel like hell, seeing how hard Mellette was working while all he was doing was standing around, twiddling his thumbs and wallowing in his just desserts.

"Anything I could do where they wouldn't see me?" he finally asked her, as she rushed into the kitchen to grab a drink of water. Looking frazzled. But sexy frazzled.

"Right. Like you really want to work," she said, not even trying to hide her contempt for him.

"I'm not saying I *want* to work. But I am saying I would, if I could." It was either that or go back to his writing, and today, like yesterday and the day before that, he wasn't in that frame of mind. In spite of an upcoming deadline, there were too many distractions. Too many things to think about. Too many humiliating memories floating around in his mind, pushing out the intelligible words that might have gone down on paper.

"Then just do it, Doctor. The only way these people are ever going to get over their grudges against you is to see you do something worthwhile. Otherwise, in their eyes, you're still a bad boy who gave his grandma more grief than she needed." She tossed him a devious smile. "And a bad doctor who lets me work my fingers to the bone while he's standing around, making an ass of himself, doing nothing to help. So take your pick... ass or bad boy."

"Do I get a third choice?"

"Two's the limit around here. So what's it going to be?" She took a swig out of the water bottle, then recapped it. "Because two people off my list and onto yours might make the difference between me making it home to tuck my daughter into bed tonight or being stuck here all night, since I don't negotiate Big Swamp alone after dark."

So she had a wedding ring *and* a daughter. Interesting information—not that he wanted to be involved with her in any way other than professionally. But he did enjoy these brief glimpses into her life and wondered what else he might see if he paid attention. "Okay, let me see what I can do." With that, Justin went to the waiting area, then continued on through and opened the front door so the people standing around on the porch and in the yard could hear his announcement.

"For what it's worth, I'm a fully qualified medical doctor. I'm sure my grandmother mentioned that to all of you at one point. I know there are a few…several of you who probably don't want me seeing you on a professional basis, and I do understand why. But if there are any of you who'd let me examine you, I'd be glad to do so. And the fewer people Mrs. Chaisson has to see, the sooner she'll get home to her…family. So I'll be in the kitchen. If you're not still holding a grudge against me, I'll be glad to see you. Actually, I'll be glad to see you even if you are still holding a grudge. Either way…" He shrugged, then stepped back inside and immediately looked at Mellette, who was standing near the room divider, smiling.

"Seriously?" she said. "That's how you tell people you're open for business? It sounded more like a challenge than an invitation. You know, come stand in my line, if you dare."

"Best I can do. If the folks here want to see me, now they know they can. And if they don't, I'll be in the kitchen, cooking up a pot of gumbo." Fixing gumbo, practicing medicine, all in the same room. What had he been thinking?

"But that's not what Eula had me taking," Miss Willie Bascomb scolded. "And you should know better than to give me the wrong thing, young man. Do you think I'm too old to see what you're trying to do to me, switching off my medicine the way you are? It's shameful. Just shameful!" She was a gray-haired lady with sharp eyes and an even sharper tongue.

"But it's a simple anti-inflammatory for your arthritis," Justin said. "The prescription's easily filled at any pharmacy, and I can write you a script for ninety days so you won't have to go to town for it very often." Her knuckles were enlarged, fingers slightly bent into an outward curve. Nothing about Miss Willie had changed since he'd been a kid, and her condition seemed stable for the most part, but he didn't want to prescribe an herbal potion when the market was full of great prescription drugs that could prevent further joint damage.

"But I don't want me no prescription, Justin Aloysius. What your grandma gave me has worked well for as long as I can remember. Cures the aches, and that's all I need." She held up her crippled hands. "They haven't gotten any worse in all this time, and it's just plain foolish, wanting me to change my medicine when things are going well. Eula wouldn't have allowed that." She wagged a scolding forefinger at him. "And shame on you for trying."

The only problem was Eula wasn't here, and he couldn't duplicate her herbal cures, which for Miss Willie's condition was sassafras combined with prickly ash, cayenne and camphor, made into what his grandmother had called her rheumatism liniment. So in practical terms he was wasting his time with this patient because she wasn't about to budge, just as he wasn't. "Then I think we have a problem, because I can't give you what my grandmother used to make. Even if I wanted to, which I don't, I don't know how to make it."

"Because you were off gallivanting in the big city when you should have been staying home, studying *real* medicine, young man!" Miss Willie sniffed indignantly. "I wanted to give you a chance for Eula's sake. She talked so highly of you, said you were the best doctor there is. But she was wrong, and it would have killed her to see just how sorry you are."

Talk about a bitter pill to swallow. "All I can do is recommend what my kind of medicine considers standard. It's up to you whether or not you want to take it."

"What I want to take is my leave, young man!" With that, Miss Willie slid off the kitchen stool, gathered up her patent-leather purse, which she stuffed into the crook of her arm, and her floral print scarf, which she didn't bother putting on her head, and headed for the kitchen door. "You tell Mellette I want my usual. She'll know how to fix it for me."

Then she was gone. Miss Willie and all her one hundred pounds of acrimonious fire stormed out the back door, but not before she'd looked in the pot of gumbo and snorted again. "I don't smell filé in there," she said. "To make a good gumbo you've got to use filé powder, or do you have some fancy prescription for that, too?"

"Seems like sassafras is going to be your downfall today," Mellette said, walking into the kitchen through the front door at the same time the back door slammed shut. She was referring to filé, a thickening powder made from dried sassafras leaves.

"She always was a tough old lady," Justin replied,

on his way to the kitchen cabinet to look for filé. "Who wants what she wants."

"She swears by the liniment. Don't think she's going to change her mind about that, and at her age I guess that's her right."

"But I can't give her the damned liniment." He turned to look at her. "And as a registered nurse, I'm surprised you would."

"When you hired me to come to Big Swamp to help your grandmother, what did you expect me to do? Dispense pills these people don't want to take? That's not what Eula wanted, not what she would have tolerated from me. So she taught me her ways and for the most part it works out."

"So I'm paying you to practice my grandmother's version of medicine? Because that's not what I wanted."

"What you wanted was to have me help her, which was what I did. On her terms, though. Not yours."

"If I'd wanted someone to dispense more of what my grandmother dispensed, that's who I would have hired. But I wanted a registered nurse, someone from the traditional side of medicine. Someone to take care of the people here the way traditional medicine dictates."

"Then I expect you've been paying me under false pretenses because I've been taking care of these people just the way your grandmother did and, so far, nobody's complaining."

"You're still doing that even now that she's gone?"

"Especially now that she's gone. They're scared to death they're going to have to give up the folk medicine they've trusted for decades, and I suppose if you have your way, that's what's going to happen. Which just adds to the list of reasons why they don't like you."

He pulled a tin marked filé from the cabinet and measured out a scant spoonful for the gumbo.

"Twice that much," she prompted him.

"You're a chef, as well?"

"I know how your grandmother fixed gumbo, and I'm assuming you're trying to copy that since it's probably the best gumbo I've had anywhere."

He shook his head, not sure if he should be angry or frustrated. Or both. "So tell me, how am I supposed to treat Miss Willie when she won't take a traditional anti-inflammatory?"

"You give her what she wants, then if you insist on one of the regular drugs, maybe you can prescribe it after she's come to trust you."

"Which will be when hell freezes over," he snapped.

"Probably. But she's reasonable. All the people here are reasonable, which is why, when malaria hit, they took quinine—"

"Quinine?" he interrupted. "Isn't that pretty old-school treatment for malaria?"

"Been around for hundreds of years, but it's cheap, and it works. And it's what I was able to get the pharmaceutical companies to donate to me."

"Seriously?"

She nodded. "That's the way it works here, Justin. For the most part we get donated drugs, prescriptions that have gone over the expiration date but are still good, partial prescriptions that haven't all been taken. And quinine worked just fine for us. But I used it along with Eula's prescribed water and orange juice fast, along with warm-water cleanses. It all worked together, and who's to say which was more effective—the natural remedy or the quinine, which is actually a natural remedy itself."

"So what you're telling me is that patience with the people here will be a virtue."

"My husband always said patience is more than a virtue, it's a necessity. But he was the most patient man to ever grace the earth." She smiled fondly. "Which was good, because I'm not and I needed that counterbalance."

"Then I say your husband deserves an award, because there aren't too many patient people around."

"He did deserve an award," she said. "For a lot more than his patience. Landry was a good man. Maybe the best man I'll ever know."

She was speaking of him in the past tense, but Justin hated to ask, because if she was widowed, that was something he should have read on her application for working with his grandmother. Truth was, he'd hardly read past her name and credentials, he had been so impatient to hire someone. "And you're not…" He glanced down at her wedding ring.

"Not moving on, like most people think I should. But I don't have to. Landry can't be replaced, and I don't particularly want to."

"How long?" he asked.

"A little over two years. Leonie was just a baby when he was diagnosed, and he didn't get to stay with us very long after that. It was a pervasive pancreatic cancer. Took him almost before he knew he was sick. And you know what? If I'd known your grandmother then, I'd have been happy to give her herbal treatments a try, because I was desperate for anything. To try anything that might save him."

"I'm so sorry," Justin said.

"So am I, every day of my life. But thank you for the sentiment."

"You're raising your daughter by yourself?"

"Yes, but I have a supportive family—mother, father, six sisters. They're so much help to me, and they love Leonie. You might have heard of my mother, actually. Zenobia."

Justin blinked hard. "Seriously? Dr. Doucet is your mother? I've heard her lecture. She's…extraordinary."

"I think so. As a mother, anyway. As a doctor, I know she has her reputation, but I don't pay much attention to that. So now, about Miss Willie…" Mellette pulled a small jar out of the pocket of her tan cargo pants and handed it to him. "I'd suggest you take this to her and try to make amends. I'm with you on getting her an anti-inflammatory prescription since I've been noting some gradual changes in her physicality, but in the year I've worked here she's refused every time I've mentioned it. Maybe if you can get on her good side…"

He laughed out loud. "Do you really think that's going to happen?"

"No. But I don't believe in giving up."

He tucked the jar of liniment into his pocket, then went back to the stove to stir the gumbo. "I'm serious about wanting you to add an extra day to your schedule here."

"And I'm serious about not having the time. I work full time in emergency at New Hope, and between that and this, there's no more time to give you. As it is, you're getting my two days off from the hospital every week."

"What about working here full time?" he asked, not sure where that had come from. Certainly, he could afford her. But he wasn't sure he wanted to.

"You don't mean that."

"Actually, I might."

"You'd have to match, maybe even exceed my entire salary from the hospital, depending on how many hours you'd want me to work here, plus make up the difference for what you're paying me when I'm here. And you'd have to cover my benefits—insurance, retirement plan, paid holiday. I'm a pretty well-paid specialist, Doctor, and I really don't think I'm the solution for whatever you're trying to accomplish."

"What I'm trying to accomplish is to offer this community more medical care than they currently have. My grandmother loved these people, and taking care of them is what she would have wanted me to do."

"Then stay and take care of them."

"Not a chance."

She smiled. "Eula said you were too good for the likes of Big Swamp. Although I think she secretly believed you'd come back to it someday."

"I'm not too good for Big Swamp. I might have thought that at one time, but I grew up. But I do have a life that doesn't include mosquitoes, muskrats and alligators, and it's a life I enjoy."

"I have a life I enjoy, too, and if I don't get back to my patients, I'm not going to get home to that life tonight." Mellette headed for the door, then spun around to face him before she went back to the room full of waiting patients. "Your grandma was proud of the work you do, Justin. *My grandson, the real doctor,* is what she always used to say. For what it's worth, I don't think she ever resented the fact that you chose the city over her."

In the city... Yes, that was where he belonged. But lately he wasn't sure why. In fact, the only thing he was sure of at the moment was that hiring Mellette had been one of the best things he'd done in a long, long time. Now all he had to do was convince her to take over here full time. Maybe then his guilty feelings would be assuaged. Or some of them.

The day went surprisingly fast, and while the patients weren't flocking to Justin, the handful he did manage to see turned out to be a big help to her. So now Mellette could get out of Big Swamp before dark and make it back to Leonie before bedtime, for which she was eternally grateful. "You going to work again tomorrow?" she asked him, as she dipped a spoon into the gumbo that had been simmering for the better part of the day.

"If you want to call it working. I saw four people, and got rejected by four people."

"But they gave you a chance, and that's almost as good as them letting you treat them. Good gumbo, by the way. I think you inherited Eula's cooking talents."

"That was one of the things I always took for granted, I think. She had an amazing way in the kitchen that I didn't appreciate until I was away from here, living on fast food and whatever else I could scrounge cheaply."

"Well, if you should ever decide to give up medicine, I can definitely see you in a restaurant kitchen."

"I'd invite you to stay, except I know you want to get back to your daughter."

"And I might have taken you up on the offer, but you're right. I need some time with her—don't get enough of it." Heading toward the door, she paused before she stepped outside. "Did you ever take that liniment to Miss Willie?" she asked. "Because if you didn't, I'm betting now would be a good time. And I think she'd appreciate the gumbo, too. She doesn't do much cooking for herself these days, and a nice, hearty meal would do her some good."

"As much good as it would do me, getting into her good graces?"

"Every little bit helps," she quipped. "Oh, and I think she probably likes her gumbo over rice."

"Can you point me in the direction of her house?" he asked. "I might have known once, but it's been a long time since I've gone tromping through this backcountry, and I don't particularly like the idea of getting lost out there this time of day."

"I can do you better than pointing. I'm going to go right by her place. I can give you a lift, and that should be good enough to show you how to get yourself back before the sun goes down."

It didn't take a minute for Justin to ladle out enough

gumbo for several meals into one bowl, and scoop up an ample amount of rice into another. "Who would have ever guessed I'd be making house calls and carrying in food," he said, shutting the kitchen door behind him, then following Mellette down to the boat dock where her skiff was moored.

It was a small boat but big enough to seat four comfortably. Not fast, but high enough to sit her above the reach of alligators and other water creatures that might get curious. Not that an alligator had ever come near enough to threaten her. But she was a city girl after all. And even though her city sat on the edge of Big Swamp, that didn't mean she had swamp experience. In fact, she'd surprised herself taking this part-time job where she had to boat in and out for easiest access, dodging stumps and roots. There'd been any number of part-time opportunities available at New Hope, or in other private enterprises, but something about the call of the wild had intrigued her.

Maybe it had been Landry's influence. He'd loved Big Swamp. Had spent part of his childhood in a community not too far from here. Being here made her feel closer to him.

"Who'd have ever thought you'd get me out on the bayou in a boat, all by myself, just to get to work?" she countered, as she took her seat and started the engine. "But never say never, right?"

"Being a Doucet, I guess this really wouldn't be normal for you, would it?" he said, setting down the bowls of food in the bottom of the boat.

"Being a Doucet, nothing's normal. We're an... I

guess the best way you can put it is an unusual family. Seven girls… My poor daddy. I know he wanted a son, but he turned out to be quite prodigious in the daughter department. And at times I think it simply overwhelmed him. Then he held out such high hopes for a grandson when I was pregnant, and got another girl."

"Whom he loves, I'm sure," Justin said, sitting back as the thrum of the boat's engine settled into a gentle cadence while they wound their way through Big Swamp trees.

"He adores her. In fact, Daddy's retired now—he was an anesthesiologist—and he's the one who watches Leonie most of the time. Spoils her rotten. But I do hope that someday one of my sisters gives him a grandson."

"Leonie's his only grandchild?"

"So far. I'm the only one who's married. My sisters Sabine and Delphine, twins, are dedicated doctors, and Magnolia's a legal medical investigator. Then there are Ghislaine, Lisette and Acadia, all of them in various stages of their medical education or careers." She smiled. "We're close in age. My mother didn't want to interrupt her medical career for too long, so she popped us all out pretty quickly, about a year apart. And so far I'm the only one to take the marriage plunge. But it's Daddy's biggest fear that the rest of them will fall in love at the same time and he'll have to spring for six weddings in rapid succession."

"I can't even imagine having that many brothers or sisters," he said.

"Eula never really told me much about your family situation."

"There wasn't much to tell. I was an only child. Didn't come from Big Swamp, although my father did, obviously, as Eula was his mother. But my grandfather took my dad out of here when he left my grandmother to seek fame and fortune or whatever it is he wanted to do, and never looked back. He pretty much poisoned my dad to Big Swamp, and the people who lived here. Including my grandmother. Anyway, my parents raised me in New Orleans, then after they were killed—plane crash—I ended up with my grandmother in the place where my dad had refused to go."

"And you forever hated it here?"

"That's what she told you?"

"Not in so many words, but it makes sense. You left here when you were a kid, hardly ever came back to see her. Probably under your father's influence in some remote way. It only stands to reason that you didn't want to be here, given the history. Still don't, I suppose." She steered around a clump of low-hanging moss, then slowed down as a meandering nutria swam by the boat, not at all concerned about being disturbed. It was his domain, she supposed, and he was simply asserting his place in it.

"Still don't on a permanent basis, but I've been back plenty of times to visit my grandmother," he said, but without much conviction in his voice. "Look, earlier when you said we need to talk…you're right. I really do want to sit down and talk to you about what I'm going to do here to take care of these people."

"Why do you care?" she asked as she veered to the left and puttered her way up a shallow inlet.

"Because my grandmother cared."

"Then that leads me to the obvious question."

"Let me save you the trouble of asking. The reason I didn't move back here, not even to New Orleans, to be closer is…complicated, and I'm not even sure I can explain it to myself, let alone someone else. It's just the way things were with me. I ended up in Chicago, liked it and stayed. And, yes, I did have opportunities here. Could have gone to New Hope, actually. But coming back here, being so close…" He shrugged. "I like my practice, like Chicago. Like the life I have there."

"And you were afraid that coming back to Big Swamp, even for visits, would overwhelm you with all kinds of guilty feelings."

She slowed the boat alongside a rickety old dock, then pointed to a shanty about two hundred feet off the water. It was wooden, painted red, with blue shutters. All the paint chipped and faded. In the yard lay three good-size alligators, looking lazy and not particularly interested in the meddlers coming around to bother them.

"Or I was afraid that coming back to Big Swamp would overwhelm me with all kinds of responsibilities I can't handle. Which is turning out to be the case."

"Look, I'm not working tomorrow evening. If you can get to town, come by the house for dinner, around seven. Not sure you'll want to travel these parts at night to get home, so you're invited to stay. It'll be at my parents' house, by the way. I don't live with them, but I'm sure they'll be more than happy to extend their hospitality. That is, if you make it through the gators tonight."

"And just how am I supposed to do that?"

"Very carefully," she said, handing him one of his bowls of food. "They have short legs, so I think you'll be able to outrun them." She laughed. "But they do have that one fast burst of energy at the start, so if you don't make it to dinner tomorrow night, I'll know what happened."

CHAPTER THREE

As the day dragged on, Justin found himself more and more anxious to go to town and have dinner with Mellette and her family. It was a kind invitation, and the idea of being around real medical people again excited him because the longer he was away from his practice the more he missed it. The most appealing part of the evening, though, was the prospect of getting to know Mellette. Even though she'd made it perfectly clear she wasn't ready to move on from her husband.

All that was fine with him, as there was no time in his life for a relationship outside a professional one. He had too much ambition wrapped up in his fast rise to where he was, and that was important to him. Maybe the most important thing. Not that he had anything in mind for Mellette other than trying to convince her to work in Big Swamp full time. Because he didn't. She was his means to an end—he hoped. The person who could put things right for a lot of people. Himself included.

And he'd done some predawn soul-searching on just how to accomplish what he needed. Tried coming up with an incentive that would work for everyone involved, but especially for Mellette, because he wanted to make this offer something that would benefit her in ways that mattered. So by the time dawn began to awaken the bayou, and all the otters and raccoons outside were taking their first morning stretches, he was fairly certain he'd hit upon the perfect plan.

Although he wasn't convinced enough to be smug about it, since he was fully aware that what he was about to offer Mellette could well fly in the face of her close-knit family and cause some blaring divisions there. Big life changes had a way of making that happen—something he knew from firsthand experience.

Still, he was keeping his fingers crossed that this plan would work out; the more he thought about it, the more he knew Mellette was his only strong answer. And a strong answer was the only thing that could work, owing to all the obstacles Big Swamp presented.

"I'm working on the book," Justin told his literary agent in a just-after-dawn phone call. "But I'm pretty busy here, taking care of all my grandmother's unfinished business." Well, that wasn't exactly as true as it should have been, as he hadn't even begun to tie up loose ends. But he *was* working on a plan to open a clinic, and it was his intention to get all the personal matters tied up in the next couple of weeks so he wasn't exactly lying. Just jumping the gun on his to-do list.

"You're not going to blow your deadline, are you, Justin? Because if you are, I need to get it squared away with your editor."

Deadlines, editor... Yes, he kept himself almost as busy writing as he did being a doctor these days. Truth was, he enjoyed his growing passion for being a medical mystery novelist. It had happened quite by accident, when he'd been asked to step in at the last minute to consult on the medical aspect of a movie being filmed in Chicago. A couple more movie and television gigs had come from that, along with the idea of writing a novel.

And while Justin hadn't been an overnight best-selling author, his career was promising enough to get him his first two-book contract for starters. Now he was on his second two-book contract, and there were faint whispers of turning his second book into a movie. It was a long shot, but exciting.

He liked writing. Didn't want to stop doing it. But he didn't know how it was going to fit into his long-term plans, because his medical practice really did take up more time than he'd ever thought it would. So that was his career crisis. How could he manage all aspects of it? Or how could he separate out the aspects he wanted to prioritize?

What he could figure out, though, was that he was staying in Big Swamp much longer than he'd expected to—it was at least giving him more time to write, to edit, to work up to that next deadline, even though he'd been brain-dead the past few days, putting off the decisions he'd have to make eventually. Putting off life in general. Also, there was something about the surroundings here that was conducive to his story setting, so much eerie nature that was a real kick to his creative mystery-writing process.

He liked that, liked the mood the Big Swamp ambiance put him in when he did write. The bayou and all its shadows and swamp creatures, the wild moss drop-

ping down from everywhere, the sounds, the smells…
"I don't need a deadline extension," he told his agent.
"Except for a few days of sluggishness trying to figure
out what I'm going to do with this place, it's been good
here. So you'll probably get this book a couple weeks
early for a change."

Normally, owing to his Chicago schedule, he was a
couple of weeks late, sometimes more, because every
aspect of his hectic life kept him on edge, aware of
every minute ticking off on the clock. Unlike Louisiana, where he lost hours, immersed in his work. So in
that respect Big Swamp was being very good to him.
Good juju, his grandma would have said. Meaning Big
Swamp brought him good luck or good fortune.

In the end, that wasn't going to matter since he was
going back to Chicago just as soon as he had the clinic
situation straightened out. Why leave when Big Swamp
agreed with him? Maybe because hectic agreed with
him more. Or maybe because hectic was his habit. Either way, it didn't matter. He wasn't staying here.

So after his chat with his agent, and as Justin settled
down by the window to edit his latest novel, he caught
himself gazing outside more than he should. Distracted.
Wondering if someone from the community in need of
medical attention might stop by to see him. Fretting a
little because they didn't.

It was odd how that need was coming through loud
and strong, because until this very morning, this very
instant, he'd had no idea he'd harbored these feelings
of wanting to help out personally here. It was strange to
discover it, and he didn't understand it. So why exactly

did he want to see patients who obviously didn't want to see him? Was it to assuage his guilty feelings over his grandmother? Or to do the right thing by the people here, the thing his grandmother would have wanted? Maybe even expected from him?

Then the oddest of all possibilities struck him. *Would this have anything to do with impressing Mellette?*

No, he was ruling that one out. She was strictly a hands-off lady who didn't want to be impressed by any man. While she definitely brought out some manly instinct in him, he was going to respect her wishes. Keep his distance. Let her stay married to her deceased husband for as long as she needed.

In which case...that meant this melancholia had to be because he was disappointed by how not one single person had stopped by. And here he was, ready to treat anything—a head cold, a hangnail, even a bug bite.

So rather than treating patients, he spent the morning editing, going back over the minute details that were so important to his brand, not to mention his reputation, checking his spelling, making sure all his periods, commas and ellipses were in the right place. All this while alternately gazing out the window then chastising himself for being distracted by things that would never happen.

But it did distract him that people deliberately avoided him...distracted him so much that he eventually gave himself over to a walk that took him down to the water's edge, where he tossed some stale bread to a fat little duck that had come begging. After that, he even spent a few extra minutes strolling along the riverbank, then down the road, hoping to see someone, hoping someone would see him. But nothing. Not a single, solitary medical thing occurred. In fact, he couldn't be sure but he felt as if he was being deliberately avoided; he didn't encounter anybody on a walk that took him almost all the way in to Grandmaison, which was a good three miles.

It sure wasn't a good feeling, not being needed by the people here. But then, he hadn't really put himself out there to let anybody know he was available, had he? Or that he wanted to be needed.

Of course, had they known, they still wouldn't have come. That was something about which he was reasonably sure. But was there some way to change their perception of him?

The bigger question, though, was why he wanted the bother. Why did it matter? Why should he care? "Because she's getting to you," he said as he kicked a stone along the road on his way back home. "You're a schoolboy, trying to impress a little girl." Pull her pigtails. Tease her until she runs home to tell her mother. Treat her patients to show her what a good doctor he was. It was all the same. He *was* a schoolboy trying to impress a girl…a girl who didn't want to be impressed. "Well, I'll be damned…" he said, as he checked his watch to see how many hours it was until his dinner date with Mellette's family. "I'll be double dogged damned."

Mellette's advice had been to prove himself by simply being a doctor to the people here, which had flopped badly. Even his attempt at liniment and make-up gumbo for Miss Willie had been received badly. She'd accepted it, given him an icy thank-you and shut the door on him with a final-sounding *thunk*.

"So what am I supposed to do?" he asked Napoleon once he was back on his front porch, laptop in position, ready to get back to his book. The tomcat, who was stretched out on the windowsill, taking in the afternoon sun, didn't show the least bit of concern. "And why do I even care? That's the real question. Why do I care? I mean, it's not like I'm going to stay here and put myself into this culture again." Not that he'd ever really been a part of it when he'd lived here. He'd been the outsider who'd never wanted to fit in.

So wanting to fit in now was the furthest thing from his mind. But he did feel the obligations left by his grandmother tugging at him. And maybe that was the real kicker. The more he didn't want to feel anything, the more he felt. Right now, he felt strongly that he couldn't let his grandmother down this one last time. There were so many things in his life that couldn't be undone, so many regrets it was too late to make right. The way he'd refused to help his grandmother was probably the biggest regret of all, because he'd lost that final time with her.

Now he lost sleep over it. He'd dropped ten pounds, too, and gained a new crease in his forehead. "But I didn't know," he said to Napoleon. "Why didn't she… why didn't *someone* tell me, even though she didn't want them to?" Even Mellette. Why hadn't she picked up the phone? One phone call. One lousy phone call.

He sighed, cursing the thought of his grandmother here alone, dying, swiping back the tears that always came when he thought about it. "She should have told me, Napoleon. I know she thought it was for my own good. That I was too busy or too important to come home... How did I ever let something like that happen?" His voice went quiet. "How did I ever let her down so much when all she did was love me?"

There was nothing to add, nothing to say. They kept to themselves, these people. Kept to themselves and shut him out. Letting out a long, anguished breath, he said, "So here I am, Napoleon. Basking in the sun like you, regretting the whole blasted mess. Wanting to change something that can't be changed." He reached through the open window and scratched the cat behind his ears. "I supposed I should be glad your life is working out better than mine. At least people around here respond to you."

Napoleon's response was to hop down out of the window, stick his tail in the air and walk away.

"You hate me, too?" he called after the haughty cat, then stretched back in his desk chair, trying hard to focus again on the page on his screen. The one where the heroine had just discovered the medication switch and was hoping she wasn't too late to save the life of the gallant and heroic young doctor. Ironic how it paralleled his life in a way, he thought as he deleted an entire page where the heroine seemed to be going in circles. Wasn't he himself running in circles, too late to take care of the things that were important to him? And he was the only one to blame.

By midafternoon Justin had finally put aside his distractions enough to allow the creative juices to flow, and they were flowing so effusively he nearly forgot about his dinner appointment. So by the time he grabbed a quick shower, changed into a pair of khaki cargos and a white cotton shirt, then climbed into his grandmother's thirty-year-old pickup truck, he was wondering if he should simply bow out since he was going to be so late. Instead, he hit the back roads at speeds much faster than were really safe and got himself into New Orleans only fifteen minutes late.

By the time he was knocking at the Doucet mansion front door he was nearly winded, not from the rush of getting there but from the nervousness of what the evening ahead could mean to him.

"Thought one of those gators might have gotten you," Mellette said, opening the door to him.

"No such luck," he said, entering the foyer to what had to be one of the grandest homes he'd ever stepped foot in. Just the foyer was lavish with French antiques—at least he thought they were French, as he truly didn't know one antique from another. There were mirrors and gold knickknacks. An ornate gold clock with fat little cherubs sitting on its base and a crystal chandelier that was so grand it overshadowed everything else in the space. He wondered how on earth it was ever cleaned since all the ceiling lamps in his condo were single white globes that dusted easily with a swipe or two.

Everything he could see from his vantage point at the front door dripped with elegance, and the doctor who normally lived pretty high-end himself was suddenly self-conscious about his casual outfit. He should have known better. No, he *did* know better. "I, um…I'm not really dressed for dinner," he said when he realized how beautifully Mellette was dressed. She wore a sleeveless midcalf floral-print dress that flowed on forever. And gold sandals. She had on just a hint of makeup and a large red hibiscus over her left ear. The one word that came to mind when he set eyes on her was *stunning*. Followed by another word of warning: *off-limits*.

"You're fine," she said. "We don't dress formally. Not with the hectic lives we all live."

"But look at you," he said. "Then look at me. One of us here isn't dressed right, and I'm guessing it's me."

She smiled. "At work I'm either in scrubs or cargo pants and a T-shirt. Sometimes it's nice to get dressed up a little bit."

Actually, those cargo pants and that T-shirt looked pretty good on her, too. "Well, I hope you didn't wait on my account. I lost track of the time…"

She laughed. "Don't flatter yourself. When my daddy decides it's time to sit down and eat, we sit down and eat. The only one he waits for is my mother, who's not here yet. But she called, and she's about fifteen minutes out."

"Would that be enough time for me to run out and buy a proper suit?" he asked.

"That would be enough time for you to meet my daddy and my daughter. My sisters Sabine, Delphine and Magnolia—we call her Maggie—will also be having dinner with us, and they're upstairs, getting ready."

"I'm the only guest?" he asked, quite surprised.

"The only one."

"Talk about making an underdressed guy feel self-conscious."

"My family's normal, Justin. We can be as mean as

swamp gators when we have to be—and that's usually to defend the family—but most of the time we're just like anybody else."

"And if I could identify one antique from another, would all this glitz and glamour around me say the same thing?"

"Family heirlooms. My great-grandmother on my mother's side decorated this house, and there's never really been a need to change anything. We like the family tradition. But I thought you had a nice lifestyle going back in Chicago. Your grandmother told me you live pretty well there."

"I do. But it's…well, not this. I keep my space sparse and scaled back."

"Eula told me about your fast cars and even faster women. She said you have quite a reputation for that."

"My grandmother had a big imagination and maybe a few high hopes, because that's not my life at all. I own a nice little European sports car and a larger car for when it snows. But as far as my women…" He smiled. "Between you and me, I haven't had a date in over a year, and the last woman I dated was fast, but not in the way you'd think."

Mellette raised her eyebrows in surprise. "Seriously? No girlfriends? From what Eula described, it sounded like you have a revolving door on your condo."

"Taking some time off. Between my medical practice, which is growing, and… You know about my writing, don't you?"

"I may have read one of your books," she admitted.

"Well, that's my life. All of it. No time left over for anything else except a few hours' sleep every night.

Sometimes not even that by the time I get everything done." His eyes traveled to the miniature version of Mellette who was being escorted down the front staircase by a distinguished, gray-haired man Justin assumed to be Mellette's father.

She was a stunning child, and identical to Mellette in every way except she had long, flowing black hair, whereas Mellette's was cropped short. They were even dressed alike, same floral print, same gold sandals. He was a man who didn't normally pay too much attention to children, but Leonie was adorable. His first thought went to Landry, and he felt an unusual tug of sadness that the man would never know his daughter. His second thought went to Mellette, who beamed with pure love when she took her daughter's hand.

"This is Leonie," she said, quite simply. Then to Leonie, "This is Dr. Bergeron."

Leonie thrust her tiny hand out to shake his. "Hello," she said, in a voice that seemed deep for a child so young. "Are you my mommy's friend?" she asked.

"This is the man for whom I work for when I go to Big Swamp, *ma chère,*" Mellette explained.

"I thought you worked for Bonne-Maman Eula," Leonie said seriously.

"I did. But remember how I told you that Bonne-Maman Eula died?"

Leonie nodded. "And went to heaven, like Daddy did."

"Well, this is Bonne-Maman Eula's grandson, just like you are Grandpère Charles's granddaughter."

"Then you're the new doctor," Leonie said.

"I'm the very new doctor," Justin replied. He turned to Mellette. "She's well-spoken for her age."

"We've noticed that," Mellette said, smiling at the compliment. "We figure at the rate she's going, she'll be taking over the medical center for my mother in the next decade or so."

"Days like this and I'm ready to have her take over right now," Zenobia Doucet said, coming in the front door. She was a stately woman. Tall, like Mellette. But with honey-colored hair, which she wore pulled tightly back from her face to reveal flawless bone structure. Zenobia was the kind of woman whose looks belied her age—she could have been forty, she could have been seventy. There was no way of telling.

"Bad day, Maman?" Mellette asked.

"One of those days that make me wish I was involved in patient care again and not working as an administrator." Zenobia dropped her purse and scarf on a bench by the door and immediately went to pick up her granddaughter. "So if anybody has a problem tonight, please, keep it to yourself. I've solved everything from a missing paper-towel shipment to an overbooked O.R., and for the next twelve hours I need a clear head." She turned to Justin and smiled. "And you must be our guest for the night. So pleased you could join us, Dr. Bergeron."

"Actually, just a dinner guest. I was raised in the swamp so I don't have a fear of negotiating it at night."

"With alligators?" Leonie asked.

"Great big ones," Justin said. "With great big eyes that glow in the dark."

"Anybody care for a glass of wine or fruit juice before dinner?" Charles asked. Then he smiled at Justin. "Full bar, my boy. Anything you like."

"Beer?" he ventured.

Charles laughed. "You're a man after my own heart. One beer coming up. Actually, I think I'll join you."

"I want apple juice," Leonie announced.

"And apple juice it will be," Charles said, taking his granddaughter back from Zenobia and heading off to the kitchen with her.

"As you can see, my parents spoil my daughter," Mellette said.

"That's what grandchildren are for," Zenobia said, then scooted around Justin. "Please, Dr. Bergeron, make yourself at home. I'm going to go get ready for dinner, so whatever you need until then, please ask Mellette. Or Charles, if you can pry him away from Leonie long enough." With that she flounced up the stairs with surprising energy, leaving Justin and Mellette alone in the foyer.

"Sorry it's so hectic," Mellette said, showing Justin through the house to the veranda out back, stopping briefly as Charles appeared with a bottle of beer for Justin and a glass of sparkling water for her.

"You don't drink?" Justin asked, again feeling self-conscious.

Mellette shook her head. "One of my sisters had a problem for a short time, and while my other sisters and I helped her recover, we…" She shrugged. "It's just a personal preference. My mother likes her evening sherry and my dad likes a good, stiff whiskey. Or, apparently, a bottle of beer."

"And I feel like a real slump. Will probably feel more so when your sisters come down to dinner and are dressed as beautifully as you are."

"We don't stand on formality, Justin. If we did, I would have told you. In fact, when we were growing up we hardly ever sat down together for a meal, we were always so busy."

"My grandmother always insisted we eat together. When I was younger it wasn't so bad, but the older I got the more I resented the intrusion in my life. She never relented, though, and now I'm glad she didn't. Those were good times."

"And your parents?"

He shrugged. "They weren't really a major factor in my upbringing. Both of them worked all the time, traveled with a major oil company, and I hardly ever saw them." He took a swig of his beer, then set the bottle down on the cement wall where they seated themselves. "My grandmother was my influence."

"I know," she said quietly. "And you were lucky to have her. She was an amazing woman."

"Why didn't you call me when she got sick? I know she didn't want you to, but why didn't you, out of courtesy? Or even obligation to the man who signed your paycheck?"

Mellette hesitated, then frowned. "I wanted to. But like you said, she didn't want me to. Said you were too busy, that your work was too important to interrupt."

"You should have called, anyway. I would have come."

"And disrespected her wishes?"

"And given me a little final time with her."

"She wasn't that sick, Justin. I mean, in that, she wasn't being very truthful with me because I'm pretty sure she knew how badly off she was. But she just wasn't letting on to anyone. Not me, not Amos…

"In fact, she never took to her bed until her very last day. She was feeling tired, but that's all. At least, that's what she was telling me. And she was working through the malaria outbreak, treating people right and left. Then she just… If she'd told me how she was *really* feeling, I would have called you no matter what she wanted. Would have gotten her into a hospital, too. But Eula was literally on her feet until the day before she died, and she got pretty fiery when I mentioned calling you."

"I should have known, though. Somebody should have—"

"And I'm sorry," she said, laying a gentle hand on his arm. "You'll never know how sorry I am, but I had no way of knowing how bad—"

"Because that's the way she was." He smiled fondly. "She always did things her way, and I guess even at the end she did what she wanted to do. I just wish…"

"So do I," she said sadly. "You don't know how often I've thought about how it turned out. The people who'd known Eula all their lives might have guessed she was sicker than she was letting on, but I'm not even sure about that." She looked over at Justin. "My husband did the same thing. He could have taken more drugs to prolong his life another month or two, but the drugs made him so groggy, and he fought so hard to stay alert. The doctors wanted him in a hospice, he wanted to stay home, which is what he did. In the end, he died the way he wanted to, just like Eula, and I don't think that's a bad thing.

"I mean, I would have loved having Landry around for another couple of months. There were so many things we didn't get to finish, and two more months…" She batted back a tear. "But it wasn't meant to be."

"We all make our choices, don't we?" He picked up his beer and took another swig.

"That's the way it should be, I think. I'm sorry you didn't get to have that final time with Eula, but she really didn't give that final time to anyone. An hour before she died she was giving me orders on how to take care of certain patients."

"You know she wanted me to come home and do my *doctoring* here, don't you? She'd asked me several times over the years…or not asked so much as suggested it could work for me, coming back to Louisiana to work."

Mellette nodded, but didn't say anything.

"That's the hard one to deal with. Because I had my life and I didn't want to change it. I got out when I was a kid, and it was never my intention to return. Sure, I could have. It would have been easy enough. But coming back… There was nothing here for me."

"She understood why you didn't. And respected you for your dedication. She had that same dedication, Justin, so she knew what it was about."

"Maybe she did, but that doesn't make me feel any better about a lot of things. Like I shouldn't have run away when I was a kid, and I should have come to visit more often than I did."

"We all have those should-haves and shouldn't-haves, don't we? But there's nothing we can do about them except maybe feel regret."

"Does the regret ever go away, though?" he asked.

"Probably not, but it mellows in time. The edges of my regrets aren't as sharp as they were when Landry died. Of course, I think part of that is because I've had to force myself to stand away from those regrets in order to keep moving forward. Life got tough, and I don't have the time, or the energy, to keep dwelling on them."

"How so?"

"I lost everything when Landry died. Not just my husband but my life's savings, my house, my car—the cost of cancer."

"Your parents didn't help?"

"They wanted to, and my parents fought me every step of the way when I refused. But I made one of those choices you just talked about."

For June, the night was quite warm, but not humid, and the cacophony of nature—frogs, crickets, all varieties of small animals—was so loud it was like an orchestrated symphony. An intricate tune composed of notes that didn't quite harmonize but still somehow fit together in their blend. "Which would have something to do with why you're not living here with them, I'm guessing?"

"They wanted me to move home." She paused, swallowed. "Begged me. Did all but drag me here. But Leonie and I need to be separate. And don't get me wrong. My family is wonderful. I love them dearly and how they want to help me means everything. But I need to establish my own family, with our own traditions and craziness, and that won't happen here, under their roof. Landry and I had very specific goals for our daughter, and part of that was helping her to become independent. So if I moved home…"

"Your parents wouldn't let you be independent."

"All done with the best intentions," she said. "But you're right. And you saw how they are with Leonie. My sisters, too. Everybody dotes on her. Spoils her rotten. Which is fine for short periods of time, but not every day, all day, the way it would be if we lived here."

"Then it sounds to me as if you're doing the right thing," he said.

"Do you think so? Because it's so difficult, and there are times when I wonder if I should give in, just for a year or two. Let them take care of me. Maybe even let them pay off the debt.

"Yet when I get down and almost give in, I just remind myself I'm doing what's right by being the best example for my daughter that I can be. You know, showing her how to be the kind of person Landry and I wanted her to be."

"He was a lucky man to have you," Justin said.

"I was the lucky one."

"Lucky, but living a tough life."

"A tough life that'll get better. I've got about another year, maybe a year and a half, then I'll be out from under the debt, and Leonie and I can start moving forward."

"Until then?"

"Until then, I work hard and my daddy gets to escort her around the house like she's a little princess."

"What if I could afford to meet all your demands? That, and figure out some way where you could bring her to work with you a day or two each week?"

"What?"

"I've been doing a lot of thinking about this, and I've decided I'd like to open up a regular clinic in Big Swamp. Something to honor my grandmother. She gave the people attention whenever they needed it, and while we're not going to be able to staff a clinic twenty-four hours a day, seven days a week, for some time to come, if ever, we could give them regular medical care five days a week for starters. Then expand as there's a need, or as we're able."

"Seriously?" she asked.

"Seriously. The thing is, you could work regular hours and go home every day at a decent time. And the best part is I've figured out a way you could bring Leonie to work occasionally. Back at my hospital in Chicago there's a child-care center, and that's maybe the biggest draw for recruiting the best medical personnel. So I'm thinking we could do something like that for Leonie right here. You know, like build a safe, fenced-in play yard for her. Find one of the local women to look after her when you're with patients. Schedule one or two light days each week so you could bring her to work and spend more time with her."

"Bring Leonie to Big Swamp…" Mellette murmured thoughtfully.

"It's just an idea. If you can think of something better…"

"It kind of scares me." She smiled. "Kind of intrigues me, too."

"So you're not ruling it out. I'm still in the running to convince you."

"No, I'm not ruling it out. Not yet. But…" She shrugged. "It's a generous offer, Justin. Generous to me, generous to the people your grandmother cared for. But you and I don't agree on the type of medicine I'd want to practice there, and that's the first problem. The second is, to have a real clinic I need something other than Eula's house to work from. Unless you're willing to convert her house into a real clinic. Then there's my family. I'm not sure how they'd take it if I quit my full-time job at New Hope to open a clinic in the bayou where I'll be dispensing herbs as much as I will medicine.

"And there's the obvious problem of my being a registered nurse who needs a physician as a medical director. I'm allowed to work unsupervised, obviously, but to make this a real clinic I need someone local to sign off as my doctor. And having you living in Chicago, as the legal owner, won't work."

"Who's doing that now?"

"No one, because it's not a licensed clinic. And when I need a prescription I can't do myself, I work it out through the hospital. But I haven't even had to do that a lot because the people in the bayou don't want traditional medicine. The thing is, I'm assuming you're going to want the emphasis of this clinic to be traditional medicine—"

"I haven't thought it through that far," he interrupted.

"Then you need to think some more, because if you build it, they're not going to come if you're only handing out pills. It has to be swamp cures and pills."

"So where does that leave us?"

"Honestly, when you first talked to me about spending more time there, then came up with the full-time offer, I didn't take you seriously because it all seemed improbable."

"Improbable or not, I'm dead serious about this."

"I know you are, and Eula would have been so pleased. I do need to think about it, though, and figure out how changing my life so drastically will affect both Leonie and me. And also the rest of my family. They're a part of this, as well."

"What about your family?" Charles asked from the doorway.

"Justin's made me an offer to come and work for him in Big Swamp."

"If I'm not mistaken, you already do work for him in Big Swamp."

"Two days a week, Daddy. But this would be more. He wants to open up a clinic there and let me run it. As in a full-time position."

Charles chuckled. "Mellette Priscilla Doucet Chaisson, swamp nurse. It has a certain ring to it. Can't say I like the sound of it, though."

"It gives me an opportunity, Daddy."

"A good one, I'm assuming."

"It will let me work fewer hours and spend more time with Leonie."

"Which will deprive me of my granddaughter throughout the day? That doesn't sound so good to me."

"Well, I haven't said yes," she told her father.

"But you haven't turned it down, have you?"

Mellette looked at Justin. "No, I haven't turned it down. Right now, I'm calling it a definite maybe."

"You do know your mother's going to want to put in a counteroffer to his offer," Charles said.

"But she can't magically produce some of the advantages Justin is offering me. Day care for Leonie, for example. New Hope doesn't have it for its employees. Also, I'll be working less hours for more money, and while I know that Mother would like to offer more, she's bound by the New Hope rules, regulations and salary guidelines. So..." Mellette shrugged.

"See how you are," Charles said. "I turn my back on you for a minute, and look what you've gone and done."

"It could be good, Daddy," she said.

He aimed his next statement directly at Justin. "For one of my daughters it has to be better than good. You remember that, Dr. Bergeron. If you intend to create any kind of a situation for any one of my daughters, it has to be perfect or you'll be answering to me. Do you understand me, young man?"

"Understood, sir."

"And if Mellette accepts this offer, also understand that I'll be coming around to inspect the facility, just to make sure it's what's best for both my daughter and granddaughter."

"You're welcome anytime, sir."

Charles gave them a curt nod, then smiled. "Dinner's ready, by the way," he said on his way back inside the house. "With the bad news you're going to be breaking to your mother, I wouldn't suggest being late to her dinner table."

"Does he know something I don't know?" Justin asked, as he escorted Mellette into the dining room.

"He knows *me*," she said.

CHAPTER FOUR

"TELL ME WHAT you need," Justin said. He and Mellette
were standing shoulder to shoulder in the front yard of
Eula's house, appraising the area to see what it would
take to turn it into a proper medical clinic. They were
also looking at the overall condition of the place and
assessing the many things it lacked.

It was an old two-story traditional house, lived in by
Eula's mother, and her mother before that. Well over a
hundred years planted in Big Swamp, it had weathered
the years with a minimum of upkeep, and while it was
sturdy, it looked tired. Its wooden clapboards needed a
good coat of paint, as the last one—applied fifty years
previously—had worn off, leaving the boards a rustic
brown with splotches of white here and there.

The handrail on the two steps up to the wooden
wrap-around porch was in serious need of some shor-
ing up from a serious left- and right-tilting wobble. And
the storm shutters, which were well worn and not dec-
orative, were ready to be replaced by new ones. Every
slat was either broken or missing altogether.

All that said, it was a clean, tidy house in spite of
its rundown condition. A house that was as welcom-

ing as the line of old handmade oak rockers sitting on the front porch, where guests, patients or anybody else who wandered by could sit for a while if they wanted to. Next to the kick line of chairs hung a swing suspended from rusty chains. That had been Eula's place to sit, especially in the evenings, when the squeak from the back and forth of the chains had seemed to be louder than during the day.

And there were flowerpots full of various herbs and flowers scattered everywhere, a worn-out mat that had welcomed more guests over the years than anyone could remember and nailed prominently over the old wooden door was a sign that read Welcome. A sign Justin had never failed to look up and read every time he entered.

Mellette stepped back from the front of the house and took a good look around to make sure she wasn't about to step on a cranky gator or some other critter that had walked, crawled or slithered up from the channel—her habit every time she walked outside.

"For starters, I need the front part of the interior gutted. The structure itself seems good enough, but I need the dividing wall between the living room and dining room removed so I can turn the area into one big waiting room and reception area. Also, the old-fashioned parlor… I'd like that to stay since it sits just off the main area. We can use it for a doctor's office. And while I can use both downstairs bedrooms as exam rooms, I'll need all the furniture out of here and replaced with something more appropriate to a clinic. Maybe give the old pieces to someone in Big Swamp who's in need.

"As for the kitchen…" She shrugged. "I suppose it

can stay like it is, which will give me someplace to escape to when I'm not seeing patients, and also a place to work with the herbs. Upstairs…I'm not sure what to do with those two bedrooms. Maybe just leave them as they are for the time being, then later convert them into hospital rooms of a sort, in case we ever have anybody who needs overnight treatment. Oh, and the back storage room… That'll make a great playroom for Leonie, because the door leading outside from it can go straight into a play yard. You still intend to build her a play yard, don't you?"

"Um…yes." He'd expected changes, but not this allout rearranging of practically everything. In fact, somehow he'd just envisioned leaving the house pretty much as it was and having Mellette continue to work here the way she had. But apparently Mellette had other ideas on the subject. Other *big* ideas. "You know this is going to take a while…all this work you're proposing."

"That's fine. I've got time, and I'm a patient woman. Oh, and the outside of the clinic…I think white would work. I know that's a little bit traditional or old-fashioned, but a nice white building just looks the part. And I'd like a new sign…I want to call it Eula's House, if that's okay with you."

"No new sign," he said. "That welcome sign has always been there, and it stays. Not negotiable."

She arched inquisitive eyebrows at him, like she wanted to ask him a question, but instead she said, "Then it stays, and we'll have some kind of sign made that we can install in the yard."

Well, she'd gone from hard to convince to exuberant overnight. The enthusiasm was cute, he'd give her that. But the project itself? He wasn't sure if he liked or hated all the changes she was proposing. They sounded practical, and they were certainly in keeping with the clinic he'd asked her to run. But it was all so…extreme.

Justin took a few steps backward to study the house he'd been raised in and his eyes immediately went to his bedroom window. How many nights had he sneaked out that window, jumped across to the old cottonwood tree then shimmied down it to freedom? And how many times had he sneaked back in the front door, pulled off his shoes under the welcome sign so they wouldn't clack across the wooden floor, glad that by some miracle the door was unlocked, then crept back up the creaky stairs, never, ever getting caught?

Sighing, with just a tinge of regret, Justin wondered if he was making a mistake here, changing things so drastically. Or maybe his own enthusiasm was dragging because he actually did have some emotional attachment to the house that had only just now come to the surface. Fond memories of his childhood he'd shoved back to the recesses of his memory were beginning to creep their way back out.

Whatever the case, he was feeling like a great big wet blanket this morning and not even Mellette's pretty smile was enough to shake it out of him. "Do you intend keeping the clinic open during renovations?" he asked, trying to focus on the goal and not the means of achieving it.

"I'd think we have to. Even though you don't approve of most of the services we've offered, people here count on them. Also, if you insist on turning this into more of a medical facility, I'm still going to need a medical director. Someone to oversee or prescribe when I can't. That's a priority, Justin. I have some leeway because I have a master's in nursing, but not enough to do all the things I think you envision here."

He knew that, of course. And so far hadn't even gotten around to thinking about that aspect of the clinic. "Any suggestions?" he asked her.

A smile spread to her face. "Maybe one, but I'd have to do a lot of sweet-talking to convince him, and especially convince his wife."

"Who?"

"My dad. He retired much too young. Had some diabetic complications, and the doctor told him the stress of his job was contributing to his poor health. He was the head of anesthesiology at New Hope. So he decided to take some time off, and that was the same time I started needing help with Leonie. One thing led to another, he decided he liked the life of leisure, and my mother especially liked not having to worry about him so much, so he resigned from the hospital to be a stay-at-home grandpa. Which he loves.

"But I really think he misses medicine, and while clinical medicine isn't what he did in the past, I think he might be persuaded to oversee operations here, maybe even see a few patients every now and then, especially diabetic patients, if we're lucky. That's if I can convince my mother that it won't hurt him. She's pretty protective of Daddy, probably more than he needs."

"Wow. You've gone way ahead of me on all of this.

I was still trying to find reasons to convince you to accept the job, and you've already turned this place into a major medical clinic with its own doctor. I'm impressed." Bowled over was more like it.

"One thing you'll discover about the Doucet family is that when we make a commitment, we follow through. Or, in some cases, plow right through. We're a pretty powerful bunch to be reckoned with."

"Then I think I should make it a point to stay on your good side."

Mellette smiled, but there was a riptide of steel and determination in that smile. "Take those words to heart, Doctor. They'll serve you well."

Damn, but he liked her. She wasn't soft. In fact, he wasn't sure she was at all bendable. And she wasn't particularly effervescent, which was what he usually found in the women in went for. But Mellette had this untempered way about her that was, well, for a lack of a better definition, sexy. She was no-nonsense. Strong willed. Straightforward. All of it a very intriguing yet feminine package unlike anything he'd ever seen or experienced before.

But he was off women for now. Totally. He was struggling enough, managing his own life right now and holding all the pieces in place. The last thing he needed was to complicate that. A woman would definitely complicate it. The funny thing was, he was okay with that. Better than okay, really. He was downright pleased with the arrangement.

Particularly since the last one had connived her way in a little too deeply for comfort. She'd been pretty to look at but pernicious in ways that still made him shudder. So he'd promised himself some time off to re-evaluate his future. To see how he wanted to proceed, whether that be as a bachelor, which wasn't all that bad, or in a committed relationship, which, admittedly, scared him to death. He'd been there, done that and pulled off an epic fail. "Trust me, I was on a powerful woman's bad side not that long ago, and it's a place I don't want to find myself again."

"Broken heart?" she asked.

"Not even close. Her daddy was a politician and I was *chosen* to join a rather high-ranking family. It was flattering being in that company for a while, but let's just say it was a family I didn't like as much as they liked me, and I wasn't even smart enough at the time to realize just how much I didn't like them, I was so busy being flattered."

"So you have an aversion to powerful people?"

"Like your family? No. But I do I have an aversion to powerful people who use their power to corrupt. Nancy's daddy dearest sat on the hospital board, and it was his goal to terminate a charity program I was involved in.

"Why?"

"Because it didn't turn a profit."

"But you won the battle, didn't you?"

He shook his head. "Just the opposite. I sat front and center on the losing side."

"What kind of charity?"

"A recovery day camp for kids who'd undergone major physical trauma."

"They yanked the funding on that?"

He nodded. "Said there were other charities just as worthy, which is true. The hospital had only so much money available for charitable works, and it seemed that Nancy's father had a pet charity in mind ready to grab the funds from our little fledgling. The thing is, his pet wasn't bad, but he had his fingerprints all over it as a founder, and he wanted to use that to catapult him into an elected office. Anyway, our little charity was new, hadn't made much of a splash yet, and he simply got greedy for our funding and convinced the board to cut it off."

"But you stayed there at the hospital after they did that?"

"I have too many years invested there to walk away. And my general surgery practice is one of the strongest anywhere. I don't want to leave it."

"Yet you left the girlfriend?"

"Actually, I was getting ready to but she beat me to it, told me she was disappointed that I wasn't man enough to beat her daddy. That's when I realized…"

"Let me guess. She knew her daddy would be waging war with you, and she wiggled her way in to spite him. She was using you as her agenda to beat him."

"Something like that. And he used me as well, because he'd hoped the charity founders would just back away quietly and I could facilitate that because of my relationship with Nancy. He didn't want to be seen as the big, bad ogre who had killed sick kids' hopes and dreams, and I was supposed to be the one who shielded him from that. It didn't turn out that way, and he took a bad hit to his reputation because of it, was forced off the hospital board, and in the end he hated me as much as Nancy did."

"And your charity program?"

"Another hospital grabbed it and ran with it."

"Then that part's good," she said.

"That part's good, and the rest of it is…embarrassing. I should have been smarter."

"You don't equate their kind of power with us, do you?" she asked.

"No. Not at all. You come from a powerful family, but there are bad ways to handle power and good ways, and your family is an example of what's good. They prove that power doesn't have to corrupt."

"Good, because I was afraid you might think we were like Nancy's family, and—"

"Not a chance. I just look at that whole incident as a bad mistake in love."

"But we all make mistakes in love," Mellette said, almost dreamily.

"Even you?"

She nodded. "Even me. I should have married Landry years before I did. He was my one and only, but I wanted to finish my education, so I kept putting him off, figuring we had a lot of years ahead of us. As it turned out, I was wrong."

"I'm sorry for that," Justin said sincerely.

"So am I, every day of my life." Mellette's eyes misted up, but she blinked back the tears before they fell. "Anyway, back to what we're going to do here," she said, sniffling then clearing her throat.

For sure, Landry had been a lucky man having someone that fiercely devoted to him. Had he known how lucky he was? "Well, you wouldn't happen to know a general contractor who could oversee the work, would you?"

"Landry's brother is a contractor, actually. I can call him and see if he'll come out and give us an estimate, then we can…" She paused and gave him a doubtful look. "You're having second thoughts about this, aren't you?"

"Yes and no. Having the clinic here's the right thing to do, but…"

"But this was your home and it's hard letting go."

He nodded. "It's my last connection to her, and I suppose that's just beginning to hit me. It's hard to believe she's not going to come walking out that front door and tell me to get washed up for supper, that we're going to have red beans and rice and corn bread. Or that she needs a mess of crawdads for the gumbo, and to make myself useful and go catch some for her."

"Your grandmother really was proud of you, Justin, and she did understand your commitments in Chicago. Probably because she was just as committed to her patients as you are to yours, which makes you a lot like her."

"I'd have to go a long way to be like my grandmother," he said. "But I appreciate the compliment."

"Like I said, we could hold back on some of the changes."

He shook his head. "No, I want this place turned into a real medical clinic, and the sooner the better."

"What about the herbs?" she asked. "Because you know Eula's regulars won't necessarily come just because you renovate her house if you don't treat them with the kind of medicine they've always known."

"I know they won't trust my medicine because they want swamp medicine." He chuckled. "And they won't trust a white clinic either, Mellette. It might look good, but I did spend a lot of years here, living with these people, and I'm pretty sure a glaring white medical clinic in the middle of Big Swamp won't fit in."

"See, you do have a feel for the people here after all."

"I *was* the people here for a while. Which is one of the big problems."

"Maybe not as much as you think. And you could be one of the people here again, if you wanted to."

He shook his head. "It's not me. I want to go home."

"This isn't home?"

"This is my sentimental home, I suppose. But it's not my real home."

"You *are* planning on staying around for the renovations, aren't you?"

"Actually, I need to go home tomorrow."

"So you expect me to do everything?" she asked. "Because that's not part of the plan. At least, not part of *my* plan."

"The problem is, I have to speak at a medical symposium in a couple of days. I was asked over a year ago, and I can't beg out of it at this late date." And he wouldn't have begged even if he could have. He needed to separate himself from this place for a little while, from the memories and the feelings that just wouldn't let go.

"But you'll come back when the symposium ends, right?"

That wasn't part of the plan, either. But he knew he needed to come back to help Mellette, and he was fighting himself on that. What he'd originally envisioned was dropping in maybe six weeks from now to evaluate the progress, then maybe six or ten weeks after that for another evaluation. Then he'd hand the reins over to Mellette and get back to their former arrangement where he sent her a monthly check. It was easier that way. A monthly dip into the trust left to him by his parents, and he had a free and clear path for another thirty days.

But he was being tugged in a different direction, too. One that kept him here for those weeks, and kept him more available to Mellette, helping her with some of the burden, since what he intended to do was, essentially, to drop it all in her lap.

Which made him feel like a real creep for even thinking such a thing. "Come with me. Come to my seminar and spend a couple of days off in Chicago with me," he said, more to keep him on the right path than anything else. Because once he got home, got caught up on the whirlwind... No, he needed Mellette there with him to pull him back.

"Seriously? Just drop everything here and go to Chicago with you?"

"Seriously, yes."

"I...I...don't know what to say. I don't live a spontaneous life. Especially now, with Leonie."

"You know your dad will love to watch her."

"Chicago," she said, as a smile slid across her face. "There's this lovely restaurant—seafood—out on the pier."

"And we can take a charter boat to see the city at after dark."

"Gosh, that sounds so tempting, but…"

"But what?"

"What about the clinic here?"

"Eula took her days off, and you deserve yours."

She thought about it for a moment, then with the exuberance of a child said, "I'll do it!" and threw her arms around his neck. "I'll really do it!" Then, realizing the position she was in, she backed away and blushed. "Sorry about that," she said.

"About what?"

"My exuberance."

"I'm not. I like spontaneous." But he'd liked the hug even more.

"I'll be fine, Daddy," Mellette said on her cell phone as she struggled her way through the masses of fellow travelers congregating in the corridors of Chicago's O'Hare International Airport, pulling her overnight bag behind her, trying to keep up with Justin, who was plowing through the crowds purposefully. "Just give Leonie an extra hug for me tonight and tell her I'll bring her a nice surprise when I come home." Something to assuage the guilt of spending the night away from her daughter.

"You just have yourself a good time, and don't worry about a thing here," Charles responded.

"I intend to have fun." What she hadn't told him was that half her reason for this trip was to make sure she got Justin back to New Orleans. Something had told her he might not have come back. At least, not in the near future. And being there with him was her assurance he would.

Mellette pulled her overnighter through the whooshing pneumatic doors on the lower level just outside the baggage claim area, and headed to the line that was forming at the curb, where at least fifteen people were ahead of her, all awaiting cabs and different destinations. It was an orderly process, with taxis lined up and approaching their pick-ups one by one. "This is crazy," she commented to Justin, as someone bumped her practically into his arms.

"Which is part of the reason I love it here," he said, laughing as he steadied her.

"It would drive me crazy having to deal with this many people all the time. I mean, I can't even begin to imagine the emergency rooms…."

"You get used to it."

"Not me," she said. "Definitely not me." She stepped up to the curb as the next taxi in line arrived to pick them up. It was old, fairly grungy looking, but it would take them away from the madness of the airport and that was all she wanted. "But you really like this?"

"I love it. Love the variety, the action, the people."

"We are different, aren't we?" A difference that, as far as she could tell, would never be narrowed. Well,

Justin was entitled to his lifestyle, just as she was entitled to hers. Only his was going to have to wait a
little while longer.

Justin gestured her back into the inner sanctum, and she
was only too glad to follow him through the hall back
to his office, which turned out to be just about the nicest office she'd ever seen in her life, and that included
all those places she'd seen in architectural magazines,
showing famous doctors' even more famous offices.

"This is it," he said, motioning for her to sit. But not
at his desk. He showed her to a sitting area where cushy
leather chairs and couches were arranged in front of a
huge plate-glass window that overlooked Lincoln Park
and, beyond that, the expansive Lake Michigan—calm
today, with its occasional whitecap lapping the shore-
line. It was a stunning view, one that suited the stunning chrome-and-leather office and, for a moment, all
Mellette could do was stand and stare at the stark con-
trast to everything at Big Swamp.

As much as she stared and admired, she wasn't envious. This wasn't her world. Wasn't even a world where
she was comfortable. "This is—" she drew in a sharp
breath, trying to gather her wits "—amazing." So different from what she'd imagined. Somehow she'd pictured
him in something far less toned and trendy.

"The building over there…" He pointed to a high-
rise buff brick building that sat kitty-corner to his office and jutted up by a good thirty or forty stories, yet
sat somewhat dwarfed by the steel-and-glass buildings
surrounding, almost engulfing it. "That's where I live.

Top floor, penthouse. Just a quick walk to work. No alligators to contend with."

"You've come a long way since Big Swamp," she said. "Did Eula ever see any of this?"

"Once. It made her…nervous. She said it was too much. She didn't like being up so high. It made her feel vulnerable."

It made *her* feel vulnerable, as well. "But it is too much, Justin. I mean, I'm on sensory overload right now." She turned to face him, was stunned by how much of a doctor he looked. Was stunned even more than she hadn't seen that until now. But in her defense, back in Big Swamp all she'd seen had been jeans and T-shirts and disheveled hair, which looked good on him. Yet here he was in a perfectly starched white lab coat, and it made him seem like more of a doctor than she'd counted on. And that looked good on him, too. Justin Bergeron was equally gorgeous in both his worlds. "It does have its appeal, I must admit."

"So you understand why I have to come back?"

"If that's what your heart dictates, then, yes, I understand. But I need you in Big Swamp for a while, Justin, even if your heart isn't there. And you've got to know that's part of the reason I accepted your invitation…to make sure you did come back with me."

He chuckled. "We're not so different, you and I. A large part of my reason for inviting you was to make sure you would drag me back. I knew that once I was back in my world I might not be so inclined to leave it again for a while."

"It's not a simple thing, trying to get the clinic up and

going, and at the same time trying to keep the medical practice there running." *And be a mother,* she thought. "I've got patients to treat, and carpenters and electricians to deal with." She shook her head. "All that plus right now I'm spending more hours there than I ever worked before, which wasn't part of the deal. This arrangement was to allow me more time with Leonie, not less, and while I agree to all this in the short term, I won't do it alone. Not even for a week or two. I just can't. I can't do it alone."

"I know that," he said, stepping up dangerously close behind her at the window. "And I'm only saying I might have stayed here, not that I definitely would have. But bringing you here was just my—"

"Insurance," she cut in.

"That, plus I really did want to show you my life, the things I love, what I have going here. And you work so damned hard I thought a couple days off would do you some good.

"So give me about an hour here, then we'll go see a little of Chicago. It's going to be a beautiful night to go down to the pier, ride the Ferris wheel, have dinner, take a boat ride."

"I need to check into a hotel and get ready."

"My condo has a guest room, so I'd just assumed..."

"That I'd stay with you?"

"It's better than a hotel. No bedbugs. None of those who-knows-what kinds of stains they find with black lights in hotels. No one boiling unmentionables in the coffeepot."

She laughed. "You're ruining hotels for me forever."

"So you're not going to argue about staying at my place?"

"I'm not going to argue, but I also may never forgive you." She gave an overexaggerated shudder. "And, please, don't ruin anything else for me, like restaurants and public parks."

"Wouldn't think of it." He was chuckling as he showed her to a seat then exited his office. "Oh, and if you want anything to eat or drink—coffee, tea—just ask the receptionist. And the office has internet access if you want to work or talk to your dad back home." With that he was gone, leaving her there all alone in Justin's world—all alone to take in a different side of him. He was a minimalist, for sure. And very modern in his surroundings. Also very tidy. And, oh, goodness, he was clean. Even though he hadn't been in his office for weeks, there wasn't a speck of dust to be found anywhere, and she didn't need a pair of white gloves to prove that.

No wonder Justin didn't want to stay in the bayou. It must be driving him crazy, being around so much chaos. For heaven's sake, on some days there might be a lazy alligator or two in the yard. It didn't take Mellette five minutes to understand a completely different Justin than the one she'd come to know, who was living in a world where everything around him was pure pandemonium. He must have been going crazy there. If ever there was a case where worlds collided, this was it.

And as it turned out, his condo was pretty much like his office. Sparse of what she considered comfort. The bare minimum in furnishings, and all ultramodern. "I'd like to say it's lovely," she commented as they entered the living room, "but there's not enough here to really call it much of anything."

"I'm a man of few needs. Like to keep my life simple, which means keeping my surroundings simple. And just so you'll know, Eula hated it, too. Said it was too impersonal and cold."

"But if you like it…"

"I don't necessary like it or dislike it. It's just easy for me to keep myself organized if I don't have much to organize. Oh, and your room is the one on the left. Dress warm. It can get a little breezy out on the water, even at this time of the year."

The Ferris-wheel ride was lovely, and she couldn't remember the last time she'd actually been on one. Normally she was wary of heights, but at dusk, overlooking the pier as well as the city skyline, for a few minutes she felt like a little girl again, almost wanted cotton candy.

"This is amazing," she said as she huddled up in the seat next to Justin and gladly allowed him to put his arm around her for warmth, even though he'd bought her a souvenir hoodie with the words *Navy Pier* on it. His arm just made her feel safe, protected, and she liked that, especially when they swirled around the top of the wheel and for just that moment they were on the top of the world. "I haven't been on one of these since I was a little girl."

On the next trip to the top he pointed out his office, and on the trip after that his condo. Then all too soon it was over, and Mellette was almost as disappointed as the child in the car in front of them who cried when she was taken off by her parents. "That was almost worth the trip to Chicago."

"And the evening has barely started." For the next hour they strolled around the various shops along the pier, went through the stained glass museum and walked as lovers might, hand in hand at times, at others his arm around her waist. There were people everywhere, and concessionaires, and the whole length of the dock was lined with tour boats, people waiting for an evening excursion just to see the magnificent skyline.

"I could be happy just buying some toasted almonds and sitting here, watching the people," she said.

"Except we have dinner reservations in ten minutes, and a boat ride of our own after that."

"You didn't have to do all this for me, Justin."

He smiled. "Yes, I did. I mean, you're enjoying yourself, aren't you?"

"Loveliest night I've had in years."

"Then I had to do this for you." He took hold of her hand and pulled her in through a door and up some steps to a seafood restaurant. Sparkling grape juice was served tableside as if it was the most expensive wine in the world, and the lobster was divine. She'd been raised on crayfish and lobsterlike critters, but eating the real thing for her first time, dipping it with her fingers into the warm drawn butter... It was so decadent, so good, she didn't want the experience to end. But after they'd shared a generous slice of cheesecake it was over.

"So I know those crawdads you eat are mighty tasty,

and I love them myself, but how do they compare to lobster?"

"Two different worlds," she said, as he slid his arm around her waist. "Crawdads, crayfish or whatever you want to call them, fit my world. Lobster fits yours. I don't think you can draw a comparison because there really isn't one. But I must admit I'm enjoying my visit to your world."

"Yet we're not so different. Different worlds maybe, but I have lived in both, and I understand yours."

"Understanding it and living in it are two different things. Admittedly, I'd hoped you would stay and run the clinic. Now I understand why you can't. This is where you belong."

Was it, though? He was beginning to question that, thanks to Mellette. He had to admit he liked being in a world where she was, and this would never be her world. "I belong there, too," he whispered. "Just not so much anymore. And I think my grandmother understood that when she came to visit me. Up to that point she'd really pressed me to come home, but when she saw my life here...I think I disappointed her. Or maybe the way I fit here disappointed her."

"You never disappointed her, Justin. I think she wanted you back again, but she understood."

As they reached the boat, the captain greeted then and showed them aboard. It was small compared to some of the other massive tourist ships, but sweet and smart, with an enclosed deck as well as an exterior one. "Make yourself at home," the captain said. "We'll leave port in about ten minutes and in the meantime help yourself to the array of desserts and fruits in the cabin. And as the doctor requested, sparkling grape juice. No alcohol."

"Why do I get the feeling that we're the only passengers?" she asked Justin as they stepped into the cabin and she saw a lush array of finger food.

"Because we are. The captain is one of my patients and he was only too happy to rent the entire boat out to me for the evening."

"Well, I must say it's much nicer than my boat."

Justin laughed as he helped Mellette out of her hoodie. "Your boat's a step up from a raft."

"It gets me to work and keeps me safe from gators. That's all I need. But I could get used to something like this taking me to work every day." She picked up a chocolate-covered strawberry and nibbled off the end as the boat lurched away from the dock. As it lurched, she lurched, too, right into Justin's arms.

"Takes a while to get your sea legs," he said, laughing, as she pushed away from his chest and noticed the strawberry stain she'd left on his shirt.

"I'm so sorry," she said. "Maybe if I could find some club soda we could get that stain out before it sets in."

"Don't worry about it. I've probably got fifty more shirts. Losing one for a good cause is no big deal."

"What's the good cause, Justin?" she asked, as they pulled out of harbor and the lights of the city began to take on a life of their own. "I know you're not trying to seduce me, so is this whole thing just a ploy to make me understand why you're not going back with me? Let me see your life and how much better it is here than in

Big Swamp so I'll understand why my trip back home will be alone?"

"Whoa!" he said. "Where's that coming from?"

"It's coming from someone who's watching you try too hard to show me how good your life here is."

"Seriously, that's what you think this is about?"

"What else should I think?"

"That I'm trying to give you the best two days off you've ever spent. You don't take time off, and you don't spend time just doing something because it's fun for you. You're a great nurse, and even better mother, but where in your life do you leave time for you?"

She turned to look out at the old lighthouse in the harbor, liking the feel of the breeze on her face. It was at that moment she slipped off her wedding ring and tucked it into her pocket to save for Leonie. Moving on… It was time. Just a quiet, private little gesture meant only for herself. "It's not the way I planned my life, but it's what I got, and I'm doing the best I can to make the most of it. If it was just me, things would be different. But I have Leonie, and being a parent… That changes everything."

"Maybe it does, but don't you still have the right to hold on to something for you?"

"Right now, holding on to my sanity is enough." She chuckled. "There are days when I'm not sure I can do it, so at the end of my day, if I'm still sane, then I know it's been a good day."

"But what about you? What do you want?"

"A life where I didn't have to struggle so much, where I could spend more time with Leonie. Where

I didn't have to make the choices I make just to stay practical. Once upon a time I used to be spontaneous. Maybe not to this extent, but Landry and I would do things…like take off for a day or two, no destination in mind, and just drive until we found the place we wanted to stay. And picnics…I loved picnics, where I could just lay back and see images in the clouds." She sighed. "That's a side of me you don't know, because I can't afford to let it out. Even this…one night, and I feel so…so guilty because I know I should be back home, working on plans for the clinic or reading a bedtime story to Leonie."

"But you're enjoying it."

"More than you can know, Justin. More than you can know."

"And you trust that there are no ulterior motives?"

"Let's just say that I half trust, and leave it at that."

He laughed. "I accept it because it's so…you. Mellette Chaisson, always on her guard."

"You have to be when somebody charters a boat for an evening sweep around Chicago." With that, she picked up a piece of pineapple and popped it into her mouth. "And tries to ply you with sparkling grape juice."

"Then you like?"

"I love," she said, turning to give him a kiss on the cheek. "Thank you for being so extravagant. I think I like this side of you."

"Well, for what it's worth, I am going back to Big Swamp with you, Mellette."

"Thank you," she said, quite simply. "For everything."

For the next hour as they cruised the harbor and,

with his hand around her waist most of the time, and her head on his shoulder, to any onlooker they would have seemed like lovers. They certainly did to the captain and crew. And while the kiss Mellette gave Justin before they left the boat was circumspect, just a brief touch to his lips, the captain was already counting on the money he was going to make the next time Justin chartered his boat for this lady. And there would be another time. The captain was sure of it.

CHAPTER FIVE

THE TRIP, HOWEVER short, had been wonderful. But the symposium was now over and they were on their way back to Louisiana. A fact that made Mellette a little sad. Another day would have been nice. Two days was more than enough to be away from Leonie, but one more day in a different world would have been nice. "Thank you," she said as she relaxed back into the plane seat, awaiting take-off.

Their hands brushed across the seat console and neither one of them made an attempt to move. It was like touching him, even so slightly, meant their brief holiday had not ended.

"My pleasure. I was glad of the company."

"Even though it was my company?"

"Especially because it was your company. I live in one of the most amazing cities in the world, and yet I never take time to experience it. So for that I should be the one thanking you."

She smiled. "Your grandmother was always so worried about you because you never took time to relax. She said you drove yourself into the ground, working."

"It's the only way to get ahead."

"If that's all your life is about. Personally, I prefer having other things around me besides my job. I have my family, and I love doing things with Leonie."

"Which suits you, and I'm glad for that. But what suits me is what you saw. I work. Period."

"Will that ever change?"

"You mean, if I meet the right person, will she change that desire in me? Honestly, I don't know because I'm not looking. If it happens, then we'll see. But I could end up with someone just like me..."

"And you'd both live the very same life doing the very same things."

"Weren't you and Landry alike?"

"Not at all. He was a... I suppose the best way to describe him was a dreamer. He had these grand ideas. So many things he wanted to try. I was the one who kept us grounded, but that was okay because it worked for us. We were...good. And the whole thing with Landry was you never knew which direction he was going. He made life a surprise, fun and spontaneous."

"And I thought you didn't like spontaneity."

"I do. Just not alone."

"I can see why you miss him."

"The worst pain has mellowed, and I can think back and even talk with fondness now about the good things we had. For so long I couldn't because it made me sad, made me cry. But I got past all that because I needed to hold on to the good times so I could share them with Leonie. I realized that all she was ever going to know about her daddy was what I would tell her, and if it came with tears…" She shrugged. "That's not the kind of impression I want her to have of him."

"So why are you doing this for my grandmother?"

"Doing what?"

"You know, trying to wrangle me out of my guilt issues. I mean, I understand the whole part about your clinic involvement and how it's your ticket to a better future. But what's in it for you to make good on your promise to my grandmother?"

"Who says there was a promise?"

"I do. You're working much too hard on me for there not to have been."

"She knew you would feel guilty about not being there, and she asked me to help you through it. That's all."

"And even though you didn't know me, you agreed to do it?"

"It made her feel better. And I owed your grandmother so much. She helped me through my crisis after Landry died, was so very kind to me, taught me how to get back out there on my own again, and one little promise was the least I could do for her."

"So that promise was what?"

"Just to help you get through it. That's all, really. I made a simple promise to someone I loved, and I want to honor that promise."

"She thought I'd feel guilty?"

"She knew you would. And, truthfully, I wasn't in favor of the way she wanted to handle her last days, but it wasn't my decision to make."

"I'm glad you respected her wishes enough to honor them, but still—" he shrugged "—it hurts."

"I know, and I'm sorry for that. I really am. But I didn't know you then, and I did owe so much to your grandmother. I'm sorry, Justin. For both you and your grandmother. And I did try to talk her out of her decision. She just wouldn't be talked out of it, though."

She refused the drink from the flight attendant; Justin took a cola. And neither of them said another word for several minutes. Mellette simply sat there with her eyes closed while Justin thumbed through the dog-eared catalog selling expensive gadgetry. So it went until the flight attendant bent over Mellette a little while later and asked, "When you booked, you booked under the name Dr. Justin Bergeron. Would you be a medical doctor, by any chance?"

Mellette's eyes snapped open.

"Yes," Justin said, instantly alarmed. "General surgeon."

"Then would you mind coming with me, Doctor? There's someone I'd like you to see."

Without another word, Justin unfastened his seat belt and followed the flight attendant forward, leaving Mellette alone to wonder who might be sick, especially as because they were sitting in first class, there wasn't much more ahead of them but the pilot's cabin.

"How long have you been short of breath?" Justin asked the pilot, who was still strapped into his seat, sweating profusely and gasping for breath, while the copilot was busy assuming charge, alternately looking at his controls and glancing across at his colleague.

"About ten minutes," the man choked out.

His color had evolved to a pasty white, Justin noticed. "Are you nauseated? Light-headed?" Justin wedged himself into the cabin as best he could, while the flight attendant, a stately middle-aged woman named Lana, stood behind him, blocking entry to the cabin. "Chest pain?" Justin asked, as he took hold of his wrist to check the pulse.

"Some nausea, not much. Thought I'd eaten something that didn't agree with me. Not pain in my chest either so much as tightness." He indicated his sternum, straight down the middle.

"Shoulder, arm or jaw pain?"

"Some, in my jaw."

Justin turned to Lana. "I need an aspirin." Then he asked the pilot, "Do you have any history of heart disease? Or are you on any kind of medication?"

"No medicine except an occasional ibuprofen when I get a headache. Haven't had one in weeks. And I passed my physical last month with flying colors," the gray-haired man said. "Is this a heart attack, Doc?"

"Might be," Justin said, taking the aspirin and popping it into the pilot's mouth. Then he turned to Lana. "I put my medical bag in the overhead storage. Would you get it?"

A couple of minutes later Justin backed away from the pilot's seat, having diagnosed a thready, rapid heartbeat and low blood pressure. "Go and get my flying companion," he instructed the attendant, as the pilot let out a groan, indicating that he was getting worse.

The copilot, who'd been doing his level best to concentrate on flying the plane, turned to Justin just as the pilot, Jack Foster, reached up, clutched his chest and fell into unconsciousness. "Do I need to make an emergency diversion?" he asked.

"The sooner we get down, the better," Justin said as he laid his fingers on the pilot's neck. "I'd like to get him to a hospital as fast as we can."

Without another word to Justin, the copilot was on his radio to find an alternate airport where they could make an emergency landing.

"Justin?" Mellette said, wedging herself into the tiny cabin. She took one look at the situation and nodded. "Has he had an aspirin?"

"Just a minute ago. BP's low, pulse thready, difficulty breathing, tightening in his chest, jaw pain…" He grimaced. "Classical symptoms."

Her natural reaction was to glance toward the copilot's seat, to make sure the plane was being flown. Once she was satisfied they were safe, that the young man taking over looked not only competent but calm, she took a step closer, then lowered her voice. "I'm going to see what kinds of emergency supplies they have on board the plane. Be right back."

Outside the door, the flight attendant pointed to a cabinet where first aid and medical supplies were kept.

"What do we have available?" Mellette asked. She was primed to spring into action. Emergencies were her territory and it was difficult simply standing around, waiting to be oriented, when she needed to be working.

"A first-aid kit, portable oxygen bottles, an AED, automated external defibrillator and an EMK emergency medical kit, with various supplies and drugs."

"Such as?"

"A stethoscope, blood-pressure cuff, bag mask resuscitator, three different sizes of oral airways, nitroglycerin, aspirin, albuterol, injectable dextrose, 1:1000 epinephrine, oral antihistamines, IV antihistamines and cardiac resuscitation drugs, including IV 1:10,000 epinephrine, atropine and lidocaine. We've also got five hundred milliliters of normal saline, an IV drip set and a variety of needles and syringes."

Mellette couldn't help but be impressed by the flight attendant's knowledge. It wasn't quelling her need to move faster, but she was relieved that the airline was well equipped.

"And if Captain Foster needs to lie down, I'll get the gallery area cleared out and recruit a couple of men to help lift him there, where you and the doctor can work on him if you have to. But let me warn you that the entire plane's going to go into a panic once they know the pilot is incapacitated. We'll make the announcement and let them know that we have a second, equally competent pilot on board, but be prepared for some panic attacks and anxiety-related conditions to pop up, because I'm betting that's going to happen."

"I can imagine," Mellette said, glad of the warning. "By the way, does the AED have an ECG screen to monitor the cardiac rhythm?"

"It does, but it's a paddles-view only."

Which meant only one type of tracing out of twelve could be viewed, but that was much better than nothing. "Let me talk to Justin—Dr. Bergeron—and see how he wants to proceed."

Mellette stepped back in the cabin, where the pilot looked even more pasty than before. And he was certainly fighting for breath harder than he had only a minute before. "We've got what we need to maintain him, I think, but there's going to be more room outside the cabin, on the gallery floor, so the flight attendant's going to get that cleared for us. Oh, and she's expecting panic attacks from the passengers. Thought you'd want to know what we're going to be up against."

"One thing at a time," Justin said, as Mellette stepped back out to the galley to get the various drugs and set-ups ready for the pilot.

Almost as he spoke, two men appeared at the cabin door, ready to lift the captain to the area just outside the door. It was a bit of a struggle, getting him out of his seat in a space clearly not intended to fit as many people as were crammed in there. So to give them more maneuvering room, Mellette stepped back, essentially to the first row of first class, and stood in the aisle.

"What the hell's going on?" one impatient man snapped at her.

"Medical emergency, sir. And everything's under control."

"Is it the pilot?" he demanded.

"As soon as things are straightened out, someone will let you know," she answered, trying to sound as calm as she possibly could. Passengers were now straining to hear what she was saying, and she could already feel waves of panic coming from a number of them.

"I paid good money for my ticket, and I demand to know now!" he shouted in return.

"In due course," she said quietly as the men up front began to move the captain out of the cabin. As that was happening, Mellette deliberately stepped forward to just opposite the front lavatory door, hoping her presence there would block the closest passengers from seeing exactly what was going on.

"Due course isn't good enough!" the man yelled, unsnapping his seat belt and lunging forward. He grabbed Mellette's arm in an attempt to move her aside, but after years of wrestling rambunctious patients in the E.R., she packed a few good defensive moves and deftly slid out of his grip, managing to grab hold of his arm and spin him around so his face was pressed tight to the lavatory door.

"We don't need any more problems right now," she whispered to the man, "so I would suggest you return to your seat and buckle yourself in, or you'll be facing a security guard the instant you step off this plane."

A bold threat, and she didn't know if that was what would actually happen. But the last thing she needed while they were getting the pilot settled into position was some bull of a man rushing forward, causing problems.

"Better sit down," the old woman with the knitting magazine said. "I heard her talking to that man of hers, and she's not a person I'd care to tangle with."

Mellette turned to smile at the old woman, who gave Mellette a mischievous wink.

"Take your hands off me," the man demanded, but his voice didn't hold nearly the same threat it had earlier.

"Fine, but if you move one inch in the direction of the galley, I'll drop you to your knees next time."

Those words brought about a round of applause and cheers from the passengers in the front section of the plane. Two men seated in the first few rows of coach class stepped forward, each one taking an arm of the belligerent man to show him back to his seat. Or, in this case, shove him back.

"That was pretty good," the flight attendant whispered as she stepped back to allow Mellette into the galley area once the pilot was flat on the floor.

"All in a day's work," Mellette said, immediately slipping an oxygen mask over the pilot's face, then she set about the task of inserting an IV while Justin got him hooked up to the heart monitor.

"Guess I should be glad you didn't manhandle me that way to get me on board," Justin said, as the lines of the pilot's heart rhythm started flowing across the tiny screen. "But I suppose I'd better keep it in mind for future run-ins with you, shouldn't I?"

"I have defensive skills and I know how to use them," she replied, smiling over at him.

Out in the cabin, you could have heard a pin drop. It was as if all the passengers were holding their collective breaths. All behaving very well, including the combatant man, who was a bit red in the face, either from agitation or embarrassment. Mellette made a mental note to check his blood pressure after the captain was stabilized, just to make sure his outburst hadn't caused him any physical problems.

"Ladies and gentlemen," the copilot announced over the loudspeaker, "as some of you are witnessing, our pilot has had a medical emergency and is currently being treated at the front of the cabin. Please do not interfere with the process, please do not leave your seats and come forward, because we need all the space we have to stay unobstructed. And rest assured that I am a fully qualified pilot with ten years' experience, and the plane is functioning exactly as it should, with no difficulties. But you do need to know that we are going to be diverting our flight…"

"I've got the IV in," Mellette told Justin as the pilot continued to go over the plan, "so our choices of drugs are atropine and lidocaine." Without waiting for his response, she readied the lidocaine.

"You're good at this," Justin commented.

"I'm an E.R. nurse, remember?" she said as she swabbed the IV port and injected the drug.

"Then you're probably better at this than I am, since I rarely get involved in emergency procedure."

She looked at him and smiled. "Probably."

He chuckled. "And modest, too."

"In the meantime," the copilot was wrapping up, "please sit back and relax. This plane is in no jeopardy."

"Unless the copilot has a heart attack, too," the belligerent man piped up, and was immediately shushed by the passenger behind him. The initial rush of panic subsided.

Back at the front, Mellette, who was kneeling over

the pilot, took a look at the heart tracing and breathed a sigh of relief—not that any bad heart tracing was a relief, but she did recognize it indicated a blockage. And as far as they went, this one wasn't too bad. "I think today's going to be his lucky day," she said, finally settling back into a more comfortable position for the duration of the ride. "If you can call a heart attack lucky. Because I don't think this one's going to turn out to be too serious."

"And he did have one semiskilled doctor and one highly qualified nurse on board," Justin added as he palpated another blood pressure, then sighed in relief when he saw that the numbers were stabilizing.

"Don't be so hard on yourself. I'm sure if he'd needed his gallbladder removed, you'd have been Johnny-on-the-spot." She laughed. "But you were good. Especially in such cramped quarters."

Justin looked around, as if he'd only just noticed how cramped they were. "Did I ever tell you that I'm claustrophobic?"

"Seriously?" she asked.

He nodded as he fought to control his own breathing, which was beginning to turn a bit shallow now that he wasn't preoccupied by the emergency.

"Need oxygen?"

Justin shook his head, drew in a ragged breath. "Need wide-open spaces."

She glanced down at their patient, who was doing nicely, then across at Justin who was not. She adjusted the pilot's oxygen mask, then took hold of Justin's hand. Held it for twenty seconds, then let go when she felt the spark that passed between then. A real electrical jolt, it seemed, even though she knew it couldn't possibly be.

"Sorry, Doctor, but that's all the bedside manner you get from me."

"You've got better things to do than give aid and comfort to a hopeless claustrophobic?"

"Actually, yes, I do." She grabbed the blood-pressure cuff, then stood and headed back to the cabin, on the verge of her own little panic attack as she marched straight over to the man who'd given her quite a struggle. He was still red in the face. Too red, considering the time that had passed since the incident, and her fingers automatically went to his pulse. But he jerked his wrist away from her.

"Don't touch me," he hissed.

She could hear wheezing coming from him.

"I think you might be having a medical crisis, and I just wanted to check you."

"You touch me, and I'll sue you! I'm warning you, lady…" He sucked in a lungful of air, and the wheezes became more apparent.

"Are you asthmatic? Do you have a history of blood-pressure problems or any other diagnosed condition?" she persisted.

His answer was to glare at her and, if anything, turn even more red.

"Are you having difficulty breathing, or chest pains?"

He still didn't answer.

"Feeling anything peculiar that you don't normally feel?"

"Would that include my anger toward you?" he snarled.

She knew it was an irrational reaction, knew his agitation was escalating by the second, yet she couldn't force her medical attention on him. So she shrugged and started to walk away. But two steps into her departure she turned back to him. "You've got something going on, and I don't know what it is. I need to examine you to be able to help you, but if you're going to sit there being so pig-headedly stupid, then go ahead and have a stroke or a heart attack or whatever it is you're going to have. Just keep in mind that you've forbidden me to help you, which means you can, and probably will, die if that happens. I have a planeload of witnesses who heard you."

Not that she wouldn't help the man, even against his orders if it came down to it. But she was hoping a little scare tactic might get him to cooperate. She didn't need another emergency on this plane.

"Nice bedside manner," Justin said as she bent down next to him, preparing to sit back down and help monitor the pilot.

"You do what you have to do. In this case, some arm-twisting."

"Remind me not to get on your bad side."

"What makes you think you're on my good side?" she asked, arching her eyebrows.

"Well, for starters, you haven't injured me. Haven't even threatened to injure me."

Mellette laughed at that. "Give me time. I'm sure you'll earn it somewhere down the line."

"I'm sure I will," Justin said, shifting his position, going from kneeling to sitting cross-legged with his back to a storage pantry.

"You doing okay on the claustrophobia?"

"Not really. The galley has shrunk by half in the past five minutes."

"Want me to see if someone on board has some alprazolam or diazepam? I'll bet if I put out the call, a lot of people will have it."

"I'm fine," he said, wiping a bead of sweat off his face.

Instinctively, Mellette reached into the medical kit, pulled out a square of gauze and handed it to him for a wipe. "I'm afraid of heights," she admitted.

"Like in an airplane?"

"No, because it's enclosed. But climbing trees, and standing on the side of a mountain, looking down. When we were young, my parents took us on a mountain vacation—rented a cabin, had a very nice week planned. But I wouldn't get out of the car and walk to the cabin door because we were sitting on the edge of a bluff. I wanted to, even tried to. But I couldn't get out of the car to save my soul."

"How old were you?"

"Seven or eight, I think. And the thing is, we already knew I had a hard time with heights. Even going upstairs to my bedroom at my parents' is a challenge, because if I look down I get dizzy, and if I get dizzy I start hyperventilating."

"So I take it you and Leonie live in a one-story?"

"Blessedly close to the ground. The thing is, I've learned to control it because I know it's just an irrational fear popping out. Heights won't hurt me—" she smiled "—unless I fall from one. Which won't happen because

I don't take the risks that will put me up very high." Except the Ferris-wheel ride they'd taken. But that hadn't been a risk as she'd been in his arms the whole time.

"So did you spend your entire vacation in the car?"

She shook her head. "After a couple of hours my dad asked me if I trusted him. Of course, I said yes. Then he promised me nothing there would hurt me, and he took me by my hand and led me inside. Once I was in the cabin I was fine, but going back and forth outside, where I could see how high up we were…that's what didn't work so well. But Daddy always held my hand, and after that we took our vacations at the beach."

"Well, just between you and me, my greatest fear is getting trapped in a stalled elevator with a bunch of people. If that ever happens to me, I'll be the one in the corner, on the floor, going fetal."

She gave him a fake frown. "I don't think fetal would be a good look for you." She looked up as the flight attendant approached. "The pilot has cleared us for an emergency landing, so we'll be setting down in about ten minutes. Oh, and the gentleman in the first row would like to see you," she said to Mellette. "He thinks he might be experiencing some difficulty."

Mellette pushed up off the floor, grabbed the emergency kit and smiled. "My adoring public waits."

"Don't twist his arm so hard it breaks," Justin teased. "Because I don't do bones."

Back in the cabin, Mellette took the seat next to the man, whose name turned out to be William, and immediately put the blood-pressure cuff on him. He didn't look at her. In fact, he kept his head back against the headrest, with his eyes closed.

"It's too high," she told him, once she'd taken the reading. "Have you ever been diagnosed with hypertension?"

He shook his head.

"Well, the good news is your pulse is fine, and the wheezes I heard earlier have diminished. I think you might have been having an anxiety attack, but I am concerned about your blood pressure because it's dangerously close to stroke territory, so I'm going to have an ambulance waiting for you once we get off the plane and send you to the hospital to be looked at."

He rolled his head to look at her, and opened his eyes. "If this turns out to be nothing, I'm going to sue you for delaying me," he said.

"I'm sure you will," Mellette said, settling back into her seat and fastening in for the landing.

Her patient merely rolled his head back to look forward and closed his eyes again. And twenty minutes later, as they strapped him to an aisle chair and took him out after the pilot had been escorted to an ambulance, he looked at Mellette. "I want you to give me your name and address and a copy of your credentials," he snapped. "Immediately!"

Mellette merely laughed as she bent down to him and whispered, "Don't hold your breath."

"Maybe you should have broken his wrist," Justin said as he pulled her overnight bag down from the overhead locker.

"As miserable as he is, I don't think he would have noticed."

They were the first two to be let off the plane, and

they followed their respective patients to the medics waiting to take them to the ambulances. Then, as was customary, they were asked to report to the airline office and give details of the event. Consequently, they missed the connecting flight that would have gotten them to New Orleans in a relatively respectable amount of time.

"And I supposed you're going to blame me for the flight delay in case we don't make it to New Orleans by tonight," Justin said as the two of them were finally free to go.

"It crossed my mind," she said, holding back a smile.

It was going to be five more hours before she and Justin and would get back to New Orleans, and by the time that new arrival time had sunk in, Mellette was too exhausted to put one foot in front of the other. She'd already spent half an hour talking to Leonie on the phone, and another hour browsing all the Lambert–St. Louis International Airport gift shops for gifts to take back to her daughter. Then she'd bought a romance novel to read. All while Justin stretched out casually on the seats and snoozed.

So typical, she thought to herself, remembering back to Landry and how easy it had been for him to fall asleep anywhere, any time. While she, on the other hand, had had a hard time going to sleep in their own bed, let alone anywhere else.

But Justin did look kind of cute sleeping, she had to admit, with his mouth half-open and his hair all mussed. He really was a handsome man. More classically handsome than Landry, who'd been a rough-and-tumble outdoors boy. He was larger than Landry, too. More muscled. Taller by a couple of inches.

Landry, she thought as she settled into a seat next to where Justin was sleeping and rubbed the empty spot on her ring finger. He'd been everything she'd ever wanted. Her perfect companion. As she slid down into her seat and shut her eyes, she counted on his image popping into her mind to comfort her, the way it always did. But tonight it didn't.

Nothing was there except the frightening void of empty, black space, which caused Mellette to sit bolt upright, blink herself back into the moment and fight off the panic rising so fast it felt like her heart was going to explode. Landry... For that instant he'd been gone from her completely, leaving her with the sense that he was never coming back. She'd forgotten what he'd looked like. How could that happen? How could his image just vanish like that?

Mellette wanted to close her eyes again to see if he would come back. But she was too frightened, and her pulse hadn't settled down enough.

"You okay?" Justin asked groggily, as he sat back up.

"Just fighting fatigue. No big deal."

He sighed and scooted over to her, until they were touching, then he put his arm around her shoulder and pulled her even closer. "You fight too much," he said. "It'll wear you out."

"I have a lot of things in my life to fight," she said, giving in to the comfort he was offering. It was a man's touch she hadn't expected to like, or even to accept. And it surprised her how easily, and how willingly, she allowed herself to practically melt into his arms. But that was exactly what she was doing and she was enjoying it more than she should have. Any other time she would have recoiled, jumped up, moved to the other side of the aisle. Right now, though, she was just too tired and, admittedly, she did like the feel of having him there with her. Liked it more than she should have, maybe even more than she'd let herself admit to.

Liked it so much she let her eyes close. And didn't sit bolt upright when she still couldn't find Landry in the darkness. As the only one she needed there was Justin.

CHAPTER SIX

IT WAS HARD, facing the changes—the changes going on inside himself to do with Mellette, after holding her for those hours in the airport while she slept. He was attracted to her. More than attracted. In fact, he wondered if she might be the one to turn his world upside down. But leaving Chicago and coming back here? Could he do it? And if he did, could he be happy? Somewhere logic needed to meet emotion, and he wasn't sure where that would happen, or how.

Also, it was hard, facing the changes going on with his grandmother's house. He hadn't realized how attached he'd been to it, or to the memories. Too much was changing…changing too fast. All of it was his doing, though. The medical clinic and what he was feeling toward Mellette.

Admittedly, his new feelings for her were what had him the most confused, because they weren't the normal physical fluff he experienced when he spent time with a pretty woman. She was substance. It just engulfed her like a cocoon. So while that probably should have scared him—and he'd have been smart to have been scared—

it didn't. It was more like it intrigued him, made him want more…more of her.

He'd been too long without a woman, he tried to tell himself. And while that was true, the other thing he had to admit was that he'd never had a woman like Mellette in his life. So maybe she wasn't really in his life so much as close to it, but she was close enough that it was making him think. Confusing thoughts. Conflicting thoughts.

"Better color?" Mellette asked, stepping up behind him.

"Much." Rather than going with white paint for the house's exterior, which she'd originally planned, Mellette had chosen a charcoal gray, which was as near to the original color as it could get. But she'd added trim colors that the house had never had before—lighter gray around the windows and a rich brick red for the chimney, door and flower boxes under the windows, which made the place look welcoming. "It's…different. Going to take some getting used to. But I like it."

"Changes aren't always easy, are they?" she asked him, giving his arm a sympathetic squeeze then looping her arm through his and pulling him toward the house. "Even when we expect them and want them."

"Even when they're for the best." The welcome sign was conspicuously missing and it surprised him how much that single, small subtraction affected him. But it did, and it caused a hard lump to form in his throat, probably because it had always been his habit to look up at the sign looming over the door every time he walked in. But times were changing, weren't they? And this was her project, not his. So he had no reason to complain. At this late date, he had no legitimate call to remind her of his suggestions, either. No reason to say put back the sign because, damn it, he missed it!

"Did you save the welcome sign?" Justin asked Mellette, on the off chance she'd tucked it away somewhere, as he stepped up on the front porch and saw that the old wicker furniture, too worn to be functional, had been replaced by new. He was glad she'd left his grandmother's original porch swing, though. "The one that used to hang over the front door?"

"Yes, it's in a safe place and ready to hang back up once the project is completed."

"Good," he said, having this sudden urge to sit down on Eula's old swing and just...swing.

"Want me to hang it now?"

He shook his head. "No, that's not necessary. Just as long as it's hung up at some point." He was surprised how sentimental he was about something so meaningless, but he was. That sign signified...home.

"Well, if you change your mind..." she said, then went chasing off after a man in a hard hat who had a stack of lumber over his shoulder.

That was when Justin went inside, took two steps in the door and was surprised to see the progress that had been made. Nothing inside resembled what had been here before...not even in the very rough stages, as this was. Walls were gone, studs and wiring exposed. The old wooden floor had been torn out, replaced by boards over which new flooring would go. Even the old windows were missing. "Damn," he muttered, impressed as hell and sad at the same time.

"You like it?" Mellette asked, stepping in just behind him.

"It's not what I expected."

"You wanted a clinic that looked like a clinic, and that's what you're paying me to give you. So...would you like the grand tour?"

He wasn't sure he was ready for it. But when he turned to look at Mellette, he wasn't sure he'd ever seen anyone as stunningly beautiful in all his life. And it was her excitement over the transformation that was making her so pretty. It shone in her eyes, in the way she smiled, in the way she concentrated on every little aspect of every detail in the front room. With her Creole mixed coloring and a slight scarlet flush of excitement rising to her cheeks, she was a real breath-taker. Someone who, under different circumstances...

No! He didn't have a right to those thoughts. There were too many obstacles, the first being the fact that she still considered herself a married woman. Her bond to that union was so strong, even now, that she wasn't going to let another man in. And even if she did, it wouldn't be him because he wasn't leaving Chicago and she wasn't leaving here. So what was the point of even thinking out the what-ifs of this situation?

Still, he couldn't help but admire beauty when he saw it. In Mellette he saw it in ways he'd never seen it before. And that included her take-charge attitude. The more he was around it, the more her strong character was growing on him and all he could think of was the missed opportunity back in Chicago. She'd kissed him as a friendly gesture, but what if he'd returned that kiss with some passion, rather than just standing there like a dope and not responding? "Sure, a grand tour would be good," he said, mentally kicking himself.

Of course, one kiss didn't change the outcome of their destinies, did it?

"Well, this is the new reception area, and I've had it enlarged so we can turn it into a proper waiting area. I think a lot of folks will still prefer to sit outside and wait on Eula's porch, the way they always have, which is why I've added new chairs. Oh, and the window boxes. I know she wasn't into frilly things, but with the new paint I just thought that the exterior needed some dressing up, and Eula did love the flowers in her garden, so I took the liberty of planting some of them in the new window boxes.

"Even though we're turning this into a more functional clinic, I still want it to have some homey touches, which is why, when this waiting room is done, it's not going to be so…traditional."

"Should I ask what you mean by that?"

She shrugged. "It's going to be about simplicity. A place to pour yourself a good cup of chicory coffee. A checkerboard to play a quick game while you're passing time. A couple of rocking chairs. And a nice sound system for some zydeco."

"Zydeco," he repeated. Music popular in the bayou.

"Of course zydeco! What other kind of music would you expect?"

Of course zydeco. It made sense, actually. In fact,

all Mellette's choices so far had made sense. "I made a good choice."

"Zydeco was my choice," she said defensively.

"But you were my choice. And you have no idea how you glow when you're working. It's very attractive on you."

"Oh," she said, as the scarlet in her cheeks flushed a little redder. "I'm not a big one for flattery," she said. "Most people flatter because they want something in return, and all you're getting is what you're paying me to do."

"Which precludes me from paying a compliment when that's what's due?"

"You picked me out of a registry. I was a name to you when you chose me, so it's not like you really chose me so much as you chose my credentials for the job."

"Like I asked before, does that preclude me from paying you a compliment when it's due?"

"And like I said, I'm not a big one for flattery. You're paying me to do a job and I'm doing it. Purely business, Justin."

"Whoever said it wasn't?"

"Flattery leads to other things."

Like sleeping together, entwined in each other's arms in the airport. And enjoying it. "It's not my intention to lead to other things, Mellette, and I'm sorry if my compliment made you feel uncomfortable."

She blushed even harder. "It was a year after my husband died. I wasn't ready to date, had no intention of getting involved. But there was this doctor at the hospital—a man I worked with occasionally. I thought he was a nice man, someone who was just trying to be kind to me. And he flattered me, Justin. All the time. Said things that didn't mean much at first, and eventually the flattery...it ramped up. Became very suggestive. I asked him to stop, told him I wasn't comfortable. But he didn't, so I went to my department head, who took it from there.

"Then this doctor had the audacity to tell my supervisor that I'd been asking for it, that I'd been the one who was suggestive, and if it weren't for the fact that my mother was chief of staff, he'd have filed a complaint against me for sexual harassment. Me, harassing him! I mean, I know I was vulnerable right then, maybe not picking up on the clues, but...but I wouldn't have done that. Wouldn't have even let him go on for so long if I'd really taken a good look at what he was doing. I was still so numb, though."

"Your supervisor didn't believe him, did she?"

Mellette shook her head. "Not for a minute. But word got out, people talked. I got shunned. You know how it is. Anyway, after that, I just don't trust people's motives unless they're pretty straightforward. And while you've been pretty straightforward..."

"I make you nervous."

"Flattery makes me nervous because you never know where it's going to go."

His heart did go out to Mellette, being so assertive on one hand and so unsure of herself on the other. To have loved someone the way she'd loved Landry... He couldn't even imagine that. "Where does complimenting you on a job well done fall in your list of things I shouldn't do?" he asked.

"See, that's well within my bounds, because it's professional. Just telling me that I look good while I'm doing the job isn't."

"Then instruct me when I get it wrong, because I do want to know, Mellette. I want you to be comfortable working here." And especially comfortable working with him.

"I will. Speaking of which, let's go to the first exam room, formerly the forward downstairs bedroom. It's had quite a transformation." Sighing, maybe a breath of relief, Mellette gestured for Justin to follow her down the hall, past a new space that was little more than the size of a large closet. "Doctor's office," she said. "I was going to have it up front in the parlor, but decided to use that as my own office space since I don't expect the doctor will be here all that often. And I need something different than the kitchen."

It was apparent she was nervous, the way she was wringing her hands, so he took particular care to stay well away from her—walked to the window on the other side of the room while she remained standing in the doorway. "When you say the doctor, I'm assuming you mean your dad?"

"My dad, maybe others if I can recruit some volunteers form New Hope. Oh, and let me warn you, the next time you see my mother, she's not going to be very cordial to you. She absolutely hates the fact that my dad has agreed to come back to work, even for a few hours a week. And you're the one who's going to feel the bite of her wrath, I'm afraid. I mean, she's not happy with me giving up my job at the hospital to come and work here full time, and you're going to get the backlash from that, as well. But when Daddy told her he'd be coming out here occasionally..."

"In other words, you've just put me in direct opposition to arguably the most powerful doctor in this part of the state."

"Something like that." Her eyes finally crinkled into a relaxed laugh.

"And she wants to kill me."

"More or less."

"Then it's a good thing I'll be back in Chicago when the project wraps up."

"Trust me, Chicago's not far enough away to escape my mother's anger."

"But doesn't she see that this clinic is a good thing?" Justin asked, as he surveyed walls now torn down to the studs.

"I think she sees that bringing our kind of medicine to the people out here is good, but not at the expense of her family. And the thing about my mother is she's still very...Creole. She's one of the most highly regarded physicians in the country, yet she still has respect for the herbal aspects of bayou medicine."

"So she's not in favor of modernizing the clinic?"

"She's in favor, but not to the point that the old traditions here will be lost. She loved your grandmother, by the way."

"She knew her?"

"Not knew. But she did meet her once. Came here

when I first took the job to see what kind of place I was working in, and she and Eula sat on the front porch and talked for hours. They talked as doctors, and talked as women who shared similar backgrounds, and my mother truly respected her for the work she did here in Big Swamp."

"But she's not in favor of getting you or your dad involved."

"She likes having her family close, and this isn't close enough to suit her. I think she believes she can't protect us well enough while she's in the city but we're out here, which is like a strange and distant land to her."

"You're just like that, aren't you? About Leonie. Your whole life is built around protecting the people you love, and especially your daughter." He sneaked a casual glance at her as she looked away because he liked the way her face lit up, but he wasn't fast enough to avert his gaze as she turned back and caught him.

"What?" she asked.

"I like the way you come alive when you talk about the things you love. It's nice to see you relax that way."

"I—um—um—" she stammered, looking for a comeback. But when she didn't find one she dived back into her protective shell. "To be compared to Zenobia Doucet... That's maybe the nicest thing anybody could ever say about me." She paused, then gestured for him to follow her upstairs, where she intended to show him that modernization and not transformation was taking place. Just new paint, new windows, new varnish on the wooden floor. Nothing else to change the bedrooms.

"You meant it as a compliment, didn't you? Comparing me to my mother?"

"Only if you don't think I'm trying to garner a favor by paying the compliment." Running his fingers over the formerly green, now light yellow walls, he looked outside to the yard, to his old escape route, and smiled fondly. "That was my old escape route. One I used so many times when I was a kid, and it was such a simple way to get away for a while.

"Out the window, down the tree, hide behind the clump of sweet azaleas to make sure the creaking caused by opening the window didn't awaken my grandmother, then, when I was sure I was in the clear, make my way along the fern bed to the hickory tree. After that, run like hell across the open expanse down to the old boathouse. Once past that I was home free!

"Then it was either grab my bike and take off on one of the back roads, or untie the canoe and paddle myself out of there, maybe meet up with Johnny Redbone and Bobby Simoneaux, go into Grandmaison and hang outside the door to Guidry's Inn and hope some of the beer bottles getting tossed in the can out the back door still had beer in them.

"Or go down the road to old man Lazier's place and sneak in the back of his barn to grab a few leaves of that weed he was always drying behind his regular tobacco. Sometimes we got lucky and found a jar of his moonshine in the rafters, one he'd overlooked when he'd taken the others into his house. Those were good nights for a bunch of fourteen-year-old boys."

Good nights, good times, he thought. Rough times,

too, that had earned him his bad boy reputation, and certainly now he'd never do those things he'd done back then. But he looked back on the old days with fondness, because he hadn't had such a bad childhood. He had been a bad child, though. One set down in the middle of what could have been a very good childhood if he'd let it happen. Which he hadn't. Even so, he'd turned out pretty good in spite of it.

"So whatever happened to your coconspirators?" she asked.

"John Redbone's now a judge on the bench over in Baton Rouge, and Robert Simoneaux is a high school history teacher. No thanks to me and the way I'd led them. And make no mistake—I was the ringleader."

"Sounds like good times for a young boy."

"Restless times. I was always restless."

"But like your friends, you found your place, and the restlessness stopped."

Except that he was feeling restless again.

"Your grandmother always knew where you were going. Did you know that?

"She told you?"

Mellette nodded. "When you thought you were sneaking out, she was sitting up, worrying. And she didn't like what you were doing one bit, but every time she tried to discipline you, you threatened to run away. She was afraid you would. So you'd sneak out the window, and she'd stay up all night waiting for you to come back, praying you'd be safe."

"Damn," he muttered. "Why didn't she ever tell me?"

"You left home when you were, what? Sixteen?"

He nodded. "Just a week shy of turning seventeen. And I was getting into all kinds of trouble by then, and she…she wanted me to fix the messes I was making for myself. Wanted me to take responsibility…" He turned to face her. "I guess I'm not really surprised that she knew. Maybe the only thing she didn't know was how to handle a smart-ass kid who wouldn't be handled."

"Her only hope was trying to teach you to be *smart*. At least, that's what she told me."

Maybe one of the reasons he didn't want to be here was that he didn't want to see, through adult eyes, the kind of pain he'd caused his grandmother. It was a bitter pill to swallow. But it was a pill he deserved. "What about the second bedroom downstairs…my grandmother's sewing room? Is it going to be turned into an exam room, as well?" he asked, deliberately trying to change the subject. Talking about the many ways he'd hurt his grandmother was still too painful.

"Identical to the first exam room."

"And the kitchen?"

"I haven't been able to make any changes there. The kitchen is where Eula most loved to be, whether it was cooking a meal for herself or friends, or fixing one of her herbal concoctions. So when I think of Eula, I picture her in the kitchen, and I just haven't had the heart to change any of it."

Funny, but when he pictured his grandmother, that was where he thought of her, too. There in the kitchen, or sitting on her front porch. "Maybe you won't have to," he said, hoping that was the way it would turn out.

"So what do you think so far?"

"I think it will work. It's going to take some getting used to, but since you're keeping some of the more homey touches, as well as keeping some of the house intact, I think people will generally respond positively."

She shook her head. "Nobody's even coming here right now. If they do, they won't come inside...prefer the porch. They think what we're doing here is disrespecting Eula's memory, and they want no part of it. So I'm either working on the front porch treating patients, or making house calls."

"House calls? Seriously?"

"Three or four a day right now. And trust me, no one out here wants the kind of medicine they think you're trying to cram down their throats. They literally peek out the windows to make sure you're not with me when I visit them."

"So I'm getting the blame for the way they're acting?"

Mellette smiled. "You sure don't think I'm going to take the blame for any of this, do you? I've got to work with the people, so I'm doing everything I can to stay on their good side. And since they need an enemy..." She tapped the air with her index finger, pointing at him. "It's all yours, Doctor, and you're welcome to it."

"Good thing I've got broad shoulders."

"Good thing," she agreed as she stepped backward into the hall. "Look, I need to go and see Paul LeCompte. He's not been feeling too well—gastric upset, and I want to take him some tea."

"Tea?" Justin questioned.

"Your grandmother's special recipe for Paul. Got to look it up and put it together for him."

"Ah, yes, her patient filing system, as she used to call it." He was referring to her volumes of old, dog-eared, spiral-bound notebooks in which she'd kept the precise instructions for the herbal remedies she used on each and every one of her patients. One book for each letter of the alphabet, except the *X-Y-Z* volume, which was combined.

Justin walked into the kitchen, opened an old-fashioned Hoosier cabinet that had seen well more than a century of use—the cabinet where she'd kept her herbs—pulled out the *L* volume and turned to the Paul LeCompte page. Not to be confused with the thirty or so other LeComptes in her book. "It says chamomile tea, with one pinch cinnamon, one pinch cayenne, two juniper berries smashed and three pinches of ginger."

"Eula was pretty precise about her prescriptions."

"One pinch, Mellette. That's the kind of medicine you're practicing? A pinch of this, two smashed berries…"

"If it works it works."

"Then why has Paul LeCompte been coming here for a quarter of a century with the same complaint?"

"See, here's the thing, Justin. Your grandmother certainly had the ability to cure certain things. She was always very humble about calling it cured. She always called it treated. But as you well know, there are things that require lifelong treatment, chronic problems like Paul LeCompte experiences that will never be cured."

"The man eats too much greasy food. Always has.

Cut out the grease, cut out the stomachaches and who knows what else his diet is doing to him."

"Are you going to be the one to tell him that? Because you know how the people are around here."

"I'll tag along, if you don't mind."

"And do what? Irritate him?"

"My presence here irritates just about everybody else, so there's no reason he should be the exception."

Mellette quickly assembled all the LeCompte tea components, put them in a small paper bag, then dropped it into her traditional medical bag and headed for the back door, which meant they were taking Eula's old pickup truck for this house call.

"I'll drive," Justin said, grabbing the keys off the hook by the back door and rushing ahead to open Mellette's door for her. It wasn't so much to be gentlemanly, since he wasn't sure how she'd take the simple gesture of courtesy. But the passenger's door had been stuck for more than twenty years, and it took some effort to persuade it to open. Like a couple of kicks, a few swear words and another kick.

"Some things never change," he said when the door finally popped open. He helped Mellette in, then shut the door and smiled. Yep. Some things never changed. And in a way, he was glad about that.

Paul LeCompte's cabin was fairly isolated in the woods, and if not for the mailbox on the dirt road, his weedy, overgrown driveway would have been easily missed. It was a pretty area, really, full of cypress trees and huge oaks, with a never-ending maze of brackish waterways separating his little piece of land from that which sat adjacent to his, and coincidentally was owned by his brother Robert.

The moss hanging down from every tree resembled a silverish-gray beard adorning the many branches, quite eerie to lay eyes on for the first time. It was still used as ticking in mattresses by a lot of the folks who lived in the bayou. Justin knew for a fact that his grandmother had occasionally used it to treat what she called sugar, and what he called diabetes.

"It's about time you got yourself back where you belong, Justin," Paul LeCompte said, pronouncing Justin's name *juice-tan,* the way most of the people in the bayou did. "Didn't think you'd ever have the guts to show your face around here again, not after the way you treated poor Eula, God rest her soul. Not being here for her last days…"

Mellette looked over at Justin to gauge his reaction, saw his jaw clench, saw him ball his hands into fists. Laid a reassuring hand over his left fist and was quite surprised how well he kept his cool.

"She was a mighty good woman," Paul continued. He was seated in a rocker on the front porch of his blue clapboard house, swatting at mosquitoes and snapping pole beans he'd picked from his garden. "Deserved a whole lot better than what you ever gave her, all that nonsense before you ran away."

Mellette stepped up behind Justin and took hold of his right arm. Could feel his biceps tense up. "Justin's just here to help me, Paul. He's very good with treating gastric upsets such as yours."

Paul's response was to snort. "Give me Eula's tea. That fixes me right up, and it's all I need." He looked up at Justin, who'd yet to speak. "And I don't want the kind of medicine you'd be having me take."

"I didn't come here to give you medicine, Paul. If you want to keep on having the same stomach pains you've been having for as long as I can remember, that's your business."

"You're right, young man. That's my business."

"But if you'd ever care to see just what the diet of yours is doing to you—to your heart and arteries, and to your blood—I'd be glad to prescribe the blood tests you'd need."

"I'm just fine," Paul said although, admittedly, he did look a little stressed. "Don't have anything wrong with all those things you mentioned."

"And you're, what? About fifty now? Bet you've never had a full physical, have you?"

"Don't need one," Paul snapped. Then he looked at Mellette. "And no offense to the lady, but even if I did get that physical, I wouldn't be having it from a woman. Just doesn't seem right."

"Well, I'll be here for a few days. And I'd be glad to accept a bowl of those pole beans in exchange for a physical," Justin offered.

"Don't you go holding your breath, young man. I've done just fine up to now without having a doctor interfering with me, and I'll do just fine in the future."

"Well, if you feel any tightness in your chest, or lightheadedness, or experience any shortness of breath…you know where to find me."

"Only if I'm looking for you, Justin, which I won't be."

"Pain in your arm or shoulder, trouble *going,* back spasms…"

"What was that about?" Mellette asked as they walked away from Paul LeCompte's cabin.

"Well, when I opened my grandmother's notebook to his page, I saw she'd written the description of a hypochondriac, so I decided to play to that a little."

"A little? It was a masterful performance, Doctor." She applauded him.

"And if it worked, he'll be coming around shortly for me to have a look at him."

"It has to be you, since he's not about to let me take a look." She laughed. "That's pretty sneaky, Justin." She pronounced his name the way Paul had.

"It's a good way to mix medicines."

"But that's only one person."

"One is a start," he said, as he kicked the truck door until it opened. "I think you need better transportation out here."

"The truck works fine. Starts up every time and gets me where I need to go. People trust me when they see me in it, but if I were to show up in something shiny and new, I can't even imagine how they'd react."

"For a rich girl, you're pretty down to earth."

"See, that's the thing. My family has wealth, but I don't. If I did, I'd quit my job and be a full-time mother."

"Is that your dream?" He shut the truck door and went around to climb in the passenger's side, then looked back at the house and saw Paul standing there, watching him.

"For now. I love my work. But I'd love to spend more time with Leonie, maybe even take a couple of years off and stay with her until she goes to school." It wasn't going to happen, of course. But it was a nice dream.

"Look, can you give me a couple of minutes? I think Paul is trying to work up the courage to tell me something, and I'm thinking maybe I should go back up there and talk to him."

"And let him take you to task the way he did before?"

Justin shrugged. "I've got broad shoulders."

"Then go, talk. I'm sure what he has to say isn't meant to be heard by a woman, anyway."

Which turned out to be the case, as far as Paul was concerned. "What you said about having trouble going," he said to Justin. "I can go all right, but sometimes it's a little…slow, if you know what I mean."

"I do know," Justin said, feeling quite pleased that someone was actually seeking out his medical advice. "And there are a lot of ways to take care of that."

"Ways Eula would have used?" the man asked him. "Not that I would have mentioned such a delicate matter to her. But are you talking about treating me the way she would have approved of?"

His grandmother had been a formidable woman, even after her passing, and it pleased him to see how much the people here were still loyal to her. "Depends on what I find when I give you a physical. But there are certain remedies of hers that might help you. The best I can promise you until I've had a look is that I'll be open-minded."

The man snorted. "We'll see about that, Justin. We'll just see."

"So are you going to get a bowl of fresh pole beans?" Mellette asked him.

"Seems so, some time tomorrow, most likely." Justin climbed into the truck and started the engine. "And he'd appreciate it if you weren't anywhere near him when I have to do that physical. Which, by the way, means I've got to get some walls up in one of the exam rooms today."

"They're not scheduled for another week."

"Are the materials there?"

"If you mean the Sheetrock, yes, it's there. But can you put it up?"

"I worked in construction for a while when I was saving up to go to college. So yes, I know how to swing a hammer."

"I'm impressed," she said. "Landry worked for his family in construction. In management, though, not in the field. They wanted him to be more involved in the business end of the company, but he loved the actual hard physical work. Said it made him a good kind of tired at the end of the day."

"I know how that feels. I had a chance to go into hospital administration, but I couldn't imagine not being involved in patient care. It's what I love, and, like Landry, I like that good kind of tired I feel at the end of the day, the kind of tired that lets you know you've done something useful."

"Well, I could ask Tom if he can get someone to help you with the walls."

Justin shook his head. "If I can get Amos Picou to come over and steady the sheetrock when I put it up, I'll be fine."

"And you'll have an exam room all ready for Paul LeCompte by tomorrow?"

"You've never had his pole beans, have you? They're worth the effort."

As they made their way back across the bumpy road, Mellette twisted ever so slightly in her seat in order to catch glimpses of Justin out of the corner of her eye. Certainly, she didn't want to out-and-out stare at him, but she did enjoy watching him. Probably because he surprised her. Just when he proved he was one thing, he changed, almost magically, before her eyes. Yesterday she hadn't been sure he'd actually return with her and today he'd just convinced Paul LeCompte to come in and surrender to a prostate exam. And now he was going to hang Sheetrock.

Justin was a man of many moods and faces, she decided. Had she'd seen them all, or were there more to come? In a way, she was anxious to find out.

"I have a good recipe for fixing pole beans," she said. "Maybe since my mother won't be home tomorrow night, we could invite Daddy out and have him bring Leonie, maybe invite Amos Picou, and have dinner? I'll cook, of course. Get us some ham shanks, potatoes and onions, maybe shrimp? And we'd need cornmeal for corn bread."

"You cook?"

"Some. After all, I *was* married." *Was* married, not *am* married. It sounded strange saying that, because she still told people she was married in the present tense, not the past. This was the first time she'd ever referred to it in the past and it was odd. Not odd in a horrible way, though. Odd, as in the way it was supposed to be. Life was progressing. Moving on.

"Sounds like a meal fit for a tired doctor, which is what I'm going to be by the time dinner rolls around tomorrow night."

"We don't have to do it," she said, suddenly feeling very unsure of herself. It wasn't like she was asking him on a date or anything like that. But this was her first real step away from Landry, and while she'd expected to feel guilty, she didn't so much. That was probably even more of a surprise than her arranging this impromptu little dinner party, which was a pretty big surprise in itself since she didn't usually have time to socialize.

So what was it about Justin that was causing her to step away from all her caution? Maybe, just maybe she liked the man. Or maybe it even went beyond that a little. Was she ready for that, though? Falling in love again? Could it be time? Was she able to move on and give herself totally and completely to another man without Landry coming between them?

These were things she needed to consider in private—far, far away from Justin's charm and influence. Because to love Justin and to have him love her back meant a compromise that scared her. It might mean moving away from here and starting over in Chicago, of all places.

She didn't know if she could, didn't know if she was ready for that drastic change. But it came with Justin, and there was no reshaping that. So she had to proceed carefully. Very carefully.

"No backing out now. I haven't had homemade corn bread in years, and you don't know how much I'm looking forward to it. But let me warn you beforehand that if the food is good, I intend to be lavish with flattery. Just want you to be prepared for that."

Mellette laughed halfheartedly. "Don't you worry about the food. It'll be good."

"Just like everything else you do," he said, then hurried to add, "Statement of fact, not flattery."

Mellette laughed again, this time a genuine laugh, and for the first time realized that she'd laughed more with Justin than she'd laughed since Landry's death. It was good being carefree again, not always having the weight of the world on her shoulders.

Impulsively, before she jumped out, she leaned over and kissed him lightly.

"Wh…?" he began.

But she held her hand up to silence him. "Don't ask, because I don't know. Don't have a clue, and I don't want your opinion."

"Well, I'm not objecting," he said, snaking his hand around her neck. "In fact, if I may be so bold as to reciprocate…" The second kiss was longer, deeper. And when Mellette pulled back from it her lips felt swollen.

"We shouldn't be doing this," she said, trying to reclaim some composure.

"You're probably right."

"I am?"

He nodded gravely. "It's unnatural. Two people attracted to each other wanting to kiss. It throws off the whole balance of things."

Mellette laughed. "You don't know how close you are to the truth."

"You're not ready? I mean, I totally understand if that's the case."

"I think it's the opposite, Justin. But I need time to figure it out. We don't exactly have a smooth road in front of us however we proceed, do we?"

"You ever heard of living for the moment?"

"You ever heard of planning ahead?" She leaned over and this time kissed him on the cheek. "I need time," she said wistfully, hating the word, hating the concept. But it was true. She did need time. And a clearer head than she had at this moment. "Now, I've got some herbal concoctions to mix, then some computer filing to do, and you've got, well, whatever it is you need to be doing."

"Buzzkill," he complained, feigning a hurt look.

Mellette laughed as she headed back into the clinic. Truth was, she hoped he discarded his shirt and got on with his carpentry. If only he knew the thrill that gave her. If only...

CHAPTER SEVEN

GUILTY PLEASURES. Okay, that was what she'd call this and she'd try hard not to feel guilty or disloyal. But she was human after all, and female on top of that. Which was why sitting in the front room, sipping lemonade and watching Justin swing a hammer, had such appeal. He was shirtless, sweaty, his jeans were riding dangerously low, and all of it together was a lethal combination. In fact, if the other Doucet sisters were here, she could just imagine them lined up together, drinking lemonade and watching the show with her.

And what a show it was. Justin was the picture of vital health and strength, everything a man should be. More so, the graceful way he slung that hammer…and the way he kissed…

Watching him gave her chills and caused beads of perspiration to break out on her forehead at the same time. Watching from afar, of course. Only from afar. And with the utmost discretion, since she would not allow herself more than a few stolen peeks from time to time as she went about the task of starting to computerize patient files—a tedious, dry task she wasn't too happy to be doing.

That was why she was allowing herself those occasional peeks at him, she kept telling herself. They were a distraction from the mundane task; something to help her refocus on what she needed to be doing.

She had to admit she enjoyed what Justin was so generously putting on display, and the only thing that might have made it better was if he'd had a leather tool belt riding even lower on his hips than his jeans.

Landry had looked good in a pair of jeans, too. Intellectually, she remembered that he had, but the image wasn't quite there any longer, and she gasped when she realized just how much she was enjoying Justin's exhibition. She felt disloyal and felt a horrible, knotting sensation begin in her stomach. She suddenly thought she was going to throw up.

Jumping up from her desk, Mellette ran to the bathroom, slammed the door shut and simply leaned against it, almost hyperventilating. What was happening to her? Why was she being so faithless to Landry? Sure, she'd taken off the ring. But the feelings wouldn't come off, and she still had these moments of panic when she wondered if she deserved to be happy again. Survivor's guilt was what they called it, even though she'd simply interpreted that to mean she was missing her husband.

She still missed him, but her heart was expanding, taking in someone else, and it scared her. Sometimes she was so sure she could move on, yet other times…

"You okay in there?" Justin called from outside the door.

"Fine," she said, her voice wobbly.

"You looked pale when you went charging down the hall. Are you sure you're okay?"

"Just a little too much heat and humidity out here in Big Swamp," she lied. "I think we're going to need some kind of air-conditioning installed." Slowly, she let herself slide down the door, until she was sitting in a crumpled heap on the floor. "Let me splash some water on my face," she said as tears streaked down her cheeks. Mellette, normally the strong one, felt so weak, so confused. She didn't know what to do. "Don't…know… what…" she whispered as she sobbed quietly into her hands. Things were changing too fast. Spinning out of control. And she didn't know if she wanted them to. Or if she could make it stop now that it had started.

And it had definitely started.

"She's a mighty fine woman," Amos Picou said, as he steadied the Sheetrock against the studs while Justin nailed it in place. "You could do worse."

"I'm not doing anything," Justin said. "Mellette's still very much married to her husband."

"Who's been gone for nearly three years. I know Miss Mellette is having a hard time moving on, and I have sympathy for what she's going through, mixed emotions and all. But one of these days she's going to be standing straight again, and you need to have yourself ready if you want a shot at her. I'm telling you, boy, she's one mighty fine woman who's going to have her pick of suitors when she wants them."

"If by standing straight you mean ready for a new relationship, yes, I'm sure she will be. But I won't be here to see it." And that was a problem both he and Mellette recognized, or that kiss would have turned into more than a kiss. Of that, he was positive.

"Is that what you think? That you're not going to be around?"

"That's what I know. As soon as this clinic is done, I'll be gone. And Mellette can stand as straight as she wants, but I'll be standing back where I belong, on the shores of Lake Michigan." He spoke harshly, trying to cover up his own mixed emotions. "I've got to be going home, Amos. I don't have any other choice."

"She could be falling for you. Those are the symptoms I think I'm seeing. Which makes that one of your choices, son. Maybe your biggest choice."

"And what makes you an expert?"

"Been in love. Know the look of it." He laughed from his belly. "Know it when I see it on two people, the way I'm seeing it on you two."

"You were in love?" Justin asked, somehow surprised to hear the confession. "Guess I never thought you were the type."

"Oh, I was the type, all right. Once when I was sixteen. Miss Xenia was my momma's friend. Beautiful woman in all the ways a woman should be beautiful. With some fine legs—merciful heaven, she had fine legs. Like Miss Mellette. Only problem was she was my momma's age, and my momma knew I was having these feelings. She threatened to hit me with a broom if I ever embarrassed myself around Miss Xenia."

"Did you ever get hit?"

"Oh, I got myself a good whamming one day. Was

on my way to fetch some sugar for Momma, and had to pass right by Miss Xenia's house. 'It's hot out there today,' she said to me. 'Bet you'd like to come in for a nice, cool glass of lemonade.'"

"Did you?"

"You bet I did. I was in that door so fast my head was spinning."

"And?"

"And her lemonade sure was sweet. Best lemonade I ever did have."

"We're not talking lemonade in the literal sense, are we?" Justin said, chuckling.

"Let's just say that Miss Xenia made that awful transition from boy to man pretty damn good."

"But your momma found out?"

"After a while. And like she promised, she took the broom to me. But it didn't matter none, because my sweet drink of lemonade had up and moved away."

"And you never saw her again."

"Nope, and I'm glad I didn't. First love was sweet... real, real sweet. You can't go back, though, once it's over. The memories sure were good. Still are. But they didn't stop me from falling in love again."

"With my grandmother?"

Amos nodded. "That love was never returned, but I never treated it the way I should have, either. But I had me a real nice friendship that lasted a long, long time. It was enough."

"But was it, Amos?"

"Most of the time," he said sadly. "Not all of the time, though, because every morning, no matter what else was to come, I woke up alone. And you don't want that, boy. It feels like there's a big emptiness in you that's going to suck you in, and no matter what you do to fill it with other things, or try to forget it, it'll come back the next morning and you've got to deal with it all over again."

"If she didn't love you, why didn't you move on?"

"And go where? This swamp is what I chose. Got myself landed here after my other life didn't work out so well, knew this was where I belonged. Had me a fine life whittling trinkets to sell in town to the tourists and picking herbs and living close enough to Eula so that I didn't always feel so empty."

"Did she know how you felt?"

"I expect she did. And she respected it. But I never got the sense her feelings for me were the same. She was so wrapped up in taking care of the folks down here after your granddaddy left her, I don't think she had room for much else. Except you."

"Ah, yes. Me. The great disappointment."

"She understood human nature, boy. Knew your disappointments and frustrations. Knew you weren't adapting well from your grand life to being raised in Big Swamp. But she did the best she could."

"I know she did," Justin said solemnly. "And for what it's worth, I'm sorry she never returned the feelings you had for her."

"Me, too, boy. Spent a lot of years being sorry, and I've got some big regrets because I never tried hard enough. And with the way I've seen you looking at

Miss Mellette, I think maybe you need to do some trying, too."

Justin took one powerful swing and hit the nail dead on, then took a couple more swings to drive it all the way in. "It can't work. Even if I could get past her husband, I'm going home and she's not about to leave here."

"You sure about that?" Amos asked, handing Justin another nail.

"I'm not sure about a thing. I mean, I'm attracted. I'm maybe falling in love. I've never seen a woman with so much strength and determination. She's a force, Amos. A real force. And I'm not sure I even know how to approach someone like her on an intimate level, let alone carry it through to wherever it might go."

"One step at a time, boy. You take yourself one step at a time."

"Not sure that's enough to get me past Landry."

"Oh, with the way Miss Mellette's been watching you for the past hour, I just have me this great big hunch that door is wide-open."

"Seriously?" Justin asked, moving back to take another swing.

"Seriously, boy. As they say, it's time to wake up and smell the coffee."

"It's been one hell of a day," Justin said, settling into his grandmother's porch swing. It was going on to midnight, and every muscle in his body was screaming.

"Starting out in Chicago and ending up here. Longest day of my life," he added, stretching, then yawning. "So why are you still here?"

"Got caught up in the work."

"It's not too late for you to go home."

She shook her head. "I respect Big Swamp, but I don't travel out here at night."

He laughed. "Some of my best times in Big Swamp happened at night. Always had a healthy respect for what's out here, but I don't think I was ever afraid of it."

"Poisonous snakes, alligators, bobcats…" She shook her head. "I'm a city girl, Justin. I might work in the bayou, but I won't put myself in danger here."

"Yet look at all the families growing up out here."

"That's their life. What they know. If I'd grown up here, I'm sure I'd have a whole different attitude or perspective. Or maybe I wouldn't. I mean, you grew up here, and you ran away when you were sixteen."

"Not because of the wildlife."

"From what I understand, you *were* the wildlife."

He chuckled. "I was restless. That's for sure."

"Why?" she asked. "Why were you so restless?"

He gazed at her in the dim yellow light, sitting in a wicker chair, legs tucked up under her. She was stunning. Absolutely stunning. And the thing was, he doubted she even knew how beautiful she was. Mellette prided herself on her competency, yet she was so unassuming when it came to her looks. They were certainly looks that could get under a man's skin.

"I've asked myself the same question a lot of times, and never really come up with an answer. Maybe it's because I saw the bayou as limiting…for me. I think I always knew I wanted to be a doctor, but how can that happen when this is where you live?"

"You leave."

"Like I did."

"But you were on fire before you left, Justin. At war with the world."

"I *was* angry. But never with my grandmother."

"Did she know that?"

"I don't know. After I grew up, and got over the rage, I tried to make it up to her. Helped her every way I could."

"But that never felt like it was enough, did it?"

He shook his head. "It might have, though, if she'd accepted anything I offered. But aside from you, she rejected pretty much everything I tried to give her."

"Because you were giving on your terms, not hers. She had her life here, Justin, and she didn't want to leave it. Just like you don't want to leave your life in Chicago. She fought to hang on to what she had every bit as much as you're fighting to hang on to what you have. And in the end you get what you get, whatever that turns out to be. For Eula, it was being at odds with the person she loved most in the world. And for you...well, I don't know, as the last chapter hasn't been written yet."

"How did someone so young end up with all the wisdom in the world?" he asked.

She scooted out of her chair and headed for the door, stood there for a minute, waiting for Justin to get up and go inside with her. "Life dealt me a blow I didn't expect. I've had lots of time to do the retrospective on it."

"We've both had those blows, but you came through yours with so much grace."

"Because I had to be an example. It wasn't just about me."

"But I made my blows all about me, which makes me selfish, doesn't it?"

"Your grandmother lost a son, too. But she turned her personal tragedy into something that was all about you."

"Until she lost me," he said, swallowing hard. "I never saw it that way before."

She took hold of his hand. "She was the one who was full of grace, Justin. Not me. I was just coping the best way I knew how, and leaning pretty heavily on my family to get me through. I don't think you've ever leaned on anybody, have you?"

"No," he said. "I've always gotten by—"

"On your own," she interrupted. "And that's sad. Because life is meant to be shared, even the bad parts of it. I'm sorry you've never known that."

Suddenly, without warning, she stood on tiptoe and brushed a light kiss across his mouth. It wasn't a particularly provocative kiss, neither was it a sexy one, but it burned all the way through to his soul. And he was the one who felt his knees go weak. Wasn't it supposed to be the other way around?

"And that's where this discussion ends. So, on that note, I'm going upstairs and to bed," she said, as if nothing had happened when, in fact, everything had just happened. "I'll be in Eula's room. You can have your old room. 'Night, Justin. Sweet dreams."

"Good night, Mellette," he said, as the screen door banged shut. "Sweet dreams back at you."

Sighing, he sat back down on the swing awhile longer, positive his shaking legs weren't ready to carry him up the stairs yet, and listened to the night sounds. The calls of locusts and frogs, the rustle of the opossum. No, he'd never been afraid here. Not of the wildlife, anyway. But something else, something very real had just terrified him, and he had no idea what to do about it. Not a single clue. Because he could feel himself being pulled in a way he didn't want to go. Or did he?

Could he live here again? Could he start a new life one more time? Could he finally come home?

"Didn't snap 'em," Paul LeCompte said grumpily as he shoved the basket of beans at Mellette when he walked through the front door the next morning. It was early, she hadn't even had her coffee yet, and she had no idea where Justin was this morning. She'd heard him come up the stairs a good hour after she'd gone to bed, had tossed and turned and punched her pillow so many times it had a permanent knuckle indentation in it. What had she done? Why had she kissed him again when she'd promised herself she wouldn't do that?

The truth was, she didn't know. It had just happened. She'd felt like it. It had seemed the right thing to do at that moment. But it had come with a lot of regrets after the moment had passed because she knew where and how this thing ended.

So she'd tossed and turned, and listened to Justin thumping around in the room next to hers for a little while. And if that wasn't bad enough, she'd tried visualizing in her head what he was doing with each little thump and thud, which had kept his image vivid in her head. Then all had finally gone quiet, and she'd been left to her explosive and confusing thoughts, the ones that had kept her awake for a good hour after that. The ones where she'd promised herself she wouldn't go a step further with Justin, no matter what.

Nowhere in her jumbled head had she made room for the notion that Paul LeCompte would be waking her up just shy of 7:00 a.m. with a bowl full of pole beans.

"I…um…I'm not sure where Dr. Bergeron is," she said, feeling self-conscious in her nightie and bathrobe.

"Well, go and find him. I don't have all day to sit around here waiting for him to show his face. I came for that physical, and if he's not here to give it to me, I'm leaving and not coming back. And I don't like what you're doing to the place. What Miss Eula had here was fine. Just fine."

She wondered if Paul would even care that Justin had worked for hours building a private exam room for him. Sure, it was still in the rough, but walls were up and there was enough equipment in there to call it respectable. "Give me a minute," she said on her way to the kitchen to set down the beans.

"Sounds like my patient's in a bad mood," Justin said as she entered the kitchen through the back door. After she'd set the beans on the kitchen counter, he poured and handed her a cup of coffee. "I'm assuming you like it black and strong," he said. "It suits your personality. Only it's not chicory."

"I like chicory."

"I like coffee the way it was meant to be…from real coffee beans. Not chicory. No chicory added, either."

Chicory was a Southern popular, earthy-tasting herb either substituted for or added to coffee.

She smiled as she clung to her coffee cup. "That's right. You're not a Southerner anymore, are you?"

"Oh, I'm Southern. Just don't have a taste for all things Southern, especially chicory. Even if it's supposed to be good for my liver, stomach and spleen."

"And your kidneys," she added. "Don't want to leave them out. Oh, and let me compliment you. You know a little more about herbal medicine than you let on."

"Eula raised me around it. What do you expect?"

"I expect that you should probably go and take a look at Paul LeCompte. I don't think he's going to wait very long to see you."

"I might need assistance."

"Do you really think that man's going to let me assist you, especially given the kind of exam you're doing?" Mellette shook her head. "Don't get me near that, Justin. I'm warning you, these people here are pretty set in their ways and that man out there is the worst of them. There's no way I'm going near him."

"Coward," he said, heading through the kitchen door.

"Darn straight I'm a coward," she called after him, then slid into a kitchen chair and tucked her legs up under her as she sipped her coffee, thinking about her promise to Eula to help Justin get through this. It had been her dying wish. What could she have done? "I'm working on him, Eula," she whispered. "He's not easy, but I'm doing the best I can." She was doing more than she'd ever expected.

The problem was, she didn't think her best was good

enough. Justin was here because she'd done everything but tie him up to keep him here, but he didn't need to be kept here under duress. For Eula's last wish to work out, Justin had to want to be here. And for that he had to be happy again, at peace with himself.

"It wasn't a promise I should have made," she said, as she took another sip of coffee. No, it definitely wasn't a promise she should have made. But Eula Bergeron had been one persuasive lady, who'd found her tender heart and gone to work on it like an expert cardiac surgeon.

Sure, she'd been particularly vulnerable because of Landry's death, which had made her vulnerable about Eula's deteriorating condition. She'd made all kinds of promises to Landry in those last days, as she'd done to Eula. That was who she was. She couldn't help it, didn't have an excuse, either. The lady with the tough exterior and the take-charge demeanor had a very soft spot at her core, and there was nothing she could do to overcome it. She probably wouldn't even if she could.

Sighing, Mellette went back to the stove to refill her coffee cup, then took it upstairs with her while she got herself ready for the morning's work. She had three patients who'd actually made appointments, which meant she probably had nine more who hadn't. Then this afternoon she had four house calls. Plus somewhere in there she had a dinner to prepare, which, admittedly, excited her as much as anything had for a little while, probably because it was as close to a social life as she'd had in months. A dinner party, she thought as she stepped into the shower. Yes, she was looking forward to it.

* * *

"He agreed to take both medicines—Miss Eula's and mine," Justin said as Mellette stepped out of the bedroom into the hall, her hair still wet from her shower. She looked so sexy with wet hair and bare feet. Such a simple look—khaki shorts and a white T-shirt—and he was all but aroused. Fat lot of good that would do him.

"How'd you work that out?" she asked, toweling her short hair.

"Honest, man-to-man talk about the consequences of an enlarged prostate, and where a treatable condition could lead."

"Ah, yes. Go straight to the manhood and they always listen."

"Of course they always listen." He smiled as he averted his eyes, even though she was fully dressed. "Those kinds of things are near and dear to a man's heart."

"Even to Paul LeCompte's?"

"Especially to Paul LeCompte's. He's quite the ladies' man in these parts."

"Our Paul LeCompte, the one who snarls?"

"He did ask if you were seeing anyone," Justin replied with a grin.

"No…seriously, he didn't really do that, did he?"

"Cross my heart," Justin said, keeping a straight face and crossing his heart.

"I hope you told him I'm not looking."

"I told him you were…taken."

"Taken? By whom?"

"He didn't ask. But I think he assumed it was me."

"Why would you do that?"

"Are you interested in him, because I can tell him—"

She swatted at Justin. "Don't you dare. You've already said enough."

"You sure? Because he does like the ladies."

"I have patients to see, and if you're able to convince any of them that you're not the idiot they remember you being, then you can have part of the patient load." With that she marched into her bedroom, slammed shut the door so hard the Bergeron family pictures hanging on the blue-and-white-flowered wallpaper in the hall rattled. The one of Justin riding his new bike on his eighth birthday fell off the wall and the glass cracked.

Laughing, he picked it up, looked at the smiling face of the boy, and thought back to that day. Eula had saved her money and bought him a brand-new bike, not a used one like all his friends had. It had been red and shiny, and maybe for the first time since he'd gone to live with her he'd felt like he belonged there.

Up until that day he'd been so…lost. Orphaned so young and dropped into a lifestyle he'd known nothing about. He'd gone from well-off to poor. Living with a woman his mother had avoided because of their differences and whom his father had escaped because he'd wanted more than she'd had to offer. Nothing had worked, nothing had fit him.

Then that day, when Eula had given him the bike… the look on her face had said everything. She'd loved him, had made such a hard sacrifice to please him.

Everything had changed that day, and for a little while he'd stayed happy. But then he'd wanted a car.

There had been no reason why he shouldn't have one, except that the money his parents had left him, and it had been a considerable amount, had been held in a trust. As an administrator, Eula had refused to dip into it. "You want a car," she'd told him, "go find a job and earn it." It had been the same with nicer clothes, electronic games. Things other boys his age had had. "You want them, you go to work and buy them."

In the mind of a young teen, that hadn't been fair. That money was his. Rightfully his. And his grandmother had no right keeping it from him. So he'd lashed out. Said hurtful things, done hurtful things. Told her he understood why his dad had wanted to get away from there and why his mother had hated her. They had been harsh, ugly words. Yet through it all Eula had held firm in her resolve, for which he thanked God now, and would do every day of his life.

But he'd been so bad to her back then that it had become difficult to get past it. Sure, he'd tried making it up to her when he'd got older and had understood exactly what he'd done. Tried to get her to accept an apartment in New Orleans, somewhere where she could take life easy. Invited her to Chicago, as well. Or anyplace else she wanted to go. She had been content with her life the way it was, and he always wondered if that was the case or if he'd broken her heart so badly it couldn't heal. It had made it dreadfully difficult to face her for such a long, long time.

But that eighth birthday… He'd been happy then. Truly happy. "Too bad I can't go back to that feeling again," he whispered as he hung the photo, cracked glass and all, back on the wall.

Too bad Mellette couldn't go back to a happy time, either.

Too bad they couldn't go forward together and find that new happy place. He could almost picture them together. But there was nothing about them that would ever work out. Nothing at all.

CHAPTER EIGHT

IT WAS AN intimate little dinner party. Amos showed up early with fresh-caught shrimp, then Mellette's dad and Leonie arrived, bringing a delicious bread pudding he and Leonie had made together. And Paul LeCompte decided to come, too, since he'd provided the pole beans. There'd been no invitation extended and apparently no invitation was necessary, as he simply strode through the door and asked when supper was ready, then proceeded to sit down at the dinner table as if he was the guest of honor. In a way, he was, as Paul merely being there was a huge show of faith in Justin, otherwise he wouldn't have barged in and made himself at home.

So they ate sausage, chicken and crawdad jambalaya, with seasoned pole beans and corn bread, and talked lightly around the table, enjoyed each other's company, complimenting Mellette on her cooking. It came as a surprise to her, since cooking wasn't exactly her strongest suit. Many nights, at the beginning of her marriage, Landry would endure the meal, tell her it was good, and eat small portions, feigning a small appetite. What she hadn't known at the time had been that he'd eaten the small portions because that had been all he could endure. Then later he'd sneak into the kitchen and fix a peanut-butter-and-jelly sandwich.

They'd been married almost a year when she'd caught him with a peanut-butter sandwich in his hand. At first he'd tried sparing her feelings, telling her it was because he loved peanut butter and jelly, then he'd finally, after some persuasion, owned up to the lie and confessed that her cooking left a little to be desired.

So she'd tried even harder, and improved some. But tonight was such a triumph, having everybody praise her cooking and genuinely like it. Especially Justin.

"She'd make some man a fine wife," Charles Doucet said to Justin after Paul and Amos had gone home for the night and Mellette was showing Leonie all the changes she was making to the clinic. Justin and Charles were standing on the front porch, enjoying a rare cool breeze blowing through Big Swamp, both of them drinking tall iced tea accented with a little splash of sweet lemonade.

"Except she doesn't want that," Justin said, looking up at the sky visible through the thick bayou canopy, seeing patchy splotches of starless black.

"You sure? Because she sure seems to have the eye for you."

Justin chuckled. "I see where she gets her straightforwardness from."

"Her mama," Charles said, without missing a beat. "God never did put a more straightforward woman on the face of this earth than Zenobia Doucet. That's what got me hooked in the first place. I liked all that opinion in her. Made her different from all the other women

I knew who went wishy-washy or giddy when asked their opinion. That, and the fact that Zenobia's as fine looking a woman as I've ever seen. Just like Mellette."

"She *is* a fine-looking woman, sir," Justin said.

"You would be talking about my daughter, I'd hope," Charles responded, chuckling.

"I would be talking about all the Doucet women I've met so far." But especially about Mellette. Her dark skin, stunning eyes. The kind of woman who naturally flowed into a man's thoughts, even when he tried keeping her out.

"Well, all I can say is that I agree with you on that. And that it's going to take some kind of a special man to win the heart of my eldest daughter again. Landry is a tough act to follow, but I'm sure the right man can find his place with Mellette. He'll just have to work hard to prove himself. But if he's willing to do that, he'll discover that she's worth the extra effort."

"Tough order, though," Justin said, turning his face to the breeze. He used to love nights like this, where the weather went from an unbearable wet heat to cool and balmy. Of course, usually after the drastic change a storm rolled in. Sometimes just a bad storm, sometimes something worse, like a hurricane. Tonight he didn't know what was coming, but his immediate concern was for the safety of Mellette, Charles and Leonie, because if they didn't get out of here soon, they wouldn't be getting out at all until the storm blew over.

"Look, not that I want to cut the evening short, because I don't. I've really enjoyed this. But if you want to get back before the storm hits, I think you'd better take

Mellette and Leonie and start out now." He looked up again, hoping to see a star or two, but saw only the same somber blackness. And the breeze was getting even breezier. "Or maybe you should spend the night here."

Charles looked up, took his own appraisal. "And worry Zenobia to death? She's not fond of this place to begin with, but if she ever knew that I'd come out here and brought Leonie, she'd have my head."

"What's she going to do when Mellette starts bringing Leonie to work occasionally?"

"Well, right now she doesn't know about it, and I'm keeping it that way for as long as I can. But once she finds out, she'll have *your* head, if you're still hanging around these parts. So, on that note, think I'll go round up my ladies and take them home."

"Sure you shouldn't stay here? It can get treacherous out there during a bad storm."

"Not as treacherous as my wife can get, so thank you kindly for the invitation, but I think it's best to, as they say, get while the getting's good. It's been a good evening, though, Justin. And I wish you success with what you want most." He gave Justin a knowing wink. "And I hope to hell you know what that is."

"I'm beginning to think I might," he said, with a sigh. "Yes, I'm beginning to think I might." On that note, he followed Charles back inside to say good-night to Mellette, a little bit nervous, especially now that he'd all but had her father's blessing and encouragement.

"She's in the kitchen, putting away the dishes," Leonie announced. "Grandpa went to help so we can go home fast."

"But you're not helping them?" Justin said, smiling at the girl. Her eyes shone with the same determination he saw in Mellette's eyes. Another strong woman in the making, he decided.

"Too short," she said, matter-of-factly.

"It's tough being short, isn't it?" he asked, heading on into the kitchen, holding out his hand to Leonie to take her with him. "But it won't last long. I promise. One of these days you're going to wake up and you won't be short anymore, and when you look at a picture of when you were short, you'll hardly even remember it because getting tall like your mommy happened so fast."

"Really?" Leonie said.

"Honest truth," Justin said, then bent and whispered to her. "I know, because I used to be short, too."

"Just like me?" Leonie asked.

"Once I was even shorter than you are. Then look what happened to me." He patted the top of his head. "I got this tall."

"Wow," the little girl said, totally taken by Justin and his story. "Will I be that tall, too?"

"Maybe not this tall. Or maybe taller. It'll be a big surprise."

"What surprise?" Mellette asked as Justin and Leonie stepped through the kitchen door, hand in hand.

"How tall I'll be," Leonie announced. "Did you know Justin used to be short like me?"

"Seems like you've got quite a way with children," Charles said, as he put away the bean pot.

"Look," Justin interrupted. "As much as I hate doing dishes, why don't you all let me finish this while you go home? I don't want you getting caught on a back road in the storm that's coming, and since your dad's insistent on getting home…the sooner the better."

"You'll be okay out here all alone?" Mellette asked sincerely, then realized that sounded a little patronizing. "Of course you will. What was I thinking?"

"You were thinking how you were concerned for a friend," Charles said, as he scooped Leonie up into his arms and headed for the front door. "A very good friend."

Both Justin and Mellette shot the man a reproachful look as he scooted outside, laughing.

"He wants me to be happy," Mellette explained, "and to him, happiness comes in the form of marriage."

"And seven daughters?"

"Probably. My dad is a very traditional man living in a family of eight very progressive-thinking women. It's not easy on him, but his heart is in the right place, even though he tends to get a little too concerned about our welfare and futures. Fact is, he would have had each of us married off years ago and producing all kinds of grandchildren for him to be fawning over. But we tend to take after our mother, who believes you can have it all—career, marriage, family—and a happily ever after that involves all of it."

"Well, he's very good in his role of father."

"Trying to marry me off?"

"Something like that."

Mellette blushed. "I'm sorry you got dragged into that, Justin. Daddy means well but, like I said, he's traditional. You know, as in a woman can't be happy or fulfilled without a man."

"And can she be?"

"Just the way a man can be happy and fulfilled without a woman. And on that note—" she headed for the door "—think I'd better catch up with them or my very traditional father will strand me out here for what he thinks is my own good."

Justin followed Mellette to the front porch and made a very big show of not getting too close to her so Charles would see there was no kiss involved. The strangest thing happened, though, just as she stepped off the front porch. He wanted to go after her. Wanted to pull her into his arms and kiss her like he'd never kissed another woman. "You shouldn't go out in this. I think it's going to be a bad one. I did ask your dad to stay overnight."

"We'll be fine," she said.

"You'd be more fine if you spent the night here."

"And I'll be better if I spend the night in my own bed. Look, Justin. I appreciate your concern, but it's not a good idea to stay out here another night."

"Why?"

She shrugged. "Honestly, I don't know. Things are getting complicated. The absolutes I've been hanging on to aren't as absolute anymore, and it scares me. So I just want to…go home. That's all."

"What absolutes, Mellette?"

She shook her head. "I need time to think before I… before I say anything, or do anything."

"Would this be about me?"

"About you…about me. There was a time when I

thought I couldn't move on, but now—" she shrugged "—it seems like I am, and I need to adjust to that before I say or do something that could affect my future or Leonie's or even yours."

"And the storm makes it convenient to run away."

She smiled sadly. "It does, doesn't it?"

"What if I convinced the three of you to stay, and promise not to talk about anything meaningful?"

"Nice try," she said, reaching up to stroke his cheek. But before her hand reached him he took hold of it and kissed it.

"Nice try," he said back.

"Look, I've really got to go now. Daddy's a good driver. We'll be fine, like I told you."

"And like I told you, you'll be better spending the night here."

She shook her head stubbornly. "No," she said in finality. "We're going home."

"Call me when you get there?" he asked.

"If I remember. But I do have to get Leonie to bed first."

Damn, she was a stubborn woman. It was as sexy on her as it was frustrating. "How about you let me do the driving as I know the roads better?"

"I know the roads, too."

"Are you trying to run away from me?"

"Maybe a little bit. But we will be fine, and I'll call. I promise. As soon as I can get reception, I'll call and let you know we got home safely."

They could have argued it into the night, and she still wouldn't have backed down. Continuing the argument only kept them here longer, so he took a step backward, threw his hands in the air in surrender and frowned. "You win, but I don't like it."

"I always win, Doctor."

"But is it always for your own good?" Without warning, without provocation and without thought, he stepped forward, pulled Mellette into his arms and kissed her hard. It was short, because he truly hadn't seen it coming, but not so short that he didn't feel the effect of it shoot straight up through to his feet. Funny thing was, for a moment it seemed like she was kissing him back, just as hard, just as desperately. Lips pressed tight, breathing slightly heavy, all in the dim glow of the yellow lightbulb.

But from the kiss there was nowhere else to go but backward, so he did the gentlemanly thing and took that step back. He'd be damned, though, if he was going to apologize. He had nothing to be sorry about. Nothing at all. So he simply stood there and waited for Mellette to make the next move.

She raised her fingers to her lips and exclaimed, "Oh, my," very, very quietly.

Oh, my, indeed. This was the second time she'd made him go weak at the knees. "Well, that'll give your dad something to think about," he responded. "Now I guess you'd better get going while you can." Before the next kiss happened. And, hand raised to God, he wouldn't let her go if he kissed her again. "Because if you don't you really might have to spend the night here."

On that note, she turned and hurried down to the car, crawled in, and then they were gone.

Justin watched until the car was no longer in sight, then returned to the kitchen to finish cleaning up, wishing he'd fought harder. But the harder he fought, the harder she countered him. Still, riding out the storm with her would have been nice. "So I'm getting myself hung up on someone who's going to change my life in big ways," he told Napoleon, who'd come around begging for his dinner. "Here's the thing, are you content to be a Big Swamp cat, or do you think you could make it in Chicago? Because those are the choices." The thing was to have Mellette and to make her happy, there really was only one choice.

The cat answered with a coarse meow.

"To have her I have to stay. She'd hate being anywhere else but here. And I'd hate being anywhere where she wasn't," he continued as he pulled a can of tuna and egg scramble from the cupboard and opened it.

Napoleon's response was to arch his back and twine himself around Justin's ankles. "So that would be my answer, wouldn't it? Arch my back and entwine myself around Mellette's ankles forever. If she'll have me."

He dumped the cat food into a bowl and put it down on the floor. "See, you've got the right idea. Go where the food is. If I'm here, you come to me. If Mellette's here, you go to her. And if neither of us is here, you wait for Amos to come round and feed you. No games, no tricks, no wondering how it's going to turn out. You already know, and you go with it, no matter who's opening your can of tuna. Makes life easier doing the simple, obvious thing, doesn't it, boy?" He reached down and stroked the cat just as the first rumble of thunder hit the bayou.

It was loud and startled him, caused his breath to catch as it roiled on and on. He and his grandmother used to sit out of the porch and watch the storms roll in like this. That had been back when the lightning and thunder had scared him. "God's way of cleaning up the bayou," she used to say. "It stirs up the water, gets rid of the dead wood in the trees and gives everything a good washing."

Well, the good washing started even before Justin could get outside to watch it. Once he was there, he settled into the swing, watched the rain start to trickle down at first then eventually turn into torrential sheets. He missed his grandmother like crazy. And missed Mellette almost as much.

"You missed the turn," Mellette said to her dad as they crept past the road that would have taken them back to the main highway. The storm was pretty bad now, changed from a moderate shower to a torrential downpour in a matter of minutes, and while storms didn't normally bother her, she rarely spent them out in the middle of the bayou where their effects seemed larger, and louder, and more violent.

Justin had been right. They should have stayed there. But staying had meant confronting her feelings, and she wasn't sure she was ready to confront anything yet. Part of her wanted to, because her feelings for Justin were getting stronger. He was nothing like Landry, no similarities, no way to compare the two, which was good. Because Justin didn't deserve that and neither did Landry's memory. But that was all he was now. A memory who held a special place in her heart. Putting him in that rightful spot was so difficult. She had to do it, though, if she wanted to finally move on. It was time. Justin was showing her what her heart was telling her.

Mellette glanced over the seat at Leonie, who was thankfully slumped over in her car seat, sound asleep. "This one leads out to Grandmaison, and that's at the literal end of the road. We need turn around and go back." Funny how well she knew this backcountry— it was almost like she'd grown up in it. Could she leave here, leave New Orleans and live in Chicago? There had been a time she would have said no. Now the line was blurred. There were no more definites; Justin was showing her how to move past them. So maybe Chicago could work. "There's a place just up ahead on the left where I think we can do it. It's a driveway, leads down to Amedee Mouton's property." She knew Amedee by the gout in his right big toe.

A tree branch came crashing down on the road in front of them, which brought the car to a stop. It was large, a main feeder from an oak tree, and it blocked the entire road, stopped their progress forward to Amedee's turnoff. While their recourse was to turn around and go back to the right road, there was no place to make that turn on a one-lane, dirt washout that artery was turning into. Plus the wind and rain were picking up, the visibility had decreased to only a few feet and the lightning was getting treacherous.

"Could we just back down the road?" Mellette asked,

turning around in her seat to get a better view out the rear window.

"We could, except I can't see the road well enough to negotiate it."

"Do you have a flashlight?" Mellette asked.

"In the glove box."

As much as she hated to suggest it, she said, "Then I'm going to get out and walk behind the car, and signal you where the road is."

"In this weather?"

"We don't have any other options, Dad. It's either keep moving or stay here until the storm passes and hope we can get out of here when it does." Much like the way she'd been living her life lately. Only in her life, she'd chosen to stay. "And I'd rather not get stranded on the road, which is what's going to happen if another tree branch comes down behind us. So how about we just get this done?"

"Can I help?" Leonie piped up from her car seat.

"No, sweetheart. Grandpa needs you to be very quiet so he can concentrate."

"You drive, I'll direct," Charles said. But Mellette was already out of the car and on her way down the road behind it. She'd never been out in rain like this. On a muddy, slippery road, with the wind gusting so hard against her she was afraid it would blow her right over. She was taking a risk that somehow seemed small compared to the one she was considering.

"Can you see my light?" she yelled, waving her flashlight in the air, in the direction of the car. "Dad, can you see it?"

If he responded, she didn't hear him because the wind was so noisy. In fact, all she could hear was her own voice blowing back at her and the low howling of wind whipping through the trees on all sides. It was eerie, being so close to the car yet so distant from it, and all she could do was trust that he followed her light and hope that whatever beasties lurked in the shadowy ditches to the side of the road were content to hunker down in the downpour, the way she wanted to.

It took Mellette nearly ten minutes to direct her dad down a stretch of road that should not have taken more than a minute to cover, and by the time they'd reached the intersection where he should have turned in the first place, she was exhausted, ready to climb back into the car and hope the rest of their trip out of the bayou was uneventful. But no such luck.

As Charles made the turn, and as Mellette was about to run to get in, a huge downdraft caught the car and spun it around, knocking it sideways into the ditch along the side of the road. In order to avoid being hit by the fishtailing car, Mellette took a leap sideways and landed flat in the mud, wrenching her shoulder and twisting her ankle. Nothing serious, but nothing she wished for in the middle of the storm, either.

"Dad!" she yelled, pushing herself out of the mud and trying unsuccessfully to rise above her knees. Between the rain, the wind, the mud and what was turning into a swollen ankle, all of that combined with no leverage from an unusable shoulder, she was pretty well stuck where she was, scared to death that either her dad or Leonie had been injured in the slide-off. "Can you hear me?" she yelled frantically, trying with everything she had in her to crawl or slither over to the vehicle. "Dad! Leonie!" Justin…

No answer, of course. And as she crawled along she worried about alligators in the ditch, and trying to get herself down the three-foot embankment. What if they were hurt? How could she help them? "Please, can you hear me?" She also worried about a flash flood coming through that could drown them. And the rain was getting worse. "Please, answer me. Or hit your brake lights or something to let me know you're okay."

No response again. So Mellette belly-crawled her way back down the road, too slow to make a difference but determined to get there no matter what it took, while feeling total despair, too worried to even think straight. Too worried to realize that anyone coming along that road stood a good chance of not seeing her there on the ground, belly to the mud, and hitting her before she could get out of the way. *What am I going to do?*

She shut her eyes for a moment, said a little prayer, hoped that when she opened her eyes this would be a nightmare, that none of this existed, that she was back at Eula's House, enjoying the evening with Justin, glowing in the praise of her cooking, showing her daughter what she was doing at work. But when she opened her eyes… "Oh, my…"

The headlights bearing down on her didn't have her in their beam. She was there, directly in front of the vehicle coming at her, but there was no way she would be seen. And even though the car seemed to be traveling very slowly, that was just as deadly as fast. So she grabbed her flashlight, tried aiming it at the car to signal the driver, but the metal casing was slick and the light slid right out of her hands. A quick, chaotic patting of the muddy ground around her produced nothing. The flashlight was totally lost.

Frantically, Mellette tried scooting herself along in the mud faster, trying to get herself out of the path of the oncoming car. The slippery road made progress at a satisfactory speed nearly impossible in her position, as the road was already turning to small streams of rushing water, reducing her to the position of a fish fighting to swim upstream. So rather than trying to crawl any longer, Mellette lay down and simply rolled, hitting her wrenched shoulder repeatedly against the road, each bump and grind making her injury all the more painful. She just hoped she was fast enough, and the vehicle continued to be slow enough…

Praying there in the mud and rain that she had enough time to get out of the way, she worried about her daughter. "Leonie," she whispered as the vehicle slogged its way on past her, missing her by mere inches as her body slid off the road onto the grassy berm separating the road from the ditch on the right side.

Truth was, she wasn't sure she hadn't been hit. Her shoulder and ankle hurt so badly the pain radiated through her body like someone was prodding her everywhere with a hot poker, making her feel like everything in her body was aching, as well. Sympathetic reaction, she told herself as she stretched up, glad to see the lights from the vehicle coming to a stop near where her father had skidded off the road. *Thank God some-*

one will help them, she thought as she sank back down in the rain and the mud, closed her eyes and hoped to be found.

It wasn't that he had his grandmother's "extra sense," as she'd called it. But something wasn't right. He could feel it. He was restless. Needed to pace off the energy. Or go running. Anything. "Did she get like this when she knew something wasn't right?" he asked the big orange cat, who was sitting in the open window behind him, grooming himself, his back turned to the storm like it didn't matter that all hell was breaking loose in the bayou since his own tiny space in the universe was secured.

Justin had seen his grandmother suddenly "know" something on several occasions, and had never paid much attention to that peculiarity of hers. Thought it was crazy mumbo jumbo. But right now he wasn't so sure because his feelings were so strong they were about to drive him over the edge. So he bolted out of the porch swing and crashed through the door, then paced up the stairs then right back down for the next five minutes, every passing second making him feel even more pent up.

"They couldn't have made it all the way out of the bayou before this storm broke," he told Napoleon on one of these trips downstairs. He paced back upstairs, got to the top stairs and spun around, then ran back down. "So I'm going out. Back in a few minutes," he said to the totally uninterested cat.

Did it make any sense that he was going to drive all

the way out to the highway? Probably not, but he didn't care. If a little drive in the worst storm he'd seen since he'd left Louisiana alleviated his anxiety, then it was all good. If it didn't, he'd take the highway on in to New Orleans, right up to their door, if that was what he had to do. What was he looking for? Nothing, he hoped. Absolutely nothing.

Hopping into his grandmother's old pickup truck, hoping it was up to the task, Justin made his way slowly along the road, glad with every passing few feet that aside from the storm and the occasional limb in the road, so far it was an uneventful drive. People didn't go out in weather like this, he thought to himself as he leaned forward to peer through a totally rained-over windshield with wipers so slow and worn they did little to disrupt the water on the glass. It was coming down in sideways sheets, hitting the truck so hard it sounded as if he was being attacked by falling rocks rather than the unremitting raindrops.

Traveling at no more than a few miles an hour, the trip was interminably long, and there was no visibility other than what the headlights picked up in their narrow beams. Even then those images were captured only mere inches in front of him, which slowed his five miles an hour to three when he thought of what he might miss if he traveled any faster.

What the hell had he been thinking, allowing Mellette and Charles to go out when bad weather was predicted, even though it had been their choice to try to get home? Back in Chicago there'd been bad storms, especially blizzards and windy thunderstorms coming off the lake, and somehow he'd forgotten that Chicago's very worst wasn't anywhere close to what Louisiana could bring on.

"They're going to be fine," he told himself as he literally inched his way along the dirt road, hoping his trip was uneventful and that they were already back in New Orleans, tucked away in that big, white mansion of theirs.

Still, he had to go on because…well, just because. If something happened to the three of them out on this road… Justin swallowed hard, blinked harder and tried to focus on the fraction of light he could see on the road ahead of him. It was there, then it was gone. A flash that could have been anything. Were his eyes playing tricks on him? Had he really seen something?

He slowed for a second, rolled down the truck window and looked out. Nothing. But that didn't mean anything, so he got out. Opened the door, stepped down onto the road that looked more like a shallow stream and took his flashlight, which unfortunately was only a medical penlight, and surveyed the area in front of him then off to the side of the road. And that was when he saw it—the shadowy outline of another vehicle sitting at an angle in the left ditch, which was approximately three feet below road level.

It was their car! That knowledge hit him like a punch to the gut, and he was away from his truck and crawling down into the ditch to assess the driver's side before he even realized what he was doing. Flashing his light in, he saw the air bag had deployed and was already deflating, with the white, powdery dust from the deployment still swirling around. He also saw Charles Doucet, who was caught somewhere between consciousness and unconsciousness, moving around, trying to extricate himself from his seat belt but not coherent enough to make the right moves to unlatch it.

"Charles!" Justin shouted, adjusting his angle to see Mellette. Only she wasn't in the front seat. So his eyes tracked back, saw a very frightened little girl strapped in her car seat, but still no Mellette. Had she been thrown clear, or was the white powder obscuring her? He didn't know, didn't have time to figure it out as he ran back up the ditch and climbed onto the passenger's side to get a better look. But still no Mellette. And the car wasn't open in any way, no windows had been shattered, so she hadn't just flown out on impact.

Stumped, he went back to the driver's side, fighting the rain that was turning the ditch into a stream, wondering where she was. Fearing the worst. He hated his fears, hated that he didn't know.

"We need to get the door open!" he shouted to Charles, who'd finally managed to beat down the entire air bag and was also free of his seat belt.

"Get Leonie first," he yelled.

"Are you injured?" Justin called back.

"Not badly. But I can't get back there to her."

"Where's Mellette?" he called, as he pulled on the driver's door, only to find it stuck shut.

"On the road. She got out to direct us. We slid off the road…haven't seen her."

And he hadn't seen her, either. Hadn't seen anyone. "Look, I need to go to my truck and get the crowbar."

The one that had been under his grandmother's seat for as long as he could remember. *Emergencies, Justin. It's for emergencies.* "Thank you, Grandma Eula," he said to himself. "I'll be back in a minute."

The climb back up the ditch wall was easier said than done, as now the water was up to his knees and flowing hard and fast. Which meant he had to get Charles and Leonie out of there immediately, before the water level got so high… He'd heard stories of where a car trapped in a ditch got caught in a flash flood, and the water rose so high and so fast that it washed the car on down the stream into the lake.

Whether or not the stories were true, he really didn't know. But what he did know was that he had two people trapped in a dangerous situation and they needed to be out of there right away. So as he slipped and slid across the road, he shone his penlight back and forth, hoping to see Mellette. But he could see nothing. And he didn't have time to look. Damn it, he didn't have time!

Once he located the crowbar under the driver's seat he ran back to the car, slipped and fell headfirst into the wash, and realized that the water level was getting higher. He pulled himself up and made his way over to the car, where the water was now about halfway up the door.

Without a word to Charles, he stuck that crowbar in the door seam and put every bit of his weight into the effort of prying it open, and for once, thank God, luck was in his favor. The door opened with very little effort, and Charles practically fell into Justin's arms.

"Get her out of the back," the older man gasped, as he tried to right himself.

In the backseat, little Leonie was crying and screaming for everything she was worth, kicking, flailing and clinging to her stuffed bear with ferocity. "Leonie," Justin said as he climbed over the seat into the back of the car. "Remember me?"

She stopped crying and looked at him. Then nodded.

"Good. Now, what I want you to do after I unbuckle your seat is to wrap your arms around my neck and hold on as tight as you can. Can you do that for me?"

"I want my mommy," she said, sniffling.

"I know you do, sweetheart, and I'm going to look for her once I get you out of here. So promise you'll hang on to me?"

She nodded. "My bear can't hang on."

"Then I'll have to put him in a safe place." Justin tucked the bear into his soaking shirt. "Now, grab hold…"

The struggle to get out of the car wasn't so bad, but the problem came in helping Charles up the ditch, and getting himself and Leonie back up the side, as well. It took several slip-and-slide attempts to get himself up to the road, but when he'd managed it he left the older man behind and got Leonie safely into his truck, then went back to help Charles make the climb out.

He lay flat on the ground and used every ounce of strength he had to pull Charles up and out of the ditch. The run-off was now threatening to suck him under, its wash was so turbulent. All the while he was scanning that ditch for Mellette, hoping she wasn't in it somewhere, because…because nobody could survive being submerged in that. "Do you have any idea where she is, sir?" Justin sputtered, once the man was seated in the truck cab, holding his granddaughter.

"She was on the road behind me."

"Behind?"

"I was backing up. Missed this turn-off, couldn't see the road well enough to negotiate it, so she took her flashlight and walked behind me, signaling the way. But I went into a skid, slid off… Don't know where she is, and the only reason she didn't come to help us… You've got to find her, son! You've got to find her."

"Are you okay for me to leave you?"

"Sore hip, that's all. No big deal."

Justin nodded, then shut the truck door and stood outside for a moment, trying to visualize the road and just where he'd seen that momentary flash of light. "Mellette?" he yelled, even though he knew his voice wouldn't carry over the wind. "Can you hear me? Do you still have your flashlight?"

There was no answer from her. That would have made things too simple—the whole rescue taking place without a hitch. Well, Mellette was his hitch, and the only way to proceed was to simply walk through the rain back the same way he'd been driving, an inch at a time. Looking for her. Hoping…praying she was okay. Praying even harder than she hadn't fallen into the same ditch the car was trapped in. The vehicle was now totally under water, bobbing up and down, getting ready to be carried off to wherever the ditch emptied. He couldn't bear to think that Mellette could be down there.

"Mellette," he screamed against the wind and the rain and the night, as he flashed his penlight along the berm and took it step by step.

She wanted to get up, but it was like there was a lead weight holding her down. As hard as she tried, she just couldn't get herself up to a sitting position. The pain had subsided some, reduced to more normal proportions, but her body was resistant, and she was so cold…so wet.

But she was awake, and if she fought to stay awake she'd be fine. She knew she'd be fine. But her dad and Leonie… She was so scared for them. Water could rush through these ditches with torrential force…. She should have listened to Justin and stayed there, instead of insisting they get back to town. But she'd been stubborn. Too stubborn. All because she didn't want to face the fact that she was falling in love with him and didn't feel guilty or disloyal.

For the first time since Landry had died, she realized she could move on and that it was starting to happen. She was starting over and it was scary and good and exciting and so many things she couldn't yet determine. But she wanted to start over now, because of Justin….

Heavy drowsiness slid over Mellette, trying to pull her into sleep. She fought it off, though. Fought it hard because back in E.R. she'd treated too many cases where unconsciousness had overtaken and killed people. She knew about exposure, knew about hypothermia…knew her body wanted to wind down and give up the battle. "No!" she said. "I won't let it. For Leonie…

have to fight." She had to stay awake until somebody found her. Until Justin found her.

"Justin," she murmured, picturing herself in his warm, dry arms. He'd come to get her. Would take her away, take her someplace safe. Protect her. "Justin…"

Five minutes of looking, then ten, then fifteen passed, but he wasn't giving up. She was out there, so close he could feel her. But he just couldn't… "What the…?" Off to the side of the road, on a grass berm, his light slid over a form. It didn't look human, wasn't moving… could have been mistaken for a rise in the weeds and fescue grass growing prolifically there. Or even an alligator crouching down, hoping to be ignored while he enjoyed the deluge.

Something compelled Justin to move to the side of the road, however, and there… "Mellette!" he shouted, kneeling down beside her.

"Justin, I knew you'd come. Knew you'd save me," she gasped, throwing her arms up around his neck and clinging to him for dear life.

"Are you hurt?" he asked, as she buried her face to his chest. "Mellette?"

"I knew you'd find me. I was waiting… Knew you wouldn't let me die out here. Knew you would come looking for me…."

"Of course I would," he said, huddling over her to protect her. And just like that, her grip on him tightened and she kissed him. Kissed him hard, and with so much desperation…

A reaction to being safe, he told himself as he pushed

himself off her and started to help her up. That was all it was. Just a reaction to being safe. A kiss anybody might give their rescuer out of gratitude, shock, fear.

Or maybe she'd hallucinated. Thought he was Landry.

It wasn't right, being jealous of a dead man. But he was. Which made him feel like hell.

CHAPTER NINE

WITH HER ARMS still snaked around his neck, and her head still pressed to his chest, there was nothing Justin could do to stop the feelings Mellette was causing to well up inside him.

"Justin," she said again.

He looked away, didn't even glance down at the woman in his arms for fear he'd yield to the temptation that wasn't rightfully his. "You're fine," he said stiffly as he fought his way back to the truck, trying to keep himself upright against the wind, trying to keep his mind just as straight against the sure knowledge that was soaking through his skin.

So what *did* you do when you were falling in love with someone who wasn't emotionally available? Because that was what he was doing. He was falling so hard he could almost see himself walking away from his Chicago life to come back here.

Just what was he doing? It was one hell of a question and it didn't have a good answer, even though it had been loitering around the edges of his mind for a little while now—loitering without being processed into full thought. The truth was, the answer was already there.

Loving Mellette was all that mattered. "Wet, chilled, probably a little hypothermic, but you're okay," he reassured her.

"I knew you'd come," she sputtered again. "Was waiting for you to find me."

"Of course I would find you." And he'd never let her go.

"Leonie? Is she okay?"

"Leonie and your dad are just fine," he said as he approached the truck. "I got them out of the car and, other than being cold and wet, there's nothing wrong with them." Opening the driver's side door, he slid Mellette into the middle spot, next to her dad, who was holding Leonie on his lap, then climbed in after her. Her head immediately went to Justin's shoulder, not to her dad's, and she snuggled into *his* side, shivering, as he maneuvered a wide turn in the road, taking great care not to slide and end up in the ditch the way Charles's car had.

Of course, he was used to driving in these conditions. He'd started sneaking this very truck out for a drive when he'd been tall enough to both see over the steering wheel and reach the gas pedal. "This is going to be a bumpy ride," he said, meaning it more in the figurative sense than literally, because now, with her head resting on his shoulder, Mellette's hand rested on his thigh. And he was fighting the urge to enjoy it with everything he had. Wondering if maybe, just maybe, she wasn't, for once, thinking of Landry.

"Not bumpy," Mellette murmured, finally relaxing into a slump. "Nice." Then she drifted off to sleep.

By the time they were back at the house, she was practically sprawled over him, in a way that no father should have to see. Which was probably why Charles hopped out of the truck the instant the truck stopped, grabbed Leonie and ran into the house, leaving Justin there to deal with a very limp Mellette.

"Wake up," he said, trying to untwine himself from her. "Mellette, wake up. We need to get you inside."

"I'm awake," she said groggily.

He wasn't convinced, given the almost intimate nature of the way she'd draped herself over him. Awake, Mellette would have never done this. Would she? "Awake with both eyes open. I need to see both your eyes open and looking at me, Mellette. Both eyes…"

"I'll open them," she purred as her hand wound its way up his chest and stopped only after she'd stroked his cheek with her fingers.

"Stop it," Justin said, totally confused.

"Why?" she asked. "Don't you like it?"

"That's not the point," he said.

"The point is I can live in Chicago, if you want us there. That's what I thought about the whole time I was in that ditch. That I love you, and when you love someone, nothing else matters. I thought I might die out there and I didn't want to die without ever telling you that I love you."

"And I love you, too, Mellette."

"Which is why I can go to Chicago. Because nothing else matters."

"We'll talk about this when you're not so tired. Right

now I'm going to carry you upstairs and put you to bed, so you can get all the rest you need."

"Thank you," she whispered, turning her face up to look at him as he lifted her into his arms and kicked the truck door closed. "For saving us. Thank you."

He loved the fact that she was so close that despite being covered with mud and grass and soaked to her skin she was still the most beautiful woman he'd ever seen...ever rescued. "Look, Mellette, we need to talk once you've rested. We both need to be clear headed."

"I am clear headed. If you want me, I'll go to Chicago."

"What if I want you here?"

"You'd stay?"

"I'd stay."

Her response was to sigh and press her head against his chest. Then she let him carry her upstairs to a room where he sat her down gently on the bed.

She gasped from pain, which alarmed him. "Where do you hurt?"

"Shoulder, ankle. Nothing broken, I don't think."

"Maybe I should take a look..." Or maybe that was something he should get her dad to do, given all the confused feelings that were now springing up in him.

"I appreciate it, although I don't think there's much you can do to help me." She smiled. "I was a bit clumsy out there."

"You were out on the road in the dark in a bad storm, directing traffic on the road. It's a miracle you weren't killed."

"A miracle," she murmured.

"Look, let me get you a pair of scrubs, and once you've dried off and changed, I'll have a look at you. Okay?"

She nodded as she sank back against the pillows. "Okay," she said as she fought to keep herself from drifting off.

"She's on the verge of going to sleep," Justin told Charles, who was scouting the kitchen for a good stiff drink of anything he could find. "Oh, and my grandmother kept it in the pantry out on the back porch. Called it her medicinal stash. Don't recall ever seeing her drinking it, but she did keep it handy for her patients."

"My wife keeps it locked up because one of my daughters had a problem. Not that Delphine would get herself into trouble again, because I don't believe she would ever do that. But Zenobia doesn't want her daughter tempted. In fact, it's only recently that she would even allow alcohol of any sort back in the house." He chuckled. "And I'm not sure but I think she measures it each and every time one of us has a drink, which for me isn't too often since I'm diabetic.

"She's a formidable woman."

"You can say that again," Charles said, disappearing round the corner to the pantry then reappearing with a bottle of whiskey. "So care to join me?"

"Actually, I need to take some dry clothes up to Mellette then have a look at her. I guess she hurt herself when she fell."

"And just how would you be looking at her, young man?" Charles asked.

"Like a doctor, sir."

"That's too bad. I really thought you had more in you than that." He poured himself a small amount of whiskey into a glass, then drank it down in a quick gulp.

"I do, but I'm not going to let it be a problem."

"Let it be a problem. That's what my daughter needs, and for you the reward will be worth the hard work. Back in the day, when I was trying to decide if I stood a shot at winning the attention of the fair Zenobia, I almost tripped myself up thinking about all the bad aspects. First, there was her status. She came from wealth, I didn't. And she always had this huge sense of rightness about her, one that could have scared me if I hadn't been so damn smitten. Of course, I never thought I had a chance with her. Even when she was in medical school you could tell she was destined for great things."

"Becoming an anesthesiologist is pretty great, too."

"It is. But with Zenobia…there was more there than I'd ever seen in any woman I'd ever met. And you know what? While I was still trying to convince myself to walk away, that I didn't stand a chance with her, she was the one who approached me, asked me out on our first date. And was I scared to go? Lord knows, I was shaking in my shoes."

"But you went and, as they say, lived happily ever after."

"Happily ever after," Charles said. "The thing is, I was on the verge of missing it all because all I saw were obstacles. And yes, my sweet Mellette has obstacles. But don't let that happen to you, son. Don't miss out because of them. Mellette may be like her mother in a lot of ways, but those are a joy to discover and an even greater joy to grow old with. So go get her settled in while I go and make sure Leonie's asleep. I've got her bedded down in one of the rooms upstairs, and unless you have other plans for me, I think I'll just give my wife a call if I can get through, then sleep there beside my granddaughter in the chair."

"Sorry I don't have better accommodation, but Mellette has been changing this place around so quickly…"

"And doing a fine job of it," Charles said with pride, as he tucked the bottle back into the pantry then headed back up the stairs.

Justin wasn't long after him, carrying a set of scrubs in his arms. "Mellette," he said, knocking quietly on the bedroom door. "Can I come in?"

Sure, it was a polite formality, but he needed to be polite with her. Besides, her dad was just next door. "Mellette?"

"Justin?" she said.

He pushed the door open, and the vision of Mellette Chaisson propped up against his pillows was almost more than he could bear. "Dry scrubs," he said. "Not much, but under the circumstances…" He sat them on the bed, then backed away.

"I might need some help," she said. "I'm not moving so well. My shoulder hurts. And my ankle is ridiculous."

"Let me get your dad.…"

"I'm not having my dad help me dress. All I need you to do is steady me when I stand up and walk into the bathroom to wash myself off. And steady me when I do that, too. Oh, and you can keep your eyes closed if the sight of a naked woman bothers the good doctor."

"It doesn't bother me so much as I'm trying to be polite, as your father is right next door."

She laughed as she scooted to the edge of the bed. "Just kidding. I'll be fine on my own. Mind if I use the shower?"

Justin rushed across the room to help her stand, steadying her with his arm around her waist as he assisted her to the bathroom, where he did the gentlemanly thing and kept his eyes shut when she dropped her muddy clothes to the floor. But even with his eyes shut, his imagination went to town as he stood there and let her hold on to him, lean on him and anything else she wanted. "You know I'm just a poor mortal," he said when his head bowed down and his eyes opened to see all her clothes on the floor around her ankles.

She laughed. "A poor mortal who wouldn't take advantage of a woman in my condition. Now, could you turn on the shower for me and help me hobble in?"

Help her? Did she think he was made of stone? Especially when one look was so close that his hands were shaking. But in spite of the beast inside that wanted to look, or ogle, or even fondle, he completed all his tasks with closed eyes, holding his breath until she was safely in the walk-in shower, leaning against the wall, and he was safely back outside it, leaning against the bathroom sink. Sweating.

"I'll just be a minute," she said, as the water splashed off the sides of the shower.

"Take your time." He wasn't ready to help her back out and do it the gentlemanly way. Being a gentleman was taking everything he had.

"I'm really not that modest," she said. "Besides, you're a doctor."

"I really don't need to see you naked. Especially since if I did it wouldn't be the doctor in me doing the looking." And that was a huge understatement.

"I might not mind. But whatever the case, can you hand me the towel? I've stood on one leg as long as I can and I'm ready to get out."

He handed her the towel then the scrubs when she asked, and before long Mellette pushed back the shower curtain to reveal a very clean, very fresh version of her former muddy self. "You look better," he said, exhaling a sigh of relief now that she was fully dressed.

"A nice shower is a miracle unto itself," she said, hobbling out as he rushed up to steady her. "So let's talk about you staying here. Was that real or my imagination?"

"As real an offer as I can make. Back in Chicago all I have is…stuff. Nothing I love so much that I couldn't walk away from it. Here, I have something I love, but more than that, someone. I'm in love. And that's the definition of *home,* isn't it? I want to come home, Mellette. To you, to the life I need to live. All of it."

"Are you sure?"

"Are *you* sure?" he asked.

"You know, you're pretty muddy. I think you need a shower." She dropped her towel to the floor. "Want somebody to scrub your back?"

* * *

Life was good here in Big Swamp. He had a new family, a new medical practice, and Eula's House was up and running and, surprisingly, busy. So much so they were already expanding. He worked there, alternating duty with Charles and several of Mellette's sisters and assorted friends. Mellette was the glue that kept it together, and with all the improvements made to the facility she was able to have Leonie at work with her every day now. That made for one happy nurse.

"It's what Eula wanted," Amos said as he and Justin sat on the porch swing, waiting for Mellette to see her last patient of the day. "She told me the first time she set eyes on Miss Mellette that she was the woman who would make you happy once and for all. I only wish she would have lived to see it happen."

Justin hadn't worked out all his guilt over his past, and maybe he never would. But it was amazing how much better he felt knowing that he was moving forward in the direction his grandmother would have wanted. That, and having Mellette's support made coming home to stay much easier.

"If that's what she wanted to happen, I'm sure she knew it would," Justin said, looking out to the fenced play yard where Leonie and several of her Big Swamp friends were playing ball together. There were so many kids here some days it was like they were running a day care. In fact, he and Mellette were thinking about adding that to the clinic's future agenda.

"So are the local folks treating you better out here now, boy?" Amos asked.

"A little. I have a few patients who ask to see me now and a couple who, when they end up with me, don't object. It's only been six months, so give it time." Time—something he never took for granted now, thanks to Mellette.

"He's being modest," Mellette said as she stepped outside and took her place on the swing next to Justin. "He has at least fifteen patients who like him, and probably that many more who tolerate him." She took hold of Justin's hand, then leaned over and kissed him on the cheek. "And one of his most faithful patients is Paul LeCompte."

Amos blinked. "You got Paul going to a real doctor on a regular basis? I don't believe it."

"I'm compromising," Justin admitted. "Giving him some of what he wants in return for him taking some of what I want him to. It works out."

"Look, we'd better round up Napoleon and Leonie and head back to New Orleans. Mother's expecting us for dinner, and we need some time to get ready."

Justin looked at Amos. "When my mother-in-law invites us, it's mandatory."

"Good Lord, man, you've surely been domesticated."

"That's what love will do to you, Amos. That's what love will do." With that, Justin pulled Mellette to her feet, grabbed the cat out of the clinic, and the two of them went to get Leonie. A core family of three with such a large family extending out from that. He was a lucky, lucky man.

"Do I have to wear a tie?" he whispered to Mellette as they headed to the boat.

"Tie. Shoes. Socks. Jacket." She kissed him then laughed. "Either that or a face-off with the Doucet family."

The thing was, he *had* faced everything. And he'd won the biggest prize of all.

"Oh, and about that last patient of the day…" Mellette said, placing Justin's hand on her flat belly. "It was me."

"As in…"

She nodded as the three of them walked along, hand in hand in hand. "As in."

Yes, he had definitely won the biggest prize of all. Somehow Justin knew Bonne-Maman Eula was up there, looking down and smiling.

* * * * *

A DOCTOR'S
CONFESSION

BY
DIANNE DRAKE

Published in Great Britain 2014
by Mills & Boon, an imprint of Harlequin (UK) Limited,
Eton House, 18-24 Paradise Road, Richmond, Surrey, TW9 1SR

© 2014 Dianne Despain

ISBN: 978 0 263 90776 6

Printed and bound in Spain
by Blackprint CPI, Barcelona

Recent titles by Dianne Drake:

A CHILD TO HEAL THEIR HEARTS
P.S. YOU'RE A DADDY
REVEALING THE REAL DR ROBINSON
THE DOCTOR'S LOST-AND-FOUND HEART
NO. 1 DAD IN TEXAS
THE RUNAWAY NURSE
FIREFIGHTER WITH A FROZEN HEART
THE DOCTOR'S REASON TO STAY**
FROM BROODING BOSS TO ADORING DAD
THE BABY WHO STOLE THE DOCTOR'S HEART*

**New York Hospital Heartthrobs*
Mountain Village Hospital

**These books are also available in eBook format
from www.millsandboon.co.uk**

CHAPTER ONE

"HE'S HANDSOME ENOUGH," Magnolia Loraine Doucet—
Maggie—commented. It was one of those hot, hot August days in Big Swamp, where her preference was to sit on the front porch swing, fan herself and sip a tall, cool lemonade. Which was exactly what she was doing with her sister Mellette on the front porch of Eula's House.

Inside, Mellette's husband, Justin, was arguing with Amos Picou on just how much larger the clinic extension should be. Amos wanted to keep everything as it was, and Justin wanted things bigger—a surgery for minor procedures, a cubbyhole where he could escape to write pages for his latest crime novel. It wasn't a lot in terms of square feet, but changes were met with resistance in these parts.

And while the argument with Amos, who was in favor of leaving things be, was not nearly as heated as the noonday sun, it had seemed the perfect time for the sisters to go outside and take a break.

"You mean drop-dead-gorgeous carpenter man without his shirt, and all sweaty. And look at his..." Mellette Bergeron teased.

"You're a pregnant lady with a husband just inside the door. You don't get to look at his anything."

"Hey, I can still look...a little."

"You've got a looker. Got him hook, line and six months into your pregnancy."

Mellette smiled the smile of a very contented woman as she laid a protective hand on her belly. "Don't I know that."

"So stop looking at that guy over there." Maggie nodded her head, indicating the big hunk of a carpenter working on framing the additional room that would be used as a minor surgery at Eula's House.

"Because you want him?" Mellette teased.

"Please. You know I'm not into relationships."

"Ah, yes. School and work, and more work. An exciting life."

"It is exciting."

"Then why are you looking?"

"I'm not looking so much as...as...admiring the physiology. And I was involved not that long ago."

"Marc the Bland and Raymond the Terrible. You do know how to pick 'em."

Maggie Doucet envisioned Marc for a moment—nice man, no wow factor. When his image disappeared she conjured up Raymond the Terrible—man's body, pig's head.

"Marc was okay, just not...not conversant or interesting. And if you recall, Marc the Bland dumped me. He dumped *me* because I wasn't interesting enough for him."

Maggie and Mellette both laughed, then Mellette

continued, "Then entered Raymond the Rebound, who turned out to be Raymond the Terrible. Misogynist pig of a man."

"I know, I know. You warned me, Mother and Daddy warned me." So had her other five sisters. "I met a street performer down in Jackson Square who was dancing for coins and even he warned me in a mime sort of way."

"Yet you didn't listen to any of us, did you?"

No, she hadn't. Because that's just the way she'd been, looking for absolution and as stubborn as the day was long. Not a good combination. Sure, it was a long, tired story about how she'd been stupid. One known to women the world over. And yes, she'd already admitted it freely. What she'd done hadn't just been stupid. It had been double stupid! Head-in-the-sand time, being dumped by someone she considered bland, then turning to Raymond.

Lesson learned from all that—she wasn't ready to jump back into anything for a long time to come. What she had suited her, kept her as safe as she needed to be. "Not doing it again for a long, long time, if ever."

"Not even with Mr. Tool Belt over there?"

"Especially with Mr. Tool Belt over there. He's…"

"Too tempting?"

"I'm not looking."

"But you took him lemonade yesterday, didn't you? Did you take lemonade to any of the other workers or just him?"

"Just him, but…I did make a pitcher full and left it out there in case any of the others wanted it."

"But he got his from you? Correct?"

"What are you trying to imply?"

"Nothing!"

Maggie snapped, "I just gave the man some lemonade, so don't make a federal case out of it, okay?"

"Which means you *are* interested, being so defensive and all."

"And just where do you get *that?*"

"You also said he's sexy, did you not?"

"I *said* the way he drank his lemonade is sexy. That's not saying he's sexy." Although he was. Very.

"Same thing," Mellette argued.

"No, it's not." Maggie turned and scowled at her sister. "Your pregnancy hormones are acting up again, which is making you irrational."

"How so?"

"You want everybody to be as deliriously happy as you are right now. Even if, like me, they don't want to be. Or if, like me again, they're satisfied with their life the way it is."

"Maybe you want to be happy the way I am, and you just don't know it yet. I was like that when I first met Justin. Wasn't ready to let go of the past and move on. It took me a while to come round, but when I did…"

"You decided the whole world has to act just like you did. Except my world is complicated."

"And mine wasn't?" Mellette asked. "I had to remove a wedding ring given me by someone I loved very much in order to make room for Justin. And I also had a daughter who was very much involved in my move forward. And you have…" She folded her arms across her fat belly and faked a contemplative frown.

"Let's see. You have none of that. You're moving away from a boring boyfriend, followed by a chauvinist rebound, you're at the top of your law school class, you have a killer job that you claim to love. And that sweaty guy over there keeps looking at you out of the corner of his eye. Nothing about that sounds complicated at all. In fact, it seems pretty straightforward to me."

"I'm in transition. Give me some time."

"Seriously, Maggie? That's the best you can do?"

Maggie took a quick peek at the guy in the jeans, then concentrated on her lemonade. "I'm sure his story is a long, sad one. You know, dumped by the love of his life who ran off to marry a rodeo clown, and now he sits at home alone every night, sniffing the scent of her left on the pillow while petting FruFru, the fluffy white poodle over which they fought for custody."

"First thing is, he's definitely not the poodle type. German shepherd, I think. Yes, he'd definitely have a German shepherd. And, Maggie, if you think he sits home alone every night, you probably don't deserve to serve him lemonade. He's one catchable hunk of man if I've ever seen one, and the only reason he'd be staying home is because he wants to." She took a sip of her lemonade.

"Or he's a serial killer."

"A serial killer with drop-dead-gorgeous blue eyes," Mellette continued.

"They're green," Maggie corrected.

"You looked!"

"And I saw his sandy blond hair, wide shoulders and six-pack abs. Sure, I noticed, and that's not counted as looking. It's being observant. And I'll have a good description ready for the police if he is a serial killer."

"He's a sexy drinker with drop-dead-gorgeous *green* eyes you can describe right down to his abs. So does he have a birthmark?"

"You said they're drop-dead gorgeous," Maggie challenged. "I didn't."

"And you're going to contend they aren't, *madame* lawyer?"

"Not a lawyer yet. And I'm not contending anything other than the fact that they're green." A very nice, tranquil green. "And that he is handsome." With coloring that nearly matched hers, with green eyes just a shade lighter than the green in her eyes.

"Because you were gazing longingly into them."

"If you weren't so pregnant, I'd challenge you to a fight, right here, right now," Maggie said in good-natured fun. "The way we used to when we were kids."

"Remember how Daddy would encourage us, even lay down bets on who'd win the wrestling match? So then we'd go at each other for a while, then Mother would come in and Daddy would pretend he knew nothing about it? Then he'd get all stern and try correcting us, and we'd jump all over him."

Both sisters laughed over the memory.

"Between you and me," Maggie said, "I'm glad you're having a girl. I like the idea that Leonie will have a sister the way I had all of you, and I love the idea of having another niece since the first one I got was so great. I mean, boys are nice, but I don't know how one would fit into the family. We're so used to girls." She was referring to her six other siblings. At age thirty-three, Maggie fell middle in line of the seven Doucet girls. With long, honey-blonde hair and green eyes, she stood out as the different one—she being fair while the others ranged in skin complexion from medium dark to dark.

Being the fairest of the group, people had taken for granted she was also the weakest or most vulnerable. Except that wasn't true. There wasn't a weak, vulnerable Doucet girl in the bunch. Admittedly, Mellette was probably the strongest of them all, and that had helped her through the death of her first husband and into a life with a new love.

Maggie wasn't far behind Mellette in strength, though. Only hers was directed at her career. First a nurse, and now studying to be a lawyer who defended medical malpractice suits—a career change that had come about after her hand, placed directly on a patient's heart with the intent of squeezing the life back into him, had saved him but also caused him an infection.

The ungrateful man hadn't thanked her for saving him but he had sued her for infecting him, which, for a while, had shattered her world and her desire to be in medicine. But like the typical Doucet she was, she'd come back swinging, decided to go to work as a malpractice investigator and, true to her strong nature, decided after that it wasn't enough. Now, with just over nine months to go, she'd be the lawyer fighting back on behalf of the doctors and nurses who got sued unjustly.

"I think Justin's glad it's a girl, too. He loves Leonie, and while he's never said as much, I think he likes the fact that Daddy reigns over an empire of girls. Maybe sees himself in a similar position."

"You want seven, like Mother had?" Maggie questioned.

Mellette shook her head vigorously. "This one, maybe one more. Although I will say that Mr. Drop-Dead-Sexy Carpenter over there looks like he's got some boys in him, in case you want to change the direction of the Doucet family."

"Pregnant or not, I *am* going to wrestle you to the floor," Maggie said, giving her sister a pretend slap on the arm.

"Over what?" Justin Bergeron asked, stepping out onto the front porch. Justin, a general surgeon and part-time general practitioner at Eula's House, was also a medical crime novelist, with a burgeoning screen-writing career added to his résumé.

Both sisters looked up at him and started laughing.

"And I'll take that as my cue to go back inside," Justin said.

"You can stay," Mellette said. "We were just… You know, sister talk." She glanced over at her sister, who was glancing out at the carpenter. "About silly things. You and Amos are welcome to join us out here for lemonade."

Amos Picou, an old Bergeron family friend, stepped past Justin and hurried down the steps. A direct descendent of African lineage, he was a part of the local legend, a friend to all and an all-round good man. "Sorry, ladies, but I'm off to catch me some crawdads for a nice gumbo Justin's going to be fixing later on. Gotta hurry since he's got to get that gumbo on to simmering pretty soon, but later, after I get back, that lemonade will sure hit the spot."

Maggie's eyes opened wider. "Did I hear someone say gumbo? And did I hear an invitation to dinner to help eat some of that gumbo?"

"I'll bet Justin will fix enough for one more, if you want to go over and ask Mr. Tool Belt to join us," Mellette said.

"I'm not going to go ask Mr. Tool Belt anything!" Maggie said, almost too defensively.

Mellette smiled and poured a glass of lemonade. "Just give this to him. Ask him if you want to, or don't." With that, she hurried inside, then watched her sister from the front window.

They were watching him. Probably talking about him. The fact was, he hated lemonade. Had hated it all his life, hated it yesterday when the looker had brought him some, and would hate it just as much this time she brought him a glass. But it was a kind gesture, and he didn't want to seem ungrateful. After all, they'd given him work and, as it turned out, he needed work. He had living expenses to meet and his own house to renovate. Although he was finding it tough working at a medical clinic, being that close to medicine again.

When he'd answered the ad, it had read that this was to be a room addition. He'd assumed a house, as the ad had said to apply at Eula's House. So if he'd known...actually, he'd have probably applied, anyway. But at least he'd have been prepared to spend his days around doctors and nurses. That was the tough part, being around them and not being part of them.

Well, money was money. And lemonade was lemonade. "I appreciate it, ma'am," he said to Maggie, as she handed the glass to him.

"There's more, if you want it," she said. "Up on the front porch. Help yourself. And tell the other workers to help themselves."

"I'll tell the others, but I think one will hit the spot for me, thanks."

"My name's Maggie Doucet, by the way," she said, smiling at him.

"And I'm Alain Lalonde," he replied.

"You're from around here, aren't you? I can tell from the drawl."

"Just moved back from Chicago."

"Chicago? Really? That's where my sister's husband was living when she met him. Justin Bergeron. You've met him, haven't you? He's the doctor on call here.

"Yes, ma'am, I've met him," he said, handing her back the empty glass after downing the lemonade in nearly one gulp, like it was bad medicine. "Now, if you'll excuse me…"

He turned his back and started to walk away. But Maggie called out to him, "Alain, would you care to stay for gumbo tonight? As your drawl indicates you're from around here, I think you'll appreciate a good gumbo for what it is, and my sister's husband is making enough to feed an army."

"Appreciate the invitation, ma'am, but I have other plans." Said politely, because he was grateful for the offer, but he wasn't in a social mood and he didn't want to drag the others down with his attitude. In other words, he knew he'd throw the proverbial wet blanket on the party and he didn't want to do that. "Maybe another time."

"Well, if you change your mind, you're always welcome…"

"Again, thanks. Look, I've got to get back to work, ma'am. The job foreman isn't paying me to stand around and talk. Thanks for the lemonade."

Well, that went badly, Maggie thought as she walked away. Talk about a polite dismissal.

"So?" Mellette asked, even before Maggie was inside the clinic.

"So, what?"

"What did he say?" Mellette asked. "I saw you two talking, so what was it about?"

"He didn't ask me out, if that's what you mean. In fact, I asked him to gumbo tonight and he turned me down."

"Seriously, you asked him to dinner after you told me you wouldn't?"

Maggie shrugged. "I was trying to be friendly. That's all."

"There are six other men on the job site. Did you ask them all, too? Or did you just single out Mr. Tool Belt?"

"His name is Alain Lalonde, and he's the only one I asked. And that's the end of the conversation, as far as I'm concerned because—" she glanced down at the floor "—have you looked at how swollen your ankles are? I want you to go sit down, elevate your legs and leave my love life to me."

"So you're thinking about Alain in terms of your love life?" Mellette teased on her way to her favorite chair.

"I don't want a love life!" Maggie retorted. "Let me repeat myself. I don't want a love life. I have work, I have school, I have my volunteer work here. I have a pregnant sister who needs me to help her. That's enough. *No love life!*"

"Yes, right," Mellette said, as she changed her mind and headed to the stairs, deciding to go to one of the two bedrooms on the second floor for a real rest. "Oh, and Billie Louviere will be here in half an hour for her three-month checkup. Pregnancy's normal, she's doing fine. Justin's available if you need him, but if you don't, tell her hello for me. Oh, and keep an eye on her blood pressure. It hasn't been high but something tells me she might be a candidate for hypertension the further she gets into this pregnancy."

"Her first?"

"After a couple of miscarriages. She's pretty nervous."

"And I'm pretty nervous about your swollen ankles. So go put them up, and call me if you need anything."

"Like lemonade," Mellette teased.

"Leave the lemonade out of this."

Once back outside, Maggie tried not looking for Alain Lalonde, but that was nearly impossible as all the building activity was directly in her line of sight as she sat on the porch. "Okay, so he's good to look at," she said as she poured herself another lemonade. Good to watch, good to turn into a little midday fantasy. After all, there was no harm in looking, was there?

After Billie Louviere's checkup, a couple of walk-ins presented themselves at the clinic, and by midafternoon Maggie had actually seen enough patients that she was getting tired. Not exhausted, but with just the right amount of weariness setting in that she really felt she'd done a good day's work. It was time to go home, though. Eat a quick bowl of gumbo and head on back to town.

Even though she was taking the summer off from school, she still had casework for a couple of legal clients to go over this evening, and she did want to read a chapter in one of her law textbooks, if she stayed awake that long.

"Time to get up," she called down the hall to Mellette, who was still napping in Justin's former bedroom. While no one actually lived at Eula's House anymore, named for Justin's grandmother, they kept the upstairs as a residence, hoping that one day it might be turned into a very small hospital ward. The downstairs had been converted into a clinic that maintained a portion of Eula's herbal practice, as well as a proper medical clinic. To outsiders it might seem a confused mishmash of traditions, but to the people of Big Swamp it was where they could seek medical help in whatever form they chose.

"Come on, Mellette. We need to eat, then I've got to get out of here. Go home, go over some case files." She pushed open the bedroom door to look in on her sleeping sister. Then gasped. Her ankles were puffier than before. So were her hands, and even her face, especially around her eyes, looked puffy.

"You okay?" she asked as she approached the bed.

"Headache," Mellette said. "A little nauseous. Think the heat's done me in." She started to sit up, but Maggie gently nudged her back down.

"Stay there. Don't get up yet."

"Why?" Mellette asked. Mellette, a nurse herself, had worked in emergency medicine at New Hope, where their mother, Zenobia, was chief of staff.

"Because you're tired, and tiredness and pregnancy aren't a good combination. I'm going to go downstairs and get you a drink of cold water, so don't get up. Hear me?"

"Hear you," Mellette said, as she dropped back into her pillows and shut her eyes.

Two minutes later Mellette had a blood-pressure cuff strapped to her sister's arm, and two minutes after that she was on her way back downstairs to find Justin.

He was outside, talking to Mr. Tool Belt. "Something's wrong with Mellette," Maggie interrupted, not beating around the bush for a more tactful way to approach it. "I don't do obstetrics so I can't tell for sure, but she's awfully swollen, her blood pressure is on the high end of normal and—"

"Where's she swollen?" Alain Lalonde cut in.

Both Justin and Maggie gave him an inquisitive look. "Feet, ankles, eyelids…" Maggie answered, not sure why she was giving a symptom list to the carpenter.

"Urinary output normal?" Alain went on.

Maggie shrugged, quite surprised by the carpenter's line of questions. "I didn't ask her."

"Nausea, vomiting, headache?" Again from Alain.

"Nausea and headache." More than surprised, she was confused.

"Onset?"

"This afternoon," Maggie said. "Why do you care?"

"Alain was probably the best high-risk obstetrician in Chicago," Justin answered.

"You knew?" Alain asked. "And you didn't ask why I'm here, doing carpentry?"

"A man has a right to his privacy. I didn't want to invade yours."

"So Mellette...I think it may be preeclampsia. If it is, we caught it in time. But I think you'd better be getting your wife to her obstetrician pretty damned fast."

Justin turned to run to the clinic, then paused and signaled for Alain to accompany him, leaving Maggie outside to wonder what had caused a doctor to quit and become a carpenter. Not that there was anything wrong with being a carpenter, because there wasn't. But why had Alain put himself through so many years of medical training just to quit? It made no sense, especially as he was so highly regarded, according to Justin.

So what made a doctor give it up to come to Big Swamp and bang out a clinic expansion? It was a question for which she had no answer. And it was a question for which she was going to find an answer, especially as this man was about to touch her sister. Darned straight, she was going to find an answer.

Instead of going upstairs to Mellette, Maggie went

straight to the computer in the office and entered the name Alain Lalonde into a search engine. The first thing that turned up was a headline about a wounded army doctor who saved the lives of his men and women. They had been under siege and he'd drawn the fire away from his escaping crew and patients. Had been shot in the leg in doing so, spent several weeks in the hospital in rehab. Received a medal.

"Amazing," she said, as the second thing that turned up was of an obstetrician accused in a malpractice suit. Something about performing a Caesarean when it hadn't been necessary. The article said he'd gone against orders from the woman's personal physician and performed an emergency C-section when a normal delivery would have worked.

"And someone sued you for that?" Maggie whispered. It didn't make sense to her as long as the baby had been healthy, which it apparently had been. Was it the lawsuit that had made him quit, or had he just burned out?

"Who are you?" Maggie whispered as she clicked out of the articles. "Alain Lalonde, just who are you? And why are you working as a carpenter and not an obstetrician?"

CHAPTER TWO

"How far along are you?" Alain asked as he checked Mellette's blood pressure.

"Twenty-four...no, twenty-five weeks now."

"And when did your symptoms start?" He pumped up the blood-pressure cuff and deflated it slowly.

"A couple of days ago, but only swollen ankles. I honestly didn't think anything about it because of the heat."

"In this heat, swollen ankles are common."

"How high is my blood pressure?"

"One-forty over ninety. Not extremely high, but I wouldn't want to see it going any higher."

Mellette gasped. "And the baby?"

"I don't have anything here to do any tests, but I heard the heartbeat, and it was strong."

Justin and Maggie, who'd finally joined them, sighed in relief.

"Look, you need to be in the hospital at least for the night so your doctor can get tests done. I think you have a mild case of preeclampsia, which can be controlled by drugs and lots of rest, but we need a blood panel, and most of all we need to get a fetal monitor on you. The problem is, the trip out of here is rougher than I want you to take." He looked up at Maggie. "Is there any way to get a helicopter in here?"

"No!" Mellette gasped.

"It's for your own good, Mellette," Alain said. "But most of all it's for the baby's safety."

Mellette shut her eyes and a tear squeezed out the side and trickled down her cheek. Immediately, Justin was at her side, pulling her into his arms. "Alain's a good doctor," he said. "If he thinks we need to evacuate you by air, that's what we'll do."

Even before Mellette had a chance to agree, Maggie was on the phone, making the arrangements. "Thirty minutes?" she questioned. "We'll get her down to the pickup spot as fast as we can."

"Already?" Alain asked, clearly impressed.

"Done deal. We need to get her down to the grocery in Grandmaison where an ambulance will take her out to Flander's Meadow where she'll be picked up. The ambulance will be there in half an hour, so I'd suggest we get going. If that's okay with you?" she asked Alain.

"Perfect plan." He gave her an admiring glance as she helped Justin bundle up his wife for the trip.

"Please," Mellette said, "I can walk down the stairs."

"And I can carry you down just as easily," Justin said.

"I want you to come along, as well," Alain said to Maggie. "I don't anticipate anything happening, but I want you to keep watch on her blood pressure while I drive."

"I can do that."

"It's going to be that proverbial bumpy ride."

Maybe it was, but Maggie was glad with everything inside her that Alain was there taking charge. No matter what the article said, she trusted him.

Maggie stared up into the sky as the helicopter lifted off, carrying Justin and Mellette. She'd already called her parents, who would be at the other end when it landed. And she'd called her sisters, as well as Pierre Chaisson, Mellette's brother-in-law from her first marriage, who would watch Leonie when everybody else was at the hospital. "You never think in terms of a pregnancy having difficulties when the mother is in such good shape. I mean, prenatal problems are for other people."

"They're for everybody, Maggie. Sometimes they can be predicted, sometimes they can't, sorry to say. I mean, Mellette doesn't seem to carry any of the risk factors, but you see the results on someone who's perfectly fine. It's frustrating for everybody."

"But Mellette's going to be okay, isn't she?"

"Once they get her blood pressure stabilized she'll be much better. The thing is, she's really going to have to be careful now, because she's not far enough along to deliver. But we have our ways of taking care of these problems, lots of new drugs and techniques, and odds are your sister is going to do just fine and deliver a healthy baby at the end of her pregnancy."

"Wish you could make guarantees," Maggie said on a sigh, as Alain slipped an arm around her shoulder. "Or promises."

"Wish I could, too. But the one thing I can guarantee

is that you did a good job, catching it quickly and responding the way you needed to. A lot of women think all that pregnancy puffiness is just part of the course. Mellette got lucky."

"That's what nurses are supposed to do."

"You're a nurse? I guess I'm not surprised because of the way you responded, but I didn't know that. I'd heard you were in law school."

"I am, but I'm a nurse first."

"Busy lady. But a very astute one. Your training shows."

"Thank you," she said. "I come from a long line of medical people. I think it comes naturally when your name is Doucet."

"Doucet, as in…?"

She nodded, enjoying the feel of his strong arm. It was steady, something to give her comfort. "Yes, *that* Doucet family. Fortunately, or unfortunately, we're known far and wide. Or should I say my parents are." She smiled. "The rest of us just try to maintain the family reputation as best we can."

Alain chuckled. "Well, you maintained it today. Did it proud. So I wonder if that gumbo is still simmering, because I could sure go for a bowl of it right about now."

"I'll bet it is," Maggie said halfheartedly.

"You want to go to the hospital, don't you?"

She nodded.

"Then here's the plan. Gumbo first, and that will give the doctors enough time to get your sister looked at and under treatment. Besides, she's not going to be allowed any visitors for a while—just her husband, and I'm sure your mother. So you might as well wait a little while here with me, then I'll drive you in to the hospital."

"You'd do that?"

"It's not out of the way. My...house is just a few blocks from New Hope, which is where I'm assuming she'll be going, so it's no big deal."

"Then I say let's go have some gumbo."

"So here's the thing," Maggie said to Alain over gumbo. "I've been giving this some thought. We need a doctor here. I'm here part time, and my sisters manage to squeeze in some hours, along with my dad when we need him. Mellette and Justin are the driving force, though, and that's over with for a while now. So I need someone who, first, is licensed here, which you are, according to the internet, and also who can guarantee me something near full-time hours for a little while, as Justin's going to be staying home more to watch over Mellette. With both of them gone, that leaves the clinic closed a good bit of the time, and since you're not working as a doctor right now..."

"I'm not working as a doctor, period. Hence the hammer in my hand." She'd been reading about his past and he wasn't sure if he liked that or not. It was all still so... touchy with him.

"But I read up on you. You're an obstetrician and a war hero. You ran a military hospital in Afghanistan so I'm sure you're up to some work here, in this clinic."

"Ran a hospital, past tense. And if you read up on me, you'll know why."

"You were involved in a lawsuit and I'm sorry about

that. Sincerely sorry it happened to you. But if every doctor who got sued stepped away from medicine, there wouldn't be any doctors left."

He cringed. "It wasn't that simple. But that's the bottom line, yes. I did get sued, and the hospital stepped back from me because the people suing me are, shall we say, prominent. They make big donations to the hospital. I did what I believed was right, which left a perfect bikini body with a scar, and the hospital walked away from me. Took a step back, threw collective hands into the air and told me I was on my own."

"Which is enough to make you bitter, and I understand that. And like I said, I'm sorry about that," Maggie said in earnestness. "It's never easy, getting sued. I saw how it devastated my parents the few times they were sued. But they were lucky that the hospital stood behind them and they came out victorious. I take it you're not doing so well in your lawsuit?"

"To say the least," he repeated. "And it's not just the lawsuit itself. It's all the other things on the periphery that get to you."

"What do you mean?"

"You can't get it off your mind. You go over everything you did, wondering if you missed something or left out something that was crucial. You wonder what you could have done differently that might have changed the outcome. But, damn, in the end it was just a scar. She has a perfect baby boy to show for it."

"Well, your insurance company should figure it out. They don't pay out on bad or false claims."

"That's the other part. I took two years off and went

to serve in the military before the lawsuit was filed and the hospital revoked my insurance in that time and fired me while I was laid up in rehab, trying to figure out whether or not I'd ever walk again. So I'm hanging out there on my own in this. Welcome home, Captain Lalonde."

Maggie's eyes widened. "I did read about your injury, and I'm sorry."

"Old news," he said. "I recovered. But while I was focused on that, the hospital did me in. And the thing is…"

"There's no loyalty," Maggie said. "It was owed you, and they took it away. But after that long?"

"Statute of limitations in Illinois is generous. The thing is, I talked to the woman who's suing me—"

"Your attorney let you do that?" Maggie interrupted.

"I don't have an attorney. Can't afford one."

"And the hospital where you worked really, truly isn't backing you up at all?"

"They claim my insurance coverage ended when I went into the military and became a military doctor, therefore they're under no obligation to cover me in a suit that was filed after I left the military. I mean, there was almost a three-year lapse in there."

"Seriously?" Maggie said indignantly. "That's what they're trying to pull?"

He shrugged. "I got some pro bono advice, which was basically to try to reach a settlement. But the settlement they want is higher than I can afford. I damaged a model's perfect body with a scar and they want a bite out of me."

"But the baby was healthy."

"It was in fetal distress. Her own doctor wasn't responding to the calls. They came in, I got assigned and knew there was no way she was going to push that baby out in time, maybe not at all because her pelvis was so small, so I did what I had to do. And now, with the lawsuit hanging over my head, no one back in Chicago will hire me because along with the lawsuit they went after my reputation, so here I am working as a carpenter, probably not inclined to ever go back into medicine, anyway. Bottom line is I appreciate the offer you gave me, but I come with built-in liabilities."

"Maybe you do, but are you contented to stay a carpenter? After all your years of education and experience, are you ready to simply throw in the towel and keep that hammer handy?"

"I've had a couple of friends who were knocked to their knees by malpractice suits. It was ugly. And while the insurance usually pays up one way or another, there's no way to fix a damaged reputation. For me, that's as important as anything in this whole mess."

"And it's a stigma for life, if you don't have the right people representing you. My parents have both been unjustly sued—my mother on behalf of the hospital more times than I can count, and it's always a horrible time for her. For Daddy, too, when he got sued, because of all the emotions involved."

"Then you understand."

"More than know, Alain. That's what I do."

"What do you mean?"

"I'm a registered nurse, and I work part time in medicine just to keep up, also because I love patient care. But

I'm also a medical malpractice investigator, and within a few months I'll be an attorney who's going to specialize in med malpractice cases, not representing the people doing the suing but the medical personnel being sued. Besides putting on a vigorous defense where it's deserved, I also want to do some reputation fixing. The thing is, insurance companies are so eager to simply give in and settle, but that doesn't vindicate the doctor or nurse being sued who doesn't deserve it. Like you, for example. You'd never seen this patient before, and she presents with fetal distress. Yet she's wanting to get into your pockets for something that wasn't your fault."

"It's not about the money. They have enough for two lifetimes. It's all ego. I suppose they want a story to tell. And they sure as hell got it. On top of that, he wants to run for some elected office and campaign on medical reform as part of his platform. He just happens to want to build that platform on my back."

Maggie paused for a moment, then a smile slowly spread to her face. "Then here's what I propose. I'll have to check with my superiors first, because I'm just the investigator. But if I can convince them to take you on as a client, in return I'd like hours here at the clinic. We'll pay you, of course. Not much, but some kind of stipend for living expenses."

"You can work in Illinois?"

"We have a registered agent in Illinois so yes, I can work there. And the thing is, Alain, while this isn't the kind of action that's going to put money in your pocket, unless you want to countersue, which I wouldn't recommend since you turning around and suing back turns you into some kind of aggressor you don't want to become, it's one that will prevent you from having to go through this alone. And there's a good possibility we can restore your reputation once we win it and it's over with.

"In other words, the best outcome would be giving you some peace of mind, and maybe the will to go back out there and practice medicine on a full-time basis. So…interested?" Her heart really did go out to the man. He was taking a beating he didn't deserve. Even without all the facts, it sounded as if he'd unwittingly stepped in then gotten hammered with a situation that couldn't have possibly been salvaged.

"Maybe," he said cautiously. "The thing is, if they sue me they can't really get anything. I wasn't kidding when I said I needed this job as a carpenter to get by. So wouldn't it be just as easy to let them sue then find out I'm not worth two nickels? I mean, I'm living in my aunt's house, fixing it up for her. She's moved to Florida and told me I can do with it what I want. She'll deed it over to me in due course if I want the place, but I don't want it right now because if I'm being sued I don't want them taking her house."

"Your reputation's worth more than a couple of nickels, isn't it?"

"It used to be."

"You've got a mighty good reputation in the military. Got a medal of honor, didn't you?"

"Are you just full of facts about me?"

"Just read the headlines, not the details." She smiled. "And that headline needs to be protected, Alain. You did something good, and you deserve to be proud about it rather than simply giving in to defeat."

"I'm not defeated. More like practical."

"Which is why I want to practice medical defense law. Someone's coming at you, going to ruin you if they can, and you don't deserve it."

"So what if you do get your law firm to take me on? What happens?"

"First, they'll assign me to investigate the case. And if I do say so myself, I'm the best at what I do."

He chuckled. "And modest, too."

"Only when I have to be."

"Anybody ever called you a pit bull?" he asked.

"A time or two. The thing is, I believe in what I do. Doctors and nurses are an easy target, especially doctors who are required to carry so much insurance. My mother runs a hospital where doctors are sued unjustly all the time, and it takes so much away from the patient care she should be giving because she has to get involved in the legal proceedings.

"The worst, though, was my dad. He suffered a huge suit, and it depressed him for weeks. He didn't do anything wrong, and the hospital eventually just settled on his behalf. He wanted to defend himself, though, and he never felt good that by settling it seemed like he was guilty of medical negligence. It broke his heart, and that hurt all of us."

"Which is when you decided you wanted to be a crusader?"

"Not a crusader. Just someone who wanted to make sure that the innocent weren't being punished. And I'm not saying that all cases are unfair, because I've seen some that are well deserved. But I've seen too many that are not."

Alain took a sip of his water then squinted up at the sun. "So what you would want in return are hours at the clinic, doing what I'm assuming will be general medicine."

"Are you good with herbal medicine? Because we do a bit of that, as well."

"I've never gone near the stuff."

"Then that's where I can help, because Mellette's been teaching me."

"You're going to be my nurse?"

"Probably. But I do have my other work, as well as law school."

"Meaning you never sleep."

"Meaning I sleep only when I have to."

"Well, I do have a commitment to work on the addition, and Tom Chaisson—"

"Mellette's other brother-in-law from her first marriage," Maggie interrupted.

"You keep things very cozy down here, don't you?"

"We try to," she said.

"Anyway, Tom just made me project foreman. He's got another job in Baton Rouge that he's got to oversee, so he asked me to take on this project for him. And I can't back out on that. So if I agree to this, when I don't have a stethoscope around my neck I'll be wearing tools on my hips. Can you deal with that?"

Could she deal with that? The fact that she could still

watch him in carpenter mode was an added bonus. "I can," she said, her voice just a bit on the wobbly side.

"Then I guess we have a deal. You take my case to your law firm and see what they have to say about it, and I'll work here as your doctor on call."

"You can live here, too, if you want," she added. "Upstairs, in one of the bedrooms."

"Might not be a bad idea, as I've got my aunt's house practically gutted and I'm reduced to living on a cot and cooking on a hot plate. Her house was one of those projects that the more I got into it, the more I found that needed fixing." He grinned. "And it's a big old plantation house, turning into a big old plantation money pit."

"Well, no promises or anything, but I do have some pull at New Hope, which could be a consideration for you after we get your lawsuit straightened out."

"Anyway, I think it's time to get you on the road. I expect that by the time we get there the doctors will know more about what's going on with your sister."

Maggie reached over and gave his hand a squeeze. "You're a good man, Dr. Lalonde, and it's my intention to make sure you hang on to that reputation."

"I like your passion," he said.

And she liked his abs.

"So you're a doctor?" Mellette said. She was on bed rest now but allowed to travel out to Eula's House with Justin when he took calls there. Her condition had much improved in a couple of days and for now she was allowed light activity.

"Depends on the time of day," Alain said as he eyed her ankles.

"They're much better, Doctor. Swelling's gone down, and they're almost back to normal. You caught it in the early stages and my physician is treating me for preeclampsia. He doesn't think I'm going to have any strong complications, though. And while I have to curtail my activities, I'm not on total bed rest yet."

"As long as you're sensible," Alain warned.

"That's what everybody keeps telling me. And with six sisters, trust me, I'm never alone to do something insensible, not that I would. But I just wanted to thank you for helping me, and for taking over the clinic."

"Your doctor's aware you're coming out to Big Swamp?"

"He's aware, and he's consented, provided I strictly limit my activities to giving advice from a lounging position. Got to have someone to oversee the medicinals," she said, smiling. "Maggie's coming along in her knowledge of herbs, though. I expect she'll know everything she needs to in the next couple of weeks. She's awfully smart."

"Nurse, herbal practitioner and lawyer-to-be. I'd call that well-rounded."

"Somebody talking about me?" Maggie asked, as she took a seat next to her sister on the porch swing.

"Saying horrible things," Mellette teased.

Alain liked the way they interacted. He'd never had brothers and sisters. In fact, his parents had been very old when he'd been born—one of those menopausal miracles that happened to a couple who'd been barren for twenty-five years and had adjusted their lives accordingly.

While he loved his folks dearly, there'd never been any youth in his life. With a mother who had been near fifty when he was born, and a dad in his mid-fifties, he'd been raised in an older world than most of his friends, and as a consequence he'd always seemed too old and stodgy. There'd been no youthful pranks, not even when he'd been in college. No frat parties. No wild and crazy dates. Just seriousness, studying and responsibility.

Yet when he saw the way Maggie interacted with her sister, it caused him to realize what he'd missed out on. And made him feel a little envious. Stirred something up in him. "She told me what a bad girl you were when you were young."

"Maybe just a little bit. But I wasn't in it alone. There was always another sister joining in, then blaming it all on me."

"Who, me?" Mellette asked, laughing and holding her belly to stop it from jiggling.

"You, Sabine, Delphine, Ghislaine, Lisette or Acadia."

Alain shook his head. "It's hard to imagine your mother having seven of you and still running one of the best medical centers in the South."

"We're strong women," Maggie said. "Had parents to support that in us."

"Strong, as in overachievers?" he asked.

"Call it what you want," Maggie went on. "But that's who we are. My mother was raised in an era where women were just on the brink of coming into their own, only in her family, because they were of a certain social status…"

"And from a very traditional Southern family," Mellette added.

"That, too," Maggie agreed. "Anyway, what was expected from her was to be just like her mother, who was…I guess the best way to describe our grandmother is a social butterfly. That's the way she was raised, and it was the world in which she raised our mother. For my grandmother, who is involved in more charitable work than anyone I've ever seen, it works. Her life exists for her causes, and she works hard at them, but she also finds time to sit down to tea with various friends every day of the week.

"But for my mother…that social hour of tea was wasted when there were things to do. She was hard-driven, I guess you could call her. So instead of following in the family tradition, she started one of her own. And we all seem to be following her example in one way or another." She smiled, then added, "As overachievers."

"So what about your family, Alain?"

"Teachers. My mother taught high school math and my father taught college chemistry. They're both retired now, living in a condo on a Costa Rican beach."

"No brothers or sisters?" Maggie asked.

"Just me. A late-in-life kid who surprised the hell out of my parents when I popped into their lives."

"Sounds like an interesting story," Mellette said.

"More like typical. We were just an ordinary family. No prestige. No bells and whistles."

"But close?" Maggie asked.

"More so now than when I was younger. But I've grown up. It happens to most of us sooner or later."

"And what do they think about you not practicing medicine any longer?" Maggie asked.

"Actually, they don't know I've given up the stethoscope for a hammer. They think I'm in Louisiana practicing medicine, and as far as I'm concerned, that's the way I want to leave it."

Maggie gave him a questioning look. "Because they're older?"

"Because they made a lot of sacrifices for me when I went to medical school, and I sure as hell don't want them knowing they wasted their money."

"It wasn't wasted," Mellette said, as Justin stepped out on the porch. "Look what you did for me. That, in and of itself, says a lot about your ability. Now all you need to do is let my sister get to work on your case and get you back where you belong on a full-time basis, rather than squeezing it in while you're letting your drywall spackle dry."

"My wife's opinionated," Justin said, taking Mellette by the arm and leading her down the stairs. "And on that note I'm going to wish you both a good afternoon and escort her home. The waiting room is cleared, and barring any emergencies or walk-ins, you're free for the rest of the day. Although I wouldn't count on it, because I heard that Ivy Comfort may be having a bout of rheumatism." He smiled. "As they say, heard it through the grapevine, which is alive and well in these parts."

Alain's expression turned to panic. "I don't treat rheumatism."

"But I do," Maggie said. "And it's me she'll want to be seeing for some special tea and maybe a liniment we make that's—"

Alain held up his hand to stop her. "I'm going to trust that you know what you're doing, and leave it at that. If Miss Comfort would like any medical treatment, I'll be glad to see what I can do. Maybe prescribe a mild anti-inflammatory drug or—"

"She won't take your prescription," Maggie warned as Justin and Mellette walked away. "It's been a real challenge here to prescribe traditional medicine. Most of the people are willing to tolerate it, since it's all they can get without leaving the area. But we have a few holdouts who absolutely refuse to give in to modern ways, and Ivy Comfort just happens to be one of them. So Eula gave her some herbs that seemed to help, then Mellette took over after Eula died, and now that end of the practice is being passed along to me. Along with any regular nursing duties that come up."

"Your family's gotten so involved here. I wouldn't have thought that, given your mother's status, you'd have been inclined to."

Maggie shrugged. "Initially, it was because my sister came to help out Justin's grandmother, who was an herbal practitioner. The people here trusted her for over half a century, and when she died the position of herbal practitioner sort of fell to Mellette because the people here trusted her, too. They didn't trust Justin, who wanted to practice nothing but traditional medicine, and a lot of them still haven't come round to his way of thinking. But I suppose because Eula trusted Mellette, and I'm her sister, that's why they trust me."

"Then what's that say about me? I'm just an interloping medical doctor who's not going to put forth any kind of effort to prescribe herbs."

"What it says is that you'll have a tough time. There will be some who accept you unconditionally because you're a doctor, and some who'll accept you marginally because they trust Mellette, Justin and me. Then there will be those, like Ivy Comfort, who won't even acknowledge you." She smiled. "Ever."

"Even if I prescribe an anti-inflammatory for her that does more for her than her herbs?"

"Even if you prescribe an anti-inflammatory for her that cures her rheumatism. That's just the way she is. The way a lot of people here are, and you'll have to accept it. As in not taking it personally when Ivy walks in that door and instructs you to fix her a cup of coffee."

Alain laughed. "Actually, I make a pretty mean cup of coffee, so Miss Ivy and I might just hit it off."

"Don't count on it," Maggie warned, smiling. She liked this man. Liked his seriousness, liked the way he fixed on his task. And, Lord knew, she'd watched a good bit of that these past few days.

"So what you're telling me is that in order to get along in these parts, I'd be better off sticking to my carpentry work?"

"Probably."

He smiled, and arched wicked, sexy eyebrows. "Then I guess that's what I'd better get back to. If you need me…" He raised fingers to his mouth and faked a whistle.

"Trust me, I will." With a fair amount of pleasure, actually. "Oh, and, Alain, I'll know more from my law firm tomorrow on whether or not they're going to take on your case. The partners are going to have a meeting on it first thing in the morning."

"Any indication, one way or another?"

She shook her head. "Although I can say that they usually go with my recommendations. In fact, the only thing they ever fully reject is my suggestion for the office Christmas party. I like glitz and glitter and all the trimmings, and they like to keep it…sedate."

"You don't like sedate?"

"For a holiday, it's boring. And why be boring when you can be over-the-top?"

"An over-the-top overachiever." He gave her a slight bow as he stepped off the front porch. "I bow to your abilities."

"And I accept that bow," she said, laughing. Yes, she really liked this man. Now all she had to do was get him out of the mess he was in. Which meant, if the partners took him on as a client, no mixing of business and pleasure. Too bad, as she had an idea the pleasure part could have been way over-the-top, as well.

CHAPTER THREE

SHE HELD OUT her hand for him to see a grouping of the tiniest marks. They *hurted* her, she told him. "My ouchie." In reality the wound was from the common stinging nettle, a very uncomfortable plant with which to make contact. But it was nothing that required medical attention, which made Alain wonder why she was here.

"And you came to me all by yourself?" he asked, quite touched by the girl. Her big brown eyes were sad, and huge fat tears welled up in them.

"'Cause you're the doctor. Aunt Gertrude told me to come over here, that you could fix it for me."

He was flattered and angry at the same time. Lilly, as she called herself, couldn't have been more than six, maybe not even that old, and a child that age had no business wandering around the bayou all by herself. "Well, your Aunt Gertrude was right about that. I can." A nice stream of hot water usually did the trick, or a generous coating of calamine lotion.

"Dandelion works," Maggie offered as she entered the exam room, carrying a glass of juice for the child.

Alain shook his head. "Nothing herbal…"

"Just saying," she quipped as she handed Lilly the apple juice.

He nodded as he led Lilly over to the sink and held her hand under the water while she was distracted, drinking her juice. "So no one's with her?" he asked, trying to sound matter-of-fact.

"Not a soul. Miss Lilly Anna Montrose was a big girl today and came all the way here from Grandmaison by herself."

Grandmaison, a good two-mile walk. Now he was downright mad, angry enough to spit nails at someone. "Well, then, I'd say Miss Lilly was one brave little girl today. That was a mighty long walk for her to take all by herself."

"People around here are independent," Maggie said, but not in defense of Lilly's aunt, who'd sent her off alone. "They start that independence young in some cases."

"Too young," he said, looking at the hand where the nettles had stung the child.

"Can't say that I disagree. I was as surprised as you when she showed up here a little while ago. Oh, and she also brought payment." Maggie held it up. It was a quarter.

"Is that your money?" Alain asked the girl.

She nodded. "I've been saving up. Aunt Gertrude told me I had to use it to pay for my 'pointment. Is it enough? 'Cause I have two more at home."

"As it turns out, that's exactly what I charge for fixing a nettle sting."

She handed the empty glass back to Maggie. "Thank you," she said. "That was very good."

"Would you like some more?" Maggie asked.

The little girl nodded shyly. "All we ever get to drink is water. Sometimes tea, if we can afford it."

"Look, Lilly, I need to go get some special medicine to put on your hand. Would you mind sitting up on the table until I come back?"

"Okay," she said, then smiled. "It doesn't hurt so much now. Maybe it was the apple juice."

"Then I think we should give you some apple juice to take home with you, in case it starts hurting later on. Do we have enough to send some with Miss Lilly?" he asked Maggie.

"Full supply of it, Doctor," she said, stepping back as Alain lifted the child up onto the exam table.

"We'll be right back," he said to Lilly, then followed Maggie into the hall. "She's malnourished, unkempt, I doubt she's ever seen a dentist or a doctor and God only knows what kind of parasites or other bugs she's infested with. And a two-mile walk?"

"I need to figure out what to do about her," Maggie said. "Because if her aunt's house is like what I'm expecting…"

"Then we can't put that child back in there. Do you know her aunt, by any chance?"

Maggie shook her head. "But I know a child social services worker and I think I'll give her a call before we decide what we need to do about Lilly."

"What I need to do is not send her back into a home where an adult would allow her to come here by herself."

"Don't jump the gun, Alain. We haven't even seen that house, and we sure don't know the circumstances…"

"Yeah, well, I can only guess!" he snapped. "I saw

those conditions in Afghanistan, where children were robbed of their youth, like Lilly is. So much poverty, so many health problems…" His eyes went distant for a moment. "Landmine victims…just children. You can't even begin to imagine…"

Maggie laid a comforting hand on his arm. "No, I can't," she said softly. "And I'm sorry you had to see such atrocities."

"Seeing them is one thing, but living them is another." Said in bitter despair. "And not being able to do anything to fix it."

"I can't say that I even have a clue what you're talking about. My life, for the most part, has been pretty sheltered. Never any hardships, never any threats."

"Then you were lucky. Because a lot of the world out there is ugly. Like I think Lilly's world is probably ugly, too. Look, she needs a bath, Maggie. And a good head scrubbing as I'm pretty sure she's got lice. Could you do that for me and give her a good going over to see what else we can find?"

"And clean clothes," Maggie said, knowing there were no little-girl clothes at Eula's House. "I'll call my dad and see if he can bring something out for her. Shoes, too. I'm betting there still some things left over from one of our childhoods stashed away in the attic."

"He'd do that?"

"My dad is a real softie when it comes to little girls. He always threatened to trade a few of us in on boys, but I think he liked sitting at the head of an all-female kingdom, being adored by his flock."

She truly liked Alain's sympathies. More than that,

she was surprised how easily they were jostled to the surface. He seemed more like a man who held everything in, yet the instant Lilly had walked into the clinic and held out her tiny, grimy hand, he'd melted. And not just a little. "I have money," she'd proclaimed. But she'd had more than that. In that very instant she'd had Alain's heart. And a very tender heart it was indeed.

"So what's the prognosis?" Alain asked an hour later.

"Lice, like you thought. I did the treatment, and cut her hair a little to get rid of some of the mats. And she's about ten pounds under her ideal weight, a little on the small side for a child her age. She has very bad skin, lots of bruises and cuts. Missing some baby teeth. No education, no attempt to teach her to read. But she's very bright. And she loved her bath. I found an old bottle of bubble bath left over from Eula, and I think this child would have stayed in the water and played all day long if we'd let her."

"Any health concerns?"

"Nothing significant that I could find. Heart and lungs sounded good, eyes are clear, ears turned out fine after I cleaned them. She does have a few open sores, probably infected bug bites. No real signs of physical abuse. More like extreme neglect. All in all, I think she's a healthy child, but I would like her to be seen by a pediatrician at some point for a complete exam."

He sighed heavily. "So what do we do in the meantime?"

"I've talked to my friend from Child Services and she's going to come investigate, but that may take a couple of days. If we think the child is in imminent danger we can surrender her to the authorities and they'll put her into the children's home until the case can be investigated."

"Which isn't a solution, either."

Maggie shrugged. "You could keep her here, if you get her aunt's consent. Provided her aunt is her legal guardian."

"And just what would I do with a child?"

"Protect her. Look, this is a gray area in the law, because the authorities don't like to separate a child from his or her family without just cause, and so far we don't know if we have that cause. We suspect it, but suspicion isn't enough."

"Bet we'll find some pretty damning evidence it if we go over to Grandmaison and knock on her aunt's door." Alain clicked into his cell phone and dialed a number. "You up to babysitting for an hour?" he said as Maggie brought a freshly scrubbed Lilly into the kitchen. She was wearing a shirt that came down to her ankles. It was cinched around the waist with some gauze strips. And she was barefoot. Clean, though. Clean and beautiful, with bright eyes and a shy smile. "I have a house call to make and I seem to have found myself a little friend to watch over for the time being."

Amos Picou, on the other end of the phone, was more than happy to do the honors, and he was there within ten minutes, immediately engaging Lilly in stories of Big Swamp. "He comes around every day, checking the work we're doing, making sure we're doing it up to Eula's standards. He seems like a nice man," Alain explained.

"A very nice man," Maggie said, changing out of her work shoes into ankle-high walking boots.

"We're driving," Alain told her.

"Maybe that's your intention, but once we get to Grandmaison, there's no telling what we'll be doing or where we'll be going." She tied her long hair up in a bandanna and, as was her habit, she grabbed up her backpack full of medical supplies. Looking more like an outdoor adventurer than a nurse, in cargo shorts and a T-shirt, Maggie was the first out the door and likewise the first one to her car.

"You're driving?" Alain asked, running to keep up with her. Like Maggie, he had hiking boots, only they were laced together and slung over his shoulder.

"My car, and I know the roads. Seems like I'm the logical one."

"Not complaining," Alain said as he hopped in alongside her. In a split second they were off, speeding down the road as Amos sat on the front porch, entertaining Lilly.

"Are you always going to get this involved?" Maggie asked, once they were underway. "Because there are a lot of people out here who could use some help. That's why I keep coming back. Mellette asked me out here the first time and it became addictive, giving medical care on the most fundamental of all levels."

"I'm not involved," he said. "Just concerned."

"Lie to yourself, Alain. Lie as much as you want, but to the people looking in, you're involved. Don't know why, not going to ask questions, not going to pry. But let me warn you. When you get too involved, it breaks your heart."

"Has your heart been broken?" he asked.

"Be more specific. Has my heart been broken by…a man, by medicine, by life in general?"

"Any, or all."

"Yes to all, I suppose. I've had a couple of relationships that totally fizzled because…because I am who I am. One man just bored me and the other insulted me. And both of them thought I should change into the woman they wanted me to be. One dumped me, I dumped the other. Good riddance to both."

"So you're an overachiever and a hard case. What other attributes are you hiding, Maggie?"

She smiled. "The ones where I march to my own drummer, as they say. Learned it from my mother, polished it thanks to Mellette, who takes stubbornness to an art form. And tempered it thanks to my kind-hearted, sweet father." She swerved to avoid a bump in the road, and in doing so hit another bump in the road. "Damn it," she muttered.

"A little temper, too?" he asked.

"No. A lot of temper. Most of it reined in most of the time."

"Remind me to stay on your good side," he teased.

"Trust me, there are days when I don't have a good one."

"Which is why you want to become a lawyer?"

She laughed. "Nothing quite so complex. I'm going to be a lawyer because I like to argue with people I perceive to be in the wrong. Oh, and win. I love winning."

"Winning for yourself, not for your client."

"One and the same. When I'm involved, it's all the way. Kind of like you and children you see as neglected or abused. When you're involved, it's all the way."

"Is my heart hanging out on my sleeve that much?" he asked.

"It is, but it's a good look." A very good look. She liked a big hunk of a man who also had a gentle side. It gave him nice balance, which, in turn, balanced her quite well, too. That was, if they got involved enough for her to even stay balanced. Which wasn't going to happen since she wasn't at the right place in her life to take on any more than she already had. Call it bad timing or misaligned karma, or whatever you liked. Alain Lalonde was one of the good ones who was simply going to have to slip on by.

The journey came to an end at a contraption that looked like an old house trailer with several shanty add-ons. Chicken bones and plastic milk cartons littered the ground outside the structure, along with various other indescribable bits of refuse. Judging from the looks of things, the inhabitants here simply opened up their windows and tossed out their trash. The newer the trash, the more flies buzzing around it.

"It's worse than I thought," Maggie said, following behind Alain up an intentional clearing that served as a path leading from where several rusted pickup trucks were parked, past a graveyard for refrigerators, stoves and other cast-aside appliances, right past an old claw-foot bathtub filled with dirt and berry bushes, and on up to the door, where a welcome mat sat askew on a rotting wooden step-up. "How could anybody raise a child in this squalor?"

"Not very well," Alain said.

She appreciated the safety behind him. He was so large, with such broad shoulders, she felt fortified by his brute strength. And while she didn't know if this was a situation that required protection, having it there in the form of a very buff man sure didn't hurt. "So what's the plan once we knock on the front door?" she whispered nervously.

"Hope someone answers."

"Someone rational," she added. "Because from the look of this place, that could be a tall order."

"Hope you're wrong about that, because I intend on telling them they're not getting Lilly back and asking them to sign the consent form you drew up." One that allowed him to keep Lilly for an unspecified amount of time until her future welfare could be determined.

"Have you given any thought as to what happens if they refuse to sign?"

"I could just keep her, as they sent her to me. Or if worse comes to worst, surrender her to the authorities. However it works out, she's not coming back here, into this mess." Alain raised his hand to knock on the front door, but in midrise the door swung back to reveal a woman who could have been Lilly forty years into the future. "Good afternoon," he greeted the filthy woman standing in front of him. She was rail thin, with frowsy hair, and looked like she hadn't seen the good side of a washcloth in weeks.

She said nothing.

"I'm, um…I'm Dr. Lalonde…the one Lilly came to see this afternoon."

"She got in the sticker bushes even after I told her to be careful, stupid girl. I was hoping you could put some sense in that head of hers." The woman looked beyond him. "Where is she? She's got chores to do and supper to help get on the table in a little while."

In the background, Alain could distinguish the form of a large man in a white T-shirt and camouflage overalls, and he wondered if poor Lilly had been raised to wait on this couple. He could almost picture it, and it made him cringe. "She's safe, Mrs. Montrose."

"Name's Aucoin. Gertrude Aucoin."

"Mrs. Aucoin," he corrected. "And she's not coming back here. I was concerned about her overall condition, and I've called the authorities, who will be stepping in on Lilly's behalf."

For a moment Gertrude Aucoin almost looked relieved. Then her face contorted into anger. "You got no rights. You hear me? You got no right to keep the girl."

"Why did you send her to me with a case of stinging nettle?" he asked.

"Don't know what you're talking about. That child was howling something awful, after getting stuck up the way she was, and I just did the responsible thing, sending her off to get it treated."

Maggie saw that look of relief again. It was there in the woman's eyes, and unmistakable. Something maybe only another woman might recognize. "We'll take good care of her," she said so quietly she almost whispered the words. "But we can't let her come back here, into this. And we need to have you sign a paper that lets us take care of Lilly until we can figure out what's best for her."

Alain held out the paper, along with a pen.

"He won't be happy about this," Gertrude said. "That child has chores that need doing and Joe's not going to be happy at all."

"And that child shows sign of neglect," Alain said, trying to stay calm on the outside when nothing inside him was.

Gertrude looked up, and he saw it in her eyes again. "Do you need help, as well?" he asked.

She shook her head. "He wouldn't dare touch me, or else who would take care of him? But I'm afraid for the child—he hasn't hit her yet, but the way he's been looking at her with such meanness in his eyes, I'm afraid he will…" She took a quick glance over her shoulder to make sure *he* wasn't standing behind her. "Joe never wanted her here, but we didn't have a choice. They just dropped her off one day after my sister died, and told me there was no one else to take care of her."

"You understand why we can't let her come back, don't you?"

The woman nodded as she took the pen. "I don't want her here. Hear me? I don't want her comin' back here." She signed the paper with a shaky scrawl then stepped back from the door. "We live our lives peaceful-like out here. Don't ask nothin' of nobody, and don't expect nothin' in return. Don't want that child around here, either. You understand me? She's yours now, and

I don't care what you do with her so long as she don't go showin' up on my doorstep again." With that, Gertrude stepped back into the shadows of her trailer and disappeared from view.

"I'm not sure what comes next," Alain said.

"Well, I think she just gave you a child."

They stepped off the wooden porch and started down the cluttered path toward the road. "She'll be better off," Alain said, hoping if he said it with enough resolution he might actually begin to believe it.

"She will," Maggie agreed. "And look, I know this isn't what you bargained for, but I'll help you with her until a better situation can be found."

Alain laughed apprehensively. "Look at us, suddenly parents."

"For a day or two."

"She wanted Lilly out of there. I think that's why she sent her to us. To get her out of that situation and hope we'd find something better for her."

"Well, she didn't hesitate to sign the papers. That's for sure."

"We do need to get her to a pediatrician as soon as possible."

"I'll give my mother a call. Back in the day, before she was an administrator, she was a pediatrician. Maybe she'll have time in the next couple of days."

They were most of the way back to the car when Gertrude Aucoin caught up to them. "Thought you should have these," she said, shoving a shoebox into Alain's hands. "They're what came with the kid when she got dropped off. I expect they have information you might want to know."

"What happened to her mother?" Maggie asked.

"Drug overdose."

"And her father?"

"Got himself killed selling drugs on the street. My Joe and I don't have much, not enough to spread around to a third mouth. We didn't want the kid in the first place, and they told us it was only temporary. But that was four years ago, and no one's come to get her. My Joe gets awfully…frustrated. He keeps telling me she's not his problem to take care of and that I got to fix things."

"So you sent her to us?" Alain asked.

"Saw you there the other day when I was walkin' by. You looked all official in that white coat and I thought to myself that you could help her. I was right. You will."

"I appreciate your honesty, Mrs. Aucoin," he said as she started to back away. After that, there was nothing left to say. The authorities would do what they needed to, as would he. Which was driving off and putting this incident behind him. So he and Maggie climbed into the car and sped away, glad to be gone from there, glad there had been no confrontation.

On the contrary, he felt some sympathy for Gertrude, in spite of the fact that she was as much a part of Lilly's condition as was her husband. The thing was, it was her choice. It wasn't Lilly's, though. And that was what he kept reminding himself as they headed back to Big Swamp, a place where he was going to take on the temporary duties of daddy, it seemed.

"It's a good thing," Maggie reassured him as they

puttered along the road without the same sense of urgency they'd felt on their way there.

"I know it is, but what about Lilly? She's been disrupted from her living situation twice in six years now, and I sure as hell don't like pulling the rug out from underneath her again."

"She was being neglected there, Alain. Mistreated and neglected."

"Which justifies removing her, and I don't feel bad about that. But she's going to have to make an adjustment to staying with me for a while then another adjustment when she's sent to a foster situation, and another when she's placed in an adoptive home. And who knows how many more placements will come in between those steps?"

"But she'll be safe, and that's the important thing."

"Maybe it is, but I still feel bad for her."

"We both do," Maggie said solemnly. "We both do."

CHAPTER FOUR

"SO THIS IS the situation. We can take her into custody immediately, but we don't have a family to place her with, and I don't know when one will become available. It could be days or weeks or even longer. The younger children who need pretty much total care always have first priority on our placements, and unfortunately Lilly doesn't fit in as one of the younger children, meaning that she's able to care for herself independently, which puts her in the position of having to go to one of our residential care facilities."

Karen White of the child welfare division was a kind woman, but businesslike. With her plain brown hair pulled tightly into a knot at the nape of her neck, and a thick bone structure that accentuated highly defined cheekbones, she looked as formidable as she was. Alain understood that with a job like hers she had to be formidable, as she was dealing with the lives of innocent children, trying to do what was best for all of them. It had to be tough, but it did bother him that at the end of this particular transaction was a little girl for whom he felt particularly responsible. "Residential care, as in how many children?"

"Forty, maybe more, depending on where we can find her a bed."

His first night with Lilly had been uneventful. Maggie had stayed over, cooked dinner, and everyone had gone to bed early. Poor Lilly simply accepted what was happening to her, no questions asked, no resistance put up. But she did like the clothes Charles Doucet had brought out for her...especially liked the brand-new stuffed teddy bear with the big pink bow he'd given her. Most of all, Alain believed Lilly liked being clean. More than once he'd caught her looking at herself in the mirror and smiling. A child like that, so fragile and vulnerable, didn't need to be warehoused with forty other children.

"And there's no way to get her an individual family any sooner?"

"Never say never in my job, Doctor, but as much as I'd like to be an optimist, I've been at this a long, long time and my gut instinct tells me that Lilly might not find placement at all, because she is able to be independent as far as her daily living skills are concerned. That puts her way ahead of many of our children."

She glanced at Maggie, who was fixing tea for the three of them. "I'm sorry, but this is an area where I can't play favorites, not even for old friends. Every child is equally as deserving of a good placement, and as much as I'd like to see that happen, it doesn't always work out the way we want it to. For now, Lilly will have to be assigned to a care facility rather than a private home."

"I understand," Maggie said, as she poured the brew

into three mugs and carried them over to the kitchen table. "But I'm disappointed, because Lilly deserves better than residential care. Especially after all she's been through…and I'll bet we don't even know the half of it."

"They all do," Karen said. "And we do our best with what's available to us. But what's available is limited."

"So in the meantime…" Alain started, then paused. This was where he was going to step in and do the kind of thing that always got him into trouble or broke his heart. Or both. "Is the document her aunt signed enough to allow Lilly to stay with me until your department can figure out what to do with her?"

"You'd keep her?" Karen asked, sounding quite surprised.

"I'd keep her. We're set up for a child here already…. I'm staying here temporarily, by the way. And I think I can count on one or two of the locals to help watch her while I'm working. So while this isn't exactly the most ideal situation, I think it would be better than sending her into residential care, where I'm afraid she'll get lost."

"We don't lose children," Karen said.

"I know you don't. But children can lose themselves, and Lilly is…very defeated right now. I think an individual situation would work out best for her."

"Plus, you'll have me here part time," Maggie added.

Karen arched speculative eyebrows. "Since when did you become mother material? I remember once, a long time ago, you told me you didn't want to be involved in all that kind of domestic stuff, that you were quite happy to be a professional woman, skip the husband and family."

"That doesn't mean that I don't like children. Just ask my niece, Leonie. We have a lot of fun together."

Karen laughed. "I'm talking long term. A few minutes here and there don't count."

"You make me sound like an ogre," Maggie accused.

"Not an ogre. Just someone who doesn't wear the domestic mantle very well. The good thing, though, is that you know your limitations. So many of the children in our system are the victims of parents who don't recognize their limitations before they do something that's regrettable."

"You make it sound like I'd be one of those who'd keep a child in squalor or abuse them," Maggie argued, not at all happy to be characterized this way, especially in front of Alain.

Sure, she had some qualms about typical domesticity, and maybe she'd said, once upon a time, that she'd never get herself hooked up that way. But she was older now, had seen more of life. Some of her ideals had changed—one of those being her thoughts on one of the things she'd most disliked when she'd been younger. For some reason, it bothered her, letting Alain know that side of her had ever existed.

"Actually, I know you wouldn't. But you'd never allow yourself to be put into a situation where you might feel trapped enough to do the things some people do," Karen said.

No, she wasn't at all happy with this characterization. Especially when she saw the questioning look Alain was giving her. What must he think of her? And how could she defend herself without coming off as looking too defensive, as defensive was often equated to guilty? So rather than standing up for herself, Maggie plastered a smile to her face, took a step back and waited until Karen had gone before she let go and kicked the door shut behind her. Kicked it hard. Put a lot of foot into that kick.

Alain laughed. "If she's a friend, I'd hate to see how your enemies would treat you."

"Years ago, when we were in school, I was more like the person she was talking about. Wanted no part of the perceived establishment. I mean, I had come out of a lot of domesticity that practically overwhelmed me, and I didn't want to surround myself with it. At least, not at that point. But people change. And while maybe I don't come by a domestic or motherly side as naturally as some of the women in my family do, that doesn't mean I don't know how to be domestic or motherly, or can't figure it out. I'm a nurse after all. A caregiver. And I think I'm pretty good at that."

"From what I've seen, you're a damn fine nurse. But in the case of being domestic, there's nothing wrong with being more professional than domestic," Alain said. "My mother was older when she had me and she gave up a brilliant career as an educator to stay home and raise me. I don't think it ever completely fulfilled her, though. I know she wanted to teach but my father was pretty overbearing about having a full-time mother in the house, and I don't think she ever knew she could have both her career and her family. That was another time, and today…there are a lot of choices available to work it out one way or another. Choices my mother never had.

"So you don't have to defend yourself, however you want to be. At least, not with me. Because I believe people should do whatever makes them happiest. Life's short, you know? Why waste it doing something you don't want to?"

"I appreciate that, Alain. I really do. Spoken by the woman whose family is the perfect example of everybody doing what makes them happy. Anyway, speaking of you…I finally got that call from my law firm, and they've agreed to represent you in trying to get the charges of malpractice dropped. I'm the investigator they've assigned, since I'm the one who brought the case. Although you will have to meet with one of our attorneys before we can get anything formal started. So I've agreed to an appointment tomorrow morning, if that works for you."

"What about coverage here? I've got a couple of patients who said they might stop by. Nothing definite, but I'd hate to miss them if they do come in."

"I'll see if my dad can come out for a couple of hours. I'm sure he'll want to watch Lilly for us, and maybe he can bring Leonie for her to play with. And in the meantime…I do have to get back to town this afternoon. I have a client to meet, and I've got to pull a split shift at the hospital this evening. So will you and Lilly be okay out here by yourself, or would you rather bring her back to town, where Justin and Mellette and my parents can help watch her?"

The idea of looking after Lilly all by himself had never really crossed his mind. Somehow, when he'd made the decision to keep her, Maggie had been in that picture. Admittedly, now that Maggie was going to take an exit, it made him nervous. "I may bring her to town for dinner, and I'd like to stop by my house and grab a few personal items, but we'll be fine."

"Well, the Doucet family will be at your disposal, if you need them. You know that, don't you, Alain?"

If he needed them... It was good to know, even though he intended on seeing this temporary father thing through on his own. "Thanks for the offer, and for making me an incidental member of the family. But I think we'll be able to get along on our own." If he could figure out what to do with a little girl.

As it turned out, the hours of the day ticked by faster than he'd expected. Lilly played quietly in the play yard built for Leonie while patients wandered in and out, and he kept her close by while he switched from doctor to carpenter mode and worked on the expansion project. In fact, he even gave Lilly a hard hat and let her carry his tools and assist in other ways where she could be safe. What he noticed was that she was a very dutiful, very hard worker. And so serious about everything. It almost broke his heart she was so serious—a little girl who had known no joy in her life.

He did want to change that for her, so after his day's activities were over, he gathered Lilly up and took her to town to shop for little-girl things...depending on the good grace of the store clerks to guide him through the task of what a child her age needed. More than that, what a child her age should have. And even though he didn't have a lot of cash to put into the effort, he did manage a stack of nice toys and games and an armload of practical clothes. None of which elicited the least little bit of excitement or happiness out of Lilly.

On impulse, he stopped in at a quick-cut shop and got her tangled mess of hair evened out, and while he couldn't tell if Lilly was enjoying the pampering, he did see that she wasn't afraid of having someone give her that kind of attention, either. And afterward he did notice Lilly looking at herself in the mirror with a kind of distant amazement as she studied her features—studied them like she'd never really seen herself before. While she didn't smile, he did see a spark of life in her eyes... and that was encouraging. He was getting through. Which meant a lot. A whole lot.

"Care for some ice cream?" he asked her.

"Ice cream?"

"You know, chocolate, or vanilla, or strawberry?"

She shrugged her tiny shoulders and seemed to retreat back into herself. Did the child not know what ice cream was? Had she never had it? "It's very good," he said. "Sweet and cold."

"I like sweet," she said so shyly she could barely be heard.

"Then ice cream it will be." On impulse, he called Charles Doucet, who was only too happy to bring Leonie and join them.

"How's Mellette?" Alain asked once they were standing in line for ice cream.

"Resting, and not happy about staying down as much as she has to. But Justin's riding herd on her, and she's just going to have to sit it out much more than she'd used to until she's ready to deliver. Good catch on the preeclampsia, by the way."

"Well, once upon a time that's what I did."

"And Maggie tells me she's on your case now, so that means you'll be doing it again pretty soon. Although I understand you're a pretty good handyman, which is just as impressive as being a good obstetrician."

"Jack-of-all-trades."

For Lilly's introduction to ice cream he chose a bowl of plain vanilla with colorful sprinkles, and the girl dug in like it was the best thing she'd ever eaten. Who knew? Maybe it was.

After ice cream, they took the girls to a nearby park, where three-year-old Leonie knew exactly how to play, and poor Lilly seemed at a loss what to do with something as simple as a swing.

"I don't think she's ever been to a park," Alain commented to Charles. "In fact, I don't think she's ever done much of anything other than being a slave to those people."

"Well, my granddaughter is a little livewire. Bring Lilly around often enough, and Leonie will teach her what little girls do. Speaking of which, why don't you leave her with me tonight, and I'll take both girls out to the clinic in the morning? That way you don't have to worry about getting her ready first thing when you need to be getting ready for your appointment."

"Then I could just stay in town tonight, which would make it easier," Alain said.

"And it will give Lilly more time to play with Leonie."

"Are you sure you don't mind doing this? Because Lilly and I would be fine out in Big Swamp tonight, or even in my house, which isn't set up for a child but will suffice."

"She's not a problem to any of us, son." Charles patted Alain on the back. "What's important is you getting to that appointment on time in the morning. My Maggie's looking forward to working on your case, so you want to make sure you make the best impression on her boss as it's her reputation on the line."

"Well, I wouldn't want to do anything to hurt her reputation," he said as they walked over to the sandbox, where Leonie was building a sandcastle and Lilly was watching intently, studying Leonie's every move. "As long as Lilly's okay with the plan…" He bent down. "How would you like to spend the night with Leonie? That will give you the opportunity to play more with her. Then in the morning Dr. Doucet can take you back to Big Swamp, and I'll see you there about lunchtime. Maybe I'll even bring pizza."

"Pizza?" she asked. "Is that like ice cream?"

"No, sweetheart, it isn't. It's like…" He wasn't sure how to describe pizza. "It's like the best food you're ever going to eat." There were so many things to teach her, so many things he wanted her to know, to experience. The thing was, he wanted to be part of that experience. Wanted to be the one to open up a world of firsts for her.

"Pizza's good," she conceded somberly.

"So it's okay if you spend the night here, and I see you tomorrow?"

Lilly nodded, and as she did so little Leonie quietly slipped her hand into Lilly's. New friends. Such a simple thing caused a lump to form in Alain's throat. He really wanted to give Lilly a hug before he left, but she wasn't ready for that. He was, though. Except this wasn't about him. And as he drove away from the park, and left Lilly standing there with Charles and Leonie, he felt the sting of missing Lilly before he was a block away.

"My dad told me about the change in plans, and as this is just a few blocks from the hospital..." She handed him a bag full of cardboard cartons, and the smell of the various mixes of Chinese foods made him aware of just how hungry he was. "I'm assuming you like Chinese. And that you've probably forgotten to eat."

It was after ten, and he'd been working on the entryway to his aunt's house, sanding off old paint and wallpaper, for hours. "Love it."

"Beautiful house," she said, looking around at the scaffolding in place.

"Potential to be beautiful. With a lot of hard work."

"That's how you view life, isn't it?" Maggie asked as she ran her fingertips lightly over some exposed plaster. "With potential?"

He shrugged. "When you're pretty much tapped out, the way I am, that's all there is."

"I like the optimism." She looked straight at him, appraised the plaster dust in his hair, the hole in his T-shirt exposing just a peek of his chest, the bare feet.

"You'll need it for the fight ahead of you, Alain. Winning a malpractice case is never easy, because the public in general is geared to believe that doctors gouge their patients. You'll be fighting a preconceived idea that has nothing at all to do with your case."

"And you're telling me this the night before your firm officially commits to representing me?"

"Just trying to be honest with you." She grabbed a container of egg rolls along with the sweet-and-sour sauce, then smiled. "Now, where do we sit to eat this stuff?"

An hour later, stuffed full of moo goo gai pan, crab won tons, egg foo young and a whole host of other tasty food, Alain retreated to the porch swing, where Maggie joined him. "You have an early-morning appointment, too," he reminded her, stifling a yawn.

"Three hours of sleep, and I'm good to go."

"I used to be that way, back in med school. Then my body protested, or maybe I just got too old to keep up the routine."

"So you're telling me to leave?" she asked him.

"Not so much telling as suggesting that if you want me to be at my best tomorrow…"

"Okay, okay," she said, laughing. "I'm out of here."

"Said the pretty girl to the really stupid doctor," he muttered.

"Said the wise man to the night owl," she responded. Then headed out to her car.

Alain followed and opened the door for her, and for a moment it seemed as if a kiss would be the next logical step. Too logical, too easy. Too tempting under the big, bright moon. So Maggie was the one who forced herself back to reality. He was her client, that was all. And she had to keep it that way. "See you in the morning, and don't be late," she said, backing away from him. "My boss judges a person on punctuality."

"I'll be on time," he said, taking his own step back, as if he'd just realized the same thing as Maggie. "Drive carefully," he said as he shut the car door after her.

And in a flash she was gone, and he was kicking himself for asking her to leave. But damn, this hadn't been a date, and she'd had no intention of staying over. Still, he didn't feel good about what he'd just done. Maybe because Maggie had suddenly become his lifeline—a lifeline he hadn't known he needed.

Jean-Pierre Robichaud decided to take the lead on Alain's case. He was an impressively large man, with dark chocolate skin, short gray hair and a deep baritone voice that drew attention even if he was only reciting the alphabet. Jean-Pierre had the experience necessary to win the very toughest cases. In point, he hadn't lost a case in over a decade. "You have a very impressive background, young man," Jean-Pierre began the meeting by saying. "Good work history, excellent military history…" He riffled through the pile of papers in front of him for a moment, then looked up at Alain. "Fighting cases like this one is not easy, regardless of the circumstances. But I don't think you deserve being destroyed for something you didn't have any control over.

"So, with the approval of this firm, we've agreed to represent you, and while we know your finances are not in good order, we believe you've paid the price with your military service. Meaning this one is courtesy of the house, Dr. Lalonde. You've done good work for the country, and from what Maggie is telling us, you're doing good work at her family's volunteer clinic."

"I didn't expect this to be pro bono work, sir," Alain responded, not quite sure what to make of the generosity being offered. He was a man who always paid his way, no matter what.

"Don't look the proverbial gift horse in the mouth, young man. It's a simple gesture—nothing unexpected is going to pop out at you later on except maybe a consultation on my niece, who's at the beginning of a very high-risk pregnancy. We may be wanting a second opinion down the line, and it seems high risk is your specialty."

"I can do that," Alain said. "But I won't step on professional toes."

"Didn't expect that you would."

"Well, then, I appreciate what you're offering me."

Jean-Pierre offered him a generous smile. "It's going to be a tough fight, Doctor. Always is under these kinds of circumstances. But our goal here is twofold. First to prove your innocence, then to get your reputation back. It's amazing how even an innocent verdict has a stigma attached to it."

"Once you've been sued—" Alain sighed "—it never goes away, even if the charges are dismissed or the case is won." One of the partners in his medical practice had won the case and lost his career because his patients had no longer trusted him.

"Exactly. But part of what we do is repair that damage, help restore the reputation. That's as important as winning the case. So whatever happens over the next weeks, don't get discouraged. You've got a good case, and we'll prove it. And prove your reputation, as well."

"Again, I appreciate what you're doing."

"Don't thank me. Thank Maggie. Normally we come in at the request of the hospital. In fact, you're the first case we've taken on a personal basis."

"She *is* persuasive, isn't she?" Alain said, looking over at Maggie, who'd been uncharacteristically quiet throughout the meeting.

"Yes, she is when she believes in a good cause. Which is why we hired her and why we're hoping to hang on to her once she gets through law school." Jean-Pierre stood and extended his hand to Alain. "I'll be in touch as soon as I know something. And in the meantime, if you need anything, or can think of anything that should be added to the case, please let Maggie know. Oh, and just to clarify a point, you're not going to countersue in this matter, are you?"

Alain shook his head. "What's the point? It just looks vindictive, and that won't help my reputation. All I want is out from under. A chance to go back to work with my reputation intact."

"Then that's what we'll go for," Jean-Pierre said.

"And what we'll win," Maggie said once they were out the door. "He only takes the biggest cases."

"So why mine? Nothing about this is exactly high profile."

"His son served in Afghanistan a couple of years ago.

Was critically wounded, and rescued by a medic who was wounded saving André. Jean-Pierre is as tough as they get in the courtroom—no one I'd ever want to go up against. But he has a soft spot for soldiers."

"Sounds like I've got a damn good team lining up on my side," he said, feeling the first surge of optimism over his future that he'd felt in a long, long time. Thanks to Maggie. "Look, I know it's too early to ask you out for a drink, but would you care to join me for a coffee?"

"Take me someplace where I can get a beignet to go with that and it's a deal. And let me warn you, Alain, I can eat my weight in good beignets."

"I know just the place, down on the riverfront. Want to take a walk or go for a carriage ride?"

"Would you believe that in all the years I've lived here, I've never been on a carriage ride of the city?"

"Have you always been alone? No marriages or near misses?"

"I'm not exactly a socialite, but I'm not a hermit, either. Back when we were kids and my parents gave fabulous parties, my sisters were always trying to find ways to sneak in or to hide somewhere and watch it. I was never that way. Never particularly interested in what went on. Didn't date in high school because I never met a boy who caught my attention. They all seemed sort of silly to me. And I barely dated in college because I was too busy studying and trying to get ahead. You know…multiple goals. Be a nurse, be a lawyer. That takes a lot of time.

"Then in my adult life…" She shrugged. "I suppose that if you don't put the signals out there, or in my case don't know how, no one's going to show much interest. I mean, I've dated, but my dad says I lack the attention span for it. My mother says I'm just too choosy."

"And you?" he asked as he hailed a carriage. "What do you say?"

"Honestly, I don't know. I don't think I've ever met anyone I can see myself with well into my future. And, see, that has to be the thing. My parents have such a good marriage, and if I ever do it, that's what I want. But statistics are against that these days, aren't they? Isn't marriage rated at, like, fifty-fifty? And I don't want one of those *trial* marriages before I do it for real."

"So you just stay away from it altogether?"

"Not altogether. Let's just say I'm judicious. Of course, that leads to spinsterhood, doesn't it?" She smiled. "And I'm very good at that. Not unhappy with it, either."

As the carriage arrived, Alain helped Maggie up and onto the seat and took his place next to her rather than across from her. It was an open carriage, very elegant. White, pulled by a white horse. Maybe something more appropriate for romance, she thought as they ambled their way through the French Quarter, by Jackson Square, with all its statue people and tourists mingling in the street. She especially liked seeing all the beautiful bougainvillea in bloom, draping itself from various doorways. And the wisteria…to die for. Her New Orleans. The reason she could never leave. She loved it all too much. Couldn't imagine her life anywhere else but here.

Using her phone, Maggie snapped multiple pictures

of things she'd seen hundreds of times before, but she was a tourist today, getting herself caught up in the festive atmosphere the way most tourists did. Once, when he wasn't looking, she snapped a profile picture of Alain against the backdrop of the President Andrew Jackson statue, then looked at the image on her phone. He was really quite handsome. A veritable prince, riding along in the carriage, looking so regal and in control of himself.

She enjoyed looking at him, from afar, or up close. Liked him best in his low-riding jeans and T-shirt, though, rather than sitting atop a marble horse like President Jackson. The rugged Alain was how she thought of him. He was a real sigh-maker. Of course, he wasn't so shabby in scrubs, or even his gray suit. Truly, he was a man worthy of a second or even a third look, she decided as they clip-clopped along the street and exited the carriage at an open-air café, where she noticed that he was a man who also drew a fair share of admiring glances from other women. And just for this little while, she was the one who had him.

It was a strange sensation, feeling the burst of pride that came from being Alain's girl, even if only for a few moments. One she'd never felt before, not with anyone. One she liked, nevertheless. Liked a whole lot. But it was also a sensation that frightened her, as she knew she might like to be in this very same position again. Maybe she would have under other circumstances.

But he was a client. *Her* client. And the law firm had a very strict policy where members of the firm could not date or otherwise fraternize with clients. One with which she fundamentally agreed. So, while she'd finally found a man who might prove to be more than a casual acquaintance, there was nothing she could do about it. Alain Lalonde was off-limits to her in every way but professional.

After beignets, she told herself. *After beignets.*

CHAPTER FIVE

"We went shopping for some basics and Lilly decided she wants new shoes other than the white sneakers I bought her." White, basic, perfect for everyday wear. "Something frilly that maybe she can wear to a party. She said she's never had anything pretty like the shoes she saw in one of the windows, and she wants a particular pair that has a bow and sparkles. Not just regular sparkles, though. Pink-and-purple sparkles."

Alain took a long drink of water from an aluminum bottle and wiped the sweat from his brow with the back of his arm. So far, he'd had no patients come in today, which worked out well since he was in the middle of setting in new overhead beams that would separate the old clinic from the small minor surgery he was building onto the rear of the building. And nearly exhausting himself doing so for the past six hours, busting himself as hard as he could to get the beginnings of the framing completed.

For once, he truly believed all the different responsibilities he'd taken on were going to be the ruin of him. Carpenter, doctor, father… He knew other men did this day in, day out: worked backbreaking multiple jobs to support a family. Did it with grace and style. And he had all the compassion in the world for them. But he wasn't one of them, and he'd admit it to anyone who was listening, because this was killing him. Physically breaking him down into an exhausted heap, as he wasn't used to it. Knocking him down with every weakness he had, then jamming them in over and over. Sissifying him. Although he sure as hell didn't like admitting he was a sissy.

So he took another drink of water, wiped the sweat off his face yet again and hoisted the shorter of the beams up on his shoulder. "I told her that I couldn't get them for her now, and while she didn't put up a fuss or even complain a little, the look of disappointment on her face... Damn, being a father is hard when that's what you're met with. How did your dad manage with seven daughters playing on his emotions, and I'm guessing that was pretty much all the time?"

"First off, he did have help. My dad was the soft one, my mother much more the one to put things in proper perspective. As in saying 'No!' But as far as being daddy to seven girls... I think with him that practice must have made perfect. You know, trial and error. Try it out on one, and if it worked, do it again on another. If it failed, try something different."

She smiled fondly. "I think he would have welcomed seven more girls into the family with grace and never complained. He's such a...good man. Nurturing. Caring. Not that my mother wasn't like that because she was. But she never let any of us get away with the things Daddy did, and still doesn't."

"Well, Charles Doucet should write a book on raising daughters, because I think it could be a best seller. I know I'd buy it and commit it to memory. And as far as the shoes go…"

"Pink *is* a pretty popular color with girls Lilly's age. I remember I had my own pink stage going on for a few years. Everything I wore had to be pink. My bed was pink, the side of the room I shared with Mellette was all decorated in pink…unlike Mellette, who tormented me with ugly colors like orange and green. On purpose."

"And what did your father do about that?"

Maggie laughed. "Taped a dividing line down the center of the room. Told me I had full control of my side, and Mellette had full control of her side. And the first one who encroached on the other lost all rights to the color scheme and the other one of us could then do the decorating."

"Man's a genius. Pure genius."

"He is. With the patience of a saint because he was the one who took each of us shopping for our color choices. My mother was of a mind to paint everything all white and let us deal with it, but Daddy was into letting us express our creativity."

"And you expressed yours in pink."

Maggie nodded. "As pink as you could make half a room. It was a hideous room, really, and Mellette and I still laugh about it, but at the time it was an important part of our growing up."

"Like pink shoes for a little girl who's probably had no other choices allowed in her life."

"Something like that."

"So now we get down to the other issue. Do you honestly think I look like someone who should go traipsing into a children's store, looking the way I do? Lilly and I went to a discount mart, so it didn't matter that I looked totally out of place in the children's department. But in a frilly little store for little girls?"

She appraised his jeans with holes in the knees, his torn T-shirt, his work boots, his tool belt and hard hat. "You do look a little...rough, now that you mention it."

"Which means the shoes will have to wait. First, until I have time to go back and buy them. Second, until I can afford them. They cost half as much as the five outfits, shoes and unmentionables I got her at the discount store. And third, I do need to find some kind of courage to get me through those doors because..."

Maggie laughed. "Too frilly for a man of your many talents."

"Would your dad go into a store like that? It had unicorns in the window, Maggie! Pink, blue and purple unicorns."

"He has, and he would."

"Then he's a better man than I am."

"Not better. Just *differently* experienced. You didn't have time to work yourself up to daddyhood. It was just thrust upon you. One day you were single, the next you were...encumbered. But trust me, in time a store like that won't faze you, not even looking the way you look right now." She took a good, hard look at him and curved her lips into a warm smile. "And I'm guessing the store clerks might even appreciate the look. But... until you get comfortable with the concept, I could take her, if you want me to," Maggie said. "And pay for the shoes. It's not a big deal, really."

"For you, maybe it's not a big deal, and I appreciate the offer. But I'm the one raising Lilly right now, and I want to be her provider. She has a roof over her head, friends to play with, she's fed and that's more than she's had before, so the shoes will have to wait."

He stepped sideways then turned to head into the new part of the structure. "And if that seems like I'm being too harsh, I'm sorry, but that's the way it is. Life isn't always fair. It's hardly ever the way you want it to be, either. Especially when pink shoes are involved."

"Spoken like a man who's been beaten down."

"Beaten down more than once. And learned some hard lessons from the experiences."

"Fine, then no shoe arguments from me," Maggie said. "And you're right. What Lilly needs can't be bought. She has everything that's necessary, and the rest of it can come…or not come, depending on what the court decides to do with her. You're doing an amazing thing, taking care of her temporarily, and she's one lucky little girl to have you."

"Speaking of which, I have a hearing tomorrow before the child services judge, if you'd care to come and stand up as a character witness."

"Jean-Pierre already told me, and I've got the time blocked out. Although these hearings are usually pretty cut-and-dried. Each side presents its evidence—our side why the child should stay with you, their side why she shouldn't. And the judge will usually decide based on the preliminary evidence given."

"And my chances?"

"With most lawyers representing you, not good. But Jean-Pierre's appearance in a juvenile hearing will have some impact, so we're pretty hopeful." She reached over and squeezed his arm. "Like I said, the man doesn't lose. Not even in a hearing like this one. But you've got to ask yourself one hard question, Alain. If you win, do you really want to take care of Lilly for what could amount to be a very long time? She's going to be hard to place in the foster system, and equally as hard to adopt because of her age."

"I've thought about it, and I want to do this. That look in her eyes…it's so sad. I know she won't have a traditional lifestyle with me, but I do think I can change that look, maybe show her what it's like to be happy."

"Just like that?" Maggie snapped her fingers. "From carefree bachelor to surrogate father? You make darned sure it's what you want before we get to court, because once that child is placed, she doesn't need another disruption."

"You don't think I can do it?"

"Actually, I think you can. But you're a little down-and-out yourself right now and I wonder if that's what's pulling you in Lilly's direction. It's a valid consideration."

"Valid, maybe. But that's not me, Maggie. If I make the commitment, I stay with it."

"Trust me, Alain. Taking care of Lilly is about much more than honoring a commitment. Think about it. That's all I'm saying. You have until tomorrow and nobody's going to think less of you if you decide it's a responsibility you don't want or can't handle."

He drew in a sharp breath. "I can do this," he said, trying to hold back his temper. Because this conversation was making him angry. Maybe he didn't have a clear-cut picture on why he wanted to become guardian to that little girl, and maybe to an outsider it didn't look like a good choice. But the fact remained that he did want her. No matter what, he wanted to give that little girl proper care until a family could be found for her. And maybe it was as simple as his mother, who always made room at the dinner table for anyone who needed a meal, or who'd offered a bed to virtual strangers who'd fallen on hard times.

Or maybe it was even simpler. He'd looked into Lilly's eyes and seen her soul—a good soul, a soul that hadn't given up, in spite of her circumstances. Whatever the case, he was sure. "It's what I want."

"Then good luck," she said, and stepped back as Alain handed the beam off to two workers and stepped aside as they lifted it into place. Then he pulled the drill off his tool belt while they steadied the beam in place for him to fasten to the support beams. "Oh, and it would be nice having you sitting there *on my side,* without the skepticism. Sometimes it feels like the whole deck is stacked against me and I don't want part of my legal team helping stack that deck."

"Not the deck, Alain. Just a couple of cards in it maybe, but not the full fifty-two."

"Well, if the majority of the fifty-two weren't tilting against me, I'd be back home, practicing medicine, instead of being in Big Swamp, trying to build a clinic for someone else to practice medicine."

"Give it time," she consoled.

"Time, I've got. And that's about all I've got." He screwed another few bolts into the wood, then stepped back to appraise his work. "It's beginning to look like what it's supposed to be," he said with some pride as he glanced across to the enclosed play yard as Mrs. Dolly Tremaine brought Lilly outside for some afternoon exercise. The people here were so good to him, a virtual stranger, helping him out the way they were. People to trust, he decided. People he liked. "And I'm hoping that inside two months it can be used as a minor surgical suite without collapsing the way my life seems to be."

"Want me to swing from your rafters in order to prove they won't fall down?" she offered.

"That's displaying an awful lot of trust. Foolish trust, if you ask me."

"But you've built before, haven't you?"

"One of the many things I did to get myself through school."

"So you know what you're doing." Statement, not question.

"Up to a point."

Maggie laughed. "Hoist me up, let me prove it."

"No way in hell I'm going to let you swing from my rafters. If anyone's going to do it…"

With that, Alain pulled himself up on the beam and did several chin-ups. Quite successfully. Nothing budged. Nothing fell down.

And Maggie fanned herself, watching all that brawn

flexing itself. "Not bad," she finally managed to say. And she didn't mean the chin-ups.

"Not bad? That's it?"

"Um, makes a respectable frame for a surgery. Especially if any of the patients who come in here want to do chin-ups."

"Very funny," he said, lowering himself back down then dropping to the ground.

"If you have a sense of humor," she teased.

It was an obvious flirt. Even he, as oblivious as he was to most things, could feel it. But what he didn't know was if she was responding to his flirting or he to hers. Whichever the case, the last thing he needed was to add one more complication to his life. Especially a complication that came in the form of one of his legal representatives. Conflict of interest, no doubt. That had been a rule between members of his medical practice and patients, and he was sure it had to be a rule between members of the legal practice and clients.

Still, he liked the flirting. What man wouldn't? "Think your sister will approve of everything we're doing here?"

"Mellette really *did* want to be around for more of this," Maggie said. "She's so invested in the changes, and I know it's got to be frustrating her that she can't be out here, overseeing everything. She's really take-charge that way."

"And you're not? Working as a nurse, working for a law firm, going to law school in your spare time, all with the goal of commingling your medical and legal careers."

"That's different."

Alain laughed. "How?"

She thought for a minute, then laughed with him. "Okay, so maybe my sister and I are alike in some ways."

"Aggressive girls," he commented.

"Which I'll take as a compliment. And thank you for my sister as well, because she'd take that as a compliment, too."

"How's Mellette doing, by the way?"

"Resting comfortably. Physically comfortably, anyway. Emotionally, she's pretty miserable, though."

"That's understandable, especially when someone who doesn't like being kept down is being kept down." Alain laughed. "I've had a lot of patients just like her, who once they hold that new baby in their arms for the first time forget everything else that came before. Mellette's going to be that way, just wait and see. Once she delivers a beautiful, healthy baby, everything will be better. Anyway, does she know if it's a boy or a girl? I'm guessing a girl, since she's carrying it spread out. Boys carry more like a basketball." He indicated a ball-shaped belly.

"Old wives' tale," Maggie said. "Same as if you tie your wedding band to a string and hold it over a pregnant belly. If it goes in circles it's a boy. If it goes from side to side it's a girl." She laughed. "Folk medicine does have some basis in truth, which is part of what we practice at Eula's House, but not in predicting pregnancy."

"Maybe you're right, maybe you're not. My grandmother claimed she always got the gender right. If it's a tight little ball up front it's a boy, if it spreads out all the way around it's a girl. She swore by it, and her patients swore by her predictions."

"Was your grandmother a doctor?"

"A trained nurse and midwife with lots of practical experience taught her by her mother, who had no formal training. They lived in a small community, not unlike Big Swamp, and the women of my family were the ones who did all the birthing. My grandmothers on my dad's side as far back as the genealogy goes. I think that's the reason I chose obstetrics, because I was always amazed when my grandmother walked into the bedroom empty-handed, and a little while later came out with a squirming, crying, brand-new baby."

"You really liked that?" Maggie asked.

"Actually, at first it creeped me out, hearing all that screaming and shouting coming from the other room during the birthing process. She had a birthing room in her house…a house with very thin walls. And if I was staying there and one of the women actually came there to give birth, I'd hide under my grandma's bed, put my baseball mitts over my ears.

"Then one day my grandma asked me to come in and help her. It was a breech birth, twins. She had me pushing down on the woman's fat belly, sort of turning the baby, as I recall. And I could feel the babies in there, alive, trying to get out. Grandma got them turned easily enough, and I saw, for my very first time, a real live birth. It was messy, it about made me sick at my stomach, but there were two little girls who'd just come into the world with my help and…"

"And you were hooked."

Alain smiled. "Hooked, end of story. After that, it's all I wanted. Anyway, my parents were teachers, so we weren't rich, but they put away every spare penny they could save to get me to medical school. And that's the end of my story. Except the part where they don't know their years of scrimping didn't pan out."

"But you took a tour in the military. Why'd you do that?"

"A hitch in the military helped offset some of my school expenses, and I stayed long enough to get all the education I needed."

"And your parents and grandmother?"

"Parents retired from teaching, grandmother was a midwife until she was about ninety. She's gone now."

"And your grandmother's percentages on predicting the gender?"

"Always right, as far as I know. Or if she'd been wrong, I've never been told."

"Are your percentages that good in your obstetrics practice? Because Mellette did have an ultrasound, and it's a girl."

"Old wives' tale," Alain said, as he motioned Maggie back from the O.R.-to-be and pulled out his hammer. "It never let my grandma down. Me, I prefer an ultrasound. That, and Justin already mentioned it to me."

It had been a while since he'd dressed in a suit, and while the necktie wasn't exactly choking him, he sure wasn't feeling easy about things, and it had nothing to do with the charcoal-gray suit he was wearing, or the black oxfords that pinched his feet. Dear Lord, how had he dressed like this on a daily basis? In such a short time he'd become accustomed to a more casual approach to life, and he liked it so much better. But court protocol being what it was called for a more formal version of Dr. Alain Lalonde, and that was what he was about to give them, as Lilly's future did matter that much to him.

He'd tossed and turned all night thinking about it, thinking how it would be easier to simply walk away and let Child Services do what they wanted. But he'd tucked the little girl into bed this evening and read her a bedtime story, and she'd been so eager to hear another one. She couldn't wait until tomorrow night.

Nobody had ever read to that child before, and it was such a simple thing. And maybe that was what convinced him more than anything that he wanted to win this fight—he wanted to read to her, and show her things she'd never seen before. Take her to zoos. And museums. Open new doors…doors every child deserved to have opened.

True to his word, Jean-Pierre, who'd agreed to handle this matter, met Alain outside the courtroom door the next afternoon, with only moments to spare before they entered the chambers. And unlike what Alain had expected—probably a TV version of a courtroom with massive mahogany wall panels, some kind of overhead gallery and enough seats to fit hundreds of spectators, this room was small, no room for a jury box and only two rows of seats for spectators.

The plaintiff and defendant tables were nothing more than what you'd see in a dated library, and the chairs were so straight-backed they were uncomfortable. To top it off, the room was dim and musty, its windows tinted over in a yellowish paint. And the judge's bench was little more than a standard library tables, like theirs was.

Alain felt mildly overdressed for the room, actually. But it didn't matter, because he was about to be judged on everything he said or did—judged and condemned or judged and approved.

"Let me do the talking unless you are specifically addressed," Jean-Pierre Robichaud cautioned him as they took their place at the table. "And quit looking so miserable. This is only a preliminary hearing, and it has nothing to do with the malpractice claims against you. If they do ask you anything about that, which they shouldn't but they might, for God's sake keep your mouth shut!"

"And, please, look pleasant," Maggie said, as she slipped into the chair on the other side of him. "Right now you look like you're about to be lynched."

"This is my first time…" Alain explained.

"Well, with what you've got coming up in the future, you'd better get used to it, because there's a whole lot more of this down the line." She gave his hand a squeeze then loosened his tie for him. "Better. Now sit back and watch Jean-Pierre work his magic."

"Are you sure you want to take custody of the child?" Jean-Pierre whispered to Alain. "It's an odd circumstance at best, and no one would bat an eyelid if you changed your mind and walked away from this. I mean, there are no blood ties, not even a former acquaintance-ship."

"I worked in squalor in Afghanistan, saw and worked with kids like Lilly every day, and couldn't do a damn thing but bandage their wounds. I volunteered at an or-phanage, and nothing I did for those kids made a real difference, but this time I can make that difference. And I want to."

"I didn't know that about you," Maggie whispered.

"There are lots of things you don't know about me," Alain said.

"But I'll find out the further we get into the mal-practice investigation, correct? Because there's going to come a time when you can't keep secrets from me." She gave him a suspicious look, one that showed she knew there was more underneath Alain's rugged surface than he let on. "And you do have them, don't you, Alain?"

He glanced over at her, gave her a curious look, one that couldn't be interpreted, and nodded. "If you have to, that's what we'll do." Secrets from so long ago, bur-ied in a court archive that was sealed. He wasn't sure he was ready to go there again, because he believed his past was buried deep enough. But who knew?

"I have to," she said, "if you want to win your mal-practice case. Jean-Pierre and I can't afford secrets com-ing out at the wrong time. Not knowing is what can lose us our case."

Knowing could cost him his case, as well. So appar-ently his choice was to roll the dice and see how lucky, or unlucky, he was. And he did always have his car-pentry to fall back on if his medical practice was taken away. "Okay, I have a juvenile record. Spent about a year being resentful because my parents were too old, and I did things like shoplifting, joyriding in a stolen car. I was a pretty good graffiti artist, too. Paid with two years of after-school and every weekend labor in a nursing home when I got caught."

Maggie laughed. "I already knew that. I called your school to check you out—part of my investigation— and let's just say that the records they read me were not glowing."

"Do you know about the scar on my hind end?"

"Cleats, when you were playing football in college."

"I had a hernia operation, too."

"Quite successfully." She smiled. "And the nursing notes showed you were a very impatient patient."

"Is there anything you didn't discover about me in your research?"

"Maybe a couple of things, but give me time. I'll come up with them."

"Why do I feel…violated?" he grumbled.

"You're going to be damned grateful for her skills one day, young man," Jean-Pierre said. "She's the best."

"Or the nosiest," Alain grumbled again, then became quiet when the social services representatives entered en masse and took a seat at the opposite table.

One attorney—a formidable-looking woman named Alvira Devereaux, a blonde, mid-thirties man-killer in looks and also by reputation; a social services representative named Olive Olivette, a gray-haired sixtyish woman who looked beleaguered and too tired to care; a young girl named Crystal, who was all shiny eyed and eager, which gave her away as an intern or new hire, as her only job seemed to be to carry the file folder.

One thing for sure, in appraising them they all seemed primed and ready to present their case. And Alain didn't like that one little bit. Over the course of his teen years he'd been in this position too many times, all on the wrong side, facing prosecutors like them. Or more like getting whipped by prosecutors like them while he was being represented by an overworked court appointee who couldn't even remember his name.

Long story short, he wasn't used to winning, wasn't used to being on the side where right and justice and a whole lot of mercy triumphed. Which gave him no confidence whatsoever at this hearing. And who the hell had called it a hearing anyway, when by all intents and purposes it was a trial, with him being placed on the hot seat and examined for his worthiness to take care of a child.

"Formidable representation," the attorney sitting across from leaned forward and said. She was a curvy woman with long black hair pulled back into a braid, and she wore a red skirt that seemed much too small and tight for the occasion, in Alain's opinion. It would have been more appropriate in a bar, after work, over drinks, where the appreciative stares might have been more appropriate. But what he noticed was that under the table, when she crossed her legs, her skirt rode up even higher, barely covering half her thigh. A sight that was definitely not overlooked by the judge, who entered the courtroom without a robe, feasted his eyes, nodded at the group, then took his seat.

Alvira Devereaux knew her way around, Alain decided. And she used it to her advantage. While Maggie was dressed in a sensible, knee-length navy skirt, white blouse, and jacket to match the skirt. Prim and proper.

He sure hoped prim and proper could win the race, because the judge had yet to take his gaze off Alvira Devereaux.

Alain gulped audibly as Judge Henri Breaux began, "This is an informal hearing. Nothing more, nothing less. We're simply here to determine the better short-term care of the child Lilly Anna Montrose, who was removed from her custodial caregivers, her biological aunt and nonbiological uncle."

The judge's eyes skimmed over the red skirt yet again, then fixed on Jean-Pierre. "It's an honor to have you in our courtroom today, Mr. Robichaud. We don't often have a person of your reputation and prestige represented here."

"It's my pleasure to be here, Your Honor," Jean-Pierre said, his voice as smooth as melting butter, even though the look on his face was clear disapproval over the way Judge Breaux was drooling over the red skirt. "It's a clear-cut case where the aunt has granted custody, and since Social Services have seen fit to challenge that, I should think we can dispatch with the matter quickly and fairly since it's all laid out before you in precise legal terms."

The judge nodded then glanced down at the papers. "And what say you, Miss Devereaux?" he asked the opposing attorney.

"What we contend, Your Honor, is that Dr. Lalonde is neither fit nor proper to care for a young child, especially given his circumstances."

"His circumstances?" the judge asked, then looked directly at Alain. "And what would those be, sir?"

"Another legal matter about which we are not prepared to disclose any information in an open situation that has yet to have its day in court, your honor," Jean-Pierre answered. "My client is here today based only on the matter before us, and it is not my intention to allow him to be tried, or even heard, on any other matter.

"Now, I do have to advise the court that I am prepared to present Mrs. Gertrude Aucoin, the aunt to Lilly Montrose, who is ready to testify that she has watched Dr. Lalonde from afar for quite a while and decided, based on what she saw, she wanted him to raise the girl. It would take a postponement and sufficient time to serve a subpoena, which I can and will do, if the court so pleases." He paused for effect then continued. "Mrs. Aucoin is in a delicate living situation herself and I'd prefer not to make that any more complicated than it already is, but if I have to…"

"Witness notwithstanding, Your Honor, there is another circumstance that should be brought to your attention."

"Moral turpitude in question, Miss Devereaux?'

"No, sir, but…"

"Prior convictions or even arrests on suspicion of child crimes?"

"No, your honor, but if you'll allow me to explain?"

"Does this explanation have any legal bearing on this case, and this case only?"

"Can I approach the bench?" Alvira finally asked.

The judge signaled them both forward, and as they

went, Alain leaned over to Maggie. "So what's this about?"

"She's trying to get your existing malpractice suit entered as proof that you're not fit to take care of Lilly."

"Yet I've delivered successfully in hundreds of high-risk pregnancies," he snapped. "Maybe I should go up there and tell him that."

"Look, Jean-Pierre knows what he's doing. Trust him."

"It's hard to trust anyone, especially the red skirt with the wiggle that the judge can't take his eyes off."

"Neither can you," Maggie teased.

"That's beside the point."

"Is it? Even Jean-Pierre, the most devoted husband in the world, is having a look. But those kinds of tactics fall short in the courtroom. The judge has seen it all before, and I mean *all*. Miss Devereaux is obviously new to this, she doesn't have her courtroom style down yet, and while she may be impressing a few of the men here, she's not impressing the legal system, and that's what you need to trust more than anything else."

"You don't dress like that for court. In fact, you're dressed rather…plainly." And in her case plain was definitely sexy.

"I don't even own anything like that."

"Too bad," Alain quipped as Jean-Pierre headed back to the table. He gave Alain a half smile, then sat down, adjusting his massive form into the uncomfortable chair.

"We're good" was all he said as Miss Devereaux yanked at her skirt, trying to pull it lower than the lack of fabric in it would allow it to go.

"So, Dr. Lalonde, your petition would give you custody of Lilly until such a time that she could be placed in a proper foster home. And according to Child Services, they can't specify a time when they can find that home for her, given that she's older, their foster-care system is in need of more caregivers and that younger or dependent children always get the available slots. I believe that about sums it up."

"Yes, it does," Jean-Pierre said, in Alain's stead.

"Also, according to our disclosure, you're not only working as a doctor but you're physically building a clinic addition in Big Swamp, where a number of the local ladies have agreed to look after Lilly during your work hours. I also have letters of endorsement from both Dr. Zenobia and Dr. Charles Doucet, stating that their family is willing to step in and assist you whenever help is required." He glanced at the social services representative. "And you have…nothing substantial to repudiate the letters of endorsement we now have on file. Is that correct?"

"My argument, Judge Breaux, is based on the child services agency contention that having a man stepping in to temporarily raise a young girl is not appropriate."

"Based on what facts?" he asked the attorney.

"Based on appearances, sir."

"Then you would condemn any number of fathers who are raising their daughters without a woman in the house? Or condemning Lilly because she is not a male child? Is that what you're telling me?"

"A father is different," Miss Devereaux continued.

"A legal parent is always different. And certainly we're not condemning Lilly because she's a little girl."

The judge sighed audibly. "This child has no legal parent, and she was willingly given away by her guardian. Given into the doctor's care. Which holds merit with this court, Miss Devereaux, even given the circumstances under which this action transpired. Unless you can produce a family I deem worthy to care for Lilly Montrose before I render my judgment, I intend to find for Dr. Lalonde, and thank him for his willingness to step in and do the honorable thing. So do you have someone right now, right this very minute?"

"No, we do not," Miss Devereaux said, her demeanor now taking on defeat. Slumped shoulders, wrinkles creasing her forehead.

"Very well. Then I find that Dr. Lalonde is a suitable guardian for Lilly Anne Montrose until such a time that better arrangements are presented to this court." He banged his gavel, then stood. And this time he didn't so much as glance at Miss Devereaux, who stood, then proceeded to tug her skirt back into its proper place.

"So what did you say to convince him?" Alain asked Jean-Pierre.

"You said it with your high-risk practice. His wife had a high-risk pregnancy, almost lost her baby and her life, and a very good doctor saved them both. He found that the malpractice suit wasn't admissible, as Miss Devereaux had hoped it would be. And while his visual attention might have been more fixed on her legs, his judicial attention was definitely fixed on the case. Oh, and I expect that Miss Devereaux will get an informal letter of reprimand about her appearance in the next day or so." Jean-Pierre smiled. "Henri Breaux is a good representative of the legal system and he doesn't approve of such tactics."

"Too bad he can't hear my malpractice case," Alain said.

"For that, we've drawn Amelia Tassin, I'm afraid."

Maggie audibly gulped. "I've read about her."

"And I take it what you've read isn't good."

"She's fair," Jean-Pierre said, but hesitantly.

"Fair, if she's having a good day. Which she doesn't have many of."

"She will side with the evidence, which we do have to prove our case," Jean-Pierre said.

"And she's chopped at least two inches of height off every lawyer who's ever come before her," Maggie went on. "I've done my homework, and she rarely sides with the doctor."

"But I've done my homework," Jean-Pierre countered, "and I never lose."

"So I'm sensing that Judge Tassin is not a good choice for us."

"She's not a good choice for anybody," Maggie said despondently as they left the courtroom. "I know Jean-Pierre is optimistic, and if anyone can win in Judge Tassin's courtroom, it will be him. But she's been accused of having a bias."

"If we even go to trial," Jean-Pierre said, then smiled.

"What's that supposed to mean?" Alain asked.

"Nothing yet, but Maggie's on your case, and that says a lot."

"Would you have some secrets, Maggie?" Alain teased.

"One or two. And that's all I'm going to say, except that when I have the time I'm going to get Lilly and bring her back to New Orleans. She needs those pink shoes, and she needs them bad!"

He had an idea that it was Maggie who needed the pink shoes far worse than Lilly did. But who was he to argue? In fact, if pink shoes fixed everything, maybe he'd just get himself a pair, too.

CHAPTER SIX

His HOUSE WAS really no place for a child to stay, at least not for the long term. Half of it was under dusty sheets and half of it was in renovation, covered in plastic and sawdust. He'd managed to make their sleeping quarters and a corner of the kitchen good for the night, but in the long term it just wasn't the place where he wanted to keep a child.

Only thing was, the sleeping quarters at Eula's House weren't much better. With the exception of the kitchen and the room they used as an exam room, it was a total mess. And like his house, only a couple of rooms remained intact. Oh, and the fenced-in play yard. He'd managed to keep the construction totally away from that.

It was strange how only after he'd been awarded custody had he even begun to think of such things— child safety, child convenience, child comfort. Lucky for him Lilly wasn't a fussy child about anything, which did worry him, as children her age had definite preferences. Or should have preferences. But she simply went along with whatever was put in front of her. Seemed content with what she had but not overjoyed with anything. Which was oddly unsettling.

"Is she better today?" Maggie asked on her way in the clinic door to start the morning shift, whatever that might be, since there were no appointments scheduled on the book. "Now that you've explained to her you'll be keeping her for the next little while, what in the world are you going to do with her?"

"I think she'll be easy enough to have around. I mean, she accepted the judge's decision to let her stay with me pretty much the way she did the white sneakers I bought her. It wasn't her choice, but she was polite about it and that's as far as it went. No opinion expressed, no temper tantrum, no resistance. She merely went along with the decision made for her... I kind of wished she'd expressed something, though. Getting through to Lilly would be good."

"You will. Once she's settled in and knows what to expect, she'll do better."

"I hope so."

Maggie stepped up to Alain, who was standing at the window, watching Lilly and two of her friends play in the yard, and gave his arm a squeeze. "Well, just give it some time. Her entire world is changing, and as bad as the one was from where she came, she's just not sure what to make of the new one. Maybe she doesn't want to get attached. Attachment is a scary thing, you know."

"Why's that?" he asked, as he shrugged into a white lab coat, ready to see patients.

"You get used to something then it's gone, as in taken away from you, and your heart gets broken."

"What did you ever have that was taken away?" he asked.

"An almost fiancé. I found him bland, but bland was

safe for me, even though I wasn't quite ready to say yes to a future with him. At the time I was trying to figure out some compromises in my life that would make it all fit together. Then he dumped me, told me I was boring, too much work, not enough fun. Can't say that it broke my heart exactly, but it sure messed me up for a while, seeing myself through someone else's eyes.

"Threw me into the arms of the worst rebound in history…. And the thing I think that broke my heart was that my heart wasn't broken. Made me realize that I was in a place where it was easier to stay…alone."

"Because you couldn't love him enough? I don't think we always have a choice in that. We love whomever we love, and the emotions and motivations directing that are often a mystery that takes a lifetime to unravel."

"But it's a rude awakening, Alain, discovering yourself the way I did. Of course, what came out of that experience is that I know who I am, know what I can and can't do and don't go places I have no place being. Like involved in a relationship. I mean Marc is a good man, to most women he's probably perfect, but I…"

"He wasn't the right man, so you sentence yourself to a life without relationships because of it," he countered gently. "It won't always be that way, especially when the right man comes along."

She nodded. "I think I was combating loneliness with him, and I suppose he knew that all along, or figured it out somewhere along the way. I truly believe he knew exactly where he stood in my life, and that's the worst part. He deserved someone and something better, and all he ended up with was me. Me, Alain! All he got was me."

"Because that's what he wanted, Maggie. He didn't settle. He chose. But you *un*chose for him and pushed him away. See, there's a big difference between choosing and settling. One's dictated by your head and the other is compelled by your heart. He knew you weren't compelled, and that's why he left. I understand that."

"Well, he was right. I wasn't the one for him. After a whole year of dating I couldn't even bring myself to give him an answer when he asked me where we were headed. A *whole* year, and I couldn't figure it out! It was just…"

"Boring."

She shrugged. "Does that make me a terrible person?"

"It makes you human, that's all. But are you going to forever lock yourself away because of that? Because you're just like everybody else and make the wrong choices and decisions sometimes?"

"Well, he did get a nice wife, they have a beautiful child and they're happy. At least it turned out right for one of us."

"So you're done trying?" Alain laughed, but sadly, in a way that showed he knew, he understood. "And you think you're able to put yourself in the position of trying to be all knowing? You think you should be able to predict life, and futures and outcomes?"

"My life, yes. Because I shape it to be what it should be."

"And what if you fall in love someday? Really in love. In love so much you can't stop it or hold it back or do anything other than let it consume your life. And while I'm not saying this will happen, take me for an example. What if you should fall in love with me?"

Her eyes snapped up at him. "Don't even joke about something like that, Alain. Of course I'm not going to fall in love with you. You're…damaged."

"And you're not?"

"Oh, I'm very damaged. But it's something I can only work through alone. Without help. Without anyone there to show me the way. But the difference between you and me is that I know that. Whereas you have some kind of optimism going on that makes you believe you can make a difference. The truth is, in the end, nobody ever really makes a difference. Not one that affects the whole picture."

"So because you can't affect the big picture, you keep yourself isolated. Change the entire world or change nothing at all."

She brushed back her hair, took a deep breath and fought hard to regain her composure. "That's not fair. I try to make a difference where I can. I volunteer at the clinic, which is helping someone. Plus I work in two careers that help. And I'm not isolated. Just look at me. I have a full life, people coming and going, fulfilling jobs with more on the horizon."

"So, see, you do make a difference. And that affects the big picture, whether or not you can see it. One person taken care of today, another life tomorrow—who's to say how any of those lives will turn out? Who those people will become, or who they'll help along the way? You don't have to see the big picture, Maggie, to be part of it. And as far as more on the horizon, more of what?

The things you think you need or the things you really want? Or are you one of those people who can't even admit what you want or need? Not even to yourself?"

"What I want and what I need are more of what I've got. More job. More time to do that job. More opportunities to advance in that job."

"Then 'all job' makes you happy, or is that just a safe place to be?"

She sat down at the breakfast table and poured herself a cup of coffee. It was fresh brewed, smelled, oh, so inviting of chicory and complemented the plate of Annabelle Hawthorne's sweet biscuits she'd brought over the day before in lieu of payment. "I like being safe, and I'm not ashamed to admit it," she said, watching him go and stand at the window and look out at Lilly, who was having breakfast with a couple of sleepover friends in the fenced-in play yard.

Alain was an amazing man, really. Totally at home wherever he was, doing whatever he was doing. Last night he'd held a sleepover for Lilly and invited a couple of the local girls, hoping they would help Lilly open up a little more. On her way in, she'd watched the girls interacting, and in a lot of ways Lilly reminded her of herself—the one always standing off to the side, watching. "And as much as you want to figure out what's going on with Lilly, it may not happen for a long time, Alain. If ever."

"She's so isolated."

"But at least she's there, part of the activity, including herself in it and not completely withdrawing. Which is a good thing."

"Delivering newborns is easier. You may have to figure out some physical problems along the way, but that's easy compared to this."

"You could be right. Being the outcast is always so… difficult. And no matter how hard you try to fit in, something never works, something that keeps you ostracized."

"Is that the way you were, Maggie? The one always off on the side, watching?"

Maggie took a sip of her coffee and sighed. "I was more like that than any of my other sisters. They were always so outgoing and I was so reserved. Sometimes to the point of being backward. At least by my family's standards."

"And your parents noticed?"

"Of course they noticed, and they worried a lot." She pulled a biscuit from the plate and broke off the end, then popped it in her mouth. Once she'd finished swallowing, she continued, "They wanted to fix me, probably like most good parents would want to do for their children. So they took me to a child psychologist, who assured them I was just being me. But that wasn't enough because I was so different. So I was taken to another psychologist and another. In total I can't even tell you how many psychologists I saw, and my parents never got the diagnosis they wanted, one that told them there was something wrong with their little girl. Something they could fix."

"So what did they do?"

"In the end, they left me alone to be the wallflower I wanted to be. I mean, what else could they do other than institutionalize me or commit me to a lifetime of psychoanalysis for something that wasn't a problem for me?"

"Was that ever a consideration?"

Maggie laughed. "No. They knew I wasn't mentally ill but, in truth, I think the reason they dragged me to all these psychologists was to make sure that they weren't being bad parents to me. After all, we didn't have a traditional household. My parents both worked long hours, we had, as they call them today, *au pairs*. Several of them, actually, since there were seven of us girls.

"But the thing is, we were never neglected by our parents. One or both were always there when we had a part in the school play or ran in a track meet. One or both tucked us in every night of our lives. And we made a point of having several family meals together each week. Had movie night, and game night, and popcorn night. My parents gave us their best, but with me I think I made them feel like their best wasn't good enough, so they were looking for help, looking for a solution.

"But all these years later, when I think about it, I think it wasn't about me so much as it was about them. They loved me, but it was difficult having a child so different from the rest of them."

"So you think it's okay that Lilly's off standing under the oak tree while Sandra and Aureille are having a good time playing with their dolls?"

"I think it's a choice that Lilly's okay with, otherwise I think she'd be playing, too. And you do have to let her make some of her own choices, Alain. Or you're telling her that what she wants doesn't matter, which is pretty much where she is right now, believing that nothing about her matters."

He sighed the sigh of a troubled man. "But with her past…"

"Those are issues that will eventually have to work themselves out, but not until she's ready."

"Which will be when?" Alain asked as he watched Lilly move even farther away from the girls.

"Tomorrow or next year or never. Give her space, Alain. Which, by the way, is the same thing as respect. When she totally trusts you, if she's ready, she'll open up. Or not. It may not be in her nature to want to confide to anyone. But, in the meantime, at the risk of sounding like someone who's about to ask another someone out on a date, how about dinner and a movie tonight? I have Leonie this evening, there's a good children's movie playing at the theater and I thought pizza would be the perfect food to go with the rest of it."

"Can I have popcorn?" he asked, smiling.

"With butter, if you behave."

"Behaving is underrated, but for butter on my popcorn…"

"Oh, and it's my treat."

It was like the room suddenly went cold. "You don't think I can spring for pizza and a movie?"

"Personally, I don't think you can spring for anything that isn't a necessity," she said. "And it wasn't meant to offend you. I just thought a nice evening out with the girls…"

"Charity date," he grumbled. "No, thanks. If I want pizza and a movie for Lilly, I'll pay for it."

Rather than being offended by his change in demeanor, Maggie merely laughed. "Male pride isn't very becoming on you, Alain. And it's going to deprive Lilly of a good time. Do you really want to be that selfish?"

"I can see why you were a loner. You were totally disagreeable, and even rude."

"Well, rude buys the pizza. Come by the house at six, and if you're still in a grumpy mood, drop off Lilly and go grumble in the swamp somewhere while the girls have a nice evening out. Oh, and if it makes you feel any better, we'll split the check. You pay for your pizza and popcorn, and I'll take care of me and the girls."

"Do you know how ridiculous that's going to look?"

"About as ridiculous as you sound," she quipped, then grabbed her white coat off the peg by the door and went to greet their first patient of the day, Minerva Jane Craig, who always refused to schedule an appointment. She was a bit of a drinker—homemade stuff— and couldn't understand the headaches that came in the morning. It was up to Alain and Maggie to sort headache from hangover.

As it turned out, pizza was good. Lilly ate with a voracity Alain hadn't seen in her yet. But the movie was another thing altogether, and it scared her to death. So much so that he cut his part of the evening short and left, carrying a very shaky little girl in his arms. Picture too large, noise too loud. Sensory overload, he supposed.

They spent the night at his house in town, a very uneventful night where they watched a little television, he popped corn she refused to eat and they both went to bed early. But in the middle of the night he got a call from Maggie, who'd gotten a call from Justin Bergeron who was on duty at the hospital, who'd gotten a call from his wife, Mellette, who'd gotten a call from Napoleon Dempsey who ran the Big Swamp gas station, and it seemed that Yasbeau Bonchance had come down sick and was close to being delirious, she was in such a bad way.

By the time Alain had cleared his head enough to pull on a pair of pants and a shirt, Maggie was at his front door, followed by her father, who had every intention of taking Lilly back to his home for the night.

"You're driving?" Alain asked.

"I'm faster than you. Know the roads better."

He couldn't argue with that. While he hadn't actually gotten lost out there, he had spent more time than he cared to admit winding the twisted roads—wrong twisted roads that lengthened his journeys. "So who is she and what are her symptoms?"

"I've never seen her before," Maggie said, phoning her sister. "Tell me about her," she said, then two minutes later related the description from Mellette. "She's in her mid-thirties, large, healthy in that she didn't ever come to see Eula as far as Mellette could remember. She's nice."

"So do we know what's wrong with her?" he asked, as Maggie took a turn in the road much faster than he would have and he ended up hanging on to the truck's door handle for dear life.

"Justin said she had a powerful hurt in her side."

"Right side?"

"He didn't say."

"So we could be looking at appendicitis. Or a ruptured cyst. Might be a gallbladder attack, depending where, on her side, the pain is located."

"Don't you ever get patients who aren't very communicative about their symptoms?" she asked him.

"Usually, by the time they get to me they're way more communicative than they need to be because they're scared to death. Seeing an obstetrician who deals with high-risk pregnancy for a problem is almost admitting to something you don't want to face—that there could be a problem with your pregnancy."

"I understand that maybe now more with Mellette than I did before, but still..." She shrugged and smiled as she rounded a gravel curve a little too fast, which threw Alain halfway across the seat until the seat belt locked down tight on him. "People will be people, I suppose. No changing human nature once it's set in."

"How about changing their driving style?" he choked out, unsnapping the belt to free himself and immediately snapping himself back into place.

Maggie laughed. "Sorry about that. One of the warnings about being the introverted girl was that when I turned sixteen and started to drive, I was hell on wheels. Guess having a big hunk of metal surrounding me made me feel brave or something."

"I think it left a bruise," he commented drily.

Maggie laughed again. "Want me to ice it up for you once we get there?"

"I want you to let me drive...always! Whenever we're in a car together, I drive."

"Talk like that could hurt my feelings," she said, teasing him as she slowed down for the next curve.

"Talk like that could save my life," he countered. "You don't drive like that with Mellette's daughter in your car, do you?"

"Actually, Mellette doesn't let me drive Leonie anywhere. That's why my dad always tags along. He's my designated driver."

"Instead of all that money they spent on shrinks for you, they should have saved it for a good driving instructor."

"You're blunt," she said as they pulled off the road onto a long, narrow lane that looked more like a pathway than a road.

"And you're not?" he countered, flinching involuntarily as various vines and branches snapped against the car.

"I would never take one of your psychological vulnerabilities, like you're a baby when it comes to riding with someone else, and use it against you."

She was really enjoying this, enjoying the teasing and the light banter between them. Enjoying it almost as much as he was, and he couldn't, for the life of him, figure out someone as engaging as Maggie could have ever been such an introverted child. "And I would never blatantly tell you you're a menace on the road, except that's a fact of which I'm sure you're already aware."

"I've never been in a wreck," she said defensively, as the house where Yasbeau Bonchance lived with her husband, Henry, came into view.

"The day is just beginning," Alain said as he climbed out of the passenger's seat and grabbed his medical bag.

Yasbeau, as it turned out, was a very large woman, with a sweet smile. She offered to make coffee even though she was definitely in some pain. And her husband, Henry, who was equally as large, brought out a plate of leftover fried chicken in case anyone was hungry. At three in the morning, the snack, while appreciated, wasn't exactly what either Alain or Maggie wanted.

"When did this pain start?" Alain asked Yasbeau as Maggie started taking vital signs—temperature, pulse, blood pressure.

"Yesterday afternoon, when I was fixing Henry's lunch. He likes a big meal midday, since he does such hard work…he's a mechanic. So I cooked him up some black-eyed peas with fatback, corn bread and a bowl of greens. The pain came on when I was greasing up the skillet for the corn bread. It wasn't much, just a twinge, and I didn't think much about it. But it kept coming back, off and on through the day, and got powerful bad when I was frying chicken for Henry's dinner. That's when I had to go sit down for a while and wait for it to pass."

"And did it?" Alain asked.

"Some. It got lighter for a while. But I wasn't much hungry, so I didn't eat much. Henry, bless his heart, did the dishes for me while I settled in and watched some television. I must have dozed off, and Henry just put a blanket over me and let me sleep in my chair. Then a couple of hours ago I awoke with a powerful hurt, and it's not going away. In fact, it's getting worse."

"Where?" Alain asked as he took out the stethoscope and listened to Yasbeau's chest.

"Vitals all elevated," Maggie said.

Alain nodded, as Yasbeau indicated right-sided pain just below her rib cage. Then also indicated some behind her right shoulder blade.

"Any nausea or vomiting, or unusual belching?" he asked.

"Got me a terrible case of nausea," she said, "but not the other."

Alain moved his stethoscope down to Yasbeau's belly and asked her to please lift her blouse, which she did, but only after a stiff nod from her husband. As she was in the process of shifting around, another one of her spells hit and she almost doubled over with pain.

"It's getting worse, Doc," Henry said. "And it's taking her longer to get over each one."

"Gallbladder?" Maggie asked. "Pain's certainly in the right area."

"Maybe, but…" Alain held up his hand to quiet everybody in the room, then placed his stethoscope on Yasbeau's belly and listened for a second. After which he indicated for Maggie to hand him his bag, from which he pulled a different stethoscope. Maggie gasped and immediately turned and ran down the hall toward the bathroom to gather up an armload of clean towels, while Alain listened to a distinct heartbeat in Yasbeau's belly. Two, in fact.

Straightening back up, he looked at her, and she was

as white as a ghost. "Have you ever had a baby?" he asked her.

She shook her head. "Henry and I've been married since I was fifteen and we haven't had the good fortune. So somewhere along the way we decided the good Lord didn't mean for it to happen for us."

"Have you had a period lately?"

Yasbeau shrugged, shook her head. "Never been regular that way. Eula wanted to give me some herbs to help fix that, but I figured I'd be better off just the way I…" Another labor pain hit, following only a couple minutes behind the first one Alain had witnessed.

"Is she…?" Maggie asked, setting the pile of clean towels down on a table next to where Yasbeau was sitting.

"Unless I heard wrong, which could happen, it may be twins."

"Twin what?" Henry asked.

"Babies," Alain said. "You wife is in labor and she's about to give birth. It might be twins."

"Can't be," Yasbeau gasped. "I'm getting too old for that. My mamma quit her childbearing years when she was thirty-five, and I'm already thirty-six." Another pain gripped her.

"Problem is, I have no way of knowing how far along these babies are," Alain said. "And since she obviously doesn't have a clue…"

"Dear God," Maggie said, pulling out her cell phone. "I don't know what kind of emergency transport we can get out here. If any…"

"Labor's fast," Alain said, standing up. "Yasbeau,

I need to get you into your bed and take a look to see how this birth is progressing."

"Ain't no man ever looked down there," Henry piped up.

Alain smiled at him. "I deliver babies every day, and there's a good chance I might be delivering two here in the next hour or so. What I need you to do, Henry, to help your wife get ready for this is to boil me some water, and get me as many fresh sheets as you can find. I'll also need two boxes big enough to hold the babies, and I'll need the sheets in those boxes ready for the babies to stay warm in. Do you understand?"

Henry nodded, then a smile crossed his face. "I did twins?"

"Don't know for sure, but you may have. Oh, and, Henry, since Yasbeau hasn't had any doctor's care while she was pregnant, this may be a little rough. When it comes time for her to deliver, I need you to stand behind her and push her back up and hold her in a sitting position. She may be screaming, but can you do that for me?"

"I can," he said in all seriousness.

"Good. Now, get that water going, and find those boxes and sheets."

"Water?" Maggie asked.

"Need something sterile if I have to do a C-section."

"Oh, no! I hadn't even thought about that possibility."

Alain shrugged. "Trust me, it's a possibility."

Maggie made her phone calls while Alain helped Yasbeau into the bedroom, and by the time Maggie had managed to find an ambulance that would meet them halfway, Alain had Yasbeau ready to examine. It took him about one minute to shout, "These babies aren't waiting. One of them's crowning right now."

Maggie looked in over his shoulder and saw the top of the first baby's head. It was covered in a mass of black curls. Curls that were popping into the world at a rapid speed. "What can I do?" she asked him.

"Take the baby, clean it up as best you can. I have some clamps in my bag so use one for the umbilicus, then get the baby warm."

"Nothing like doing it the old-fashioned way," she said, as Alain helped maneuver the first baby into the world. A boy, fairly good-size, thank heavens. One who started thrashing and screaming the instant he had his first chance. "He looks good," she told Alain as he began his exam for the next baby.

"My kid?" Henry sputtered, with great emotion from his end of the bed.

"Your son," Maggie said, giving Henry a quick peek at the baby before prepping him and tucking him in to a sheet-lined box that had once cased canned green beans.

"Just the one?" Henry asked anxiously, as he held his wife's hand.

"Doctor is checking now to see if there's another one."

"And I'm sure there's one more on the way," Alain announced. "Just a little slower than the first one."

"We've got two," Henry announced pridefully to Yasbeau, as if she didn't already know.

"How far along?" Maggie asked Alain.

"I'm guessing somewhere close to thirty-four

weeks," Alain said. "Breathing seems fine and everything looks normal, but I still want them to go in for a good checkup. Yasbeau, too, since she's done this thing without medical care."

"Go in, as in the hospital?" Henry asked.

"It's best for everyone."

"We don't like hospitals around here," Henry argued. "And my wife and children will be fine without them."

"They probably will," Alain argued back, "but do you want to take that kind of a risk? If everything goes well, they'll be in and out in a day or two."

"I think we should," Yasbeau said as the next labor pain struck. It had been fifteen minutes since the first baby, and a quick check showed that the second one was on its way, in a big hurry just like its big brother.

Ten minutes later, another fine little boy pushed its way into the world, and seemed as healthy as the first one, who'd already been named Henry John Bonchance, Junior. The second was tagged with John Henry Bonchance. Thankfully, there were no more babies to come.

"So what do we do about getting them to the hospital?" Maggie asked as she helped get Yasbeau cleaned up and ready for the trip while Alain examined the twins.

"One of us will have to take the babies to meet the ambulance, and one will take Yasbeau and Henry. And I'm telling you right now, I'm driving the babies."

"You don't trust me?"

"I don't trust you so much that I've already asked Henry to drive his truck so you can look after his wife."

"I should get angry over that," Maggie said, "but I

won't. It was an amazing night." Said as the sun was beginning to wake up over the swamp. "It's been a long time since I've assisted in anything like that and it kind of makes me miss nursing. Makes me wonder if I can squeeze in a few more hours at the clinic, or even at New Hope."

Alain smiled. It had been a good night. Two healthy twins had come into the world to a mother who hadn't even expected them but who was already proving she was going to be the best mother in the world. And he and Maggie had worked so well together. Yes, a good night all the way around, he decided as he handed off the babies and mom to the waiting paramedics at Dempsey's Gas Station a little while later.

Times like this made him want to get back into his kind of medicine so badly he could feel the physical ache of it. But there was also something else bothering him, something that would never be allowed. He'd enjoyed Maggie. Enjoyed her too much. Could even see the two of them, well... No point in thinking about that. She'd made herself perfectly clear on the subject, and Maggie didn't strike him as the kind of woman who'd change her mind once it was set.

Too bad. Because he could almost see great things with them.

CHAPTER SEVEN

"NOT BAD FOR a night's work," Maggie said, kicking off her shoes, pulling her feet up under her on the porch rocker and making herself comfortable in the throw pillows. They were sipping iced sweet tea and eating leftover sweet biscuits.

"Not bad for someone going in expecting appendicitis or worse and ending up with babies. It's been a long time since I've done any of the other procedures and trust me when I say I'd rather deliver twins any day of the week."

"Those babies were over five pounds each, and she never knew she was pregnant. How does something like that happen? How can a woman make it to almost full term and not even suspect she's pregnant?"

"Not enough education, for starters. People here, especially the women, could use some prenatal classes. Also, she didn't go to doctors, which didn't help matters any. That, plus she's a large woman. Some women close to menopause age never suspect that the end of their periods could signal a pregnancy and not the end of child-bearing days. My own mother thought she was in menopause and didn't even suspect pregnancy until she was well over six months along.

"So what happened isn't unheard of. In fact, it's more common than most people know. In fact, cryptic pregnancies—that's what they're called—happen where one woman in four hundred and fifty doesn't know they're pregnant until week twenty or later, and one in twenty-five hundred never know it until birth."

"Well, it scares the bejeebies out of me. So many things could go wrong, especially carrying twins. And she delivered less than a month early. Without complications. And the babies are perfect."

"As they say, ignorance is bliss. But she was a healthy woman to begin with. Strong. Ate good foods, even though she's large. Didn't drink. Exercised. Had everything going for her that a doctor would prescribe. As a result, mom can come home today, and the babies will probably be home inside the week."

Maggie stretched back and looked up at the early sky. "How would it be to get up one morning without any knowledge that you're going to have a baby, then end up being a mother by the end of that day?" She took a sip of tea, then looked out over the yard at the lush greenery. The more time she spent in Big Swamp, the more it was growing on her. She liked the nature here. Especially liked the people.

In fact, she could almost see herself giving up the creature comforts she'd come to expect just to live in a place like this. How would it be to come home after work, spend her evenings and nights working in virtual solitude? No one interrupting her, no one expecting anything of her.

Where she lived, her condo was surrounded by people, and shops, and blaring horns. People whizzed by all hours of the day on bicycles and scooters. Tour buses that made regular routes to the cemeteries, the Garden district and Jackson Square also slowed down so eager tourists could look at the front of the building where her condo was located.

See, what she hadn't learned until after she'd bought her condo was that the building was actually designated as haunted, making it one of the frequent stops on both bus and walking tours filled with people wanting to experience, firsthand, a real live ghost. Amazingly, on Fridays and Saturdays, she even had walking tours that came by at midnight, of all things!

So the solitude out here in Big Swamp was nice. Relaxing. Something she envied. Only thing was, the internet reception was spotty, and cell phone reception came and went, and she needed those connections to the outside world for her work. And the most convenient way in was by boat, right straight through the swamp, which she wasn't fond of. Still, it was a pleasant, if impractical, daydream.

"Actually, that did happen to me just recently. I woke up one morning all free and clear then ended up with a six-year-old child. For sure, it's a life-changer."

"But you're not going to keep her permanently, and that's the difference. There'll come a time when a nice foster or adoptive family will take her, and you'll be able to go back to being free and clear."

"Except children her age are hard to place. I talked to her social worker yesterday and, so far, no luck. No interest in anything, even temporary, and there's a long list of children younger than her waiting to be placed."

"But her placement eventually is something you're going to have to brace yourself for, Alain. Lilly is not your ready-made family and she won't be staying here. I know it's hard not to get attached to her, but on the other hand you could wake up any day and have her taken away from you, and that's just something you've got to be prepared to deal with. Just because she's hard to place right now doesn't mean she won't be placed."

"I'm aware of that, and I'm also aware that would be best for her," he defended himself. "And I want what's best for her, whether or not you think that."

"Oh, I think that. But your given choice in careers is delivering babies, so you must love them, maybe have a stronger bond than most people do because of your career choice, and it scares me to death that you're going to get too attached, then get hurt."

"I know what I'm dealing with here, Maggie. Professionally, emotionally…I go through this every day and know the end results. I don't keep the kids I deliver, and I don't expect to. But I do everything humanly possible to help them while they're under my care. That's what my life is about."

"But the babies you deliver aren't six, and in so much need."

He blew out an impatient breath. "I can draw the line."

"Can you?" she challenged.

"Why do you even care?"

"Because I like you, and I don't want to see you get hurt."

"I suffer through."

"Maybe you do, maybe you just keep it all in. Whatever the case, I'm betting that all that time in Afghanistan was difficult, seeing all those children in need and not able to do a thing to help them."

"That's a different story."

"Is it, Alain?"

"Okay, so maybe you don't get used to what you see going on around you every day, and you try to harden your heart to it. But there's so much of it, and when I was…injured…and I was in the hospital, recovering at first then doing light duty for several weeks, I was in the same hospital where they were taking civilian casualties and it was…tough. I'll admit it. But working in the orphanage, then being there, that didn't make me want to take every single one of them under my wing, so to speak. It just made me glad that in some ways I'd been able to help."

"But Lilly reminds you of one of those children, and it's become personal. She's the one you can do more for than just help. And even if you don't know that intellectually, you feel it emotionally."

"Or you're completely wrong. Maybe I'm just being a doctor who cares for his patient, and Lilly's a patient with extraordinary needs."

"Maybe." Maggie nodded, but she wasn't sure his heart was in his defense. Alain Lalonde was a hard person to get to know, and while on the exterior he just didn't seem the type who wanted that kind of intense emotional involvement with a child, on the inside was he as different as he claimed to be? She did question that. More than that, she was attracted to the part of him he denied. Pretty package to look at, but even prettier down deep. Except she didn't do the down-deep part herself. It was too risky, and more than anyone she knew, she knew exactly who she was and what she wanted.

Also, she was very unbendable about those things. Not even when it came to Alain, a man she was finding herself extremely attracted to. "You may understand all that intellectually, but it's still difficult having people ripped out of your life, especially once they've found a place in your heart."

"The heart heals."

"Does it?"

"Something bad happens, a heart breaks, but people move on with their lives."

"They move on, changed. Because the heart doesn't heal so much as it bends to accept whatever happens." She shook her head. "And while the heart may have this amazing ability to stretch itself in new directions, I don't think it ever really heals from being broken. My sister, after her first husband died, found a new love, but that doesn't mean her heart isn't still broken over her first love. It's just…"

"Reshaped?"

"Reshaped," she agreed.

"Then what you're telling me is that your heart could

reshape, too, to where it includes wanting a different life. Maybe a home and family."

"I...I don't think so. That's a whole different argument."

"Is it?"

"Of course it is. We were talking about broken hearts, not reshaping a life."

"Well, for whatever it's worth, I think you'd be a sensational wife and mother, and I don't think there needs to be that much reshaping."

"A sensational mother who would be more devoted to her work than her child. That's not a good definition of sensational, Alain. That's more a definition of someone who'd suck at it. Look, I've got a legal client to see at noon, and a full afternoon of research ahead of me. Then tomorrow I've got to go into court with Jean-Pierre in the morning, and I've got promised hours at the hospital on the evening shift.

"Most likely I'm not going to make it back out here to help you for at least two days, maybe more than that, depending on how my casework goes. Will you be okay on your own? Because if you think you'll need help, I'm pretty sure Daddy would love to come out and put on his stethoscope."

"I think I'll be fine."

"But with taking care of Lilly? Are you sure?"

He smiled. "Where there's a will, there's a way. And that goes for everything in life."

"Unless your will gets stretched too thin."

"Like yours does sometimes?"

"That's not a nice thing to say. I manage to manage

quite well, thank you very much." She was actually offended that he thought she tended to overdo things. If
nothing else, she'd shown him how utterly efficient she
was in everything she did. Maybe even went out of her
way just a little to prove it to him.

"Look in the mirror, Maggie. You're a beautiful
woman, but you don't smile much, and you look just
plain tired. And you can't deny it because you can't be
objective."

"Nothing a good night's sleep won't fix."

"If you allow yourself that good night's sleep. Which
you won't."

She squared indignant shoulders. "Why do you even
care?"

"Because you work for my defense attorney, and I
need my team fresh and eager, not tired and cranky."

"You're being serious, aren't you?" she asked him.

"Dead serious. You push yourself past the point of
common physical sense and you, with your medical
background, should know better than most people."

Part of what he was saying was right. She did push
herself. Got by on too little sleep and too much caffeine.
But that wouldn't last forever. Thirty-four weeks, count
them. Thirty-four weeks and she'd graduate from law
school. Then she could cut that activity out of her life
and move on into something better. It was a plan…her
plan. And the end was finally in sight. "What I know
is that you don't have the right to interfere."

"Maybe I interfere because I care."

"Well, don't. It won't get you anywhere." That was
the truth, plain and clear.

* * *

True to her word, Maggie was nowhere to be seen for three days, which left Alain plenty of time to be doctor, carpenter and even father. He and Lilly were falling into a routine, though. They'd have breakfast in the morning, after which he'd spend a couple hours homeschooling her. Apparently Lilly had had no formal or informal training whatsoever. She couldn't read or do the simplest math, let alone do any rudimentary writing or printing, but she was an eager, smart learner, and he'd have been willing to bet that she'd catch up to children her own age in no time at all.

After homeschooling, he either worked as a doctor, if he had patients to see, which was becoming more and more the case. Then Lilly would play in her play yard, looked after by one of the local ladies who'd volunteered to help. More like, she held back and simply watched what went on around her. Then Alain would take a quick lunch break with Lilly, after which he went back to work. But as he doctored he supervised the building crews, who were getting closer to finishing the surgery.

Then in the evening he'd spend another couple of hours homeschooling Lilly, they'd have dinner together, she'd refuse to play games but she would settle into watching television occasionally. Then off to bed. Lilly first, then himself a couple of hours later, after he'd read some articles in various medical journals.

And with each passing day he was becoming more and more frustrated that he couldn't draw Lilly out of her shell. "Be patient with her," the social worker had said. But it wasn't Lilly he was losing patience with.

It was himself, for not finding a way to get through to her. Which made him feel like a failure more and more.

"She's come up in uncertainty," Amos Picou said one evening as he stopped by for coffee, and to bring by a batch of herbs he'd picked fresh that day. "And that's all she knows."

"What she knows is that she doesn't trust me," Alain snapped.

"You're right about that. That child doesn't know how to trust anybody, and how can you blame her, coming from where she did, always getting yelled at no matter what she did?"

"I don't even want to think about where she came from," Alain said. "It's depressing, and so damned frustrating not to be able to change the way she was raised. Makes me want to go hit something or someone."

"Ah, but there's where you go wrong. You have to think about where she came from, and what happened to her there, which will help you understand what scares her so much. They're tied together, Doc. Part of who she is, part of who she'll always be."

"Then you don't think she can overcome her past."

Amos laughed. "No, we can never overcome it, and maybe we shouldn't because it's what makes us who we are, gives us the strength to get along in this world. But we can get past it. We all do, if we're strong enough and want it badly enough. Although I think some folks like using it as an excuse. But not Lilly. I see real strength and determination in that child."

"But how do you help someone get past it? I guess

that's the question I have. How can you help someone get past something that's changed their life?"

"You wouldn't be talking about Lilly now, would you?"

"It's that obvious?"

"You get that moony look every time Maggie comes around. Anyone with any sense can see it."

"Except the one who's supposed to see it."

"She's just set in her ways. Knew me a gal like that once. Stubborn. Dear heavens, she had a stubborn streak in her that wouldn't have budged for anything. And I obliged that in her because I was always too afraid that if I did anything else she'd send me packing. Miss Eula Bergeron…"

"As in Eula's House?"

Amos nodded. "The sun rose and set in her as far as I was concerned, but I never took the chance to tell her because having her on her terms was better than not having her at all. When I was younger I should have done something about it. Should have taken that woman in my arms and told her how I felt and accepted the consequences one way or another, but I didn't. Then time passed and we got stuck in our routines."

"You never knew if she reciprocated your feelings?"

"Never knew. Never will. And that's the worst part. If I'd known, I could have done something about it. Maybe fought harder to win her hand if she wasn't in the mood to get caught, marry her if that's something she had had a mind to do, or get on with another life altogether. But my choice was to stay here, look after my herbs and be her friend. It was good, but it was never enough. And I've got to tell you, son. You've got one a lot like Eula. But if you want my advice, you'll be smarter than I was."

"She doesn't want a traditional domestic kind of life. No entanglements—husband, kids or otherwise."

"Then you intending on keeping Lilly?"

"Haven't given it a lot of thought yet, but I might. We seem to work out well together, and she does need consistency."

"Boy, you sure got some learning to catch up on. Consistency is never any reason to adopt a child…or go after a woman. You'd best get to thinkin' hard on your real feelings before it's too late, because if you think the adoption board's going to give you that child because you have a consistent relationship, you're in for a rude awakening. And I hope to God that word never comes into play between you and Maggie or you'll end up like me, picking herbs in the swamp all alone and swapping stories with neighbors."

Amos stood. "I've got a good gumbo on the stove and some corn bread just waiting to be cooked. Call Maggie, and I'll see the three of you around seven. Oh, and I'd be obliged if you'd tell Maggie to let her sister know I'll be sending a pot of leftovers her way. Mellette and Justin love my cooking. I'd like to think it's one of the things that got them together. That, and a relationship that wasn't based on consistency."

"I didn't say Maggie and I had a relationship based on consistency."

"Didn't have to say it, boy. It's written all over you." Laughing as he walked away, he called out, "'Consistent man looking for consistent woman for a consistent relationship.' Now, that's a lonely heart ad that'll have 'em lining up at your door."

Alain's response was to pick up a piece of pea gravel and throw it at the man. It landed about a foot away from Amos's boot, and Amos just laughed as he continued to amble on. "Not very consistent with your throwing aim either, are you, boy?"

"It's not a date," Alain told himself as he looked in the mirror to make sure he looked presentable for an evening of gumbo at Amos Picou's. A plaid cotton shirt, jeans, boots—nice but not overdressed. The event had grown to include Maggie's parents, a couple of her sisters and even Justin was going to bring Mellette out for the evening because she was going stir-crazy, staying all cooped up and in bed much of the time. A few of the locals were stopping by, as well. Everybody bringing food. In other words, party!

Yet it felt like a date to Alain, probably because Amos had called a while ago and told him his date for the evening had accepted the invitation.

"Will there be lots of people there?" Lilly asked as she shied into the corner of the bedroom.

"Maggie and her family will be there. You remember Leonie, and she'll be there. And a few friends from Big Swamp will be stopping by, as well."

"Don't want to go," Lilly said, big tears welling in her eyes.

This was, perhaps, the first time Lilly had expressed

an opinion, and it surprised him. "Why not?" he asked her. "Everybody there will be very nice."

"*They* might be…"

"Be what?"

"Stealing things from people who go to parties, when they left their houses to go." She was referring to her aunt and uncle. "They would make me sneak in and take things like money and pretty things on shelves, and sometimes if I got caught or took the wrong things they'd…"

"What, sweetheart?" he asked gently.

"They'd lock me in the closet, or make me stay outside all night, all by myself."

Dear God, what she must have suffered. "But they won't be there at the party. And what if I promise to hold your hand and never let go of it?"

Lilly shook her head adamantly. "They'll come and look in the windows to see who's there, so they can go steal from them. They always do and no one sees them. If they see me there, or you…"

"Are you afraid they'll come here, too?" he asked, wondering if she also lived in that sort of terror. "To this house?"

Lilly nodded. "If we go to the party."

"Then we won't go," he said, even though he was disappointed to miss the evening, and the chance to spend time with Maggie. But none of that mattered. Lilly was terrified of being in crowds and he wasn't about to put her through any more hell than she'd already experienced. "In fact, how about we go to town and have pizza?"

That brought a wan smile to her face.

"Then there's this place we could go get ice cream."

"Can Maggie come, too?"

"She's going to be spending the evening with Amos Picou and his guests so, no, not this time. But you like her?"

"She would be like my mommy, if I had one. Someone who was nice, and never yelled."

"Was your mommy like that?"

Lilly nodded. "She made me nice clothes, and sometimes, when she could, she bought me toys."

Yet left her child to people like the Aucoins. Of course, Lilly's mother might not have known. Or there might have been extenuating circumstances that forced such a choice. But, still, to leave your child to people like that? It made him shudder, just thinking about it. "Well, when I call Amos and tell him we won't be there, I'll let Maggie know you'll miss her tonight. Will that be okay?"

"Thank you," Lilly said shyly.

Several minutes later, after he'd made his apologies to Amos, he found himself on the phone with Maggie, explaining the situation. "Oh, and just so you know, Lilly said if she had a mother she'd be just like you. That's in case you want to dispel the myth that you're not parenting material."

"A mommy like me? Are you sure that's what she said?"

"Exact words. Because you're nice. She thinks you'd make her pretty clothes."

"Except I can't sew, I can't cook and I don't know

how to relate to a child for more than a couple of hours. Great mother material that is."

"Well, you may have yourself convinced one way, but Lilly is certainly convinced another."

"We all do that, don't we? See what we want to see. Anyway, sorry you can't make it. Amos makes the best gumbo in these parts and this is turning into quite the party."

He was sorry, too, but about more than just the gumbo. "Well, be on the lookout for Lilly's aunt and uncle peeking in the windows, because that's the kind of event they like to stake out." Except for this once, they wouldn't have Lilly to do it for them. Would that throw them off their game? Or did it really matter?

As he took her hand and led her to the truck, he wondered about a lot of things. About Lilly, first and foremost. And about Maggie. Then somewhere in there he did let the thought enter that he might just like to keep Lilly, adopt her and raise her the way she needed to be raised. But he feared that would preclude Maggie from ever being more than she was to him, and one of those thoughts went far beyond friendship.

It was an impossible situation. No matter how it worked out, he couldn't have it every way he wanted. But he sure didn't like the idea of picking and choosing, either.

"Pepperoni?" Lilly asked when she climbed in the truck.

"Extra pepperoni." No, he sure didn't like the idea of picking and choosing. Wasn't sure he could. Or how he would, if it came right down to it.

CHAPTER EIGHT

"LOOKS LIKE YOU two are having all the fun, and I'm missing out." Maggie sat down at the extra chair at the table and signaled the server over. "Mind if I join you?" she asked Alain. "Or is this a private party?"

Lilly's face lit up. "I wanted you to come with us. He didn't," she said, pointing a serious and accusatory finger at Alain. "He said you had other things to do."

Alain chuckled. "It's not that I didn't want you to have pizza with us. But I did explain your previous engagement with Amos Picou to Lilly and told her that's where you'd be this evening, having dinner there with those friends and family."

"An extra plate and an iced tea," she said to the server, who scurried right away. "Well, that's where I started my evening, but this sounded like more fun. So if you don't mind sharing your pizza with me, I'd love to stay." She smiled. "Besides, as much as I love a good gumbo, and I must admit that I had a taste of Amos's and it was heaven, I do like a good pizza just as much." She turned to Lilly. "Especially the pepperoni."

"Pepperoni gumbo?" Lilly asked innocently. "Maybe

you should tell Amos his gumbo needs lots of pepperoni."

"And maybe I will next time I see him."

"Well, as you can see, we have plenty to share." Almost two-thirds of the entire pie was still uneaten, still warm and, oh, so inviting so she dug right in. "So why are you here with us, Maggie, when Amos was throwing the party of the season?"

"Too many people. Too much noise. I was already tired, and by the time I left, half of Big Swamp had dropped in, bringing their own gumbos, etoufees, jambalayas, okra casseroles, bodin sausages, dirty rice, crawfish pies… It was overwhelming and yummy, but the walls were closing in. I'm not so…"

"Social?" he asked.

"I'm social, but in smaller proportions. Especially when I've had a long, long day. And people were just falling all over each other there were so many of them, so I was glad when Amos made your excuses because that gave me my own excuse to crawl out the door and sneak away. So why didn't the two of you go over there?"

"Pretty much the same reason. Lilly's not fond of large crowds, and I can take them or leave them," he said, dishing up another piece of pizza. "Well, it sounds to me like a brilliant idea, coming here."

"Can I go play in the balls?" Lilly asked shyly. She was referring to a large castle-like blown-up contraption filled with soft balls, designed to let children play and bounce in it. "I'm done with my pizza."

"Think they'll let me play in the balls, too?" Alain asked.

"No, silly. You're too big."

"Then I guess you can go play, but I'll be watching."

With that, Lilly scampered off to join three or four other children in the balls.

"So what's the story?" Maggie asked.

"Her aunt and uncle are sneak thieves who have a habit of robbing people's houses when they attend parties. Apparently they put her to work at it as well, and Lilly was afraid they'd be at Amos's party, looking in the window to see who was there and see me, then go and rob the clinic. So she didn't want to go."

"You're a good temporary dad, bringing her here," she said, reaching across the table to squeeze his hand. But the squeeze turned into more of a hand hold, where their fingers entwined, then lingered that way much longer than either of them had intended.

"It's not so bad when you're being daddy to someone like Lilly. She's easy to care for."

"Have you ever thought of having children of your own?" Maggie asked him.

"Not really. It takes two, and I've never found my other half. I suppose when I do, a family won't be out of the question. And you?"

"I don't have time. I've made choices that…" She looked down at their entwined fingers and pulled her hand away. "That wouldn't leave me time to be a mother."

"Conscious decision?"

"Not that so much as the way it worked out. You know what they say about making your bed then having to lie in it."

"But you can always shake up the bed, can't you? Or buy a new one?"

"I like my old bed. It suits me. No shaking, and no new bed needed."

"To bad. You'd be a brilliant mother."

"Seriously? How do you figure that?"

"I see the way you look at Lilly, with…I guess you'd call it longing. And the way you love your niece. I think you underestimate yourself."

"Or you overestimate me."

"Hey, you're here with Lilly and me tonight, eating pizza, rather than being at Amos's, eating his world-famous gumbo. That says something."

"Maybe it does, but I'm not sure what." She sat back in her chair and fixed her attention on Lilly, who was having the time of her life jumping up and down in the blow-up castle filled with balls. If only life was that simple.

Ten minutes later, when Lilly had returned to the table, Alain suggested they leave and go for ice cream.

"Ice cream?" Lilly practically squealed.

"A little girl's dream night," Alain said.

"It would be her dream night if someone would allow me to buy her pink shoes, as well."

He smiled. "That from the nonmom type."

"I was a little girl once and I know how important these things are. So are we in for the shoes, as well?"

He looked across the table at Maggie and her eyes were shining almost as brightly as Lilly's, and for a second a lump caught in his throat when he thought of them as the perfect little family. They weren't, of course, and he knocked that notion out of his head almost as fast as it entered. This was temporary, he told himself as they finished up the pizza. It might last another few days, maybe a week or two, but then it would be over with. Over. Done. He'd be back to being on his own without the responsibility of one little girl. The thought of that didn't settle well with his pizza.

"If they're really that important…"

"Trust me," Maggie said. "They are. So do either of you know of a place where we can find some pretty pink shoes?"

"I do!" Lilly exclaimed as she took Maggie by the hand and led her in the complete opposite direction from which they'd come. "And they have sparkles on them. And purple stars."

"Oh, my," Maggie said as they passed the window of the shop for little girls' things. "Is that them?"

Lilly nodded. "They're beautiful, aren't they? Like the shoes a fairy princess would wear."

"Well, they look a little small for me, but maybe they might have a pair that would fit you."

"Really?" Lilly looked up at Alain. "Would it be okay to go see?"

Damn, his heart just swelled every time Lilly looked at him, especially with such wonderment. She was such an abused little girl, yet she was such a typical little girl in so many ways, and he was glad that Maggie had had the common sense to know that Lilly not only wanted these shoes, she needed them to help make her normal. Glad she not only knew but had banged it through his thick skull.

"It would be very okay," he said as he opened the door for his two ladies.

An hour later they emerged with shopping bags full of shoes and socks and clothes—nothing practical the way he would have picked them all. But everything was frivolous and feminine and every six-year-old girl's dream. "See, now, that's the way to go shopping," Maggie commented as they wandered on down the street, hand in hand in hand.

"My idea of shopping is get in, get what you need, get out as fast as you can," Alain replied. "Anything else is a waste of time."

"Typical man," Maggie snorted.

"Typical man," Lilly echoed, and they all laughed as they headed off for ice cream.

Maggie had really given this a tremendous amount of thought on the way over here this evening. Why had she wanted to come? What did it mean? Why, if she knew she didn't want to get involved, was she putting herself in the direct line of involvement? And nothing could have possibly been more direct than this.

Okay, so maybe she just liked the male companionship. It had been years since Marc and she was, after all, human, subject to the same frailties and foibles all humans were. So maybe she was simply in the mood for some male companionship, and Alain was safe owing to one little girl tagalong. Nowhere in her arguments did she simply make a case for wanting to see Alain on his own, without child. No, that had never entered the mix because Lilly made it safe for her.

But when she'd stepped into the pizza parlor and hidden near the door, simply watching them interact for five minutes, why had her heart knocked a little harder than it usually did? And why had her cheeks flushed a little more scarlet? Was it because she was afraid that was what she wanted deep down, and didn't even know it or recognize it or want to know it? Or was it because she was afraid she'd get entangled in it somehow when she knew she didn't want it?

So maybe she was choosing Alain because he was safe. Why not? There was safety in numbers, especially when one of those numbers came in the form of a child.

On one hand he would take care of a certain need in her for male companionship, which she did sorely miss. But on the other, he had Lilly, the ultimate safety net. Also, there was that little clause in her contract that wouldn't let her outright date him, either. Meaning she was playing it safe all the way around with a man she found attractive. Whatever that meant.

"By the way, I have an appointment in Illinois on Monday to interview the woman who's suing you," she said casually as they headed toward the ice-cream parlor and Lilly stopped at practically every shop to gaze in the window.

"That easily?"

"No, nothing's ever that easy. But her attorney is paying me the courtesy of a short interview, with the stipulation that you're not there. She doesn't want to face you, which is exactly why I think you should go with me."

"Why?"

"Mrs. Gaines, the woman suing you, has guilty feelings. In my experience, people with guilty feelings are hiding something. It took some convincing to get her agree to sit down with me informally, and I promised you wouldn't be in that meeting, but nothing says you can't be in the hall outside. Or I might just insist on having you in the room, anyway. Who knows?

"Anyway, they're willing to talk settlement now. I put it out there on the table, and it wasn't flat-out rejected, which makes me even more suspicious." She smiled. "I've got a couple more hunches to play out, but I think that by the time I get to the table with the opposition, we're going to be in a pretty good position."

"You're that optimistic?"

"I'm never *that* optimistic until I've played all my cards and come up with the best hand."

"Which you expect to have?"

"Which I hope to have, otherwise I wouldn't have called the meeting. Oh, and Lilly's not cleared to leave the state, so my dad will look after her for a couple of days."

Alain swallowed hard. "I don't know what I'd do without the Doucet family. It's like you've stepped into every facet of my life and made it better."

Maggie smiled. "We're like that. Once we take you in, we don't let go very easily."

The next thirty minutes in the ice-cream parlor turned out to be the best for Lilly, who never stopped giggling as she ploughed into her bowl of ice cream. Afterward, she proclaimed, "This was the best night I ever had," then smiled all the way back to the car, juggling her packages, wearing her pink shoes, with a belly full of chocolate with sprinkles.

To be honest, it was one of the best nights Alain had ever had as well, and he hated seeing it come to an end. But it was over sooner than he liked, and Lilly was asleep almost before she'd climbed into the car.

"I'm glad she had a good time," Maggie said.

"And I'm glad you came along. The pink shoes…"

She shook her head. "It wasn't about the pink shoes. I enjoyed the company. Being with the two of you this evening was nice, and while I don't usually relate so well to children, Lilly is an exception. She's very… mature. Fun to be around, like my niece is."

"Maybe you like children more than you think."

"It's not that I dislike children. It's what I said earlier about not seeing myself in the role of mother and protector on a daily basis. My sister Mellette is a natural, and she'd be happy with a dozen children. They complete her life.

"But for me…I don't know how to explain it other than I don't need a child to make me feel complete. I'm already a complete person and I don't have any burning desire to pile onto that." She looked into the backseat at Lilly, who was snoozing peacefully. "She's an amazing little girl who's got a lot ahead of her to face. Have you ever considered keeping her? Because I think you'd be a perfect father for her."

"Actually, I have given it some thought. Haven't come to any conclusions yet, but I do like having her around. She seems to fit into my life quite easily, like she's supposed to be there."

"Well, for what it's worth, I watched the two of you this evening, and you seem natural together. I think you make her feel safe because she comes out of her shell when the two of you are interacting. At times, it was like watching a little girl who adores her daddy."

"My only fear is that she's going to become too attached to me, then the court will place her with someone else. I mean, what's that going to do to her?"

"Don't let them place her with anyone else. Fight for her, Alain. I'm sure Jean-Pierre will be glad to handle the legal end of it. Two of his children are adopted, and he's very much an advocate for placing children in the right situation."

"Sounds like you're trying to push her on me."

Maggie smiled. "Maybe I am. Just a little. Anyway, it's time to get her home and tucked in. You're not going all the way back out to the swamp tonight, are you?"

"I think we'll go back to my place," Alain said. "Lilly's too tired to take very far, and I'd like to get her settled into bed sooner rather than later."

"Mind if I come along and help tuck her in?" Maggie asked impulsively. "It's on my way home, and since its Friday night I don't mind avoiding the walking tours for a little while longer."

"Ah, ghosts." Alain laughed. "Hope your ghost is amiable."

"Can't say that I've ever had the pleasure of meeting him, but he must be somewhat amiable to put up with me and all my strange hours. Or maybe ghosts don't really have a connection to real time the way we do."

"Well, you're welcome to come back to my place where there's a definite connection to real time. I can't promise you ghosts and tourists, but I do have my share of scaffolding and paint buckets and furniture covered with sheets."

"You don't mind if I follow you home?"

He shook his head. "And I'm sure Lilly would love to have you there for her bedtime story, if she's awake enough to hear one tonight."

"You read her bedtime stories?"

He nodded. "It just seemed like the right thing to do. And she enjoys them."

Maggie was touched by all the efforts Alain made to make Lilly comfortable in a world that had been pretty cruel to her. More than that, it was occurring to her that she, Maggie, was becoming more and more attracted to Alain, which didn't make sense because while he was everything she wanted in a man, he was also everything she didn't want. That, plus she'd actually encouraged him to adopt Lilly.

Maybe that was her out strategy, her way of making sure the attraction didn't go any further than attraction. Because his legal case would be over with one day, maybe even by Monday, then she'd have some real emotions to deal with. So build up the man she could want into the kind of man she didn't want...

It was too confusing. Too manipulative. Better to just let it turn into whatever it was meant to be and deal with the consequences at the time. Besides, she'd made a pretty strong case against wanting the domestic life, and Alain certainly seemed like that was what he wanted. So she'd thrown out all the signals, and she was damned sure he'd read them. Meaning she was safe.

But she wasn't sure if being safe made her happy or sad.

Maggie followed Alain to his house, where Alain carried Lilly up his front stairs and through the front door. "No ghosts, but lots of activity. Or, at least, I've never encountered a ghost. Maybe there used to be one until I started all the banging and ripping out walls."

"Could be your ghost hooked up with my ghost and they've gone off to find someone better to haunt." Maggie pulled off Lilly's shoes and socks, then took the child from Alain's arms. "Which room?"

"We're staying downstairs, first one on the right. Eventually it'll be the parlor, but for now it's set up to be her temporary bedroom."

"And where are you staying?" she asked, once they'd tucked Lilly into bed.

"Next door to her, in the dining room. Sleeping on a cot." He smiled. "Not exactly the best accommodation, but it beats sleeping on the bare wooden floor."

"It's a beautiful house, Alain. How did it become so...rundown?"

"My elderly aunts owned it and never really trusted caretakers to do any of the odd jobs a place like this requires. Then one of my aunts passed, and the other one just moved out and shut it up for nine years. Left it the way it was the day she walked out, including a stained porcelain teacup in the kitchen sink. Anyway, after all the legal proceedings against me started, and I was virtually penniless, she just gave me the house. Said it was my inheritance anyway, and that I could sell it or keep it and live in it, whatever suited me.

"And since this had been my great-great-grandparents' home, and also because I was basically homeless, I decided to fix it up then figure out what to do with it. But the more work I put into it, the more I'm inclined to want to stay here."

"I can't blame you. All the fixtures are original—gas converted to electric. And the trim work… It's like my parents' house in elegance, or could be like their house when it's completed, but I think it will be even nicer because it has a family history." She pulled back a dusty old sheet and looked at the gold silk settee underneath. "Original furniture, too? Real Victorian?"

"Everything's the way I always remember it being, and I suppose that would be Victorian. I'm betting you'll find some old Victorian clothes in the wooden chests in the attic. Something my great-great-grandmother might have worn. I know I used to play with the toys and clothes I found in those chests when I was a child, and it was like stepping back in time."

"Oh, my. And it just sat here empty all this time without being vandalized?"

"Maybe because it looked so rundown no one would have guessed what was inside. Or maybe because my family hooked up a modern alarm system to it even before my aunt moved out, and it's been monitored all these years, even though it was deserted."

Maggie brushed her fingers over the settee. "Once upon a time I pictured myself living in a place as amazing as this. I was quite a reader, did that rather than watch television and play. And I read about all these beautiful Southern mansions, and how life had been back in the 1800s when they were built. I used to fantasize about making a grand entrance down a staircase just like the one here, and being the belle of the ball."

"So what happened to the little girl with the big dreams?"

"She started reading her parents' medical texts and couldn't put them down. Got hooked on the more practical side of life. Pretty soon the belle of the ball wanted to be a nurse."

"Just as admirable," he said as he took one more look in at Lilly and shut her door all but a crack, then turned to face Maggie. "But did she ever go back to revisit her belle-of-the-ball days, even for just a few minutes, or did that dream just disappear?"

Maggie shook her head. "Her life got involved in other ways…ways she liked better. Ways that suited her better, too."

"So withdrawing from the ball was your idea?"

"Withdrawing from the ball seemed the more practical thing to do in my case. I had sisters who also wanted to be belles of their own balls, and it just seemed silly for me to have those kinds of dreams, especially since…"

"Since you were the practical sister in the family."

"Something like that. We all have to grow up some time, don't we? I just did my growing up a little early."

"Maybe, but didn't you deprive yourself of a childhood? Because you didn't even allow yourself to have any fun when you'd hit that stage where a young person is supposed to experiment to find out which way their life is supposed to take them. Is that what happened to you, Maggie? You purposely stalled yourself?"

"Not stalling, because I already knew where I was going."

"Something else could have been out there for you, if you'd looked."

"Except I was pleased with my choice. Got even more pleased when I found a way to merge my love of medicine to my love of the law. Both things are pure. They don't let you down."

"And you never, ever let down a little, just to have fun?" he asked as he stepped closer to her.

"Never. Not enough time."

"Because you don't want to make the time," he said, reaching out and stroking her cheek.

"Alain, we can't do this. It's in the contract..."

"You'll always find an excuse, won't you, Maggie?"

"But we have this legal agreement."

"And if we didn't, what would be your next excuse?"

"I don't need an excuse."

"Then let me tear up that contract so we can see what happens. No one can force me into honoring it, especially as it's all pro bono work."

"But it wouldn't be ethical," she argued, holding her ground, not backing away from him even a few inches.

"Not if you were to tell anybody, which you wouldn't. But what goes on between you and me privately..."

"Why are you doing this to me?" she asked. But there was no challenge in her voice. More like giving in.

"And why are you staying here, asking me, if you really weren't opposed to it? In fact, why did you come and have pizza with us, and spend the evening with us, and follow me home?"

"Because you're my client, and—"

"And your client is about to kiss you. Which is what you want, isn't it? Oh, and if you need a reason for what I'm about to do, one that would hold up in a court of law, it's because…"

"Because why?" she whispered as his lips dipped down dangerously close to hers. So close she was on the verge of melting into him completely.

"Because I want to," he said as his lips sought hers. "Even though I know you're doing your best to push me away from you, I still want to."

"I'm not pushing," she argued.

"Sure you are. You tell me how you don't want children, don't want to be involved in any form of domesticity, then plead your case for my adopting Lilly. Yet you stand here, wanting this kiss as much as I do. Knowing full well one kiss could turn into so much more."

"That's not true. I wasn't…"

He chuckled. "Sure you were. And I'm on to you, Magnolia Doucet. You're human. Have human needs and wants and desires just like the rest of us. And as you try to distance yourself from all that, you really don't want to be distanced. It an excuse that keeps you safe, though. Except nothing about us is safe, and you already know that. I was aware of it for a full week when you watched me from the porch while I was working and you were sipping lemonade with your sister. Watching me, Maggie. Watching *me*. Not the work, not the other shirtless men. But me!"

"You were a hard worker."

"And you're lying to yourself."

"There was nothing else to watch."

"You could have been reading one of your medical or law texts."

"I wasn't in the mood."

His lips dipped even closer. "Because you were in the mood for me. Admit it, Maggie."

"You looked good in…sweat." She swallowed hard. "Great in sweat." She shut her eyes, felt the sweat rising up between the two of them. "But you're not what I want, Alain. We need to be practical about this. I don't want—"

"Just for once, let's concentrate on what you do want. And you do want this, don't you?"

"No, I…"

"Admit it, Maggie. You want it."

"No, I don't." His lips were so close to hers now, a hair couldn't have separated them.

"Give in to it, Maggie. Take what you want, not what your head dictates. Only your heart, Maggie. Only your heart."

"Yes, I…I…"

The kiss was light at first. More like a gentle brushing. Or tickling. But when she didn't resist it, he pushed harder, pried her lips apart with his tongue and delved in like a starving man. A man who hadn't had the taste of a woman on his tongue for decades or beyond.

Her response at first was almost a paralyzing shock. Even though she expected the kiss, maybe even wanted it in some way she didn't understand, she stiffened under it, didn't melt into him naturally. Didn't fit the curves of her body to his. In fact, she felt like a board she was so stiff and frightened, felt like she would break in two if he held her any tighter. Yet she didn't want to stop. And in an instant when he let up to catch his breath, her heart pounded hard against his chest and she thought that this would be the last of it, that Alain would come to his senses and end it.

But his breath was his second wind, and the next time he kissed her he ground himself hard into her, his body matching equally to hers, knocking out all her stiff reserve and demanding the truest melding of man and woman. Which she gave him. Weakly. Without breath. And with more passion than she'd ever known in herself.

"I… We…" she gasped, trying to pull back, but he wouldn't let her pull back, and she didn't fight him to get away. "We can't do this," she finally managed. "Really, we can't."

"I'd say we do it very well."

"My job… That really is an obstacle."

"Who's to know?" he said as he kissed his way around her neck, taking pleasure in her shivers.

"I'm to know."

"And will you report yourself?" he continued as his tongue grazed across her jaw and down her throat.

"No, but…" She wanted to shudder, to give in to the pure pleasure and forget about the rules, but that wasn't her. And she prided herself on being staunchly loyal to what she believed in. "But I'd have to withdraw from your case," she whispered as the moment suddenly froze between them.

"Seriously? Over a kiss?"

"I follow the rules, Alain. Always have. And this… this whatever it is won't work because it's not allowed. I can't kid myself over that. It was nice…good… sensational. But I really can't."

"Damn," he grunted out of pure frustration as he stepped back from her. "Leave it to me to find the only girl who's made me want to do that in a long, long time and she's a stickler for the rules."

"I'm sorry," she said, biting her lip to stop the tears that wanted to flow. Because he was the only man who'd ever made her want to break the rules. Break them, throw them out the window, all caution be damned. But that simply wasn't in her makeup. Never had been, never would be. At least, not break the rules and be able to look at herself in the mirror ever again.

"I'm sorry," she said again, this time her voice even more wobbly then before. "I do want to be able to represent you, and I can't do that and…and this. It doesn't work that way for me."

Alain leaned back against the wall and simply shut his eyes. "I think one of the things I like best about you is your ethical principles, but, damn, I never expected it to come back and kick me in the…"

She reached out and took hold of his hand. "It wasn't your fault."

"Because I'm a man and men are expected to be weak in these kinds of situations?"

Maggie laughed. "No. Because I let you down and

thought for a few moments that I could have it both ways. For what it's worth, I'm glad you tried."

"For what it's worth, I hate like hell that I failed."

"But getting your life straightened out is more important than anything we might have done here tonight."

Alain let out a jagged sigh. "Just for the record, counselor. Would something more have happened here tonight?"

"I object on the grounds that would be pure speculation." She smiled, kissed her fingertip then brushed it across his lips. "Or I might just have to perjure myself, and you wouldn't want me to do that, would you?"

"Well, then, I suppose court is adjourned."

"For now," she said as she headed for the front door. Then she turned and gave him a serious look. "It was the right thing, Alain. We shouldn't have let it get out of hand and I shouldn't have let it get out of hand. I'm going to have to have a serious talk with Jean-Pierre tomorrow to make sure he wants me to remain on the case, since I did cross the line."

"You think he'll withdraw you?"

"Probably not. Not for one kiss. But I'm going to be treading on thin ice."

"Call me when you know."

She nodded, then disappeared out the door, leaving Alain so disappointed and frustrated that he kicked a hole through the drywall in the newly walled hallway. "Of all the stupid things…"

Yes, he knew her principles. Yes, he even respected them. But nowhere…*nowhere* in that addled brain of his had he thought he'd be the one to step over her line.

He had now, and tomorrow he'd know the consequences. "Damn it to hell," he muttered as he plopped down on his cot and stared up at the ceiling for the next hour, berating himself until he finally fell asleep.

CHAPTER NINE

THREE DAYS LATER on the plane to Illinois was the next time they actually spoke. Maggie had texted him that she had squared the situation with Jean-Pierre, and she'd ignored his text back where he asked about getting together over dinner to talk about the particulars of their case before they left for Illinois. Even on the plane they didn't talk, because they sat distanced by half a plane. Had she purposely booked seats so far apart?

His guess was yes, and when he'd asked her about it in the cab, she simply said that was the way it had worked out. From then on, she was all business, talking about his legal case, maintaining a very hard defining line between them.

So he went along with it. What else was there to do? She was setting the rules and he had no other choice but to follow them. Like Amos and Eula and their unspoken set of rules...rules that had kept them apart for half a lifetime.

"Do I get to talk to Mrs. Gaines when I'm there?" he asked her. "Because I'd like to know why she's choosing me to sue. And I'd also like to find out why her doctor didn't bother to come in for the delivery and pushed it off on me. Did he know about her wish not to have a scar and was that his way to avoid a lawsuit against him? That her pelvis was too narrow for a regular delivery?"

Maggie smiled. "I have an appointment first off with Dr. Green to ask him the same question. I have a hunch we both know the answer to that one, but I'd like to see him squirm a little, and also see how much he's lawyered up. See if I can fight my way into getting you off the hook."

"You really think he'll be there with an attorney?"

"If he's smart, he will be. Anyway, I've also got to meet with Lana Andrews, who's the counsel on record to represent us here. I've already talked to her, and she's going to be on hand if I need some help, but chances are I won't. Her law firm has a reciprocal relationship with ours, so if this thing actually does go to trial, Jean-Pierre will be the one to represent you. But for this little fishing expedition, which is all it is, Lana's going to appear as our attorney of record." She chuckled. "Unless I land a whopper of a deal, which I just may do."

"A whopper?"

"Come and watch me work, Alain. See what I do, and maybe you'll understand better why I have to do it."

"In other words, seeing is believing?"

"It is. And I'm pretty sure you will."

The meeting with Dr. Green was short and not so sweet. He'd lawyered up, as Maggie had expected, and the only thing she was told was that if this matter went to trial, the only way his client would appear was under subpoena, and even then there was the doctor-patient confidentiality agreement, which would be honored.

But Maggie hit him with a doozy of a question then watched his face for his answer. "Did she threaten to sue you if you left a scar and is that why she ended up with my client?"

Naturally, he refused to answer, but they said one picture was worth a thousand words, and they'd hit the mark with Dr. Green. Which gave Maggie all the ammunition she needed.

Lana Andrews, the next person they met, as it turned out, was a tiny older woman. Gray hair pulled back in a bun, no-nonsense handshake, stern scowl. Not very formidable looking, to be honest, but Alain was beginning to understand that looks had nothing to do with skill. Lana had the reputation of being a shark, Maggie told him, but a very nice shark, Alain soon discovered as she went over her stipulations for representation.

She was going to allow Maggie to take the lead, and her only part would be to jump in when legalities were close to the edge, or when Maggie was being challenged. "Since this is an informal Q&A and nothing more, I don't expect to take part unless I have to. Oh, but I'd like to have Dr. Lalonde present at the table, and not in the hall. I know that's not what they're going to want to do, but if his presence makes their client so nervous, that tells us more than they want us to know. And I do like to see them squirm."

Maggie laughed, and whispered to Alain as they entered the room en masse, "She's as formidable as Jean-Pierre. I'd hate to see them go head to head."

Admittedly, Alain was the one who was nervous. This was his butt on the line here. Maggie assured him they'd persuade the hospital that they couldn't drop mal-practice coverage on him as he'd been employed at the time of the incident, but that was yet another legal action he'd have to endure.

It seemed like all the legalities were just piling up on him and all he could do was stand back and hope that Jean-Pierre, Maggie and now Lana were as good as he thought they were. It was an ugly mess over a simple scar and a beautiful child, and it seemed like such a waste. Ego. Greed.

"We've decided that since these proceedings are about our client, Dr. Lalonde, he should have the right to sit in on them," Lana announced, even before Alain and Maggie were all the way into the room. "And I'm sure you find no objection to that since you believe, in all sincerity, that your client was the wronged party."

"But we stipulated—" John Butterworth, opposing counsel, began.

"Duly noted," Lana said, "but, like I said, the accused has the right to confront his accuser, and doing it here, informally, seems much easier for your client than letting them go at each other for the first time in court. Which, I promise, will make for a very uncomfortable situation." She smiled sweetly, then went in for the kill. *"Very uncomfortable."*

Butterworth, a pudgy red-haired man with freckles, dressed in an impeccable hand-tailored blue suit, conferred with his client for a moment while Lana took her place at one side of the table, seated Alain next to her and gestured for Maggie to take her seat in the power position at the end.

"This is always the fun part," Lana whispered to Alain. "Where you can visibly see that you've shaken them up. Good luck, by the way. Jean-Pierre stands behind you, otherwise you would have had one of my junior associates." She gave his arm a squeeze, then sat back in the chair to observe the proceedings.

"Mrs. Gaines has agreed to allow Dr. Lalonde to sit in on the stipulation that as you will be questioning her, we will be allowed to do the same with him."

"Feel free to question away," Maggie said. She spread her notes out in front of her and clearly looked like the person in charge of the room. "But be advised that my client may or may not answer, depending on how his answer could affect the outcome of the end proceedings."

Alain blinked hard. Maggie was in command of everything. Not just her team, but she had it all over the opposition, and the interesting thing was he didn't believe that the opposition was even aware of it.

Alain was impressed. Truly impressed. And for the first time he really thought he understood her. Not all of her but the parts he'd never seen before. This was who Maggie was. Who she was meant to be. Who she had to be. In defense of the doctor... That was her. Nothing there made him doubt that.

But nothing made him regret that kiss, either. And he still believed she could divide herself and be the belle of the ball as well as master of the courtroom. If she wanted to. Question was, did she want to?

"So, as I called this meeting, I'll be the one to start

the questioning, and I'd like to keep this brief, if you don't mind."

"We have no objections," Butterworth said.

"First, Mrs. Gaines, I don't see your husband here with you today. I'd requested him to be present. I hope he's not ill."

"He's fine," she said. "Just…working. Couldn't afford to take the time off."

"I understand," Maggie said, folding her hands on the table in front of her. "Today is his weekly golf game with the heads of several corporations, and I can imagine how important that is."

"It is very important to our corporation," Mrs. Gaines said defensively. "You have no idea."

"No, I can't say that I do. Which leads me to my first question. Why, when Dr. Green had already advised you of the likelihood of having a C-section, are you suing my client?"

"I had specifically stated that I wanted no scars. Your client scarred me."

"Let me make you aware that I talked to Dr. Green just an hour ago. Isn't it true that he warned you of the likelihood of a C-section?" In reality Green had said nothing of the kind. This was only the first part of her fishing expedition.

"You don't have to answer that," Butterworth advised.

"And didn't he describe the kind of scar it might leave?

"Again, don't answer," Butterworth went on.

"And isn't it true that you threatened to sue Dr. Green if he left a scar?"

"Again, I'll advise my client not to answer!"

"You threatened to sue even though Dr. Green advised you there was no other choice?"

"There are always choices!" Mrs. Gaines snapped. "And even though my former doctor, Dr. Green, couldn't seem to find one, Dr. Lalonde worked with high-risk pregnancies and he should have known what to do."

"You mean deliver a healthy baby?" Maggie asked.

"I *said* no scar!"

"Your baby was in fetal distress. Labor was progressing too long."

"But it could have gone on longer. The baby was in the birth canal."

"In danger of dying." For effect, Maggie leaned forward in her chair. "Did that matter to you?"

"Yes, of course it did, but we could have tried a while longer."

"And in Dr. Lalonde's opinion, that was too risky."

"It was only his opinion. I had an opinion, too."

"And a medical degree in high-risk obstetrics to back it up, Mrs. Gaines?"

The woman was beginning to look distressed. "Aren't doctors supposed to do what the patient tells them?"

"Your baby was not going to be delivered alive, Mrs. Gaines. That's the bottom line, and I have affidavits from everyone in the delivery room stating that he tried everything possible to deliver that child naturally, but it wasn't going to happen." Maggie took a deep breath.

"So let me ask you this question. What was more important to you? Your scar or your son?"

"That's a despicable question," John Butterworth interjected. "My client's only contending that your client didn't explore all his avenues."

"Her doctor passed off the delivery to whomever was on staff because he didn't want to get sued," Maggie continued. "He knew it was going to be a tough delivery most likely ending in a C-section, and he didn't want to get sued. But your client also knew the odds that she wouldn't be able to deliver naturally, and I have statements from three other obstetricians she visited who will testify to the same thing.

"She suffers from a condition called cephalopelvic disproportion, which means a baby's head will be too large to pass through the pelvic opening. It resulted from a traffic accident in her late teens where her pelvis was fractured. She was aware of the condition and aware of the outcome of any attempted pregnancy."

It was obvious Butterworth had been caught completely off guard. "Your, um…your client didn't try hard enough for a regular delivery. He was with my client only thirty minutes when he made the decision to do a C-section."

Mrs. Gaines sat straight in her chair, her hands folded on the table, looking quite the ice queen. "And my pelvic injury is not the problem here. It healed nicely."

"You're forty-two years old, Mrs. Gaines," Maggie countered. "At least, that's what you claim, even though I've found records showing you are forty-six. Whatever the case, this was your first delivery, which was destined to be difficult due to your condition, and you knew that going in. I'm sorry a C-section scar marred your perfect body, but you have a perfect son as a result.

"Now, here's what I'd like. You knew the risks, you knew the eventual outcome, knew you were likely to have a C-section no matter who delivered your baby. You drop your charges against my client, and we won't take action against you for a wrongful lawsuit. In other words, we'll keep all your dirty little secrets out of court. Because, trust me, if we go forward from here, you won't have any secrets. Which could affect your husband's golf game, I'm sure."

"We have a right to our day in court, Miss Doucet," Butterworth interjected.

"And your day in court will be spent going up against Jean-Pierre Robichaud. I'm sure you know who he is. He'll win this one easily, Mr. Butterworth. I assure you, you will not stand a chance."

Butterworth conferred with his client for a minute, then said, "For the sake of her son, Mrs. Gaines has opted not to continue with this lawsuit. Consider it dropped."

"And what about Dr. Green?" Alain asked.

"He's a victim, like you are. So I don't think we should pursue him."

"And the hospital?" Alain asked.

Maggie smiled. "Lana's agreed to fix that mess, pro bono."

"Then it's over?"

Maggie nodded. "Most of it is. We still need to convince the hospital to confess the error of its ways and make that right."

"And I can kiss you?"

"Circumspectly, as this is a legal chamber."

But the kiss he gave her was anything but circumspect, and Lana simply smiled at them as she walked out the door and shut it behind her.

Maggie and Alain greeted each other with a cordial embrace three days later. Except for a friendly parting at the airport, they'd had no contact, and he'd wondered if that was because he was pushing her too hard. Women who kissed back the way Maggie had that day after the hearing had feelings, and maybe she just didn't want to confront them, or didn't know how. Whatever the case, he'd decided to give her the space she wanted then see what might happen in due course, when she was feeling comfortable again.

God only knew how anxious he was to see her, to kiss her or even just talk to her. But Maggie was making it quite clear that they were on her terms now. She took his calls but cut them short, texted him back with brief one- or two-word answers and refused pizza with him and Lilly.

Which meant she was seriously resisting him now that the case was over.

The thing was, he didn't know what to do about that because he wanted Maggie in his life not just for himself but also for Lilly, who missed her and moped around without her. Wouldn't even wear her pink shoes to pizza because Maggie wasn't coming.

"What have I done?" he asked himself as he sat on the porch one afternoon and watched Lilly sulking around in the play yard while two of her little friends played there with her and seemed to be having a good time. Lilly, who'd finally been coming out of her shell, thanks largely to Maggie, was now in full retreat again, and he felt bad about it. Felt bad about everything.

"She can be had," Amos Picou said as he settled in across from Alain. "Just not in the way you're used to."

"I don't want to just have her," Alain snapped.

Amos let out a low whistle then laughed. "You got it bad, and that ain't good. Mellette and Justin were easy to get together because they both knew what they wanted. Had a few rough patches to fix up, but true love always wins."

"The difference is they loved each other."

"And you and Maggie don't?"

"It's not that simple."

"Love is never that simple. It's not meant to be, or else you'd be falling in love with every girl who ever crossed your path."

"Well, one did cross my path, but she doesn't want to have anything to do with falling in love or having a relationship. Which means she doesn't want anything to do with me."

"Do you think she loves you?"

"She might. For a few days I deluded myself into thinking she did."

"And do you love her?"

"Against my better judgment, yes. Didn't mean to, especially since she's such a challenge. But it happened."

"Then you just go get her."

"Sure. I'll go all caveman, force my way into her office, throw her over my shoulder and carry her out."

"If that's what it takes. Because sitting here complaining to me sure won't do it."

"Says the man who never went out and got the woman he loved," Alain snapped, then immediately regretted his words. "Look, I'm sorry. I shouldn't have said that. But I'm so damned frustrated I don't know what to do."

"You don't do what I did, which was spend a lifetime wishing, without ever telling her."

Alain looked up at the sign over the door. "Eula's House," he said aloud. "From what I understand, it's come a long way."

"Folks in these parts weren't so trusting at first. Kind of like your Maggie. But they're settling in to the idea of having a legitimate practice here. We still like our herbs, and that's not going to change. It's not right, going against the general nature of things. But compromising is good, and that's what we're doing here with Eula's House." He smiled. "Compromise is a mighty powerful thing if you do it right."

"But Maggie's not willing to listen to a compromise."

"You're sure of that?"

Alain thought for a moment. Then smiled. "I don't suppose I'm really open to one, either. My idea is to get my life back on track and go back to work the way I used to."

"Which was what?"

"Ten or twelve hours a day."

"Leaving how much time for Maggie, who'll be

working that much, too, if you were so lucky as to reel her in?"

"Leaving not much. And I've been thinking about adopting Lilly, as well."

"Ah, see, the plot thickens. You and Maggie want the same things, only differently. Truth is, to get what you want, you've got to be willing to give up what you want, as well." Amos rose from his seat and headed off the porch. "You're not going to get twelve hours a day at work, a wife and a child. Won't happen, Alain, so don't delude yourself. Change that plan of yours and maybe that woman might see fit to change that plan of hers. At least it gives you something to talk about."

"Easier said than done," he muttered as Amos walked away.

"I've got mighty good hearing for a man of my years, son. And if you want that woman, you'd better make it easier done than said." With that, he laughed and disappeared down the trail.

"I can take the house call," Maggie said three hours later as she sat her medical bag on the table in exam one. "You can stay here with Lilly."

"Lilly's really missed you. She won't even wear her pink shoes. You sure you don't mind staying here with her while I run out and check on Zerelda's bronchitis?"

"I'd love to stay with Lilly. I've missed her. But remember that Zerelda prefers a decoction of colt's foot."

"That, and a good antihistamine."

Maggie shook her head. "Colt's foot. She won't stand for anything else."

"I know, but I always live in hope."

"If it works, it works. Anyway, tell her I said hello and that I'll stop by and see her in a day or two." With that, Maggie flitted out to the play yard in a way that almost seemed like she was brushing him off. Certainly, her friendliness was superficial. Nothing substantial about it, the way it used to be. And here Amos thought all he had to do was tell her how he felt then start making compromises. The only way Maggie would react to that was to run away entirely.

"So get over her," he said as he climbed into the truck and headed down an overgrown path to see Zerelda Lavache and give her the herb of her choice.

No one had made an appointment, and the knock on the front door wasn't unexpected, as people stopped by all the time. But this knock was loud, abrasive, angry, and Maggie's first instinct was to tell Lilly to run upstairs and play in the bedroom. She wasn't sure why she did it, but that was what her gut was telling her to do, and it was exactly what she did.

By the time Lilly was safely out of the way, the person outside had banged twice more, each time louder. So she approached the door cautiously and looked out and saw someone standing on the porch with a hand wrapped up in a bloody towel.

Normally, they kept the door locked and people were used to knocking, so this was nothing new, but when Maggie saw the potential injury she threw open the door and was immediately shoved back into the room, where she hit her head on the opposite wall. As it turned out, the bloody towel was a ruse. The man charging the door was as fit as anybody she'd ever encountered.

"Where is she?" the man shouted. He seemed vaguely familiar.

"What?" she said, trying to pull herself upright. But as soon as she'd pulled herself partway up, he shoved her flat onto the floor again, so hard she found herself fighting to breathe again. She opened her eyes enough to see him tearing up the office, knocking over chairs, breaking windows... It was the man from whom they'd taken Lilly. Joe Aucoin.

Dear God! He was here to take her back.

"Where is she?" he screamed when he realized Maggie's eyes were following him around the room.

"House call with the doctor," she lied, praying to God that Lilly had heard the noise and hidden herself somewhere.

"I don't believe you. Tell me where she is."

He went into the kitchen, which gave her enough time to push herself up to her hands and knees and look for a weapon...anything. But there was nothing there that would hurt him or incapacitate him. Everything she could see would only make him even angrier, so her only alternative was to get upstairs to Lilly and see if there was any way they could hide or even get out of the house.

Even though she was injured, Maggie pushed herself all the way up and made a mad dash for the stairs. Got up them and into the room where Lilly was. Found Lilly under the bed, trembling.

Lilly immediately started sobbing the instant she

saw Maggie, and Maggie shushed her with a finger to her lips. "We've got to get out of here," she whispered to the girl, "so when I tell you to run, I want you to run as hard and fast as you can down the stairs and don't stop until you get to Amos Picou's house. Do you understand me?"

Lilly swiped at the tears running down her face, and nodded.

"Then tell Amos I need help. That your uncle is after me. Can you do that for me, Lilly?"

Lilly nodded.

What Maggie didn't want to say was that Lilly's uncle wanted to kill her, and that was what she feared he'd do. "Okay, now I'm going to call…" She reached into her pocket only to discover that her cell phone must have fallen out during the altercation. "I'm going to go through to the next bedroom and make some noise, Lilly. Your uncle will hear it and come upstairs. As soon as he gets in the room where I am, I want you to run. Please, run, Lilly! As hard and fast as you ever have."

"Will you come?" Lilly asked.

"In a while. But I've got to make sure you get away from him first. Okay? Now, be brave. And run hard, Lilly."

"I love you, Maggie."

"And I love you, too, sweetheart." And she did, truly. Like a mother would, she suddenly discovered, because she knew she would literally give her life to save this child. "Now get ready." Maggie pulled away from the bed and made her way quietly down the hall. Found a glass table lamp that might stun her attacker, grabbed it and purposely knocked a figurine onto the floor, then dived under the bed.

Instantly she heard thundering footsteps on their way upstairs, and she prayed that Lilly wasn't too afraid to do what needed to be done. Otherwise there was no telling what would happen to either of them.

"Where the hell are you?" he screamed. "I know you're up here, so show yourself so we can talk."

He stomped very slowly down the hall. Too slowly, and Maggie heard him stop at Lilly's bedroom for an instant. Her stomach churned and she retched involuntarily. Which was all Joe Aucoin needed to find her huddled under the bed in the back bedroom.

"I know where you're hiding!" he screamed at her. "Won't do you no good, 'cause I got you now." He grabbed hold of her left ankle and started to pull her out from under the bed, but she fought him. And when she realized she wasn't going to win this battle, she latched on to the nightstand lamp and pulled it along with her, hoping that somewhere in all this she might just have one element of surprise.

But that wasn't to be the case, because he picked her up as easily as if she were a rag doll, then threw her on the bed and pinned here there. "We can do this the easy way, or it can get ugly," he said.

"She's not here," Maggie said, trying to extricate herself from underneath his weight. "She's with the doctor, so you'd better get out of here before he returns."

His response was to laugh. "I saw the doctor leave, and he wasn't dragging the brat along with him, so you've got her hidden. All you've got to do is give me what's mine and I'll be done with you."

Maggie didn't say anything. There was no point in provoking the man any more than she already had. So she went limp, shut her eyes, stayed limp when he yanked her up off the bed and started shaking her. "Give her to me now!" he bellowed, even though Maggie was feigning unconsciousness.

"Leave her alone!" a tiny voice screamed.

Maggie opened her eyes just in time to see Lilly run across the floor, make a lunge for Joe Aucoin and grab hold of his leg. In that instant he dropped Maggie and she immediately grabbed the table lamp and came right back up, swinging. Hit him in the head, left shards of glass everywhere, even though the hit only stunned him, caused him to start swinging blindly as blood dripped into his eyes. And his target…Lilly. He hit her and knocked her down to the floor, then immediately picked her up and started to run out the door with her.

But Maggie flew after him, grabbed hold of him from behind before he got to the stairs. His only reaction was to swing round and kick her so she fell backward and couldn't get up. Still, she crawled over to the steps, pulled herself up on the banister and forced herself to remain standing as the man made his way down with the child in his arms.

"No!" Maggie screamed. "You can't take her."

"She's right," Alain said, appearing at the bottom of the steps. He was holding a walking stick, no other weapon. And his form filled the entire opening, dwarfing Joe Aucoin. "Put the child down and walk away."

Maggie dragged herself down the steps, one by one, until she was standing directly behind the man. Her immediate action was to pound him directly on the back, and as he spun to take a swing at her, Alain lunged forward and grabbed Lilly away from him. Then he set her on a chair out of the way of the fighting and went back in with his walking stick and took a crack at Joe Aucoin's face, then another one at his chest. It was enough to bring the man to his knees and cause him to topple onto the floor at the bottom of the steps.

Maggie immediately threw herself over the man to keep him from getting back up while Alain went to get rope to tie him. But as he did so he noticed that Lilly was slumped over in the chair, her pallor the color of paste. So he tossed Maggie the rope and immediately began to assess the child. "Broken ribs," he shouted, as Maggie tied the man up in several knots of her own making. "Probably from the way he was carrying her. I think she might have a pneumothorax." Punctured lung. "She's struggling to breathe."

Immediately, Maggie went to Alain's medical bag and found an eighteen-gauge needle and attached it to a syringe. He listened to her chest through his stethoscope, an over the top of one of the ribs in the area where there were no breath sounds. The reason it was over-the-top and no deeper was to avoid a nerve, artery and veins that ran underneath each rib.

As soon as Alain found the spot, he inserted the needle and pulled back on the syringe. Immediately he started pulling back air, which was where he stopped, as if he'd gone any farther he could have stuck the lung and made the condition worse. "Do you know how many years it's been since I've had to do that?" he asked, wiping the sweat off his face with the back of his hand. He glanced over at Aucoin, who was squirming around on the floor like the worm that he was.

"I've called the authorities to come and get him, and a helicopter is en route to get Lilly, so we need to get her over to Grandmaison, where they'll meet her."

"Looks as though you've taken a few good licks yourself," he said as he bundled Lilly up in a blanket and got ready to take her to the truck.

"A few, nothing serious."

"You sure?"

She nodded. "I was just so…so scared for Lilly."

"She's going to be fine, Maggie. Once we get her to the hospital…"

Because Maggie had taken a beating herself, it was decided she'd fly in by helicopter and meet her entire family, who'd be waiting for her in Emergency. Since she felt like death warmed over, she didn't object, but she sure wished there'd been room to accommodate Alain, too. Because she didn't want him to let her go as he carried her to the helicopter. But they had to part, and he left her with a tender kiss. "One more?" she asked before he backed away.

Alain laughed. But obliged. One more kiss, and then the woman he loved was lifted into the clear nighttime sky.

CHAPTER TEN

"You look as if you've been through a battle," Alain said as Maggie reached up and ran her fingers over the bandage on her head, slightly above her left eye. She was wearing a lovely pale blue cotton hospital gown that would make even the most robust person look sick, and she was lucky enough that her name afforded her a private room so no one would have to see her looking like that unless she wanted them to.

Like Alain… If ever she wanted someone to see her when she wasn't at her best, he was the one. He'd been with Lilly, and she knew that, but she'd waited hours for him to find a minute or two for her.

"Just a small one. No big deal. But how's Lilly? I keep getting reports from various members of my family, but I want to hear it from you."

He brushed his thumb over her cheek. "Lilly's fine now, and she's resting comfortably in the pediatric intensive care. Asking for you, by the way. She's worried her uncle might have hurt you."

"I'll dab on some makeup in a little while and go down to see her. And Joe Aucoin? What happened to him?"

"From what I heard, Gertrude Aucoin was smiling when the authorities carted off her husband."

"Does she want Lilly back now?"

Alain shook his head. "She's going to Mississippi to live with her cousin. Said she's packed her bag, and that's all she's going to take with her."

"Which means…?"

"Lilly's officially abandoned now."

"Which is good for her?"

"Maybe good for me, too. The court is going to leave her with me for the time being until she's over the trauma."

"How long have I been sleeping?"

"Why?"

"I've missed so much."

"Eighteen hours."

"Seriously? I've slept for eighteen hours?"

Alain nodded as he took hold of her hand. "With the help of some medication. You were exhausted. Your doctor decided you needed some time to rest."

"My doctor?"

"Sabine Doucet."

Maggie smiled and sighed, and her eyes started to flutter shut. "She's good."

"So are you, Maggie. You saved Lilly's life."

"All I remember for sure was a kiss."

"Like this?" he asked as he touched his lips gently to hers.

"So nice…" she murmured, as she faded out.

It was two more days before Maggie was released from the hospital, and she was only released because she was going to have round-the-clock medical care at home. For the first day her whole family hovered around her, treating her like a fine piece of porcelain.

Alain, who was spending most of his time at the hospital with Lilly, did manage to find time to stop in and check on her, but he nearly had to stand in line to do so. On the third day, though, when Maggie was up and about on her own, everyone left the two of them alone.

"I've got good news for you," he said as they sat together on the veranda and he gave her a circumspect kiss on the cheek, which had turned into their custom when any of the other Doucet family was lurking nearby. Or, in this case, just inside the house, probably peeking out of the window.

"Lilly's mine, if I want to adopt her."

"That's great news!" Maggie exclaimed. "I'm happy for you." She paused for a moment, saw the concerned look on his face. "So what's the problem?"

"Frankly, you are. You and I have barely started something, and it's something I don't want to give up on. But I don't know where we stand now, and I don't know how you feel about starting a new life with an instant family."

"I love Lilly," she confessed.

"Just Lilly?"

"I love you, too. And I don't mind if it's a package deal."

"You won't be getting much from me in the way of worldly goods. At least, not for a while."

"I don't need worldly goods."

"And the mansion is a long way off from being ready to live in comfortably."

"I don't mind roughing it."

"And I'm going to be working a lot of hours between all my jobs, because your mother's offered me a position at New Hope in Obstetrics—I'm going to head up the high-risk cases. Plus I've got work to do at Eula's House to get it finished, because I promised, and I don't break promises."

"So are you proposing to me or backing out?" Maggie asked.

"Just letting you know what's entailed."

"When you get mixed up in the Doucet family, everything's entailed," she said, reaching over to take his hand.

"I sort of figured that out while you were in the hospital. They whooshed in en masse and took over."

Maggie smiled. "So are you up to it?"

"They don't scare me."

"Especially when you become one of them."

"Is that a yes?"

"A definite yes to you, to Lilly and to us as a family. Oh, and all the malpractice charges against you have been dropped and Jean-Pierre has a nice settlement check waiting for you from the hospital. After all the glowing publicity from what happened here, plus your war record, no one was about to go up against you. So you win…everything."

"Then allow me one thing to make this right with your family." He got up from the swing and steadied it, then went down on one knee. "Magnolia Loraine Doucet, will you marry me?"

Inside the house the curtains parted.

"Yes," she said quietly as he placed a large diamond-

and-emerald ring on her finger. It had been his grand-mother's ring, held ready for him until the time he proposed. "Yes," she said again, only this time loud enough for everyone inside to hear.

Then cheers erupted.

But Alain and Maggie didn't hear them, for they were already locked in a kiss that carried them far, far beyond the Doucet front porch to a place where only the two of them existed.

* * * * *

A sneaky peek at next month…

MEDICAL ROMANCE™

THE ULTIMATE IN ROMANTIC MEDICAL DRAMA

My wish list for next month's titles…

In stores from 1st August 2014:

❏ Tempted by Her Boss – Scarlet Wilson

& His Girl From Nowhere – Tina Beckett

❏ Falling For Dr Dimitriou – Anne Fraser

& Return of Dr Irresistible – Amalie Berlin

❏ Daring to Date Her Boss – Joanna Neil

& A Doctor to Heal Her Heart – Annie Claydon

Available at WHSmith, Tesco, Asda, Eason, Amazon and Apple

Just can't wait?

Visit us Online

You can buy our books online a month before they hit the shops! **www.millsandboon.co.uk**

0714/03

Make it a summer to remember with the fantastic new book from Sarah Morgan

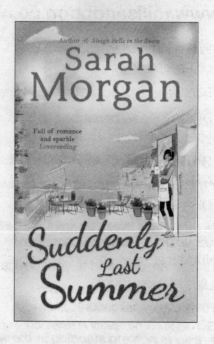

Fiery French chef Elise Philippe has just heard that the delectable Sean O'Neil is back in town. After their electrifying night together last summer, can she stick to her one-night rule?

Coming soon at millsandboon.co.uk

Discover more romance at

www.millsandboon.co.uk